Heartless
a suspense novel

John Matthew Walker

Copyright © 2022 John Matthew Walker

All rights reserved.

The characters and events portrayed in this book are fictitious. Any similarity to real persons, living or dead, is coincidental and not intended by the author.

No part of this book may be reproduced, or stored in a retrieval system, or transmitted in any form or by any means, electronic, mechanical, photocopying, recording, or otherwise, without express written permission of the publisher.

ISBN: 978-1-7355975-6-0
Library of Congress Control Number: 2022901678

Edited by Robin Patchen

Cover Design by Brett Grimes
Cover Photos licensed from Shutterstock

Published in Indianapolis, Indiana
Printed in the United States of America

What makes a someone heartless?

ACKNOWLEDGEMENTS

To my readers

To Luanne Bucci
who gave me a love for writing

To Robin Patchen, my editor, mentor and friend
who made me a better writer

To my critique partners
Linda Samaritoni, Joyce Long, and Ann Coker

To my beta readers

To my wife and family

To God
who gave me a new heart

Chapter1

He curled his bottle of Xanax in his fingers, rubbing it like a rabbit's foot. He had imagined keeping her hostage, bleeding her for the truth, then taking her deep into the woods to bury her as he had tried to bury himself, but the Xanax gave him a better idea.

Walking into the kitchen, he opened the fridge and pulled out a bottle of grape juice. It smelled a little old and had a funny taste, so she wouldn't notice the drugs. He plucked a glass from the cabinet and set it on the table beside the juice.

He dumped four Xanax into his hand. His racing heart said four pills were not enough, so he tapped a few more into his palm, dropped them into the glass and crushed them with a table knife.

Biting his lip, he thought about adding all of the pills and drinking it himself, but he stuck the bottle back into his pocket. His hands trembled as he stirred until the pills were dissolved. Lifting the glass, he sniffed the drink and swallowed his tears. He clutched his chest and slammed the glass on the table, spilling a few drops. Lips quivering, hands shaking, he wasn't sure he could go through with it.

He had never imagined killing a person in the first place, and he certainly never thought he would do it again.

Opening the cabinet, he reached for a bottle of inspiration and took a few swigs. The oaky flavor and gentle burn felt good and melted his inhibition. One more sip for good measure, then he poured a couple of shots into the glass of grape juice.

He took a deep breath, picked up the glass, and walked toward the basement door. A soft voice whispered in his mind. *This is not who you are. Don't do it.*

He flipped on the light switch and tromped down the stairs. There she sat zip-tied to a stripped-down chair. Her eyes screamed as she moaned against the strip of duct tape across her mouth.

She was the only thing out-of-place in his tidy workroom.

"I figured you must be thirsty. I brought you some juice." He set the glass on his workbench. "I gave it a little kick to make you feel better."

As he stepped toward her, her face tightened, and she recoiled. He held up his hands and said, "I'm not going to hurt you. I just want to remove that tape, so you can get something to drink."

As he ripped off the duct tape, he said, "You can scream if you want to. There's no one to hear you except me, but if you scream, I might keep this little drink for myself."

Color rushed into her swollen lips, and tears spilled down her cheeks.

"Sorry about that," he said, looking at her blistered lips. "No one deserves to have their mouth taped shut and be locked in a dark basement, but you left me no choice. Now drink your juice like a good girl."

The pain in her hazel eyes tested his resolve.

"Drink it fast, and it won't burn as much on the way down."

* * *

Brooke tightened her lips and shook her head as he held the glass to her mouth. When he relaxed, she said, "Let me drink it myself."

When she refused to blink, he set the glass on the workbench, grabbed a pair of wire cutters and snipped the zip-tie from her right wrist. Trembling, he handed her the glass.

Brooke held it to her nose and smelled the juice and the alcohol. The knot in her stomach told her the juice was spiked with more than alcohol. She didn't want to die, but she didn't want to be awake for whatever was coming next.

The glass in her hand was the one thing she controlled. The only thing. Fear squeezed tighter than the zip-ties, tightening her throat, tightening her chest, but not tightening her resolve. Her hand quivered. Lips trembled as she pulled the glass away from her mouth. The juice rippled and almost spilled until the glass rested on the arm of the chair.

"I've done nothing to deserve this." Her words sputtered like a little girl exhausted and frozen from playing in the snow.

He stared at the juice in silence. Silence drowned by her pounding chest and screaming doubts. His forehead wrinkled as tears crept down his cheek.

Brooke sensed that the man who had seemed so kind, genuine, even vulnerable was still there. The man she had thought of as the father she never knew was still there. Buried somewhere deep inside the skeleton-of-a-man.

Tears filled her eyes as his glossed over.

He was in the room but a thousand miles away. Staring. Standing. Still. Silent. He drew a slow, deep breath, shook his head and walked toward the workbench like a robot.

A drawer squeaked open. The shuffling of tools quickened her pulse.

When he pulled a roll of duct tape and some zip-ties from the drawer, Brooke screamed, "Why are you doing this?"

Her already-racing heart thumped louder and faster as he mumbled and ripped a fresh piece of duct tape. Her head swam. Her throat ached. Muscles tightened. As she twisted in the chair, the glass bobbled, and he snatched it from her hand.

She screeched, rattling her own ears, stifling her own blood. She flailed her arm, trying to slap him, scratch him, grab his hair, anything.

He grasped her wrist with an I'll-never-let-go grip, forced it against the chair and wrapped a zip-tie around it. His eyes narrowed and teeth clenched. Her wrist burned beneath his weight as he leaned into her and said, "No one deserves to be strapped to a chair and left in the dark, but no one deserves to be betrayed either."

Crushing her wrist, he held up the duct tape with his other hand and dangled it in her face. "We can start over, or you can drink your juice."

Warmth surged through her arm, throbbing into her tingling hand as he released her wrist. She closed her eyes and nodded in surrender.

He handed her the glass.

She lifted it to her mouth and looked into his eyes. Deep, dark wells full of pain she didn't want to imagine. Her eyes pleaded for mercy.

His eyes showed none.

Brooke closed her eyes and downed the whole glass.

Chapter 2
Nathan and Donna

Nathan Fortune sat in the vinyl-covered chair hunched over his walker, panting as his oxygen whistled. Waiting on Dr. Wells as usual. Staring at the same gray walls and the same glossy posters. Waiting for a miracle or waiting to die.

Cold sweat speckled his face as though he had walked through a sprinkler.

His wife Donna's gentle touch released him from his trance as she squeezed his hand. Her hand felt so warm. He gazed at her wedding band still wishing he could have bought the bigger diamond, the one she deserved.

She lifted his chin and smiled through a film of tears.

He didn't see the lines in her face, the furrowed brow, the thinning hair, or the scattered age spots. He only saw the young beauty who had captured his heart, the heart she still held in her hand, the heart that couldn't hold on much longer.

Their hands held the years, years they had invested in each other, years that were slipping away with his weakening grip and failing heart.

He smiled between breaths then looked away, shielding his tears, pretending to read the dated weight-loss poster that had been there for years.

Too exhausted and too proud to let his tears show, he read and re-read it, killing time the best he could while time was slowly killing him.

After two taps on the door, Dr. Wells nudged it open, stepped into the room, and set his laptop on the counter. He sat on his stool without a "good morning" or a "hello" and flipped open his computer.

Nathan was used to Dr. Wells entering with a smile, balancing a cup of coffee and his laptop. He would awkwardly open the door with his foot and close it with his elbow. But not today. He was all business. Nathan bit his lip while the man who normally smiled and talked up a storm wouldn't even look at him. As the doctor stared at his screen, Nathan felt a burning in his chest, blinked his eyes at the feeling that he might pass out, and breathed faster than he thought possible.

Donna's hand felt suddenly warmer as she tightened her grip.

After everyone else had abandoned him, she held on, always looking beyond his flaws as though they never existed. Her soft caress and warm smile let him know that she didn't see him laden with pain and short of breath. Although he saw himself as a man aged beyond his years, in her eyes, he saw himself as the young, vibrant man who had stolen her heart.

He squeezed her hand and nodded for her to do the talking. Getting dressed had taken most of his strength. Walking into the office took the rest of it. He wanted to kick himself for not letting Donna grab a wheelchair.

When Dr. Wells finally looked up from his computer, Donna's face flushed. Tears swelled. She covered her mouth and shook her head.

Dr. Wells scooted his stool closer and placed his hand on theirs.

Tears filled the room like a tiny funeral parlor. Mourning death as Nathan's life withered. Bitter acid rose in Nathan's throat and seeped into his dry mouth. His lips sticking together, he couldn't speak either. He coughed and sputtered as he sniffed his tears.

Donna looked at Nathan and stuttered. "It's not much of a life." Wiping her tears and taking a long breath, she said, "He can barely get to the bathroom and back to the recliner. That's where he stays most of the time, day and night."

Nathan's chest ached as he looked at Dr. Wells. He had seen his share of doctors over the years, but he had never seen one with tears streaking down his cheeks. It struck him that Dr. Wells would probably be the last doctor he ever saw.

This is it, Nathan thought.

The silence lingered as Dr. Wells grabbed a tissue to dry his tears. His doctor of many years took a long, spluttering breath, puckered his lips and exhaled like a flattening tire. He returned his gaze to his computer.

Nathan remembered the first time he saw Dr. Wells. They had hit it off right away when they discovered their common interest in fishing, and Dr. Wells always asked him how the furniture business was and wanted to see every photo of his latest re-upholstery project.

He wished this day was just another chance to reminisce and get Dr. Wells in trouble for getting him off topic. "You're making me run behind, Nathan," Dr. Wells would say.

Those days were long gone. Dying was the topic of the day, and no one wanted to talk about it.

Nathan never imagined fever and chills could turn into heart failure. The flu should have stolen a few days, but it had changed his life forever. How he wished he could turn back the clock.

Dr. Wells looked Nathan in the eyes and folded his hands in his lap. "Nathan, I'm sorry."

Those words hung in the air.

Nathan prayed for a miracle or a release from his burden. Swallowing his tears, he choked and sputtered. His gray face turned red, and his head pounded with each cough as he tried to clear his lungs.

Donna patted his back.

When he finally stopped coughing, Dr. Wells scooted closer. "We're out of options. We've fined-tuned your medications and done everything we can do to treat your heart failure, yet you've been in the ICU this year more than you've been at home."

Nathan didn't say a word.

Donna spoke while sobbing. "So, is this it?"

"No." Dr. Wells offered her a smile and focused on Nathan. "You'd be a good candidate for a heart transplant, but you have to quit smoking, avoid salt, and take your medications religiously."

Donna smirked. "Smoking hasn't been a problem. He's been too short of breath to smoke anyway. He quit two months ago because he couldn't even finish a cigarette."

Nathan breathed between each word as he said, "Do. What. You. Can."

Donna asked, "Is he even strong enough to survive the surgery?"

Dr. Wells pressed his hands together as though praying. “There is no guarantee. But one thing is certain. He won’t survive without a new heart.”

Chapter 3
Brooke

The discarded ashtray of a man stood in shadow at the top of the stairs. He cringed at the idea he might find Brooke dead, and the dark stairwell still gave him chills even after forty-some years. He flipped the light-switch. His knees felt like pudding as he wobbled down the steps. Not a lack of strength but a lack of nerve.

His stomach rolled as he stood over Brooke's limp body. He rubbed his wrists imagining the pain she would feel if she were awake.

Grabbing the wire cutters from his workbench, he stepped toward her, ready to cut her loose, but his hand trembled. He dropped to his knees in front of her and had to catch his breath. He pressed the back of his hand against his nose and mouth—a failed effort to stifle his tears.

Her broken life strapped to his broken-down chair reawakened the pains of his childhood. That gentle voice in his mind whispered. *She doesn't deserve this.*

He closed his eyes. His tears turned into anger, and he tried to convince himself she deserved every bit and more.

He had thought he knew her. She had seemed innocent, even caring, but the secrets she had uncovered changed everything. He was not about to be found out, which meant she had to disappear.

He snipped the zip-ties around her ankles, unbound her waist, and snipped the ties on her wrists. Her barely-breathing body slumped in the chair. The mix of his sweat and tears dotted her shirt as he leaned into her chest, and wrapped his arms around her.

Straining, he pulled her close and hoisted her over his shoulder. He ignored the gnawing in his gut and marched up the stairs.

Chapter 4
Brooke

Brooke awakened to darkness and seizing pain. Pain that quaked through her spine, her wrists and ankles, and pounded in her skull. She choked on exhaust and bounced on her side in the pitch-black trunk of a car. The duct tape and zip-ties were gone. Her mind still cloudy, she rubbed her face and smacked herself to wake up.

She gently touched her lips. Dry and cracked from the duct tape. They burned, and she wanted to scream, but no one would hear except him.

Her dark, cramped world paralyzed her with fear, heart-pounding, mind-bending fear as she imagined being murdered. Her heart ached at what she had thought of him and the puzzle of how and why he snapped. That kind, understanding man she thought she knew had become a monster.

What a man could do when he's lost his heart and his mind.

As the engine rumbled and fumed, the trunk seemed smaller and smaller. She pressed her hands against the ceiling awakening searing pain in her swollen hands. She patted them against her chest, trying to shake off the painful tingling.

Everything inside her trembled. Her eyes swelled with uncontrollable tears. Sniffling, she choked and sputtered. Despite pain wracking every part of her body, nothing matched the ache in her heart.

Brooke had thought she knew him. She remembered how helpless he was the first time they met. How she felt needed, and, over time, even loved. She had loved him and looked up to him. Never knowing her father, she had quietly adopted him.

Nothing had prepared her for what was happening.

As she bounced in the darkness, she hoped for a miracle.

He had only drugged her. He hadn't killed her. The realization gave her a sliver of hope.

I'm still here. Still alive.

She drew a slow, stuttering breath and smiled despite the darkness. *I'm not going to die, not without a fight.*

The car jolted over rough pavement, slamming her up and down. Tears unceasing, her hands rushed to find a tool, something, anything she could use to escape. No tire iron. No jack. Not even a spare tire.

The floor felt crinkly, almost plastic. Another chill shot through her as she realized he had laid her on a tarp. He was not going to leave any clues. She remembered the pristine basement. Everything in its place. Every detail covered.

She clamped her jaw. Scrunching to one side of the trunk, she pulled back a corner of the tarp and felt carpet. Running her fingers across the carpet, she found an edge and peeled it free, uncovering the bare metal floor. *Perfect. He might night not leave any clues, but I will.*

Biting her lip, she tasted a hint of blood. Her lips were dry and cracked. She bit harder and squeezed the blood onto her fingertip. In the dark, she wrote her name on the metal floor with blood.

As the car slowed, she touched her bleeding lip again and wrote faster. When she finished writing her name, she licked her finger clean and replaced the carpet. As the car stopped, she stretched the tarp back into place and pretended to sleep.

The car shifted as she felt a door fling open. Through quivering lips, Brooke told herself to breathe. She squeezed her eyes tight and prayed for a miracle as his footsteps clomped over the pavement. Taking a deep breath, she held perfectly still, listening as his footsteps slowed and stopped at the back of the car.

The key turned, and the trunk popped open.

She remained limp as he nudged her. He stepped back and grunted. As the trunk squeaked, she realized he was closing it, and she took a chance and opened her eyes.

Twilight. Tree-covered hills and a huge nest, high in a tree. Based on the hills and lack of corn fields, she guessed she was at least 50 miles south of Indy.

Her blood turned to ice as the trunk slammed shut, and darkness swallowed her again.

I can't die like this. God, help me find a way out!

She pulled back the tarp, stretched her hand into the deepest part of the trunk until she found the edge of the carpet. It peeled easily, revealing the back of the seat.

As his footsteps paused and the car door creaked, she stiffened, waiting until the engine revved, and the car began to move. The noise of the motor and tires on asphalt would cover any other sounds.

She pressed against the back of the rear seat. It squeaked. She froze at the sound. When she gently released the pressure, it squeaked again.

The car accelerated and tossed her backward. *He must have heard the squeak.* She curled into a ball and listened to the engine rumble.

Each time the car slowed, she thought it would be her final stop.

Then she heard another car drawing closer. *This might be your only chance, Brooke.* She cast aside her fear and thrust her feet against the backseat, knocking it forward. She forced her way over the seat, leaving her killer little time to react.

"What are you doing?" he shouted. His left hand gripped the wheel while his right swung over the seat trying to grab her.

She shoved the backseat into place as fast as she could and tried to become flush with the floor. Slapping his hand, she slid toward the right rear door, stretched her arm and flipped the lock. Still squirming and fending him off, she pulled the latch and opened the door.

Her head dangled over the edge as she held the door with one hand and tried to scoot closer to her escape.

Summer night air blew in her face as the pavement roared past. Ignoring the inevitable pain, she dug in with her heels to thrust herself toward the open door.

Her captor slammed the breaks and swerved to the right throwing her against the front seat. He grabbed her shirt. She jerked, but his grip grew tighter as the car slowed.

Trailing headlights flickered across his face. Sweat beaded above his blazing eyes as he pulled her closer and shouted, "You are not getting away."

Her head ached, and her heart pounded in her throat.

"Now close the door and sit there like a good girl."

She stretched her hand toward the door as headlights grew larger behind her. "I can't reach the handle."

"You think I'm stupid? Get down."

He shoved her head down, and she muttered, "Shut it yourself."

Yanking her shirt collar, he tapped the brakes, throwing her against the front seat. When he lost his grip for a second, she dove out the door.

Her already-bruised body slammed against the pavement, ripping her clothes and tearing her skin. Her head thumped against the asphalt as though all-at-once reawakening every headache she had ever had.

Out-of-control, she rolled across rough rocks and into tall weeds. No time to think about the fresh wounds that burned in every scrape or the blood that stained her clothes. Ignoring the pain and the fog in her mind, she scrambled to her feet and ran toward the oncoming lights.

The oncoming car stopped. She ran to the passenger's side and grabbed the handle. A wide-eyed woman pressed down on the door lock.

Brooke shouted, "Let me in. Please help me." She slid to the back door. The handle would not budge.

Looking through the window, she saw a well-dressed, middle-aged couple. The woman stared at her. She looked as startled as Brooke felt. The man looked back-and-forth between Brooke, his wife, and the car ahead of him.

Brooke pounded on the window as she sobbed.

The man prodded his wife and motioned for her to lower the window. As the woman cracked the window a smidgen, Brooke shrieked, "Please! He's going to kill me!"

She looked up the road. Just fifty yards ahead, a pale blue car sat motionless. No exhaust. No engine noises. Lights turned off. She stared at the silent, eerie scene. She had expected him to come running, arms flailing, screaming, gun-in-hand, but there he sat, his steely gray hair captured in the headlights.

Brooke stood bewildered at his stillness. She grasped the door handle with her right hand, kept her eyes fixed on him, and rapped on the window with her left hand.

Suddenly, he leaned to his right. As he straightened, the shiny reflection of a revolver flashed in the headlights and his door opened.

Brooke pounded the window, screaming madly as his feet hit the pavement. She imagined three gun shots and three victims.

The doors unlocked, and she jumped inside.

* * *

He gripped his .357 magnum. Sweat soaked. Hands trembling. His stomach lurched as though punched in the gut, and he tasted bitter acid.

He glanced both directions. Not another soul for miles. He could end this quickly, but his young heart wasn't up for killing innocent strangers.

If he let her go, Brooke would ruin him. If he didn't, he would have to kill her and anyone who might try to save her.

A fawn darted out of the woods and paused in the road. The oncoming car squealed and careened sideways. The deer scampered into the darkness.

The flash and disappearance of that fawn awakened long-buried memories. Painful memories tried to speak to him, but he silenced their whisper. *I can't let it go. She was going to expose me, ruin me.*

His eyes watered, and his heart pounded like that day years ago when he hurtled through the dense woods, running to save his life. He gritted his teeth and lifted his gun.

Headlights grew closer. He raised the gun higher. *I don't know if I can do it again.*

He had let her slip through his fingers, and soon she would be gone forever, exposing his secrets to the world.

Everything and everyone he had lived for had been buried. He was all that was left, and he was no one worth living for. He stood in the middle of that road leveling his gun toward the oncoming car. *Brooke. Why?* He couldn't see her face, only headlights coming closer. But he remembered her bright smile, soft voice and gentle touch, the way she had boosted his heart and helped him through a difficult time. He buried his anger in his thoughts and realized he was no one worth dying for.

The gun wobbled in his hands, and he shook with tears. Every painful memory tormented him at once. They had to end. Once-and-for-all.

Closing his eyes and holding his breath, he lifted the gun toward his head. The engine surged, tires squealed, and rubber burned onto the pavement. With eyes tightly shut, he braced for impact then heard the abrupt crunch of metal and branches.

The car hissed as he opened his eyes. Another failure. He was still alive.

* * *

Brooke opened her eyes to darkness and choked on smoke and fumes. Her head ached, and her face felt sticky and wet against the floor. She pushed herself onto her knees, her nose running and dripping onto her hands and the floor. In the darkness, she could not see that it was blood.

Pain quaked through her skull as she lifted her head. A soft moan from the front seat snapped her back to reality. Her mind flew to the image of her captor standing in the road holding a gun. She glanced at the man and woman. They were moaning but not moving. She climbed out of the car, ducked below the low branches, and crawled into the woods. It felt like one of those dreams where you're trying to run but not able to move. Every joint, every muscle screamed with pain and stiffness, but she ignored her pain and fought her way through the trees.

Chapter 5
Nathan and Donna

Nathan sat in his chair—a chair he'd loved when he'd first spotted it—a lightweight yet sturdy, pushback recliner. It was in shambles then, but he pictured it beautifully restored with fine upholstery, cabriole legs, and antique bronze upholstery tacks.

He'd taken the aging, abused chair and had given it new life. But his chair had lost its luster from the wear of every useless moment as he sat in it day after day—staring at his silent pager. Hope waned as the pager lay still on the end table. Like every day for the previous six months, Nathan stared until his eyelids drifted shut, and he nodded off.

He jolted awake as the pager bounced and beeped along with his cell phone. His heart couldn't race any faster, and he was already panting.

He reached for the pager as Donna shot into the living room, tears streaming as she held her phone to her ear. Nodding her head, covering her mouth, smiling, crying, almost-laughing all-at-the-same-time, she drew the deepest sigh possible and said, "They've got a heart, and an ambulance is on its way."

He smiled between breaths at the excitement in her voice. Her hands felt warm and soft as she cradled his face and kissed his forehead. Her eyes fixed on his. Nothing else mattered. All the waiting. All the hoping. All the trips to the ER. The days and weeks in the ICU. All of it would soon be behind them.

Her tears kissed his forehead as she wrapped his neck in a hug.

"You're getting a new heart, Nathan. A new life."

Time stood still as he hung onto those words and her sweet voice. The whir of a siren and the flashing lights of the ambulance broke his trance.

The next ninety minutes ran together. Paramedics, ambulance, wires, monitors, needles, lights, running stoplights, and rushing through the ER. Lights and voices zipped past him as a team of nurses and doctors whisked him toward surgery.

Despite the commotion and all the risks, he felt a sense of calm. He played Donna's words over-and-over in his mind. "You're getting a new heart, Nathan. A new life."

As they lifted him from the gurney to the operating table, he pictured Donna as a young woman. It was the first day they met. The first time he saw her smile. The first time he tasted her lips. She was his life, and his life was good. He realized in that moment between life and death that she was enough. The years didn't matter. None of it mattered.

This was it. One way or another. He would either walk out of that hospital with a new heart, or all of his pain and suffering would be over. Because of Donna, the end of his suffering wouldn't be enough. He wanted to live.

As the team prepped him for surgery, he tried to speak, but his throat was too dry, and his lungs were too weak. He looked at the nurse and hoped she could read his lips. "I want to live."

His arm felt strangely warm as a doctor leaned over him. His world went dark.

* * *

Donna sat alone in the surgery waiting area. Fear clung to her like a dense fog after a storm. Her stomach churned as she imagined Nathan stiff and cold, the doctors shaking their heads, the monitors silent.

The TV played mindless chatter while she stared out the window, watching cars go by. They told her Nathan's surgery would take a few hours. No one told her those hours would feel like days.

The clock ticked louder and louder, and she began to sweat. She reached into her purse for a cigarette. Acid rose in her chest as she stared at the cigarette. That poison stick she had thrown away years before but picked up again during Nathan's first stint in the ICU.

Being a nurse, she was well-aware of the many reasons to avoid smoking, and she was also familiar with every hospital's no-smoking policy. She tossed the cigarette back into her purse, stood, and walked toward the door.

"I'm going to catch a smoke," she said to the volunteer at the desk. "You have my cell number in case they come out."

She trudged down the sterile hall, feeling invisible as she waded untouched through the mass of numb faces, blue scrubs, and white coats. Everyone in the same world but different worlds. Each one focused on their own problems. Each one falling apart.

Donna could see them, but none seemed to notice her.

She bit her nails and counted the seconds and the footsteps until she could light that blasted cigarette. Navigating the colossal maze of Methodist Hospital took forever. Finally, she reached the entrance, took a deep breath and walked outside.

Frantic hands fumbled through her purse for the cigarette and lighter. Her fingers fumbled but managed to grab them.

As she touched the cigarette to her lips, she imagined Nathan with a tube down his throat. She envisioned him choking, unable to breathe. Tears welled as she feared the thought of life without him.

He was a long way from the brown-eyed rebel without a cause whom she'd met decades before, but she'd grown used to the feeble, breathless fool he'd become. He was completely dependent upon her, but she still felt completely dependent upon him.

She didn't miss his temper. She'd always blamed it on his illness. Hopefully a new heart would bring back the man she'd first met, the rugged but gentle hands, the arms that used to hold her close and made her feel safe.

She lit the cigarette, drew a long hit and tried to ignore her fears. It tasted like an old ashtray. Staring at the slowly-burning death-stick, she decided, *one last puff, then I'm done.* She tossed it and rushed back into the hospital.

Chapter 6
Nathan and Donna

Donna sat in a wingback chair in the corner of the waiting room. She sipped her coffee and stared at the clock. Nathan had been in surgery for over three hours, and she swore the clock wasn't moving. At first, she jumped at the sound of every cell phone, every alarm, and even quickened footsteps in the hall.

The lump in her throat was still there. It had been there since the pager and phones woke them. It wasn't going away. She imagined his lifeless body on the operating table, balancing between life and death, dependent on skilled hands, expensive machines, and the mercy of heaven.

Every muscle tightened as she folded her hands and prayed for Nathan.

She wanted *her* Nathan, his mysterious brown eyes and his tender heart. The comfortable warmth and sheer joy of his smile. The way he used to look at her like a child gazing in wonder at Christmas presents under the tree.

Her mind drifted. She was a princess in her pristine gown, simple yet elegant. Nathan was everything she ever dreamed of, and she knew she was his dream-come-true by the light in his eyes and his unforgettable smile. As he stood in his classic tux, her face flushed and her heart skipped a beat. His lips quivered, and his eyes watered as she walked the candlelit aisle to meet him.

On their special day, Donna felt beautiful like never before. She had considered herself neither homely or particularly attractive until she met Nathan. The way his eyes had studied hers… He had memorized every part of her face, every wave of her hair, every pout and every grin. He knew her inside-and-out and loved every part of her. His love inspired a self-confidence she had never experienced before and hadn't even thought possible.

She glanced at the clock again. Almost five hours into his surgery, past time for the nurse to bring another update.

His chances slipped a little with each passing minute. The longer the surgery, the longer the anesthesia, the longer he would be on the heart-and-lung machine, the longer his recovery, the longer the longshot of making it out alive.

She squeezed the arms of her wingback chair. The faded leather reminded her of her grandmother's chair. Once a stately House of Presley tufted masterpiece, the chair had been abused, neglected, and discarded in her father's barn, ready for the trash heap. She knew that's how everyone looked at Nathan—everyone but her. She saw him, not for the frail shell he had become but for the man buried deep inside.

Donna dreamed of resurrecting that man.

* * *

The nurse stuck her head through the door. "Mrs. Fortune?"

Donna swallowed then matched the nurse's smile and nodded.

"Mrs. Fortune, everything went well. They will be taking your husband to the cardiac surgery unit soon. I'll come get you as soon as he is ready."

As the nurse turned to leave, Donna's tears flowed. Her whole body shook, and she felt like she could breathe for the first time all day.

Nathan had a new heart.

Chapter 7

Nathan and Donna

Nathan opened his eyes. Lights drifted above his head in a blur. Beeps and chirps, footsteps, voices, and squeaky cart wheels jumbled together. Immense fear gripped him as he tried to move and realized he was strapped to his bed and choking on a plastic tube.

His pulse raced with the blips of the monitor as a silhouette hovered over him.

"Mr. Fortune. It's okay."

The calming voice ended his nightmare.

"Mr. Fortune, you're in the cardiac surgery unit. Your surgery went well." His nurse grasped his hand as it drifted toward the tube. "You were fighting the breathing machine, so we kept you sedated for a while. If you can tolerate the tube, we can keep you awake. We should be able to remove it very soon."

He released his grip, listened to the beeps that matched his slowing heart rate, and drifted back to sleep. The nurse's soothing voice followed him, and he pictured Donna calling from a distance.

* * *

He was back in Farmer's Park, a broad meadow split by a rippling creek and surrounded by rolling hills and forest.

He felt that strange pit in his stomach. His throat was dry and sour as he thought about what he planned to do. Life had been unkind. He felt alone, rejected, at the end of his rope, but that's not how he wanted to end.

His plan had been to visit the park one last time. It was one of the few places he found joy as a child. Nathan waded in that creek so many times as a child. His grandmother had told him the story of how she met Jesus in that creek, but he didn't see Jesus anywhere, and there were no miracles for him. Life had been one disappointment after another.

"One last time," he whispered as he pulled off his shoes and rolled up his jeans.

He stepped into the cold, clear water and watched minnows and suckers darting to get out of his way. "Grandma, I don't know if you can hear me. I don't know if there's a God who can hear me or a God who cares, but it's over for me unless something happens real soon to change it."

His mind drifted back to the gun in his glovebox. He kicked at the water as he thought about where to do it, who might find him, and how long it would take. Would anyone even notice he was gone?

He breathed a sigh and turned around to head to his car, but a tender voice and a sweet smile changed his plan.

"Aren't you a little old to be playing in the creek?"

He turned and saw sunshine for the first time in a long time. She wore a simple dress from a simpler time. Her smile and her silky brown hair lit the sky for him.

He looked around acting like she was talking to somebody else.

Her giggle and coy smile brought him back to life.

His pulse quickened like it hadn't in years. "Well, *I'm* not too old to play in the creek, but apparently, you are." He taunted her with his smile then turned away.

She didn't say a word.

He imagined her walking away, but he turned around to a huge splash in his face.

"Who are you calling old?"

He stood dumbfounded, soaking wet, and melting inside.

* * *

The nurse's soft voice snapped Donna back to reality. "Mrs. Fortune, you can come with me. Your husband is in recovery."

Donna glanced at the textured ceiling, her thoughts stretching to heaven as she whispered thanks.

She felt strength in the nurse's smile and her gentle hand on her shoulder. "He is sedated but doing very well. He should be extubated shortly."

Donna braced herself for what she might see then stepped into his room. She rubbed her shoulders at the coolness of the dimly lit room. The smooth cadence of his heart beat on the monitor soothed her fears.

She stepped toward him. The nurse still at her side with her arm now stretching around Donna's shoulders.

His eyes were closed. The pasty gray was gone from his face, and his face looked soft and warm and alive. Donna smiled through her tears. Relief surged through her like the warmth of hot chocolate after a winter stroll. Color filled his cheeks, and they felt warm. Not pasty. Not cold or clammy. Alive.

Although his eyes were closed, she saw life in his face for the first time in years.

He was no longer a prisoner to his failing heart. He was finally free.

Chapter 8
Joe and Peggy

Joe Novak wriggled his shoulders against the stiffness of his new suit. One of his mom's old friend's idea to make sure he looked good for his mom's sake. His mom's friend had been especially kind to ensure Joe's car, his father's car. It would be waiting for him at the prison along with the suit.

Sitting behind the wheel of his father's old car should have felt great after so many years, but Joe felt alone and empty. He tugged his starch-laden collar, loosened his unyielding tie, turned on the radio, and shifted the car into gear.

"You Light Up My Life."

He had never heard the song.

Debbie Boone's easy-going voice played on his emotions and squeezed his heart. "Could it be, finally, I'm turning for home? Finally, a chance to say, 'Hey, I love you.' Never again to be all alone."

He couldn't feel the "hope to carry on" as he turned the car toward the funeral home.

* * *

It had been two months and six days since his mother's last visit. Even longer since their last hug. His heart ached for her, for himself. Seven years without a home-cooked meal. Seven years without sharing a cup of coffee. Seven years in a cage, separated from everyone he loved.

The moment they opened the gate and he walked out a free man, he should have felt liberated. Instead, he'd walked from one prison to another.

Your mother died, Joe. The words stung like a pounding gavel and hung over him like a life sentence. His hopes of holding her again, protecting her again, being with her and watching her smile. The hope of showing the ring he would pick out for his bride, of handing her a grandchild to cuddle and spoil. Dead. *Your hope is dead, like your mom.*

A voice behind him said, "Joe, I'm sorry about your mom, but it must feel good to be out of prison."

Joe turned his head and faked a quick smile then stared at the casket again. "Yeah. It feels good." He spoke like a robot but kept the words he wanted to say locked inside.

He stood stiff. Still. Unmoved. Yet everything moved inside. Boiling. Writhing. Screaming. He wanted to kick the casket, punch the stodgy-stuffed-shirts behind him, the ones who offered no respect but came to pretend. He wanted to scream, to shriek like a terrified child. To explode on the town that ruined his life then gathered to bury his mother.

He had heard that prison hardens the soul, but Joe felt like a helpless child. He thought of the many times he skinned his knee or scraped his elbow, of the time he'd busted his chin on the sidewalk. His mother cleaned his wounds, careful not to worsen the hurt. She would nestle beside him with a book and read until he fell asleep. Sometimes she would make up wild and imaginative stories. Strange beasts riding camels through rainforests. Monkeys swinging from chandeliers.

He remembered traveling in her stories to places beyond imagination, into worlds that made him forget his pain, but, standing near her casket, he knew there was no such world. Her body lay cold and empty, and this world only reminded him of his pain.

He stepped closer, grabbed at the pain in his knee. Leaning on the casket, he tried to ignore his pain and hide it. He stared at his mother's face, wishing for one last moment, and pulled a neatly-folded note from his pocket. He read it one more time then gently tucked it into her folded hands.

A hand gripped his shoulder with a quick squeeze. "Joe? Are you ok?"

Joe stood unflinching and stared at his mother. "Just thinking." It didn't matter who spoke. It could have been any one of a hundred people. He was no one to them, and they were no one to him. He sniffed and swallowed every tear. "It's hard."

The quick squeeze turned to a patronizing pat. "That's normal, buddy. It'll take a while to adjust. Margie was good woman, and she'll be sorely missed by everyone. I guess we'll all have to adjust."

Joe clenched his teeth and held his words.

He stepped away from the casket to breathe. He glanced at the back of the funeral parlor, and there she was.

Peggy.

The only woman he ever loved more than his mother.

There she stood, pen in hand, leaning toward the guest book. She wore a deep blue tea-length dress with a high neck line and lace sleeves. The dress complimented her striking black hair in its carefree shag. It didn't matter what she wore or how she styled her hair, Peggy was beautiful to him in every way.

Her foot nervously tapped the floor while the pen tapped against her lips. She drew a deep breath, tucked her hair behind her ear, then touched the pen to the page. When she finished signing the guest book, she looked up and met his gaze. Joe lost himself in her soft blue eyes. Instantly, they were playing the sandbox in Peggy's backyard.

Joe remembered the warm sand running down his back as Peggy poured shovel after shovel onto his neck and shoulders. It felt so good. It even tickled, and they both laughed, but then she poured sand onto his head. He sputtered to blow it from his mouth. Eyes burning, crying with sand on his lips and tongue, he ran into Peggy's house. It wasn't funny at the time, but Joe was laughing inside as he remembered the innocence of their beginning. He would let Peggy pour hot coffee on his head if that's what it took to get close to her again.

If only life were as simple as that sandbox, but when he looked at Peggy across the funeral parlor, her lips trembled, and her eyes welled with tears.

She dropped the pen and scurried out the door.

Joe had waited seven long years to see her. He had written her notes almost every week. Sometimes more often, but she'd never visited, never called, never responded to any of his letters. Thinking of her was the one thing that kept him going while he served his time, and there she was. He couldn't let her go. He squeezed past relatives and friends to run after her, but the tiny funeral home was too congested. By the time he wiggled his way to the door, she was in her car and pulling away.

* * *

Peggy glanced over her shoulder and caught a glimpse of Joe sprinting out the door. She knew he was coming for her, and she knew what he would want. But there was no going back. With tears in her eyes, she slammed the gas pedal. She couldn't escape her past quickly enough.

Her love for Joe had only brought heartache for both of them. She couldn't let herself fall for him again.

After all these years, she could still hear her father's stinging words. *Joe is nothing but trouble.*

But, Daddy...

There's no but. He can no longer be trusted.

Chapter 9
Joe and Peggy

The doorbell rang and rang. Peggy lay on her bed, watching the ceiling fan. She knew it was Joe, and she knew she could never let him back into her life. Even if she tried, her father would never allow it.

Tears streamed at the familiar rhythm of the doorbell. Joe tapped S-O-S as he rang the bell over-and-over.

Peggy heard the tiny footsteps of her daughter thumping down the hall.

"Mom, there's a man at the door."

She stared at the ceiling and said, "He'll go away soon."

"Aren't you going to let him in?"

Her daughter flopped beside her on the bed. Peggy's tears answered the question, and her daughter wrapped her arms around her neck as the doorbell continued to ring.

* * *

Joe stood at the leaded crystal door. He was clearly not good enough to enter, not anymore. After all those years, he could still hear her father's words. "You've had your chance. You are not welcome here anymore."

Chapter 10
Joe and Peggy

Joe paced outside her door, periodically knocking.

"Peggy, I know you're in there."

He closed his eyes and leaned his head against the door. The sound of his voice used to move her heart, but there was no movement inside, not anymore, not for him.

How could she go to the funeral home and just leave without a word?

He peeked through the sidelight. The lights were out, but he knew she was home. He could feel it.

He stepped to the edge of the stone porch and sat with his legs hanging over the edge. How many times had he sat there waiting for Peggy?

He could still hear her giggle as her mom yelled, "Get out of my flowers. Have you no sense?" He'd jump up and run for his life. Peggy would chase him into the backyard and knock him to the ground.

Those days were never coming back.

He kicked at the rose bush in front of him. Peggy didn't take care of the flowers like her mom had. Guess she was still a tomboy.

She was a tomboy, but she was most definitely a girl.

When they were only five years old, she showed him "the secret."

They were sailing across the sea on her swing set. He was Peter Pan, and she was Wendy. They were poised to defeat Captain Hook when Peggy's mom walked across the grass lagoon with two glasses of fresh-squeezed lemonade. "Mom, watch out for the crocodile."

"Oh my!" She tip-toed carefully across the waves to sate the thirsty crew.

They climbed off the ship and stepped ashore into the sandbox.

"Thank you, Mrs. Landrum," Joe said as she handed him a tall glass of lemonade. Joe held the cold glass against his face, then downed the whole thing.

Their faces were red and drizzled with sweat, and they plopped down in the sand.

Peggy said, “I’m hot,” and she cooled off by pulling up her dress. She was not wearing any panties.

Joe’s eyes doubled in size. He had never seen that. He instantly understood how doctors could tell the difference between boys and girls. His innocent excitement turned to shock as her mother yelled.

“Margaret Ann, pull your dress down this second.” Her mother’s scream still echoed in his ears. *“Joey, it’s time for you to run home.”*

Looking back, he wished it had ended there, but those afternoons on the swing set grew into evenings and late night talks. Wrestling grew into hugs, and a punch in the arm turned into holding hands. But those days were over. He had buried his heart in that sandbox.

He tapped his heels against the porch like a clock ticking away the time. As the shadows grew, he knew he had waited too long. She was never going to come to the door. Stay any longer and she might have called the police.

As he stood up to leave, he caught a glimpse of a young girl staring through the glass.

She looked so much like her mother.

* * *

“Mommy, who was that man outside? He looked sad.”

Terror shot across Peggy’s face. She hadn’t realized Joe was still there, and she no longer knew what kind of man he was.

It doesn’t matter how good-hearted he is. She grimaced at her father’s words. *Prison changes a man. He will not be the same when he comes out.*

She sat up and grabbed her daughter’s shoulders. “Oh, Honey! Stay close to me while I call the police.”

“He sat there for a long time, Mommy, but then he just got up and walked away. Do we know him?”

“Baby, don’t think about him. Mommy knew him a long time ago.” *But I’m not sure I know him anymore.*

Chapter 11
Joe and Peggy

Peggy sat in silence on the edge of her bed. Memories spilled down her cheeks.

"Mommy, why are you crying?"

She smiled at her daughter's tender face.

Two little feet clomped onto the floor, and a tiny hand stretched up to hers.

"Mommy, come read me a book."

Peggy took her daughter's hand and followed her to the sitting room and her grandmother's overstuffed chair.

How many times had her grandmother read to her in that chair? How many times had she read to her and Joe? The wide-bodied chair was big enough for the three of them. She used to feel like a princess sitting beside the queen in that chair.

She pulled her daughter onto her lap. "What book would you like to read?"

"Alexander."

Peggy reached for the bookcase beside her and pulled out *Alexander and the Terrible, Horrible, No Good, Very Bad Day*.

She sighed and opened the book. "I'm not having such a good day myself, Alexander." She pulled her daughter close and read robotically.

Tiny eyes looked up at her, and Peggy could see the boredom all over that precious face. She smiled and said, "I'm sorry, Honey. Mommy's not much fun today. Let me try harder." She turned the page.

She could still hear Joe giggle and squirm as though her grandmother were reading to the both of them. Whenever her grandmother was visiting and Joe came over, he would practically tackle her with that book. Her grandmother would corral the two of them and plop down in her chair.

When she was a child, Peggy could never help but laugh when she read about Alexander's invisible castle picture. That page always took a few minutes, because Joe could never stop laughing at Alexander's blank sheet of paper. She felt a lump in her throat and her tongue stuck to her palate. She couldn't go on.

Her tears spattered the aging pages. She wiped them off and closed the book. “We need to read something else, Honey.”

Her daughter slid off her lap. “It’s okay, Mommy.”

Peggy pulled her close and hugged her tight, then she kissed her cheek and her forehead.

Her daughter’s hazel eyes looked puzzled. “Are you sad because of that man?”

I am so sad because of that man. She drew a deep breath and held her daughter’s hug as long as she could.

* * *

She and Joe were like a comfy pair of socks, always together, comfortable, a perfect match. How could she ever forget him?

They never had any terrible, horrible, no good, very bad days. The only problem with their time together was that the days were never long enough, and summer always ended too soon.

When other kids were ready to get back to school, she and Joe were just getting started. Baseball, running through the creek, climbing trees, skipping stones, wrestling, just doing nothing, but always together.

Once school started, they counted the minutes until they could play together. She was one of the boys and his best friend.

But things changed, and one day turned out to be a terrible, horrible day.

One autumn afternoon Joe slid beside Peggy on the school bus and said, “Tomorrow, Dad’s taking me hunting. He says I’m old enough, and I’m ready.”

“Can you even carry the gun?”

He elbowed her, and she punched his shoulder. “Of course I can carry the gun.” He flexed and almost growled.

Peggy giggled. “There’s no way your dad’s letting you carry his gun. He might let you shoot it, but you’re only eight. He’s not gonna to let you carry it.”

“Oh yeah? I may *have* to carry it, so he can drag the deer.”

“Either way, be careful.”

He smirked. “You’re only jealous.”

That next day was a blur. Peggy remembered her mother dashing out of the house after breakfast and running to Joe's. She didn't see Joe that day or the next. She didn't see him that whole week.

The following Saturday, her mother made her wear a fancy dress. She wasn't much into that kind of stuff, but she didn't fuss because her mom and dad were strangely quiet.

At the funeral home, she saw Joe for the first time in a week. He sat next to his mother, wearing a cast on his leg and a way-too-big blazer. She would ordinarily have laughed at his appearance, but no one was laughing. No one was talking.

Quiet condolences. Hugs. And tears. Lots of tears.

When it was finally their turn, Joe's mom gave her a kiss and a hug, then Peggy stood in front of Joe. Those few seconds seemed like forever. They didn't say a word, they stared into each other's eyes. Tears flooded and lips quivered.

Her father placed a hand on Joe's shoulder and said, "I'm sorry, Joe. Sorry about your dad and sorry about your leg."

Her father tried to edge her along to keep the line moving, but Peggy squeezed around him and gave Joe the biggest hug. She wanted to hold him and never let go. "I wish it was my leg instead of yours, Joe. I'm sorry about your dad."

She wanted her hug to erase the pain. She stayed in that hug as long as she could. She held him until her father gently pulled her away.

But she could still see pain in Joe's eyes, pain like she had never seen before.

Chapter 12
Joe and Peggy

Joe felt pain with every step as he left Peggy's house one last time.

I'm done chasing you, girl. It's time to move on.

He didn't mean a word. He pretended to feel tough, but she had always been the strong one.

As he walked toward his car, he felt the tug of memories from the house next door, his old house.

He stared at the car door, feeling lost and detached. It had been his father's car and had sat unused and neglected while he had sat in prison. He felt the same. Neglected. Empty. Not really belonging to anyone and going nowhere.

He looked at Peggy's house. *I'm not welcome there anymore.* He looked at his old house. It hadn't been his home for years, but it was the only real home he remembered, and he wanted to see it one more time.

After he'd paced for hours, his leg ached. It hurt with each step and reminded him of his worst pain, the pain of that cold November morning.

* * *

"Joe, come on. Wake up."

He could still hear his dad's voice and feel him tugging his arm. Three AM. He had never gotten out of bed that early.

"The deer aren't going wait for you. Let's go!"

As they tip-toed through the dark house, his father whispered, "Don't wake your mother or your sister."

* * *

Mr. Jenkins had given them permission to hunt on his property. It was only a few miles from their home. Joe's father turned the car onto the gravel lane and parked. Joe offered to carry the gun, but his father said nothing. His look said enough. He had taught Joe how to respect a gun, how to handle a gun, and to keep his hands off any gun without Dad's supervision—until he was old enough. That meant keeping his hands clear of the shotgun until Dad handed it to him, and keeping clear of the gun Dad kept locked in the car as well.

His dad smiled, patted Joe's shoulder, then grabbed the leather strap and slung the shotgun over his shoulder.

Joe held on to his father's coat as they followed the cleared path through the woods. Silent footsteps. Always staying downwind of the deer trail.

"He we are."

That memory stung, but Joe could still see the tree stand as clearly as if he were standing under it.

"You first, Joe."

Eighteen feet above the ground, and it felt like a mile. The stark frame towered over him. His cold hands gripped the dew-covered rungs as he climbed the ladder.

As he remembered that fateful day, he wanted to go back in time. He pictured himself gripping the ladder with his father behind him, encouraging him, ready to catch him if he fell.

He wished his father were still there, still behind him, encouraging him, ready to pick up the pieces of his broken life. Life felt like an impossible climb. A cold, steel ladder in a dark, unforgiving world. A climb he wasn't sure he could make with his dad no longer there.

No one was there. No one to catch him. No one to stop his fall. No one to care.

He wished he could leave those dark woods, go home, crawl into his warm bed, and wake up from his nightmare.

* * *

When he reached the top of the tree stand, he couldn't look down. The cold November air stung his face. He was expecting something warmer. He wasn't used to tromping through the woods in the middle of the night. The shadows and the noises played tricks on him, but he didn't whimper. He didn't make a sound. He sat in the dark silence and waited for his father.

The tree shook with each step as his father climbed the ladder. Joe held his breath and held on for dear life as he imagined the tree snapping or the stand coming loose.

He sighed when his father reached the top and the shaking stopped.

His father slid under the aiming bar, sat against the tree and caught his breath. Joe felt secure as his dad patted his knee.

"Where's the gun, Dad?"

His father smiled and held up a small rope that was tied to the stand.

Joe marveled at his father's ingenuity as he hoisted his gun.

"Never carry a loaded gun up a ladder, Joe. Seems like common sense, doesn't it?"

His dad propped the gun against the rail and grabbed the safety harness. Joe lifted his arms as his dad secured him in the harness and fastened it to the strap on the tree.

Once the harness was secure, Joe's dad lay the gun across his lap and loaded four slugs, one at a time, then pumped the shotgun as quietly as he could. Clunk. Clunk. He whispered, "There. We are ready. Now we wait."

Joe remembered feeling like a spy waiting on the enemy, and he remembered it was cold, damp, and dark. Three things that would have worried him, but with father beside him, nothing could go wrong. He felt safe, safe enough to nod off.

Chapter 13
Joe and Peggy

Joe heard the gunshot like it was fresh, and he felt the wound in his leg just the same. As he walked past his old house, his mind was in that tree stand with his dad. The pain jolted with every step, like the blast that had awakened him.

Joe didn't know what happened that morning. His last memory was drifting to sleep eighteen feet above the ground. His next memory was waking up to bright lights and the silhouette of his mother saying, "There's my Joe. You're going to be okay, Honey." She leaned over him, gave him a kiss and caressed his cheek.

He tried to sit up, but stifling pain held him fast against the bed. His leg felt like concrete.

"Where's Dad?" He looked around the room. His sister sat staring out the window. No one else was there.

His mother sat gently beside him. "Your father's gone, Joe."

"Gone? Did he get a deer? I heard the gunshot?"

She looked down at his leg. "No, Honey. We're not sure what happened, but…" She choked on her tears, unable to say it.

His sister, Jane didn't flinch as she stared at nothing and said, "Dad's dead, and it's your fault."

"Jane!" His mother's angry glare could quiet any room. She turned toward Joe and smiled through her tears. "It's not your fault, Joe. The sheriff thinks your father fell asleep. The gun slipped. He tried to grab it. The blast hit you in the leg, and your father fell from the stand. He fell, Joe. It was an accident." She turned toward Jane and said it louder. "It was an accident."

Jane muttered, "Either way, Dad's dead, and it wouldn't have happened if he hadn't taken dork with him."

"Jane, please go to the waiting room."

Joe knew it was his fault. His dad was always about safety. That's why he'd insisted that Joe wear the safety harness instead of himself.

"I was wearing the harness, Mom. *I* was wearing it." He flubbed through his words, sniffing his tears. "It *is* my fault, Mom. If Dad had been wearing the harness… If I hadn't been there, Dad would have worn it, and he'd still be alive. It's all my fault."

"Joe." His mom squeezed his face with both hands and commanded his eyes. "It's. Not. Your. Fault." She hugged him tightly. "Your father could have taken two safety harnesses, and if he didn't have two, he could have bought one. Those are not decisions for an eight-year-old boy. Those were your daddy's decisions.

"Jane didn't mean what she said. She's just angry right now. When you lose a loved one, you get mad, and sometimes you take it out on the ones closest to you. You'll see. It's not your fault, baby."

It's my fault.

Chapter 14

Joe and Peggy

Peggy sat on the edge of her bed with her hands in her lap just like she had that chilly Saturday in November. Her daughter nestled against her and held onto her arm.

As she sat staring, she could still picture Joe's tear-swollen face like his daddy's funeral had been yesterday.

* * *

The funeral swelled into the parking lot. The tiny chapel couldn't hold half the people who'd come to pay their respects.

Peggy sat between her mother and father. Unable to see past the shoulders in front of her, she sat with folded hands, listening.

The people muttered in hushed tones.

"So young. He left a wife and two kids."

"Pity. He was a good man."

Peggy tried to climb onto her father's lap, but he motioned for her to sit still and held his finger to his lips. She tilted her head, straining to see. She couldn't see anything.

As the number of mourners swelled, her father scooped her up, slid into her seat, and held her on his lap.

An older woman nodded as she took the empty seat.

The organ groaned *The Old Rugged Cross* as the last few who squeezed through the doors found their seats. The music covered the tears and sniffles.

On her daddy's lap, Peggy could see almost everyone. She could only see the top of Joe's head. He was turning around now-and-then trying to find her. She was afraid to wave, so she waited until he caught her gaze.

"I see you," his half-smile said despite his tears.

She smiled, but her heart ached for him, even more when her mother said, "Oh look. Poor Joe. His life will never be the same."

What does that mean? His life will never be the same. Her eyes swelled with tears as she realized the finality of that fancy box. There lay his dad. So peaceful. So still. So dead.

They are going to bury him in that box, and Joe will never see him again. She glanced up at her father. His sturdy chin. His thick, dark eyebrows. His warm eyes that melted when he looked at her. She couldn't imagine her life without him.

Looking back at Joe, he had his head down, leaning into his mother.

She leaned into her mother and whispered, "Is Joe going to be okay?"

Her mother kissed her forehead and smiled through her tears. "Yes, Honey, but it's going to be hard growing up without a father.

Chapter 15

Joe and Peggy

A few weeks after the funeral, Peggy heard a familiar tap on the back door.

Joe.

She ran to the door. He smiled, but the light in his eyes was no longer there, and the smile took effort. He wasn't the same carefree boy she'd known. Life had become a burden for him. How desperately Peggy wanted to lift that burden.

"Come in." She opened the door but stood in the way until his smile grew wide enough. It was an unspoken password. *You can't come into this house without a smile.*

Peggy's mother said, "Joe, you look hungry. Have you eaten dinner?"

"Mom's not home yet, and Jane can't cook."

"What about you?" her mother asked.

"Mom's afraid I'll burn down the house."

* * *

Joe held back his tears as he stared at the familiar kitchen, at Mrs. Landrum, at Peggy, at the home he missed, at the family still intact, at the table set for dinner. His second home. The home that still had a father, that still had smiles and reasons to smile.

Peggy's mother stood beside him and rested her hand on his shoulder.

He could smell the roast she had just removed from the oven.

His stomach rumbled.

In the weeks after his father's death, beef was never on the menu at his house. Hamburgers turned to bologna. Bologna turned to peanut butter and jelly, and peanut butter and jelly turned to whatever the local food pantry was offering.

He had to use a special voucher to get his lunch at

school. He always felt like the lunch lady looked at him differently, and so did the other kids, but hunger spoke louder than pride.

His daydream turned to a hopeful smile when Peggy's mother said, "Well, you should stay for dinner. I'm sure your mother won't mind."

Joe sat down to steaming roast beef, drizzled with gravy and surrounded with potatoes. He felt a momentary pang of guilt for Jane. No doubt she would be eating peanut butter and jelly by herself.

When Joe had cleaned three plates, Peggy's mother chuckled. "Have you had enough to eat?"

Joe covered his mouth. "Yes ma'am. Thank you."

"You're more than welcome, Joe. Are you and your family doing all right? Because you ate as though you haven't eaten in a week."

He half-frowned and averted his eyes. "Yeah. We're doing all right. Mom just has to work a lot now on account of Dad being gone."

"Well, Joe, you're welcome here anytime, and keep your chin up. Things will get better. You'll see."

He forced a smile, waved a feeble good-bye to Peggy, then trotted home in the dark.

The lights were off in his house. Mom's car wasn't there, and Jane had already gone to bed.

He flipped on the kitchen light and saw the mess his sister had left. "Man, she can't even put away the peanut butter." He tidied the kitchen for his mom, putting away the peanut butter and jelly and loading the dishwasher.

He lay on the sofa, closed his eyes, and tried to sleep, but his thoughts raced.

What if she's been in an accident? What if she doesn't come home? The what-ifs seemed endless. His young heart didn't know how much more it could take, and the tears trickled down his face as he sat alone and waited.

Chapter 16
Joe and Peggy

The door barely made a sound. Joe's eyes opened. His pulse quickened, his mouth dry. Then he recognized the familiar jingle of his mother's keys as she plucked them from the door and dropped them into her purse. Her shadow moved across the wall as she walked through the kitchen.

Joe rubbed his eyes and sat up.

His mother's shadow stopped then disappeared when she turned on the light. "Joe, are you still awake? You should be in bed."

"You weren't home, and I couldn't sleep."

"Where's your sister?"

"Asleep. In bed." He nodded and sniffed to stifle his tears. Images of losing his mother faded as she stepped closer.

She dropped her bags and the mail on his father's easy chair and wrapped her arms around him. "Joe, it's okay. I thought I told you I was working late."

He buried his face in her embrace.

"I'm sorry, Joe. I try to be home when you are, but I have to earn money so we can keep our home, so we can live."

She knelt to pick up her things. Joe snatched up the mail that had scattered on the floor.

Past Due? "Mom, this looks important. It's in red letters."

"Don't worry about that." She kissed his forehead and took the mail. "Come on. It's time for bed, past time for bed."

She tucked him in like she used to do and kissed his forehead. "Goodnight, my Joey."

"Goodnight, Mom."

Joe lay in his bed staring at the ceiling and listening. Dull thuds across the carpet. Clunking heels on the kitchen floor. Rustling paper bags. He heard the refrigerator open and close, the squeak of a chair scooting up to the table. His heart ached for the memory of his mom and dad talking into the night. Instead, his mother sat at that table alone. He imagined her drinking a glass of water and eating a piece of toast, all they could afford.

The chair squeaked across the floor again. The splash of the faucet and the thump of her glass on the counter followed by dull thuds across the carpet and down the hall.

He listened and waited until he knew she had gone to bed, then he snuck into the living room. Everything was in its place. She had stowed the mail somewhere.

He opened the corner desk drawer as slowly as he could. He flipped through the mail until he found the notice. There it was in bold—PAST DUE. He looked over his shoulder and listened for a moment. Silence. He opened the notice, and his stomach jumped into his throat. *Your mortgage payment is now three months past due. Please contact us immediately to make payments.*

* * *

The next day was a blur. He pushed through the day at school seeing PAST DUE in everything.

He hopped off the bus and saw his sister's rust bucket in the driveway. He dashed into the house and flung open the door. Jane sat at the kitchen table staring at a bowl of cereal. Her long auburn hair hid her face.

"What's a mortgage?"

Jane slurped a spoonful of generic oats and cardboard. Watered-down milk dribbled over her lip as she glared at him. "What? No hello. No Jane, 'how was your day?' No hug."

"Sorry." He swallowed and slid toward her with arms open.

She turned back to her cereal and brushed off his hug. "Dork. A mortgage is a loan from the bank to pay for your house."

"I thought we owned our house."

"Well, sort of. It's ours, but we're still paying for it. The bank loaned Mom and Dad the money. That's the mortgage. We have to pay the bank everything we borrowed plus interest. Why?"

His heart sank.

"Joe. What is it? You look like I just knocked over your army men."

"What happens if you don't pay?"

"You lose your house. Duh."

* * *

Joe made it his mission to help his mother pay their bills. Selling lemonade from a stand, delivering newspapers, mowing lawns. His days of playing with Peggy grew fewer and farther between, and he didn't see any more envelopes with bold red letters.

He never said anything, but once a week, he would slip his extra money into his mother's purse. He knew it was a no-no. Her purse was sacrosanct, organized, personal, and off limits, but he overlooked the rules for the sake of their home.

One evening while his mother was winding down from a hard day, he snuck into her bedroom to make his contribution, and there was another notice with huge bleeding letters: FINAL NOTICE.

Chapter 17

Nathan and Donna

Donna awakened early. Today was a new day. It felt so good to breathe, to stare out the window at nothing in particular, to fix a simple breakfast for the two of them.

A gray squirrel scampered over fallen leaves and shimmied up the redbud to sneak some birdseed. Things were getting back to normal. That's what she kept telling herself. She had the day off and hoped she and Nathan could do something together. She thought a good breakfast would get Nathan started on the right foot.

But as she scrambled the eggs and sliced an avocado, his footsteps padded across the carpet, and he landed in that blasted chair, the chair that had consumed him for the past couple of years.

No more heart failure. But his new life was pain and self-pity. He stared at nothing and pouted like a little boy who had to stay in from recess.

She turned off the stovetop and stomped into the living room. "Why are you just sitting there in pain? Why don't you take your pain medicine?"

"That stuff scares me."

"You sitting in that chair like a pathetic old man who's given up—that's what scares me."

"I think it's too strong."

"So take half-a-pill or ask Dr. Wells for a different prescription."

Nathan went to the bedroom, opened the drawer, and stared at the bottle of pills like it was poison. He didn't like the feeling of not being in control, but he couldn't function with the pain, so he took a pill.

One. Pill.

* * *

One pill turned into too many pills to count.

Hydrocodone became Nathan's escape and his prison.

He smiled at his salvation, the compressed chemistry rolling between his thumb and finger. He popped the pill and waited. The pains in his chest and soul eased as the medicine transported him into another world.

But with each successive pill, the hint of pain grew. His bottle of escape shrank. The hours between doses felt like days.

He took more pills more frequently, but it was never enough. His supply dwindled. His hands shook. His stomach knotted, and his temper wore thin.

One morning, he waited until Donna had left for work then snatched the bottle from his drawer. Three pills danced about as he shook it.

Nausea surged, and he broke into a sweat.

With trembling hands, he reached for his phone and almost dropped it. He fumbled through his contacts and called Dr. Wells.

Voice prompts. On-hold music. Five minutes. Just to leave a voicemail for the nurse. "Nathan Fortune. I need something stronger for pain…"

The clock seemed to stall, and the phone remained silent. Five o'clock came and went, and he had given up when the nurse finally called. "Dr. Wells is not going to prescribe any more pain medication without an appointment."

"But I only have three pills left. I need to see him."

"I'll have to check his schedule and call you in the morning."

As soon as Nathan hung up, the phone rang and he heard Uncle Charles's familiar "How you doin'?"

"It's still gonna be a while before I can come back to work."

"Take as long as you need. Is everything okay?"

"My heart is fine, but I tore some muscles, and I'm not allowed to do much of anything. I'm supposed to do some shoulder exercises, and I've been eating pain pills." His voice broke, and the pains in his chest and shoulder ached. "I'm in bad shape without my pain medication, and I'm not sure doc's going to give me anymore."

Uncle Charles cleared his throat. "I've got plenty left from my hip surgery. I'll give you some of mine."

Chapter 18
Nathan and Donna

Donna could hardly wait to get home. Too many patients. Too many orders. Too many unhappy doctors. Too many hours of work and not enough hours in the day.

Daylight faded a little more each day, and her drive seemed a little longer and little lonelier. As the streetlights and headlights turned on, she made the final turn towards home.

Her heart skipped a beat as she pulled up to the house. Not one light on. Not even the porchlight. Her mind jumped to an image of Nathan cold and unresponsive on the floor.

She couldn't get into the house fast enough. She slammed the door. Flicked on every light. He was nowhere. Her pulse slowed from dizzying to pounding as she saw no signs of trouble. Walking back into the kitchen, she found a note on the table.

Don't be scared. Just went for a ride with Uncle Charles. Needed to get out of the house.

A deep breath, and she opened the pantry and pulled out a bottle of Oliver Red. Not enough hours. Not enough wine.

She carried her filled-to-the-rim glass to the living room and sunk into the sofa. His empty chair seemed out-of-place, and she couldn't imagine what inspired the man who hadn't left his chair in days to leave the house without her.

She gazed out the window every few minutes as though watching for the car would bring him home sooner. But the street remained quiet as her thoughts churned. Everything inside told her he was taking more pills than he should. And he was hiding them from her. His top drawer had become sacrosanct. She felt his suspicious stare every time she walked near the dresser.

She scarcely recognized the man she'd married, the man who'd melted her heart with that very first smile. She could still see the candlelight flickering in his eyes at Iaria's Italian

Restaurant and couldn't help but laugh at the memory of spaghetti sauce on his cheek.

He had shrugged it off, fluffed his napkin, wiped his cheek, and knocked over his water.

The lifetime of laughter they'd shared began on that first date, and Donna had thought it would never end. Nathan had lifted her heart every time they were together and with every thought of him when they were apart.

She still trembled at the memories—all the firsts. The first time he held her hand, their first walk beneath the stars, their first kiss. It was as if no one else existed. The world stopped spinning. The birds paused their singing. The stars seemed bigger and brighter, and the universe seemed too small.

Nathan had stolen her heart. Nothing would ever steal her smile again.

Or so she'd thought.

* * *

Headlights slowly turned onto the lane then into their driveway. Five minutes passed, and the lights remained on, and the motor kept running.

Eventually Nathan crawled out of the car, leaned against it and heaved his supper onto the side of Uncle Charles's car and on the driveway.

He wiped his mouth with his sleeve and turned toward the house.

Donna held her tears and her anger as he staggered through the door. "Where have you been? What were you thinking? Do you know what time it is?"

"I needed to see the doctor." Nathan stumbled past her with a glazed look.

"Was his name, Captain Morgan?"

He collapsed on the sofa. Instantly snoring with his mouth wide open. Shirt crawling up his belly. One foot on the floor and one on the armrest.

Donna lifted his leg onto the sofa and pulled down his shirt to cover his belly. She tucked a pillow under his head and gently closed his mouth. She rubbed his forehead. *It wasn't supposed to be like this.*

As she sat beside him and watched him sleep, she remembered their first night in their first home.

* * *

"Nathan, can you believe it?" She spun in a circle in their nearly empty living room and surveyed their very own ceiling. And walls. And floor.

She could still hear his voice and see his smile was as wide as the horizon. "I never thought it would happen, never thought it would happen to me. A wife and a home. Donna, you have made me the happiest man alive."

They didn't have much, but they had each other, and they had the quiet but beautiful dream of a simple, sturdy life together.

"I don't want anything fancy, Donna. Just you and me, and maybe some kids if it works out. Nothing fancy."

* * *

She looked at her disheveled, drunken husband and whispered to his stoned skull. "I hope those drugs and all that booze mixes well with your immune pills."

She left him on the couch and went to bed.

So much for a new heart.

Chapter 19
Nathan and Donna

Donna stood in the shower. Steam rose and surrounded her. She soaked in the warmth and wished she could stay there all day.

If only she could feel as warm on the inside. If only the warmth could stay with her all day. But the shower ended, and the air chilled her wet skin. The days of Nathan stealing her towel and teasing her with his garish eyes were long gone.

He no longer felt like the man she married. His anger and erratic behavior made it seem as though someone had stolen his body.

She longed for the old Nathan. The mysterious bachelor with an unspoken past who'd swept her off her feet with his gentle touch, his hungry eyes, and his boyish smile.

He had seemed so real.

"You're not from around here, are you?" She remembered his soft voice like it was yesterday. "You can't be, because I don't remember ever seeing such a ray of sunshine in this little town."

* * *

The warmth of the shower was no match for how she had felt in that moment. She desperately longed to feel that way again. She had hoped a new heart would rekindle his passion for life, his passion for her, but Nathan could no longer see the ray of sunshine for the clouds that hung over him.

* * *

"I'm from North Vernon," she said.

"North Vernon? So, what are you doing here?"

"I'm a nurse. I'm on my way to Indy to start a new job."

"But you're thinking about settling down if you meet the right man?"

She blushed. "You don't waste any time, do you?"

"You never know how much time you've got."

I'm not one of those girls, she thought. She gave him a look to match.

As she stepped back, he said, "I'm looking for a good life, not just a good time."

He waded toward her and stretched out his arm.

She reached to shake his hand, and he gently held her hand. He cradled her fingers with both hands.

Goosebumps tingled up her arms as she imagined his arms wrapped around her.

He gazed deep into her eyes, and she lost herself in his longing.

“Your hands are soft,” he said. “I’ve never felt a nurse’s hands.” He lifted her hands to his lips, gently kissed the back of her hand. “I think these hands could save my life.”

Chapter 20
Nathan and Donna

Nathan awakened to Donna's car rumbling out of the driveway.

No kiss on the cheek. No good morning. No good-bye. Not even a good scolding.

He squinted at the ceiling light, clutched his pounding head, and gagged at the taste in his mouth.

He remembered talking to Uncle Charles and some guys at the bar, but he had no idea how or when he had gotten home.

Nathan blinked at yesterday's wrinkled clothes. He had even worn his shoes to bed. He sat up and rubbed his face. He scowled at his own smell and the dried vomit on his cheek.

He imagined Donna had worried into the night as she waited and wondered where he was. She hadn't woken him, yelled at him, or kicked him out. She hadn't done any of the things he might have expected. She'd dressed for work in silence, eaten her breakfast, and sneaked out of the house as quietly as possible.

I don't deserve her. Why does she put up with me?

As he stood and slipped off his jacket, a plastic bag full of pills fell to the floor.

Hydrocodone. He didn't remember buying it. He shook at the thought of it, at all the ugly memories, but his need for the feeling was palpable, faintly pulsing like his discarded heart.

What am I doing? He was staring down a long, dark road, one he had already traveled and never wanted to see again. He knew the end of that road too well, but his pain and his craving called like an enchanting siren.

His pain buried his doubts, and he tossed two pills into his mouth and swallowed.

The rest, he hid in his safe.

Nathan plodded into the bathroom. He couldn't wait to get the stale vomit taste out of his mouth. He brushed his teeth then stared at the old man in the mirror. He didn't like the etched face. The years had carved their marks and drained life from his bristly, white hair. The dried vomit on his cheek didn't help either.

He splashed cold water in his face and smacked his cheeks. A shower and shave should have helped, but they didn't. He still felt like one of his unwanted, secondhand chairs, not even good enough for the fireplace, tossed by the road for some garbage sifter.

As he stared at himself, he wondered *who would want that?* He imagined Donna leaving him on the street, a discarded relic.

He glared at the tired, disgusted face in the mirror. *I don't like you. I don't know you.*

Tears clouded his reflection. Sniffling turned to blubbering. He was thankful Donna wasn't there.

His hand reached for the medicine cabinet. No hydrocodone.

He sighed as he remembered stashing it in his safe.

As he stared at his tear-stained reflection, he longed for the man he used to be.

* * *

He imagined himself young again at Farmer's Park.

Sitting alone in his '63 Olds Ninety-Eight, he gazed across the broad green meadow, the gentle creek that slowly wandered toward the lake, the trees that surrounded the valley and climbed the hills. He relished the solitude. It was a taste of heaven and the only place he had truly felt any sense of home. It was his escape. His final escape.

He checked the glovebox to make sure the revolver was secure. He closed the tiny door and locked it.

He climbed out of the car as the serenity around him begged him to take *one last look.*

* * *

The old man in the mirror had that same feeling. *One last look.*

He imagined downing all of his hydrocodone at once. His stomach churned at the thought. *I don't want to die, but I'm not living.*

You want to live.

He jumped at the voice inside his head. It wasn't his voice. It was a young girl's voice.

"You're still drunk," he told himself.

He slapped himself a few more times to sober up.

Chapter 21
Joe and Peggy

Joe stood, one last time, in front of his old house. Tears trickled down his cheeks as memories flooded his mind. Saying good-bye to that house felt like saying good-bye to his dad all over again. It seemed much smaller than he remembered it, and the yard between his house and Peggy's seemed like nothing at all. But this house was huge for him.

It was where his life had started—and where it had ended. It seemed fitting to give it one more look.

It looked good. Whoever had bought it had put something into it, more than his mom could afford on her own. The bricks had been power-washed or sand-blasted. There were no loose or chipped bricks. The trim was fresh and tidy. Milk chocolate shudders and golden yellow bricks. Sharp edging around the sidewalk and driveway. Neatly trimmed bushes and dwarf spruce trees flanked the new solid oak door.

He desperately wanted a closer look, but the new owners wouldn't want any ex-cons lurking around the property, and he could see all he needed to see from the sidewalk.

He was glad he didn't have to see the dent in the old storm door.

Remembering it was enough.

* * *

He imagined that door swinging open and his mother saying, "Welcome home."

It's never going to happen. He kicked the door again in his mind.

That house had let him down and left him empty and alone like everything else in his life.

He pictured himself sitting on the sunken sofa, watching the hand-me-down black-and-white TV. His stomach rolled as it had when he first heard that voice.

The door swung open to the sound of laughter. *Mom and... who's that?* Extra footsteps and a man's voice.

"You must be Joe. Your mother's told me so much about you."

Joe felt a chill as the stranger looked him in the eyes. Joe looked at his mother. *Who is this guy*?

She smiled with a sideways nod, but Joe refused to acknowledge the man. He wasn't ready to share his house, his life, or his mother with another man. His father hadn't even been gone a year. He bolted past his mother and out the door. He headed for Peggy's ignoring everything else.

As he reached the gate, a powerful grip seized his arm.

"Boy, have you no manners? Your mother was talking to you."

Joe stood in numb silence, looking across the yard at Peggy, waiting for him as always, but her smile fell when that man grabbed his arm.

His mother cried from the doorway. "Joe, it's ok. You don't need to run." She stepped toward him and placed one hand on him and the other on the man's arm.

"Joe, this is Frank Mueller. I met him at work. He's a very nice man, and he's going to stay for dinner tonight."

Frank was an unyielding man with a stern jaw. He was lanky with salt-and-pepper hair and thick eyebrows that hid his eyes when he spoke.

* * *

Joe kept walking. He couldn't look at that house any longer. All the best days of his life were trapped in that house.

All of his best days had come and gone before Frank Mueller had ruined his life. Joe had grown to think of him as dishonest Abe because he looked like Abraham Lincoln without the beard and without the bullet hole in his head. Joe had fantasized about being the assassin.

When he'd dreamed of shooting Frank, he would always find himself in the woods, in the deer stand. As he'd pulled that trigger in his mind, he'd heard the shot, the shot that still rang in his ears and rattled his conscience.

He never wanted to hear that gunshot again.

* * *

That one dinner turned into multiple dinners and late nights alone for Joe and Jane. Frank always brought flowers for Joe's mom and sometimes gifts for him and Jane, but flowers and gifts weren't going to pay the mortgage, and smiles could not remove the sting Joe had felt when Frank grabbed his arm and shouted at him.

One night after dinner. Frank said his good-byes to Joe and Jane then led their mother outside for their usual thirty-minute good-bye.

Joe stared at his folded hands resting on the table. *It was just one time.* He rubbed his arm as he remembered the sudden fear that shot through him at Frank's grip.

"He's going to marry her, you know," Jane said.

"He can't. He can't marry her." Joe pounded his fist and fought the instant tears. He imagined the *just one time* turning into many times or even all-the-time.

Chapter 22
Brooke

The long stretch of wet pavement reflected a hint of moonlight. The road was eerily silent. Not another car in sight.

He knew if Brooke survived the crash, she would be running with nowhere to go. He pulled his car to the shoulder and hopped out.

He grabbed a flashlight from his car and scurried to the edge of the road. He slid down the grassy drop-off and climbed through the brush toward the wreck. He glanced through the rear window. The backseat was empty. The woman in the passenger seat was not moving, but the man moved his head and his arm. There was no sign of Brooke.

He pressed through the briars to the driver's side. His pulse drummed in his ears and his chest. Dry mouth. Sweat-drenched palms. And a nasty taste climbed his throat. He pulled the door handle. His wet fingers slipped and he stumbled backwards into more briars.

The beam of his flashlight glanced across the driver's bloodied face. The man slumped against the steering wheel.

He hadn't counted on anyone else getting hurt. He rubbed his face, prayed his supper would stay down, then opened the door. "Are you guys ok?"

The driver's phone slipped from his limp hand. The screen, still lit, read 911. The man wasn't moving. No breath. No pulse. His skin was still warm but pasty.

He untucked his shirt and used it to wipe off his fingerprints and close the door. He felt his own fiery pulse slowing, and he smiled, half-crying, half-laughing. He patted the gun in his pocket, glad he hadn't used it. When the car had sped toward him with Brooke beyond his reach, he had given up hope. The oncoming headlights had pressed toward him like prison walls closing in—in fast forward. His fingers tingled as realized how close he had been to pulling that trigger and ending his life.

But the couple died in what anyone would think was a simple accident. The driver simply lost control on damp pavement. Probably saw a deer or something. Nothing could tie him to the crash. He was free to pursue his revenge, but seeing the phone still lit with 911 told him to clear out.

He slid along the side of the car, trying to leave without a trace. He cringed as he eyed the slick grassy slope back to the road. Coming down had been easy, but he couldn't get back up without leaving impressions.

He pushed some briars aside and walked parallel to the road until he found an easier spot to climb. His boot slipped and he fell onto his knees. He winced at the pain in his leg as he slowly stood. Two streaks of mud on the ground and on his knees. Hopefully no one would notice. No time to worry. He had to get his car out of there. Then he'd be back to find Brooke.

Still no noise and no headlights approaching. He eased his car onto the road then floored it. The lonely stretch turned to winding curves and hills. He knew Brooke would try to get as far from the road as she could. Running through the woods would take her straight to the creek. He imagined her following the creek until she came across any sign of civilization.

He spotted a lonely cabin ahead on the left. No car. No lights. He pulled in and parked. After grabbing his flashlight, he got out, slammed the door, and jogged back down the road toward the crash.

Chapter 23
Joe and Peggy

Joe admired the new look of his old house, but the house had never been the same for him since his father died.

There's no going back. "I miss you, Dad. How I miss you." He felt that familiar twinge in his knee as he took the next step down the side walk.

He passed house after house. *Nothing in this little town changes,* but everything had changed, and Joe knew it, and with every step his knee screamed it.

Nothing will ever be the same again.

He passed Danny Miser's house. *I hated that kid.*

Danny called Joe a girl for playing with Peggy and called Peggy a boy ever since her mom made her wear pants to play with Joe and the other boys. He had no real reason to be mean, he was just mean. Joe always figured Danny was jealous of him and Peggy.

More than he knew.

He imagined that brat bursting out the door screaming, "What's the matter, Joella? Did Peggy steal your favorite doll?"

Joe wasn't one to pick a fight, and he could handle being insulted, but when Danny would pick on Peggy, that was Joe's hot button.

"What did you say, Danielle?" he asked and kept walking. He knew that little coward would never lay a hand on him.

When it was just the two of them, Danny Miser wasn't so bad.

One Christmas when Peggy and her family went to Florida to escape the cold, he and Danny went sledding every day for two weeks solid.

As soon as one of them was awake, he'd call the other, and they'd make a plan. Danny's house was more fun, because they had a better hill, steep at the top and tapering into the woods at the bottom. Up and down the hill all day. Each trip down was a different game: racing, cops and robbers, search and rescue, just two boys playing. The game didn't matter. It was pure, unadulterated fun.

They played until their pant legs were frozen and crusted with snow, their long johns and underwear were soaked. They would run into the house. Danny's mom always had the hot chocolate ready.

They would strip to their skin, wrap themselves in warm towels straight from the dryer, toss their cold, wet clothes into the dryer, and play games until their clothes were dry.

Joe remembered the soothing feeling of hot chocolate warming him all the way to his toes while watching little football players vibrate across their metal football field.

Nothing felt better than putting on those ultra-warm clothes straight out of the dryer.

Then it was back to the "slopes" and sledding until it was almost too dark for Joe to walk home.

But that kind of fun could never happen when Peggy was home. Daniel would always pick a fight, trying to make one of them choose him over the other.

Joe seethed as he stared at Danny's old house. When a hand pulled back the curtain, he realized he had better keep moving.

Chapter 24
Joe and Peggy

When Peggy was home, things were drastically different. She was Joe's other half.

He enjoyed sledding with Danny, but Danny always had something to prove.

With Peggy, Joe could just be Joe.

Despite the sandbox secret, Joe had never really thought of Peggy as a girl but as a friend. Her mom helped with that by teaching Peggy some appropriate points of etiquette, but mostly by making her always wear pants, or sometimes shorts when playing with boys.

Joe hadn't thought much more about "the secret" until middle school when Peggy began to change. He realized he was looking up to her. Her clothes didn't hang as loosely. The way she walked made him want to follow her anywhere.

When they walked through the woods or waded in the creek, she wanted to hold hands.

Once when she grabbed his hands, he felt a sudden warmth, and every part of him was on full alert. She was one-hundred-percent girl, and he was one-hundred-percent boy, and it was starting to show.

His body tingled from head-to-toe. Butterflies danced in his stomach, and his palms began to sweat.

"Joe, are you okay?" She let go of his hand and stepped back. "Your cheeks are flushed."

He touched his face and felt its warmth. His tongue stuck to the roof of his mouth, and he couldn't speak.

Peggy glanced at the bulge in his jeans and blushed. "Joe, maybe we shouldn't hold hands for now."

Without thinking, he nodded. He wanted to hold her hand and never let go. He didn't understand everything he was feeling, but he understood enough that he could not imagine life without Peggy. Ever.

As he walked home that afternoon, he felt like things would never be the same between them. Peggy was becoming a woman. He could no longer treat her like one of the boys.

As he lay in his bed that night, he realized he could no longer think of her like one of the boys either. She was all girl. For the first time in a long time, he thought about the sandbox secret and imagined what other secrets she might have.

He had never really paid attention to her crystal blue eyes, her smooth black curls, her perfect lips, her slender neck, and her cute little nose. He had never felt her touch as he had that day. Her hands were not just strong, they were soft. Her legs were no longer as fast as the boys' legs were, but they were slender and toned. Everything about her melted his eyes and his heart.

Chapter 25
Joe and Peggy

Joe's summer dreams faded as Autumn approached. He lay staring at the ceiling, dreading the coming of school. Dreading fewer moments with Peggy. Dreading the approach of Fall and the aching memories that would never leave. Most of all dreading the thought of Frank in his life more-and-more and eventually every day.

Frank and his mother were out to dinner. Jane had already gone to bed. Joe couldn't sleep. Even when he could, he could never rest. His uneasy feeling about Frank would never let go.

He heard the side door open, and his mother called out, "Joe. Jane."

He rolled out of bed and plodded into the living room.

There stood Frank, Dishonest Abe with his awkward smile and his bullet-free head.

Frank wrapped his arm around his mother and gave Joe a smug grin.

"Frank and I have an announcement." She smiled from ear-to-ear. "Frank has asked me to marry him."

Joe's stomach leaped into his throat. He remembered Frank's angry grip and knew there would be more to come. He forced a smile but could not stop the tears.

Jane plucked her keys from her purse, hugged her mother. "Mom, I'm happy for you." She glanced at Frank, slung her purse over her shoulder and headed out the door. "I'm going to Nick's to study."

Instant loneliness poured over Joe. Everything was about to change. Frank lived in a big, fancy house outside of town, and they were about to lose their house to the bank. He would have say to goodbye to the only home he had ever known. He would say goodbye to… Peggy. He couldn't contain his instant tears. He pressed toward his mom. Leaned in, almost eye-level with her and whisper-blubbered. "I don't want to move."

She squeezed him. Kissed his nose and looked in his eyes.

But her eyebrows crinkled and her eyes wet with tears when she turned her head and looked at Frank.

Frank subtly winked at her and shook his head.

Joe pulled free from his mother's embrace. Almost pushing her away, he shouted. "No!"

I have to see Peggy. Maybe I can stay with her family. I could sleep in their garage or the shed.

He bolted toward the door with Frank on his heels.

Squeezing pain shot through his arm as Frank grabbed him. *Again.*

His mother's voice followed him, sounding confused and hurt. "What do you mean, you don't want to move?"

Joe didn't realize he'd spoken.

He glared at Frank until the man released his arm. He stood in the doorway as his mother approached. Her face streaked with tears, she placed her hands on Joe's shoulders and said, "Frank and I are getting married. It will be an adjustment for all of us. Please think about the whole family and not just yourself."

His heart sank as she patted his head as though reminding him he was only a child. *Wasn't I thinking about the family when I started delivering papers and mowing yards to help you pay the mortgage?*

He looked at Frank with don't-beat-me eyes. He feared Frank's grip on his life would only get stronger, more frequent, and more painful.

Joe stared at his mom. "I'm sorry."

Frank chuckled as Joe ran out the door.

Chapter 26
Joe and Peggy

Peggy pulled back the curtain and watched the moving truck back up to Joe's house. The day she'd dreaded had finally come. It didn't matter that Joe was only moving a mile down the road. It felt like part of her soul was moving away.

She never remembered meeting Joe. They had always been friends, always been together, and life was just getting interesting.

The truck blurred with her tears as it rumbled to a stop and the movers hopped out.

"Aren't you going to say good-bye, Peggy?" her mother asked.

She turned and buried her face in her mother's chest. Her mother held her tight as Peggy's whole body shook.

Peggy tried to speak, but she couldn't.

Her mother cupped her hands around her face and kissed her forehead and her nose. "It's okay, baby. I know it's hard, but I think you should go over there for Joe's sake."

"I don't want him to see me like this."

"He won't, Peggy. He'll see you as his beautiful friend, and it's not good-bye. You'll still go to the same school, and you'll see him at church."

She tried to smile and headed out the door.

* * *

Joe kicked at some loose gravel. "I can't believe this day is here."

"Me neither." Peggy put her hand on his shoulder. When he looked up, she grabbed his hand and tugged.

He followed her toward the backyard.

"We could use a little help here," Frank shouted.

Joe barely heard the man and chose to ignore him. His mind was replaying every memory he and Peggy had shared.

They walked toward the creek, and Peggy pulled him behind the sturdy oak. They used to sit behind the tree when they were hiding from their parents. It was a home of its own with great shade and sturdy branches.

The broken rope was still hanging. Joe smiled as he remembered slipping from the rope and plunging into the creek. His memories halted as Peggy pressed him against the tree and planted a sturdy kiss on his lips.

Tingling warmth surged through him as her arms wrapped around him. He held on as though falling. His chest ached as he swallowed his tears. A few miles down the road felt like a thousand miles. His lips quivered and his body shook.

Peggy looked into his tear-filled eyes. "Don't cry, Joey."

He chuckled briefly and tried to smile. She hadn't called him Joey in years.

She kissed him one more time, slowly, gently, deliberately. "This is not good-bye. There'll never be a good-bye for us."

* * *

"They're over here."

Daniel! Joe's joy turned to anger at the sound of Danny's whiny voice.

Danny Miser wore the most ridiculous smile, wide enough you'd have thought he'd one some sort of contest. "Well, what are you two doing over here when you should be helping load the truck?"

Joe killed him with his stare.

Danny made those big eyes like he was acting scared.

Joe and Peggy knew better.

Joe shoved him in the chest and pushed past him toward the house.

* * *

"Your mom sure has a lot of stuff," Frank said as he carried another box. "We're going to have to get rid of some junk." He stumbled as he bumped into an over-stuffed chair. "We can start with this chair right here."

Joe didn't say a word, he just picked up the chair and carried it to the moving truck.

Box after box, chairs, beds, the kitchen table—it all went faster than anyone had imagined. So many came to help, it almost seemed like their neighbors were happy for them to move.

Joe glared at Danny as he leaned against a tree—watching and smiling, arms folded. Danny's smile grew into a chuckle as Joe carried box-after-box to the truck.

Joe's hate for Danny grew with each step. He imagined that brat running to Peggy's house every day—thrilled to have him out of the way. As he grabbed a shovel from the garage, he pictured himself slapping the selfish smile off Danny's face. He stared at the shovel, squeezed the handle like it was Danny's neck, then imagined digging Danny's grave.

* * *

As the furniture and boxes thinned, neighbors and friends began to leave. Some were heading to Frank's house to unload the truck. There wouldn't be much to do, since Frank was going to put most of their things in storage.

Joe carried the last piece of furniture onto the truck then stared at his memories—all crammed together. His scalp tingled and he froze at the still, empty-handed shadow looming over him. He whirled around. "What?"

Frank rushed toward him, grabbed his right arm and slapped him across the face. "That's the last time you will ever ignore me, son."

Joe touched his cheek with the back of his hand and tasted blood. He pressed his hand against his lip, swallowing blood and tears.

He jerked his arm free and bolted past Frank.

"Joe!" Frank shouted. "Don't ever ignore me again."

Joe kept walking and muttered, "Don't call me son." *You're not my dad. You'll never be my dad.*

His leg throbbed as he ran into his house for the last time.

He ducked into the bathroom, avoiding his mom. He didn't want her to feel any more pain than she already did. She and his father started their family in that house. Joe had never known another home.

He held a wet paper towel against his lip and checked it in the mirror. It felt a lot worse than it looked. *How can such a tiny spot bleed so much?*

Watching himself in the mirror, he realized he could stop the bleeding by curling his lips between his teeth and pressing them together. He stuffed another wad of paper towel into his pocket just in case, then he made one last trip through his home.

He pictured his dad resting on the sofa in the empty living room. He was smoking his pipe. His mom wasn't too happy about that, but Joe liked the sweet smell.

He could still smell the tiniest hint of tobacco in the carpet.

The curtains were gone, but he could still see himself hiding behind them, watching Peggy sneak out her back door to meet him. He looked at her neglected sandbox and smiled.

He heard the door open through the kitchen. He knew it would be Frank, so he ducked into his bedroom for one last sweep of the room, and one last look.

The brown paneling seemed drab. He'd never paid any attention to it before. His poster of Roger Staubach was gone, the one that hid the poster of Farrah Fawcett. He always suspected his mom knew about it. He shrugged his shoulders and moved to the closet. Empty except for a few wire hangers.

He remembered all the times he'd hidden behind his mound of clothes on that closet floor waiting for Mom to quit shouting. He'd thought he was so clever, waiting for her anger to cool, escaping another otherwise inevitable spanking. But Mom always knew, and she wasn't much for laying a hand on him or his sister.

He stood on his tip-toes and checked the closet shelf. "Wow. I almost forgot my men." He grabbed one of the hangers, raised up on his toes, stuck his tongue sideways, and strained to reach the worn shoebox in the back corner of the shelf. With a little bounce and few grunts, he slid the box into his reach.

He opened the lid to the whole of World War II. His tiny soldiers had entertained him on many rainy days throughout the years. "No man left behind," he said as he closed the box and laid it on the floor.

He could still see those army men scattered across the threadbare carpet in battle formation, and he could see Peggy dropping a cupcake on his tank battalion. It wasn't funny at the time, but he relished the memory and swore he could still see a smudge of icing in the carpet.

He drew a deep breath and stepped back into the closet one last time. He slid his hand along the inside wall until he felt the loose panel. He pried it away from the stud. Holding the gap open with his left hand, he slid his right hand up behind the panel until he felt the smooth wood of his father's shotgun. He eased it off the stud and lowered it through the gap—thankful his mom had forgotten about it.

His grandfather had given it to his dad on his sixteenth birthday. "Dad, you should have waited until I was sixteen to take me hunting," he whispered as he gripped the stock.

He left the room without looking back, sneaked out the back door and hid the gun under the backseat of Mom's car.

Chapter 27
Joe and Peggy

Frank's house stood at the end of a long lane near the edge of town. Two stories. White with ornate gray trim. Wrap-around porch with white wicker rockers and a swing. Manicured lawn and a picket fence. The property stretched deep into the woods, followed the creek, and opened into a lush meadow. There wasn't another house in sight.

A sturdy old-style barn nestled between the trees near the house. It set perfectly amid the pines and poplars, shielded from view by the house and the woods.

Everything was so perfect, too perfect.

Joe slid out of the moving van. His stomach rolled, and his pulse quickened with each step toward the perfect house. The house of anyone's dream. But it was his nightmare.

He imagined Peggy saying *it'll be ok* as he opened the leaded glass door and stepped into the entryway. He took off his shoes—afraid to make even the least little mess. He had never seen a floor shine so.

The walls were a pale lime green with glossy white crown molding, chair rails, and baseboards. Each wall had its own oil painting. Solid oak spindles framed the stairs.

His mom had always done her best to keep up with the house, but balancing work, her children, and household chores hadn't been easy. Their house was usually chaos.

Joe realized Frank was not going to tolerate anything out of place, let alone a mess.

How is anyone supposed to live here? Joe wondered. "I'm afraid to touch anything."

"That's a healthy fear." Frank patted Joe on the shoulder. "Everything has its place in this house, and I know where everything is." He looked Joe straight in the eye. "Do you catch my meaning?"

Joe nodded as he stared at their reflections on the floor.

As Frank walked away, Joe asked, "Where do I put my things?"

With his hands on his hips, Frank said, "What you can neatly fit into your room, you can keep. Everything else goes into storage."

"Where's my room?"

"Upstairs. Turn right. Open the door at the end of the hall."

Joe followed the directions and opened the door to a closet.

Frank followed him, chuckling.

"I'm sorry," Frank said sounding anything but. "I meant the last door on the left."

Very funny.

One by one Joe carried his memories from the truck into his new room. It was at the opposite end of the house from the master bedroom and as big as his old room and Jane's combined. The walls were a deep olive with mahogany trim. Too fancy and obviously not meant for him. He knew that giving him such a room was a concession and not a gesture of love. He stared at the dainty bed with fancy pillow covers and a quilted comforter and imagined Frank laughing.

His old bedroom closet had a flimsy sliding door. His new room had two closets with double doors. Solid oak. Six-panel doors.

He opened the empty closets and smelled a mix of untouched carpet and moth balls that reminded him of his grandmother's basement.

After only a few trips, he had filled the closet and the shelves. The things that were dearest to him, he put in his night stand—the Bible his grandmother had given him, his mostly empty journal, the coins his father had given him (a few silver dollars, some buffalo nickels, and wheat pennies), his dad's wedding band, and his photo album. When the nightstand was full, he stashed his remaining things under his bed, then he sat on the edge of the bed and opened his photo album.

Memories might take his mind off the cold, austere house he could never call home.

He knew Frank wanted his mother all to himself, and he wanted Joe as far away as possible. Frank was less worried about

Jane, because she was older, never home, and would soon be moving on with her life anyway.

Joe decided to cling to the isolation. He didn't want any part of Frank and wanted to stay as far away from him as he could.

He opened the memories and saw himself in his daddy's arms. You could barely see his eyes behind the squished baby face. He was more a bundle of cloth than anything else. His dad looked so happy, so proud.

He held his tears and did his best to keep fingerprints off of the pictures. Christmas, Easter, vacation in Wisconsin, Grandma and Grandpa, Jane's first dance. What a stodgy dress. Fishing with his dad. He couldn't believe they took a picture of such a small fish, but what huge smiles.

He stopped when he came across the picture of himself and his dad raking the leaves in the woods to clear the trail to their tree stand. He imagined the wind blowing all the leaves back into place and their footsteps going backwards.

He rubbed his leg as he felt that familiar twinge. He closed the album and slid it under his bed.

"What are you doing?"

Joe's heart jumped. He hadn't known Frank was standing in the doorway. He wondered how long he had been there.

"I was just putting away my things."

"Putting away your things? You call shoving stuff under the bed putting things away? I don't expect to see *dust* under your bed. Anything else I find there goes in the trash."

Joe imagined reaching for his shotgun as he reached for his photo album, but he buried his hate—for the moment and said, "I'm sorry. I'll find a better place."

He waited until Frank had gone to sleep to sneak outside and get his father's shotgun. The faint hint of gunpowder and oil reminded him of his dad. The thing that had separated them made him feel the greatest connection to him. He stashed the gun in his closet, buried it beneath his clothes, and prayed Frank would never find it.

Chapter 28
Joe and Peggy

Joe couldn't sleep. He couldn't stomach the sterile darkness of that soul-less house. The only sunshine in his life was Peggy. He had to see her. He had to at least try.

Walking a mile to her house was not a big deal—in the daytime. But at night, it was downright freaky. Every creak, every shadow sent a chill up his spine and set him to walking faster. The nighttime air grew colder by the minute.

When he finally reached her house, only the porchlight was on.

He climbed the tree next to her window and swung onto the roof. He leaned against her window to catch his breath.

* * *

Tap. Tap. Tap.

Peggy jolted from her sleep. Suddenly awake but not alert, she screamed at the shadow outside her window.

Then the shadow came into focus. "Joe?" Her heart melted as she looked at him through the glass. She felt the same ache in her chest as she saw in his eyes, then she opened the window. "Joe, what are you doing? How did you get up here?"

Peggy helped him crawl through the window as her door swung open.

Her father stood in the doorway in his boxers and T-shirt holding his 12-gauge. "What in God's name?" He flipped on the light. "Peggy, cover yourself."

She blushed instantly as she realized Joe had seen her in nightshirt. As she grabbed her blanket to cover her bare legs and thin shirt, her father shoved her onto her bed and stepped toward Joe with white knuckles squeezing his gun.

He lay the gun across his left elbow, then poked Joe in the chest. "Daniel Miser tells me you tried to trap my Peggy against a tree and force a kiss on her. I didn't believe it. But now you're sneaking into her room in the middle of the night."

Peggy's already-racing pulse accelerated as her father leveled his shotgun towards Joe's chest. "Daddy, please."

"Be quiet, Peg."

She scooted back against her headboard, bunched her blanket in her hands, held it to her face and mumbled frantic prayers as her father took another step toward Joe.

Her father glanced at her as he pumped his shotgun. "Joe, I'd better not see you sneaking around here at night ever again, and I don't want to see you here period for the next month. After that, I'll think about it."

He grabbed Joe by the shirt. "I'll show you out."

* * *

The door slammed behind him. Joe slumped to his knees, bent onto all-fours, then thumped his head against Peggy's front porch. Tears dribbled onto his hands and the stone floor as he shook uncontrollably. The porchlight clicked off behind him.

He had never been so close to Peggy yet so far away. He had never felt more alone or more terrified. He imagined Peggy's father sitting in the overstuffed chair with his shotgun across his lap, and he imagined Frank sitting up waiting for him with his twisted smile and tight fists.

He wanted to run, hide, disappear, or do anything besides go back to Frank's house. For the sake of his mother's heart, Joe walked back toward Frank's house.

He had only climbed the tree outside Peggy's window to avoid waking her parents. He didn't really think about it as sneaking or peeping. He hadn't expected to startle her. He hadn't expected her to scream, and he certainly hadn't expected to meet her dad with bed hair, wild eyes, and a shotgun.

A vision of Peggy in a thin nightgown that clung gently to every curve. He hadn't expected that, either.

He relived their brief kiss as he walked, then he thought of Danny Miser.

He envisioned stomping Danny's head with every step.

The sky turned from midnight to royal blue as he got closer to Frank's house.

He slid around to the back of the house and tried to sneak in quietly. Locked. He tried the door to the garage. The same. Every door was locked.

Joe stepped back to get a look at the trees near the house, thinking he could climb one and sneak into his room.

The lights flicked on. His eyes widened and his chest pounded as the back door opened.

Frank stepped outside and rushed toward Joe, towering over him.

Joe stepped backward. His neck and shoulders tightened.

Frank inched closer. “Couldn’t sleep?”

“I thought I’d go for a walk.”

“A walk?” Frank nodded. Lips tight. Eyes glaring. He walked a slow circle around Joe.

Eyes closed. Joe swallowed the salty brash in his throat. His mouth was instantly dry. Pulse pounding in his ears. He thought of running but had nowhere to run.

Then he felt Frank’s fingers dig into his shoulder.

“Peggy’s dad thought you were out climbing trees and peeping on his daughter.” Pain quaked through Joe’s shoulder as Frank tightened his grip then smacked him across the back of the head.

Frank grabbed Joe’s hair and pulled until his face tightened and he couldn’t close his eyes. Joe trembled as Frank continued to squeeze. Then Frank leaned into his ear. Hot alcohol-laden breath whispered, “Listen, Joe. I don’t know what you’re used to, but in this house, I expect you to keep your nose clean and everything else as well. I hoped we would get off to a better start, but it’s not looking good for you right now.”

“I’m sorry, Frank.”

He smacked him again, this time across his face. “My name *is* Frank, but you will call me sir. And I don’t believe you’re sorry, and I don’t really care. You live in my house now. You’re going to live by my rules. My roof. My rules. And if you can’t understand that, I’ll make you understand. Now get yourself upstairs and in bed.”

Chapter 29
Brooke

Brooke panted. Sweat dripping. Chest aching. She stumbled in the darkness. Briars tore her clothes and her skin, but she pressed on through the woods.

Every snapping branch, every crunch of leaves stopped her heart. She'd seen his headlights back away and speed down the road, but she still feared he was there, chasing her through the woods.

She collapsed against a sturdy oak and sobbed. She flopped onto her back and heaved giant breaths.

The hint of stars flickered between the swaying branches, yielding their tiny light in unfettered silence like a far-away god.

No one cares. No one even knows.

Pain awakened in her wrists and ankles. Her hips and back ached from the hours strapped to the chair. Every scratch and scrape stung. She swallowed her tears as she looked at the sky through the trees.

"God please help me."

Someone help me.

Twilight had faded to midnight as treetops and drifting clouds shrouded the stars. She prayed the darkness would hide her. She held her breath and listened. Nothing. Not a sound.

But it couldn't last long. He would be coming. And she needed to get moving, but her legs refused to move.

Then she heard the distant crunch of sticks and brush.

He's coming. She sat up, slid back against the tree, and covered herself with leaves. When the rustling stopped, she held her breath.

His footsteps grew louder, closer. Her heart pounding with every snapping twig.

"I know you're out there!" he shouted.

She didn't move. Night wrapped around her. Never before had darkness been a comfort to her. She breathed a slow deep breath, then softly gasped at the click of a flashlight.

Dear God, please protect me.

The light bounced between the trees and brush, but the shadow of the sturdy oak shielded her.

* * *

He looked for the biggest tree. His eyes trained on the fat trunk of an old oak. As he gradually inched toward it, he kept the light darting about as though he were still searching. He lowered the flashlight behind him, silently killed the beam, and listened.

She was breathless. Restless. Terrified.

His heart raced. He knew hers did too. He drew a deep breath and exhaled as slowly and quietly as he could. His hands trembled and dripped with cold sweat. He wondered if he could do what he had to do.

Chapter 30
Joe and Peggy

Joe sat in the pew beside his Mom and Frank. It was their first Sunday in worship as husband and wife. They were all smiles, and Frank couldn't stop rubbing her neck and shoulder.

Joe loved to see his mother smile, but it all felt so wrong. What could she possibly see in Frank Mueller?

He hung his head. Stability. Of course.

His mom didn't love Frank. She couldn't love Frank. She loved having her bills paid and having a nice house, a house she could keep and care for, a life that didn't make her work a job *and* work at home.

She'd never had that before. When Joe's dad was still alive, she'd always had to work, but surely she loved him. They had a good life.

The pastor said, "Let us pray."

Everyone bowed their heads.

Church couldn't end soon enough for Joe.

He hadn't even tried to find Peggy. He'd tried to be invisible. Now, he tried to follow the preacher's words.

Just before the amen, one of those stubby church pencils thunked against the back of his head. He twisted around in time to see Danny Miser laughing silently. Danny was stuffed into his Sunday best, a hideous orange-and-brown plaid suit that clashed with his red wavy hair and freckles.

As Joe glared at Danny, he felt a sharp pain in his ear as Frank flicked him with his finger.

He could feel Danny's laughter as he sunk into the pew.

Chapter 31
Nathan and Donna

Donna sat alone in the break room cradling her Styrofoam cup. She wished it were something stronger, but coffee would have to do. As she stared into the steaming black liquid, she felt like she was falling into a dark well—her problems tumbling upon her, burying her.

She'd almost lost Nathan, couldn't stop thinking about him, and couldn't help but feel she was still losing him. She saw his eyes in every patient. Heard his voice in every distant conversation. She felt him in everything she did, and she wondered if their life would ever be what it had been.

Nathan had been her salvation. She'd felt inadequate and insecure until she met him. His strong arms and gentle heart had been healing to her soul, which had wanted to surrender to death, to end-it-all. Instead, she'd decided to run away, to start a new life.

She didn't know why she'd stopped at Farmer's Park that day. She'd been escaping to a new town and a new job when she'd stopped on a whim to enjoy the trees and the sun, and maybe dip her toes in the creek.

When she saw him for the first time, she thought it funny to see a grown man with his jeans rolled up, wading in the creek.

Looking back, she realized she'd never asked him much about himself. She was entranced by his gentle eyes and the softness in his voice as he'd questioned her about everything. And she was eager to share. No one had ever shown such a deep interest in her. No one decent.

Nathan had seemed like a lonely sponge ready to soak up every bit of affection she could give. She immersed him in her story and loved every moment.

He wasted no time asking her for her phone number, then he called and kept calling, almost to the point of annoyance. He was like a 12-year-old chasing his first girlfriend, full of passion and energy but void of sense.

For the first time in Donna's life, she'd found someone who made her world go around and someone whose world revolved around her.

Nathan was her dream come true.

But some dreams turn out to be nightmares.

* * *

One evening, years before Nathan's heart surgery, he and Donna were enjoying the simple quiet when the phone rang. Donna answered. Her crinkled brow told him it was not a voice she recognized. She shrugged her shoulders at him as she hung up.

Nathan asked. "Who was that?"

"Wrong number."

Nathan thought little of it, until the phone rang again an hour or so later.

He snatched it quickly and held the receiver to his ear without saying a word.

Part of him wanted to run away from the forgotten yet familiar voice from his past, the past he had buried. Part of him wanted to scream into the phone, but he pulled the receiver from his ear, buried his anger and his fear, and gently lay the receiver in its cradle.

"Wrong number?"

He stared at the phone and nodded. His stomach burned and rumbled. Acid crawled up his throat. His mouth suddenly dry. Cold sweat covered him as though a ghost had called his name.

On the surface, life went on as usual, but Nathan felt the unwanted grave opening and the life he had buried haunting him. Every few weeks, the phone would ring. The same aging man's voice. The same silent answer. He hung up a little quicker each time.

But one day when he answered, Donna picked up the phone in the bedroom and said. "You again? You need to stop calling. There is no one here named Joe. Call again and I'll call the police." She hung up and focused on Nathan. Her lips quivered. "Persistent devil. I wonder how long he's going to keep calling?"

Nathan said nothing, just flipped on the porchlight and went outside.

* * *

Donna eased into her recliner and picked up her book. After reading a few lines, she held the book against her chest and sniffed. She smelled smoke drifting in through the open window. She looked outside and saw him smoking a cigarette.

When did he start smoking?

Until then, Donna had never seen him smoke, but she remembered smelling it on him the first time they met and always suspected that he had quit smoking for her.

When she first saw him, she didn't know who he was, didn't know his past, didn't know his fears, and, initially, didn't care to know. He was an ornery boy in a man's body who needed a good splash in the face, and his smile and strong arms begged for a whole lot more.

When she looked into his eyes, the world seemed smaller, less threatening. Her face warmed, and she smiled and held his gaze. His timid smile grew, and his eyes brightened. She let him take her hand, and they waded in the creek together.

Her arm lurched as he stumbled and fell to his knees with a splash. She couldn't keep from laughing until he pulled her down with him. There they lay in the creek, soaked to the skin without a care in the world.

They couldn't stop laughing. They were just big kids in a shrinking world.

Nathan stood and caught his balance. He lifted her up and set her on a sturdy rock on the creek bank. He climbed up, slid next to her, and held her hand.

She felt like a school girl holding hands during recess. She leaned closer to him, feeling brave yet trembling. Her gaze wandered over his face. "You look like you need a friend."

Her heart fluttered, and she wondered what she was doing. She had never been so bold with anyone, let alone a man she didn't know, but her fear vanished when he sniffed away his sadness, half-smiled, half-chuckled, and squeezed her hand.

Nathan looked at his feet bobbing against the rock with water rippling by. "I have no friends."

Donna pecked his cheek with a kiss and said, "Well, you have a friend now."

* * *

Suddenly, he felt alive again. The warmth of that simple kiss radiated through him like the magic of true love freeing him from his curse. He squeezed her hand like he was holding on for his life. He never wanted to let go.

He was so glad he stopped, so glad his gun was locked in the car, so glad he gave hope one last chance.

He pulled her hand to his lips and pressed it with a sturdy kiss. She was his angel sent to save him from himself.

They held hands in silence, soaking in the beauty around them, wishing the moment would never end.

Creek water dripped from her hair as she leaned against his shoulder. Nathan felt a cold drip on his arm. He watched it trickle down to their joined hands.

He reached around with his other hand and touched her cheek.

She lifted her chin and look into his eyes.

Everything inside him wanted to wrap her in his arms and give her the deepest, most heartfelt kiss, but he was trembling, and he still tasted that last cigarette.

But Donna apparently didn't share his fear. She matched his touch, gently caressed his cheek, then pulled him too close to resist, and they kissed.

Nathan forgot everything in that moment.

Nose-to-nose and eye-to-eye, they were no longer in the park, no longer on the planet. They had died and gone to heaven. He was sure of it, because he was staring an angel in the face, and she had just kissed him.

She kissed him again.

They rolled off the rock onto the grass.

Nathan pulled her closer still and buried his face against her neck. His tears swelled, ran down his cheeks and spilled onto her neck.

"Are you crying?"

He squeezed her tighter and nodded. He was trembling.

"Are you okay?" She held him until he stopped shaking, and his breathing slowed.

He relaxed his hug and gently took her hand in his. As he lifted her hand to his cheek, he said, "I'm sorry." He wanted to tell her so much more, but he didn't want to scare her away.

"It's okay."

He drew a deep breath, looked at the ground, and shook his head. "Today didn't start so good." *My life didn't start so good.* "I came to the park to say good-bye to my past." *I thought of killing myself. But I hadn't decided where I'd want to be found.* "But then you found me."

"Your past couldn't have been all bad." Her hands cradled his neck as she leaned into him. "Your past made you into the man you are, the man I'm holding, the man who saved me from drowning in those raging rapids." She giggled.

He smirked. "No. It wasn't all bad, but saying good-bye today... I didn't know what to expect." *I didn't want my life to end here. I just wanted to escape the pain.* "When you kissed me, nothing else mattered."

"You're right. Nothing else matters." She kissed his cheek again and smiled. "Without love, you've got nothing."

Her eyes, her smile, her slender neck, her smooth, flawless skin, and everything about her held him in a trance, but the shadows grew longer, the gentle breeze felt cold, and the chill broke his trance.

Nathan looked at himself. Soaked to the skin with her wet dress snug against his soaked shirt. He gave her a good looking over and couldn't find a dry thread. He smiled at her soaked chest. "So, you're a nurse?"

She smiled, nodded, and elbowed him for staring at her chest.

His smile turned to laughter. "It looks like you're a wet nurse."

Her eyes popped, and her mouth fell open. She smacked his shoulder, blushed, and smiled. "Men are all the same."

"Just joking."

"Hmpf." She climbed onto the rock, leaned back, and tossed her hair. When he tried to climb up beside her, she shoved him off the rock into the creek.

Water rippled around him. He sat up, rested his dripping wet elbows on his knees, and said, "You're a pretty *brave* nurse." He hopped to his feet and scrambled out of the water.

Her eyes widened. Like a little girl at play, she ran away, laughing.

She ran straight toward the sturdy porch swing that hung between two large oaks. She plopped down on the swing and waited. As he approached her, she patted her hand on the seat beside her.

Panting, he bent over in front of her with his hand on his knees. He raised one finger, signaling her to give him a second to breathe. Then he leaned in with puckered lips, smiled, and shook his soppy hair, spraying her once more.

She wriggled and squinted as the drops dotted her face. He sat like a wet little boy who'd just caught a spray bath from his new puppy.

Maybe his life wasn't over after all.

* * *

Nathan let the waning sun and the breeze dry his clothes while the woman beside him warmed his heart.

"Okay, so I told you I'm a nurse. What about you?" Donna touched his hands. "Tell me about Nathan."

The softness of her skin and the sweetness of her voice enthralled him. He was all hers, but he had to come up with a story quickly.

"I've seen enough of this town," he said. "I'm planning to move to Indy. I have an uncle in Beech Grove who owns a furniture store."

At least part of it was true. He knew an old family friend he called Uncle Charles who did, in fact, own a furniture store. Uncle Charles had always said he could use someone to do repairs, refinishing, stain removal, and reupholstering.

Nathan was the perfect candidate. He was young, he had no family and no other prospects, and he would do whatever he was told to do.

It didn't really matter what he said, her eyes locked on his. It didn't matter that his voice quivered. Her baby blues told him the only thing that mattered was that he was going to Indianapolis too.

He snapped her out his spell when he asked, "So where in Indy are you staying?"

She nibbled her lip. "I haven't signed a lease yet. I was planning on staying with a friend for a while." She almost giggled as she said, "I might follow you to Beech Grove."

His face warmed as he studied her eyes. He could see the sun, moon, and stars in them. She was a whole new world.

Chapter 32
Nathan and Donna

The stars peeked through the branches overhead as Donna leaned back in the swing. The gentle breeze caressed her hair and slowly dried her dress as she and Nathan swung. The barred owls filled the silence when they ran out of words, but words no longer mattered.

The whole universe was reduced to one swing in Farmer's Park. The past didn't matter. Nothing they had ever done or ever dreamed before mattered. They'd found each other, and new dreams exploded in their minds. Their hands fit perfectly together like two lost pieces to a puzzle waiting to be complete.

The sound of tires on gravel and the sight of headlights aimed straight at them pulled them from the trance. A door slammed, and a man's voice hollered through the headlights. "It's time for you lovebirds to leave unless you're fixin' to stay the night. I'm here to lock the gate."

Nathan leapt from the swing and shouted. "We'll be right there."

Donna giggled as he grabbed her hand, and they ran through the dark toward the parking lot.

Nathan said, "Just pull outside the gate. I don't want to let you get away just yet."

* * *

They parked their cars across the road from the park, stepped onto the road, and waved to the attendant as he drove away smiling.

Nathan reached for Donna's hand one more time. "This beautiful skin on your hands is going to rub off from so much attention." He kissed it and led her to his car. He could feel her pulse quicken. "Don't be scared. It's not what you think."

He turned to face her. "I'm not in this just for tonight. Trust me." He lifted her hands onto his shoulders, then placed his hands firmly on her waist and gently hoisted her onto the hood of his car. He hopped up beside her, crawled backwards, and leaned against the windshield.

She slid beside him and laughed.

"What's funny?"

"It's just that my dress finally dried out, and now I'm sitting on cold dew."

They both chuckled as she slid across the wet hood and lay beside him.

"Your car is huge."

Nathan wrapped his arm around her. "Yeah. I used to fit all my friends on this hood at the drive-in."

Donna rolled onto her side, looked into his eyes, and placed her hand on his pounding chest. "Nathan? Where do we go from here?"

A lifetime of emotions danced through his head. He wanted to kiss her again. He wanted to do so much more than kiss her. At the same time, part of him wanted to run and cry. He wanted to dance. He wanted to scream, but most importantly, he wanted to let Donna know she was something special to him. She was new life. She was redemption, and he didn't want to scare her away or make her think he was a freak or desperate, so he spoke slowly and deliberately.

"Donna, today has been more than a dream come true. I had given up on dreams until I met—"

She interrupted his words with her lips pressed against his.

* * *

Donna held on to the memory of that kiss as long as she could.

She peered out the window and caught a glimpse of him puffing on a nasty cancer stick in the chilly night air. Her memory of their first kiss faded in the light of the tiny red glow.

When the cigarette shrank to nothing, he dropped it and crushed it with his boot.

A moment later, the door opened. "Take off your boots," she said.

He groaned, kicked them off, and set them inside the door.

"When did you start smoking again?" she asked.

Nathan didn't look up but stared at the mail as he walked past her to their bedroom. He kicked himself for smoking and for ignoring her. He felt his unwanted-old-self coming back from the dead, the man he'd tried to kill, the man he had hoped to bury, but he could no longer control how he felt, not without his hydrocodone.

He could no longer control his feelings. He could no longer control his need for hydrocodone. Hydrocodone controlled him.

He half shut the door and opened the letter from Dr. Wells.

Dear Mr. Fortune,

Because of your violation of our controlled substances agreement, I am no longer willing to share responsibility for your health care. In accordance with Indiana State law, I will be responsible only for emergency issues for the next thirty days, giving you the time required by statute to find a new physician.

As he stared at the letter, he wondered how long he could hide the truth from Donna.

How he wished he could go back in time, back to the day they'd first met, the day when he buried his past, the day when he knew no pain.

He was lost in thought when she crept up behind him and wrapped her arms around him. He jumped, tossing the mail. He wanted to scramble and hide the letter, but that would make it too obvious, so he spun and embraced her. Looking deep into her soul, he planted the biggest kiss he had delivered in years.

The warmth of long-buried love rekindled and sparked a forest fire in his body. Donna pulled him against her and matched passion for passion. It had been ages since they'd spent themselves on such a powerful kiss. A kiss that took them under the covers and reduced them to exhaustion and laughter mixed with tears.

After they caught their breath, Donna brushed the mail off the bed, rolled onto Nathan, and placed one last, soft-as-a-falling-rose-pedal kiss on his flushed lips.

He instantly felt her very first kiss all over again. It took him back to that day, and how he wished that day had never ended.

* * *

That first kiss had lingered to midnight. It was too late for either to drive alone on winding, country highways. So,

Nathan followed Donna to Indianapolis to make sure she made it safely.

He was not about to let her disappear. He was alive again because of her, because of her giggle, her soft touch, and her enduring kiss. He would have followed her anywhere. Anywhere.

He followed her to her friend's apartment. The apartment was dark and quiet. Nathan parked on the street, climbed out of his car, and scurried toward Donna's car to help her with her bags.

But Donna shook her head and held up her hand signaling him to wait. "Thank you, Nathan, but it's late. I'll get my bags in the morning." She looked at the dark apartment. "Samantha's asleep, and I don't want to wake her."

She gave him a peck on the cheek and whispered, "Call me" then tip-toed up the steps onto the porch. Silhouetted against the porchlight, she waved and blew him a kiss.

The hurried thank you and good-bye told him she was embarrassed to be arriving so late. As much as he wanted to follow her inside, he couldn't.

He sat in the car, hands on the steering wheel. His heart warmed at how differently the day ended from how it began. The emptiness was gone. Buried. Forgotten. His old life was over. After a light flicked on upstairs, he watched through the window at her silhouette waltzing around the room. She was dancing, and he knew she was dancing with him. He imagined her flopping onto her bed and drifting to sleep still remembering their beautiful day together.

* * *

Sunlight peeked over the flat-roofed shops and into Nathan's car. He rubbed his eyes and awakened in front of Uncle Charles's furniture store. He tapped on the door soon after Uncle Charles arrived at the store.

"Uncle Charles, It's me, Nathan."

Uncle Charles squinted through the window. "Nathan?"

"That's right. I'd like to take that job after all—if it's still available."

Uncle Charles opened the door and scratched his head. "Sure. It's yours."

* * *

Nathan soaked up the work like a sponge in a bathtub. All the passion he felt for Donna, he poured into his work. Nothing else mattered.

The past had no hold on him.

Everything focused on Donna. Her face. Her smile. His hope. His future.

As he sanded a worn end table, he imagined her silky-smooth shoulders. As he rubbed in the deep glossy finish, he dreamed of her gorgeous hair. Donna was everywhere and everything to him. He was unstoppable as long as he thought of her.

Charles enjoyed the effort. Nathan's work brought a smile to the old man's face, and his store became fun again. "I ain't seen energy like that around here since I was your age and my daddy was teaching me everything I'm teaching you. You're doing real good, Nate."

Nathan shrugged his shoulder and let it go. He was happy to be alive and happy to have a reason for living.

Charles let him use the apartment above the store rent-free. It seemed like a good deal for both of them: free living for Nathan and free security for Charles.

* * *

Donna felt much the same. Every patient began to look like Nathan. When she was helping an elderly gentleman adjust to using his walker, she imagined being married to Nathan until they were both ninety-years-old.

Her smile and gentle touch did not go unnoticed with the old man either. He smiled at her as though he felt alive for the first time in a long time.

"You have a superpower, Honey."

"A superpower?" Donna chuckled. "Pff."

"You bring people back from the dead," he said. "I haven't felt this alive in years. You can walk me anywhere."

She blushed. *I attract all the eighty-plus men.* He no longer looked like Nathan to her, and she moved on to the next patient.

* * *

When Donna received her first paycheck, she was eager to find her own apartment, ready to be closer to Nathan. But she didn't want to seem desperate or aggressive.

She also didn't want Samantha to feel tossed aside. They had grown up together on neighboring farms. They had shared everything except their boyfriends and had always talked about life in the city. They had dreamt of living next door to each other, raising their kids together, and that was a dream Donna still cherished.

But she didn't cherish Samantha's heaping mess. By the look of her apartment, Samantha didn't just grow up on a farm, the farm had followed her into her apartment. Everything everywhere. Donna loved her friend but loathed the mess. And the smell. Moldy broccoli and dirty socks. Not what she had dreamed of.

She fussed about, picking up junk mail, dirty clothes, and a shriveled banana peel. "Sam." She shook her head as she pulled a tee-shirt from under the sofa cushion. "Just because you're a slob doesn't mean I have to put up with it." *Nathan, here I come.*

As she lifted yesterday's newspaper off Samantha's armchair, the tattered upholstery reminded her of her great-grandmother's old chair, the one she had hoped to restore someday, the one stowed in her parent's attic.

Nathan could restore the chair. It would give her a good reason to see him without seeming aggressive. And the chair would look great in her new apartment.

* * *

"So, this is Beech Grove?" Donna pursed her lips. She had hoped for a little more charm and a little less blech.

"Not much to see," Sam said as they drove down Troy Avenue past the golf course and the hospital, and finally down Main Street.

After crossing Lick Creek, they turned left and parked in front of the store. As they climbed out of the car, Samantha did a slow twirl with outstretched arms. "Well, that's about it. Beech Grove. This guy had better be something special."

Donna drew a huge breath and blew it out. She kept telling herself he was worth it. She looked at the gray streets and aging buildings and felt like she was in an old black-and-white movie.

Samantha looked at the storefront and scratched her head. “Fortune Furniture? It looks like an old gas station.”

"He’s here.” Donna beamed and nodded. “That's enough for me."

Samantha shook her head, walked around the car, and untied the knot that held the chair in her half-open trunk. “A little help?”

“Sorry.” Donna stopped staring at dullsville and helped Sam untie her chair.

They strained and grunted as they lifted it and set it on the pavement.

“Did your grandma put bricks in that thing?”

Donna rested her hands on her knees to catch her breath. “It’s solid. That’s for sure. Let’s leave it here and get some help.”

“Are you kidding? We aren’t going to go in there acting helpless. Come grab this chair.”

They lifted the chair and shuffled toward the door like an awkward crab missing a leg. When they finally reached the store, Samantha tapped on the door with one hand while balancing the chair against her thigh with the other.

An older gentleman came to the door. His gray wavy hair was smooth and well-groomed. It did not match his wrinkled shirt and jeans.

“How can I help you young ladies?”

Samantha said, “My friend, Donna is hoping you can restore this chair.”

He nodded, smiled at Donna and said, “I’ll certainly do my best. And it’ll look brand new when I’m done.”

He stretched the door open and motioned for them to bring it in, pointing vaguely toward the back of the store.

They dragged the chair through the door, casting thanks-for-nothing glances at Uncle Charles, and left the chair in the middle of an aisle.

* * *

The back door opened.

Donna felt like she was in one of those movie scenes where the orchestration builds, everything happens in slow motion, and two long lost lovers see each other from across the room. She stood trapped in a maze of furniture.

Nathan stumbled, when he saw her. He made a beeline toward her, running into a wall of end tables. She giggled as he twisted through the maze and ran down the aisle, flailing his arms as he bounced off her great-grandmother's chair.

Donna pushed the chair aside and wrapped him in a hug.

* * *

Her warm squeeze almost brought him to his knees. Her unrelenting hug felt like a come-to-Jesus moment. He was the sinner. She was the saint. He was the lost soul, and she was his salvation.

Hallelujah, he thought as she leapt into his arms and wrapped her legs around him. His elation turned to laughter as they stumbled and fell into the chair.

It squeaked across the floor as he held her tightly.

He grimaced and held his breath until the chair stopped just short of knocking over a cluster of lamps.

"It didn't break." Donna said.

Nathan rubbed his head and fixed his hair. "These old chairs were built tough."

Uncle Charles offered a hand to help Donna stand, looked at Nathan, and said, "I take it you know this girl."

Nathan blushed and smiled.

"So, who's your friend?" Uncle Charles measured her curves with his eyes and a wave of his hands.

Nathan smacked his arm. "This is Donna, *the princess of the universe,* and hands off, old man."

Uncle Charles smiled at Donna and jokingly shoved Nathan and messed his hair. "He's like the son I never had."

Nathan shoved him back.

Donna and Samantha smirked as the two of them jostled.

When the two boys stopped shoving each other, Uncle Charles stepped toward Donna, leaned close to her face, placed his hands on her shoulders, and sniffed her perfume. He stepped back and smacked Nathan on the shoulder. "So this is the girl you're set on marrying."

Nathan's face warmed instantly. Donna blushed and offered a shy smile.

"Well, if she'll take you, I'd say you've done all right." Uncle Charles patted her on the shoulder. "Good choice."

Nathan half expected Uncle Charles to check her teeth.

Samantha rolled her eyes and pretended to barf.

Uncle Charles opened his arms and looked around the store. "It's not much, but it's like home to me. I should probably keep it neater, but we move a lot of furniture through here, and neatness is often overlooked."

"Always overlooked," Nathan said.

Donna smiled and gave Uncle Charles a hug.

Nathan cringed. *Uncle Charles is not the teddy bear you think he is.* He patted the old man's shoulder like it was his turn to dance.

Chapter 33
Nathan and Donna

In the months that followed, Nathan brought a new dimension to the store. Uncle Charles was no longer simply reselling used furniture. Nathan was creating treasures, and Fortune Furniture transformed into a thriving business.

Nathan restored furniture. The irony was not lost on him. He had seen himself as damaged goods, empty, ready for the trash heap.

But Donna had seen so much more. Her love had restored him, built him into a man and a husband. Beech Grove had become their new home, and life had begun again.

Each time Nathan worked on a piece of furniture, he saw a piece of himself, and he saw Donna. Making things new made him feel new.

What others discarded, he salvaged and revived. He went so far as to make runs through neighborhoods and suburbs collecting trashed furniture and giving it new life. He went beyond reupholstering to repairing, refinishing, and even creating new designs.

On one Saturday afternoon, the pickings had been slim. Nothing but junk. "You can't make trash into treasure if there was never any treasure there to begin with."

Nathan had gone out of his way to hit some north side neighborhoods, and when he couldn't find anything worth salvaging, he decided to try a different route. He avoided 465 and headed straight down U.S. 31 toward Monument Circle. He remembered the stately older homes along North Meridian. "Maybe I'll run into some luck."

After about twenty minutes, there it was. Another piece of junk that wasn't junk.

"Do people never take care of anything?"

He pulled his truck to the side of the road and hopped out. He paid little attention to the Tudor Revival home with its arched casement doors, small central portico, and broad hip roof with hipped dormers. The kind of home people slow to a near stop to see.

All he could see was the discarded yet dignified Queen Anne. He walked around the chair, eyeing every detail. He wasn't yet an antique furniture expert, but he had seen this chair before or one much like it. He could still hear the sweet, crackling voice that boasted of its gracefully curved cabriole legs, ornate claw-and-ball foot, and foliage marquetry. As a child, those words just meant, don't spill anything on it, in fact, don't touch it.

This one had a few scratches. The shellac worn thin. And the upholstering thin from neglect. But it was still a Queen Anne.

He propped his hand on his hip and shook his head. "How can you live in a pristine mansion like that and treat something so rare like a piece of garbage?"

Others might see a tattered chair, but he saw what it had been and what it could be. He pictured the oversized chair with soft, sturdy fabric drawn tight and smooth across every surface. No creases except those precisely intended around the face of the chair and diving into the deep tufts. A subtle floral design to perfectly complement the wall he imagined behind it, and two school-aged children in knickers and polished shoes posing for their portrait.

The chair had no doubt been a cherished heirloom at some point and likely for a long time, but years and generations caused people to forget. Perhaps a coffee stain or wine? Maybe a careless cigar or cigarette burn? Something diminished its value to someone who never appreciated its value in the first place, and like an unwanted child, the chair was orphaned, tossed out on the street and left to fate.

He clenched his teeth as though looking at a younger version of himself. Unwanted and discarded.

He grabbed the chair as if he were wrestling a child from undeserving foster parents. He carried his prize to his truck and secured it with tie-downs.

* * *

"Any luck?" Uncle Charles shouted as the overhead door rattled open.

"This one chair was worth the whole day."

"One chair, huh?"

Nathan unfastened the chair and set it on the workroom floor.

Uncle Charles walked around it with a wry look.

"You can raise your eyebrows, but a brand-new knock-off of this chair would sell for twelve hundred. When I'm done with this baby, I'll list it at thirty-five hundred."

Raised eyebrows turned into an ear-to-ear smile and dollar signs. "Nathan, you see things I could never see."

Chapter 34

Nathan and Donna

Donna smiled as the door swung open, knowing Nathan was home. She covered her mouth and tried not to laugh as he waltzed through the door with his hand behind his back.

"You look happy. Did you win a million dollars?"

He danced toward her, pulled her close, and planted a kiss. "I don't need a million dollars. I have you."

Donna shrugged and blushed. "What do you want?"

He pulled his hand from behind his back and waved a mix of black-eyed Susans and daisies in her face.

She gave him a you-shouldn't-have smile, plucked her frequently-used vase from atop the fridge, grabbed the flowers, and gently arranged them.

She felt his warmth on the back of her neck as he stepped up behind her, kissed her neck and wrapped his strong arms around her. Her skin tingled as it did the first time they touched. She let herself go and leaned into his arms.

He whirled her around, pressed his face into her chest, his arms around her hips. Her heart fluttered. Her face flushed, and she knew that devilish look in his eyes. She nudged his shoulder and said, "Okay, what did you do?"

He lifted her and carried her toward the bedroom. "It's not what I've done. It's what we're going to do."

Donna fake pounded his chest as though protesting, but her heart raced as it always did when he held her in his arms.

She watched his eyes as he carried her through the house. She smiled as he stuck his tongue to the side while nudging open the bedroom door. She closed her eyes, trusting him completely as he gently laid her on the bed.

Her skin tingled as his fingers crept over every inch. His lips caressed her neck. Heat pulsed from his face and his body as he pressed into her.

She wrapped her fingers around his head and pulled his

lips to hers. As they kissed, she slid her hands toward his shirt. And one-by-one his shirt, her blouse, her skirt, and his jeans drifted to the floor.

Love's embrace bound them together—captives of love with no escape.

* * *

Nathan lay with his hands behind his head, Donna's perfect body lying against his, her arm resting on his chest. He stared at the ceiling and wondered how he'd never known life could feel so good.

Her soft whisper filled his whole world. "I love you."

There was no room left for any fear or doubt. No past heartaches. No bitterness. Not a hint of sadness anywhere. Only Donna.

He rolled toward her, pressed his body against hers and softly kissed her face. "You are my world," he whispered.

She absorbed his tender kisses, then he teased her with his roaming fingers until she climbed on top of him once more.

* * *

Donna slid back into her skirt and blouse, then stood in front of the mirror and tried to salvage her hair.

Nathan snuck up behind her, hugged her waist, and set his chin on her shoulder.

She chuckled at his crazy hair. "Get your clothes on."

He pecked her cheek with a kiss then grabbed his jeans.

Donna nodded toward the bed. "What was that all about? You're usually tired and hungry when you get home."

"Today was a good day. You remember your great-grandmother's chair?"

"Of course!"

"I found one just like it today in someone's garbage."

"Garbage? What's wrong with it?"

"Everything is wrong with it. It's trash, but that's what's so great about it. No one else wants it. It's been used and abused and left on the curb, but I can make it just like new."

"Cool."

"Cool, yes. And, when I'm done with it, it will be worth about $3500, but it will only cost me about $200 to make it gorgeous."

"Nathan, you amaze me. You can truly see beauty in everything."

They stood face-to-face again, eyeing each other's lips and smiling.

"I see beauty only where beauty is." He lifted her hair and kissed her neck. "It's only because of you."

"Me?"

"You taught me to see beauty that others can't see."

"How's that?"

He held her shoulders and looked her in the eye. "I am the chair. You saw me as I am now when all I could see was a wasted life that no one wanted." *I was ready to end it all, but you snatched me out of the garbage.* "You restored me."

"Well, I love you, but I'm not sure I did all that."

Chapter 35
Nathan and Donna

Nathan arrived at the store early, as usual. He was still smiling from the night before. He shoved the door against a solid oak desk, squeezed through, and flipped on the lights. The tight path between projects was no longer a path at all, and Nathan couldn't move without climbing over furniture.

"Uncle Charles is such a hoarder."

Nathan surveyed the mess, but he couldn't see his prized chair. He pushed through the maze until he found it. He gritted his teeth as he dug the chair out from under an end table. "I'm taking you home."

The chair clunked against a dining table as Nathan turned and saw Uncle Charles squeezing through the door.

"Having trouble?" Uncle Charles shouted.

"I'm taking this chair home to work on it. We have too much stuff here."

"It's mostly your junk."

Nathan shook his head. "Junk? It's all in how you look at it. When I'm done with it no one will see it as junk."

Nathan chuckled as he wedged the chair into his trunk and tied it down. Uncle Charles could be prickly, but the old man had to appreciate him. He had resurrected that store. Dressers that looked better than new. Four poster beds without a flaw, sturdy and stable with no squeaks. His work was amazing. Anyone who saw it knew it. Uncle Charles had to know it.

Nathan shoved his way back into the store, climbed over a bulky bedroom set and stepped from the bed to the dresser. But the dresser slid, and his foot slipped. His knee crashed into a solid oak bed frame, and he fell to the floor, writhing in pain.

"You okay?" Uncle Charles shouted.

Nathan scrunched his face in pain and nodded as he clutched his knee.

* * *

It was the first time Nathan ever visited Dr. Wells.

They shook hands, and the doctor asked, “You hurt your knee at work?”

“I can’t blame it on work. I was careless and climbed over some furniture and fell.”

Nathan grimaced as Dr. Wells manipulated his knee. He just about came off the table when the doctor pressed the tender spot on the inside.

“You may have a fracture.”

“You mean I broke it?”

“We will need to get X-rays to know for sure, but I wouldn’t be surprised. You’re obviously in a lot of pain.”

“You’re telling me.” Nathan’s face was splotchy and pale and covered with sweat. He rubbed his knee as he waited. What would Donna think? How much work would he have to miss?

The handle creaked and Dr. Wells stepped into the room. “It’s broken all right.” Dr. Wells held the X-rays against the light and pointed to a compressed area in the bone. “You can have surgery with a plate and screws, or you can wear a post-op splint for six weeks.”

Nathan stared at the films in disbelief.

* * *

Six weeks seemed like forever. Nathan hobbled around the store and hobbled around the house. His only reprieve was the narcotic Dr. Wells had given him. His knee ached and burned. The pain was crippling if he stepped the wrong way.

He could manage with crutches at home, but at the store, crutches were just in the way. Each piece of furniture became a crutch for him as he limped from one piece to the next.

Work piled up as he was working at less than half his normal pace. He began to feel like an old man as Uncle Charles worked circles around him, and he could tell the old fart loved every minute of it.

"It's pretty sad when the old man's faster than the kid," he said, half-joking, half-frustrated as Uncle Charles would set a nightstand in front of him and hand him sandpaper, stain, and varnish.

At home, Donna took good care of him, but the frustration grew a little each day. He tired at the pain in every step.

Chapter 36

Joe and Peggy

Joe crawled out of bed. Monday morning. Time to get up and get ready for school, but he was ready to throw up. Last night's spaghetti wanted nothing to do with the notion of waffles and blueberry syrup, his favorite. His mom was trying to soften the pain of so many things at once.

Joe ate a few bites to avoid hurting her feelings. She buzzed around the kitchen as if she were happy to be covered in powdered sugar and flour.

She poured Joe a glass of milk. "I want your first breakfast in our new house to be something to remember."

"Frank's house."

She gently rubbed his moppy head. "Our house. You don't have to call Frank dad, but he is part of our family now, and this is our house."

Joe squinted and fake-smiled.

His mother sighed and poured herself some coffee.

The sweetness of his mother's waffles softened his heart and the roar in his stomach. He smiled at his mother, finished his waffles, and downed his milk.

"Thanks, Mom." He grabbed his back pack and slid out of his chair.

She captured him on his way to the door and kissed his forehead, and his cheek, and the top of his head, then she gave him a hug until he finally laughed.

"I love you, Mom."

"I love you too, Joe." She rubbed his head and sent him out the door.

He patted off the flour and powdered sugar his mom had left all over him and walked to the mailbox to wait for the bus.

Bus 42. New bus. New bus driver. New kids. At least his school would be the same.

He stepped on the bus to new stares, new snickers, and the same old empty feeling. He found the last empty seat and slid to the window. He plopped his backpack beside him as a buffer against anyone who might try to join him.

The pavement whirred past, and he imagined himself flying out the window slamming into a utility pole. *At least it would be quick. I probably wouldn't feel a thing.* He looked around at the empty bus. It was full of kids but felt empty and silent, although everyone was talking. He sighed as he leaned his head against the glass.

I don't feel a thing now. I must already be dead.

The bus stopped, and a freight train of an eighth-grader climbed up the steps and looked right at Joe, but Joe didn't notice until he heard shouting and felt the sudden burning in his shoulder.

Goliath punched him hard. "Hey, doofus! Move your purse."

Joe winced as he grabbed his backpack and pulled it onto his lap.

The world felt bigger. He felt smaller.

Although the bus driver shouted at Goliath, it sounded like a distant whisper to Joe. *God, help this day to get over.*

* * *

Joe walked straight to his locker. He felt like an invisible zombie, a rotted corpse trudging through the school completely unnoticed. He fumbled through the combination and stuffed his backpack inside. He couldn't even remember what class he was supposed to go to first, and he certainly couldn't imagine why it mattered. Who needs an invisible zombie in their classroom anyway, and who would miss him?

Joe heard a miserable, whining, mocking voice in the distance. The whining and footsteps grew louder, but he didn't hear any words, just a shrill drone like fingernails on a chalkboard.

Danny Miser.

Joe pretended to be deaf and waited until Danny had passed by and disappeared into the next hallway.

The bell sounded.

The hallway noise diminished and the throng of students thinned to only a few scrambling to grab the right book or remember their calculator.

Joe slowly shut his locker. He leaned back against it, folded his empty hands over his face and slid to the floor.

The hallway was empty when the second bell rang.

Joe sat alone feeling barely alive and unable to move. He closed his eyes, listened to his own breathing, and imagined himself in the woods.

He couldn't help but remember his dad's words. "Shh. You don't want to spook the deer."

He hushed his breathing and listened.

Footsteps.

He imagined a young doe crunching leaves beneath her hooves.

The sounds started slowly and gradually grew louder and closer together, then he flailed his arms and bounced at the sound of books crashing on the floor beside him.

"Joe, are you okay? You weren't in class."

Peggy's voice was like hot cocoa on a frosty morning. The zombie was gone. He felt alive and visible.

As he bent to pick up his books, she knelt beside him. Her subtle perfume, silky smooth hair, coy smile. He imagined her in her snug, little nightgown.

"I'm sorry I snuck into your room."

She blushed. "I'm sorry I screamed."

He rubbed his neck remembering her father's grip and his stinging words. "I don't know what I was thinking."
Peggy nibbled her lip and they locked eyes. He felt an embarrassing warmth rush over his face, sweat beaded on his neck and forehead.

She elbowed him and slowly stood.

His eyes followed the smooth curves of her snug jeans as they rose before him.

She smiled at his glazed eyes, then lifted his jaw shut with her finger. She left her books on the floor, reached out her hand, and pulled him up. "You know, a gentleman would help a lady with her books."

He looked around as if searching for a gentleman, and she swatted him. They knelt together to pick up her books.

He couldn't help staring at her lips as he blindly reached for her books. She laughed and knocked him on his behind.

"What was that for?"

She puckered her lips, squinted, then turned to walk to class.

His eyes followed the bouncing design on her jeans.

She stopped at the corner of the hallway, waved, and said, “Come on. We’re already late.”

Chapter 37

Nathan and Donna

One Saturday morning, Nathan decided to revive the neglected Chesterfield. He had stripped the worn fabric, careful to avoid any injury to the fine woodwork. He gently buffed out nicks and scratches until a sudden chill ran through him. He felt dizzy and out-of-control. His body shook. His trembling hands dropped his tools, and he collapsed.

Nathan lay flat on the unforgiving concrete. He wanted to move, to get up, to scream. He wasn't paralyzed, but felt frozen, stunned by shaking chills. He was powerless until the shaking stopped.

He shook his head and tried to gather his thoughts. As soon as he felt able, he grabbed the chair and pulled himself up.

He sat for a moment, catching his breath and straining to focus.

He struggled to stand but feared he might pass out. He surrendered to the feeling and sat still.

Footsteps thundered through the kitchen toward the garage door. *Donna.*

He closed his eyes and surrendered to the chills.

* * *

Nathan opened his eyes and squinted at the blinding lights above him. His head pounded. His back ached as though he had been lying in the same position for days. He let out a moan and heard Donna's familiar voice.

"Nathan. You're awake." She stood over him, smiling, rubbing his forehead and blocking the blinding light.

"Where am I?"

She kissed his forehead. "You're in the hospital."

He squinted and frowned. He wanted desperately to sit up, but he felt winded and weak. "What's wrong with me?"

He knew it must be bad, because Donna bit her lip. She

forced a smile and kept rubbing his face. Her eyes swelled with tears, and so did his.

Without doing a thing, he felt like he was somehow breaking her heart. As bad as he wanted to know, he didn't want her to have to say it. "It's okay. I can hear it from the doctor."

He closed his eyes imagining cancer, a stroke, a heart attack. He took a deep breath, or tried to, but he couldn't. He was panting. He turned toward the sound of beeping over his left shoulder and watched the waving green and red lines and the blinking heart in the upper corner. He felt the plastic prongs and the oxygen blowing into his dry nose.

"I'm so out-of-breath."

Donna squeezed his hand as the nurse walked in.

"Mr. Fortune, you're awake."

Thank you, Nurse Obvious. I already knew that much. He tried to force a smile through his pursed lips.

Hefty, mid-forties with limp brown hair but a smile that could end a war. She patted his foot through the blanket and said, "Your cardiologist, Dr. Jackson will be here soon. I'm sure you're eager to hear from him."

"Nurse, do you mind turning off those lights."

He smiled as the lights dimmed.

"Do you need anything else, Mr. Fortune?"

"I could use a shot of Southern Comfort."

The nurse looked at Donna. "I guess he's doing better than we thought." She left the room.

Donna smiled and swatted him on the shoulder. "Why'd you say something like that?"

Nathan chuckled. "Well, it's true."

Donna crossed her arms and smirked.

He opened his eyes wide as he pressed his hands against the bedrails. He coughed and panted as he tried to scoot up in the bed. How could one simple task be so exhausting?

Nathan had never been one to sit around. He had to

always be doing something, but even trying to sit up in bed had become work. For the first time in his life, he understood why hospital patients needed a button on their beds in order to sit up. Even that was too much apparently.

Donna pushed the button for him and kissed his forehead.

He felt his breathing ease a little as he sat upright. He leaned forward and placed his elbows on his bent knees.

"Watch your gown." Donna pulled the edge of his gown over his knees and covered him with his sheet.

"Sorry. Not used to wearing a dress." He chuckled and coughed. "For that matter, I'm not used to not wearing underwear."

Donna smiled and swatted him again. "How long have I been here?"

A deeper voice answered from the doorway. "Three days." Long white coat. Stethoscope. Necktie. Fifty-something by the salt-and-pepper hair and crow's feet. "I'm Dr. Jackson."

He walked in and nodded to Donna. "I met your wife while you were still in the ER." He shook Nathan's hand with a firm, smooth grip. Nathan smirked at the soft baby-butt hands that had never done a day's work.

The doctor crinkled his brow, leaned on the bedrails and smiled. "Mr. Fortune, you were in bad shape. We had to keep you sedated on a ventilator." He spread his arms wide. "But look at you now. Breathing on your own and wide awake. How are you feeling?"

"I have no idea. I don't even know what happened. The last thing I remember is I was leaning over an old Chesterfield."

"A cigar?" Dr. Jackson asked.

"It's a fancy, tufted chair."

"That was right before you collapsed," Donna said as she reached for his hand.

Her tired eyes and furrowed brow told him she'd been

with him through it all. He squeezed her hand. She was his lifeline as he was drowning in his thoughts. Her grip, her eyes, the doctor's tone, all told him he'd almost died. He swallowed hard, coughed and looked at the doctor.

"You passed out," Dr. Jackson said. "When you arrived via ambulance, you were unconscious and barely responsive to painful stimuli."

"You're looking at me like I almost died."

The doctor looked at Donna. His face tightened.

"You're scaring me, doc."

The doctor nodded. "You were scaring us too for a while, but you're stable now. You had the flu, and it hit you extremely hard, affecting your heart."

"What does that mean?"

"The virus attacked your heart. You have heart failure."

Heart failure. Nathan stared at the clock on the opposite wall. Unstoppable ticking. The second hand marching away, stealing tiny bits of his life. His chest ached. He coughed and panted, chasing air but never catching it. Heart failure pressed against him like a smothering pillow.

"Doc, tell me I'm not going to feel like this forever."

"Time will tell. Some people, if not most, recover at least a good bit of their cardiac function, but some don't. We have to wait and see which group you fall into."

Wait and see? Nathan fixed his eyes on Donna.

She squeezed his hand. "We'll get through this."

Chapter 38
Brooke

Brooke froze against the tree and strained to listen.

Time stood still. She strained to hear footsteps, breathing, anything that would tell her where he was. Her pounding heart told her he was close. But all she could hear were birds, leaves rustling in the breeze, and scurrying squirrels.

Finally, she saw headlights through the trees. A car passed, turned around, and pulled to a stop. She could hear faint voices but was too scared to move. The car sat there, motor running, headlights and flashers on. She wanted to run, wave her arms, and scream, but fear paralyzed her. She knew he was right there waiting for her to give herself away, so she dared not move.

She breathed a little easier when she heard sirens and saw flashing red and blue lights atop an over-sized SUV. She slowly pulled herself up and turned toward the lights.

The SUV stopped. Lights flashing. Spotlight on the crashed car. The siren stopped, and two officers climbed out of the vehicle. Heart racing, mouth dry, Brooke stepped toward the light, but when she opened her mouth to scream, a powerful hand slapped her across the mouth. And her eyes shot wide open. She screamed against his firm hand and recoiled at his hot breath on her neck. He leaned into her, shoving her against the tree. His forehead slamming against her ear. She couldn't move.

He whispered in her ear. "Hello, Brooke."

She kicked and scratched and tried to bite him, but she was too weak, and his grip was unshakeable.

"Don't fight." He spit the words through gnashed teeth as he slammed her head against the tree once more, then he wrapped his left arm around her neck, his right arm behind her head, and he choked her.

"Goodnight, Brooke."

She fell limp, and her world went black.

Chapter 39
Joe and Peggy

Joe felt like his life was over until he saw Peggy or thought of Peggy. When his father died, his joy had faded. Then, when his mother married Frank, he couldn't imagine life getting any worse. Peggy became his reason for living, his reason for getting out of bed in the morning.

She made it a point to find him every morning so they could walk to class together. Thank God they had first period together.

"I don't know what I would do without you, Peggy."

She slugged him.

He grabbed his shoulder and moaned. "Oh! Okay, maybe without you, I wouldn't have to go to the doctor for my broken arm and my broken heart."

They both smiled, and she punched him again. Harder.

Then she ran.

It was the last bell, and the halls flooded with students scurrying to leave the school.

Peggy stuffed a note in his hand and blew him a kiss, then an air punch, as she trotted off toward her bus.

Joe stuck the note in his pocket and warped back into invisible zombie mode. He ran toward his bus. He was not eager to get on board, but he wanted to find a seat that didn't leave him at the mercy of Goliath.

He bounded up the steps and thought *where's the nerdiest little sixth grade girl?* As he took the final step, the bus driver's hand pressed against his chest.

"The principal's talking to you. Can't you hear?"

Joe felt a tug on his jacket and turned around to see a fiercely bald head and furrowed brow.

"Young man, come with me."

The walk seemed to take three times longer than normal as he plodded back into the school. He had never been to the principal's office.

Mr. Downs was a stodgy character. Over-worn plaid blazers. Bow ties. Balding and badly needing a haircut for what was left. His office smelled of dust and cough drops. Dusty shelves lined with books, pictures, and bowling trophies.

Joe had always imagined the principal's office as something more cryptic: a huge chalkboard with knife marks instead of chalk marks, one for every kid who'd gotten paddled, and special ones for the kids who'd gone to the hospital or been suspended. He wondered about the poor kids who were never seen or heard from again. He imagined a chair with leather straps and buckles on the armrests and front legs to strap down the trouble-makers and make them listen to classical music and poetry.

But Mr. Downs's office was nothing like that. No instruments of torture. No bright lights, not even a paddle hanging on the wall with his fraternity letters. His solid oak desk had a few books, a calendar, a notebook, and some neatly-placed pens.

Mr. Downs leaned back in his leather chair, clasped his hands behind his head, and swiveled back-and-forth.

"Joe. I noticed you were quite late for Mr. Wilkins's class this morning. Can you tell me why?" He folded his hands on his desk. "Is there something wrong?"

Joe stared at Mr. Downs's shiny dome. He tried looking at his eyes, or his tie, or anything else, but every time Mr. Downs shifted, a glint of light would bounce off his head. Part of Joe was laughing inside, but the bigger part of him was dying, wondering why he was there and how he would survive.

He lowered his face into his hands and tried to breathe. His heart was pounding, and his mouth was dry. His stomach lurched, and he tasted acid.

He lifted his head and looked at Mr. Downs. Lips trembling, he didn't know what to say, and he was afraid to say anything.

Mr. Downs slid out of his chair and sat beside Joe.

"Joe, breathe. You were late to Mr. Wilkins's class. It was one class. That's all, but that's not like you, and Mr. Wilkins was concerned. He said you were not only late, but you seemed upset and didn't participate. Are you okay?"

Joe's breathing stuttered as he thought about trying to speak. His life had gone from feeling like a whirlwind to feeling like a toilet flushing, and he was caught in the downward spiral. His eyes were glued to the floor. His hands were slippery with sweat. Every muscle quivered.

He looked up at Mr. Downs, and the flood gates opened. All the emotions of the last few years came gushing out. Without a thought, he clutched Mr. Downs's suit jacket and buried his face in his chest.

His principal wrapped him in a firm embrace. "It's okay. I know you've been through a lot. I'll call your mother and tell her you missed the bus."

Joe's heart skipped a beat at the thought of Frank answering a call from the principal. "No! Please don't. She's not home. She doesn't get off work until five. I don't want my step… Frank to come get me." He looked back at the floor and mumbled. "I don't want him to know I got in trouble."

Mr. Downs's face turned red. His jaw tightened. "Joe, I need to know what's going on."

Joe lay his head back against the bench. Tears streamed as he stared at the ceiling. He stared until the tears slowed to a trickle, then the looming presence of Mr. Downs stood over him.

"Joe. You can talk to me."

Joe sniffed to stifle his tears. He wished he were the invisible zombie again, so he could skulk out the door and leave little pieces of himself everywhere until there was nothing left.

Mr. Downs's hands on his shoulders reminded him he was very much alive.

"Joe, I'm sorry you were late for class, but that's not the problem here. It's obvious you're having a tough time, and you're not yourself. I'm willing to listen, and I want to help."

Joe looked at him and thought *a tough time? I'm having a tough life. My dad's…* He couldn't even think it.

He blew out the heaviest sigh. "Mr. Downs, I'm sorry. I didn't mean to be late to class. I just had some trouble with my backpack this morning."

Mr. Downs squeezed his shoulder. "You're a good kid, an honest kid. I can tell because you're a terrible liar." He wafted his hand to encourage him to stand. "Let's go."

As they walked, Mr. Downs said, "I had a step-father too. Life was never the same. I got used to him after a while, but I never considered him a father, not to me."

Joe smiled because Mr. Downs was making such an effort, but he couldn't let him know anything about Frank. He pictured himself locked in a closet, forced to sleep in the barn, thrown down the stairs, or worse. No way was he going to tell anyone anything about Frank—not even Peggy.

* * *

Mr. Downs gave him a ride.

When they turned onto his street, Joe said, "Can you stop here? I don't want Fr… my mom to know you brought me home."

"I'm sorry, Joe. I'm responsible for you. I have to take you to your house."

The invisible zombie was back, at least for a minute. As soon as Frank saw him, the zombie would be gone, and miserable Joe would be fresh meat.

Joe leaned his head against the window. He imagined hurling himself from the car. *With my luck, I'd get run over. I'm dead meat either way.*

He jolted as Mr. Downs said, "You know, Joe, I said I could never think of my step-dad as my dad, but that doesn't mean he wasn't a good man or a good husband to my mother. Maybe you should give Frank a little time and try to see things from his point of view."

Frank won't give me the time of day.

"I know it's hard. I lived it too. I also know you're a good kid. I knew your father, and he was proud of you. Don't you think he would want you to try?"

Joe turned to face him and gave a fake smile and nodded. "Please don't say anything. You can talk to Mom, but please don't tell Frank." *It'll only make things worse.*

"Don't worry. You're not the first student I've had to drive home."

* * *

Joe's stomach jumped into his chest as they made the final turn toward Frank's house. There it stood. The austere museum of a house where Joe was afraid to breathe or touch anything.

Mr. Downs killed the engine and sat for a moment watching the silent, sterile house. He patted Joe on the knee. "Ready?"

Joe tried to not throw up as he grabbed his backpack and slid out of the car. Mr. Downs followed

Joe thanked God his mother answered the door.

She looked beyond Joe to the principal. "Mr. Downs? Is something wrong?"

The pain in her eyes weighed on Joe, but he looked past to see if Frank was home.

"It was all my fault," Mr. Downs said. "Joe was helping me deliver supplies to some of our classrooms. I lost track of the time, causing him to miss his bus. I hope you don't mind me bringing him home. He's a fine young man."

Joe smiled as his mother's face lit up. He hadn't seen that smile in months.

* * *

As Mr. Downs backed his car out of the driveway, he winked at Joe. That man earned a special place in Joe's heart that day.

"Joe, I'm proud of you for helping Mr. Downs," Mom said. "I was afraid something had happened at school. Peggy's mom called asking how you were doing. She said Peggy came home worried saying you weren't acting like yourself. I'm glad you're okay."

Splashing and sizzling noises came from the kitchen, and she dashed back to check the stovetop. Joe followed, hoping he wouldn't need to grab the fire extinguisher.

As his mother pulled the smoking skillet off the burner, the basement door banged open, and Frank shouted, "What the blazes! Isn't someone watching the stove?" His unforgiving eyes cut through any amount of joy that tried to make its way into that house.

"It's my fault," Joe said.

His mother almost dropped the pan as she waited for Frank's next move.

"What am I going to do with you?" He sneered and turned on his mocking whiny voice. "'It's my fault. It's my fault.' Are those your favorite words? Because you sure say them a lot. Once in a while, I would like to hear that no one is at fault because whatever it was was done right the first time."

How long can a person's stomach stay in his chest? Joe was apparently trying to find out. He ran to the bathroom and threw up. As bad as he felt, he was thankful none of his vomit got on the floor. One less reason for Frank to yell.

He used AJAX cleaner and a wet paper towel on every affected surface in the bathroom. He rinsed his mouth, brushed his teeth, and slid to the floor. With his face in his hands, he sat between the toilet and the sink.

Talking turned to yelling through the door until he could hear the muffled voices turn to clear threats.

"You want to give this all up and go back to squalor because you can't control your son? Do you?" Frank screamed louder. "Do you!"

His mother's "No," barely made it through the closed door.

Mom's life was over. She'd died when his father died. All that was left was the miserable shell of a woman who didn't want her children living out of the family car.

Joe clenched his teeth. He'd had enough of Frank. He stormed out the bathroom and ran into the kitchen. "You can yell at me all you want. You can beat me. You can tie me down. I can take whatever you're dishing, but you will not yell at my mother. I said it was my fault. Are you deaf or did you just not hear me?"

"Why, you little brat." Frank started toward him.

Joe's mother tried to step in the way, but Frank shoved her into the sink and kept pressing toward Joe. He spoke at her as he walked. "Isn't it time for you to go to your women's Bible study?"

She tried to grab his arm, but he slapped her across the temple. "I said go. Now go."

Joe charged at him like an undersized cornerback, tackling his waist and driving him into the refrigerator.

Frank tossed him aside and opened the door to the garage. "Don't worry. I'll see Joe gets his supper and gets an early bedtime."

She glanced at Joe.

"Go, Mom. We'll be fine."

With trembling hands and tears streaming down her face, she grasped her Bible and walked into the garage.

The engine started, but the garage door was still closed. For a moment, Joe wanted to join her and leave the garage door closed. He pushed past Frank and pressed against the driver's window. Mom's eyes reflected his pain. As they looked at each other, Frank smacked the wall and depressed the garage door opener.

Mom glanced at Joe as she backed out. His stomach knotted as he feared it might be his last time to see her. As she turned her attention to the driveway, Joe felt the sting of Frank's grip on his shoulder. The garage door closed, and Frank dragged him back into the house.

Frank shoved him into the kitchen. He scowled and spit his words through gritted teeth. "Look at this kitchen! Do you know what it looked like before you came here? Do you have any idea?" Frank stepped toward the grease-spattered island and eyed the knife block as he spoke. He touched his index finger to the cleaver handle, smiled and wriggled his finger over it.

Joe's heart raced. Skin tingled. Sweat beaded on his forehead. All of his fight-or-flight senses launched into full terror mode.

He glanced at the backdoor. The creek was not too far from the house. Joe was certain he could jump the creek, run deeper into the woods, and find a place to hide. He grabbed a plate and flung it toward Frank. He missed, and the plate bounced off the refrigerator and shattered on the floor. It drew Frank's attention long enough for Joe to snatch his backpack and bolt out the back door.

Joe sprinted toward the creek. His lungs burned. His chest ached. He couldn't run fast enough or far enough. He glanced behind him and saw that Frank wasn't following him. He looked through the trees and saw him leaning against the door frame. He imagined his sinister smile.

Joe slunk behind the nearest tree. He leaned against it to catch his breath walked deep into the woods and along the creek. No need to run or jump over the creek. Frank wasn't coming.

A towering sycamore seemed like a safe spot to rest. He leaned against the tree and watched the creek. His tears dribbled like the water rippling over the rocks.

It didn't matter what was going on. The gentle, ceaseless flowing of that creek always brought him peace. Like the intoxicating song of a siren, the water soothed him. Light flickered across the water. Tiny rings gurgled around the smoothed stones. His eyes caught the subtle dance of water striders and marveled at how they could walk on the surface.

The shadows grew longer. The water turned black as the sun sank behind the creek bank. Joe rubbed his goosebumps and his tears, then pulled his sweatshirt out of his backpack.

You can't stay out here all night, he imagined his father saying.

"I don't want to go to Frank's. It's not home. He doesn't want me there, and I don't want to be there."

What about your mom? She wants you there. She needs you.

You're not here, and neither is Mom.

The horizon faded from pink to red to deep blue. Joe was cold, but he found comfort in being unseen, unheard, and unhurt.

Twilight slowly turned to midnight. Cold turned colder. If that wasn't enough to spoil his comfort, the woods seemed alive. Crackling sticks, rustling noises in the thicket, treetops creaking in the wind.

His eyes were wide open, and he strained to listen. The rustling and crackling grew louder and closer followed by panting.

His pulse pounded as he imagined the worst, then a familiar bark calmed his fears.

Scamp. Peggy's dog.

"What are you doing all the way out here, buddy?"

"I came by to check on you."

He startled at Peggy's voice. "How did you get here?"

"I used Scamp to sneak out. I dropped by earlier as your mom was leaving. I stopped at the road as the garage door opened. All I could see was smoke, then I saw your mom backing the car out of the garage. She backed out onto the road and about jumped out of her seat when she saw me. She stopped beside me, said I shouldn't go inside because Frank had been drinking, and he was mad, then she drove off."

Peggy sat beside Joe and continued, "I was scared so I walked around back to listen in case I needed to call 911."

"911? What did you think was going to happen?"

"I don't know. I just know you look scared when you talk about Frank's temper—especially when he's drunk."

Joe raised his eyebrows. "Yeah." He said nothing more to avoid adding worry. Frank was scary. Joe didn't want to be around him. Ever.

"So, you came around back..."

"Then you came running out the backdoor making a beeline for the creek. When it was obvious Frank wasn't coming, I knew you were safe for the moment. I went home. After Mom and Dad had gone to bed, I took Scamp outside to do his business, but I couldn't stop worrying, wondering if you were okay. So, I grabbed Scamp, hopped in my car and drove to Jenkins's place. I pulled into the lane and parked out of sight, then I followed the creek."

With tears and a smile, Peggy leaned over and hugged Joe.

They sat in silence. Moonlight flickered on the creek as the magic water striders defied gravity.

Peggy lay her head on his shoulder. His skin tingled and warmth surged through his entire body. He wanted to wrap her in his arms, run to her car, drive away, and never look back. She was the one thing in his life that still felt like home.

But he couldn't run away. He couldn't leave Mom with Frank. His throat ached. He wished he could go back in time to change everything. What he would give to get Frank out of his life. Even as Peggy slid her hand into his, he couldn't stop thinking about Frank. His evil eyes and his smug smile.

He held Peggy's hand and stared at the creek.

Peggy squeezed his hand, lifted her head and kissed his cheek. "Do you think God puts people together?"

"Sure. Why not?" He chuckled. "I mean people would look funny with scattered parts."

Peggy knuckle-punched his shoulder.

"Ouch."

"I mean it. Do you think God brought us together?"

"Never really thought about it. It sounds nice, but I don't know if it works that way." He looked at the tiny hint of light still clinging to her perfect face. "I sure hope it works that way. I would love to think that God brought you and me together." He lowered his head and said softly, "I would love to think nothing could ever tear us apart."

Peggy pressed him against that sycamore and planted another kiss. On his lips. Deeper. Stronger. And longer.

He offered no resistance. He was hers, and in that moment, Frank and the rest of the world disappeared.

Until he heard the faint sound of the back door opening. They both flinched and looked toward the house. Frank's daunting silhouette stepped into the backyard.

Frank shouted, "I'm locking up in five minutes. You need to get a shower, then get to bed."

Joe squeezed Peggy and planted one last kiss on her unforgettable lips. "I've got to go before Lurch locks the door."

She hung onto his hand until the last second, then let go as he ran to the house and slid in the back door.

He was tempted to drop his backpack by the door like he had in the old days, but he knew better. He trotted up the stairs and tossed the backpack on his bed and closed the door. He kicked off his shoes and was pulling his shirt up over his head when he felt Frank's unyielding arms wrap around him.

Frank grasped Joe's wrists and held them behind his back. "Did you really think you could just run away from me, son?" He said "son" painfully and slowly like grinding a dull dagger into his chest.

I'm not your son. Joe swallowed his pride for the sake of his life and the sake of his mother. "I'm sorry, sir. I regret my mistake."

"That's a good boy, but I'm not sure you've really learned your lesson. Come with me."

Frank held Joe's wrists behind his back as he led him down the hall, down the stairs, and to the basement. The dark, musty, single-lightbulb-dangling, torture room basement. The one part of Frank's house unfit for anyone.

His spindly fingers dug into Joe's neck as he shoved him down the stairs. Joe tripped and tumbled. His hands and knees stung as he skidded across the damp, uneven stone floor.

"Well, your mother's not back yet. It looks like her Bible study is turning into an overnighter, so we, or I mean you, can have some alone time to better think how to live your life. Imagine all that your mother is learning about being a good Christian and think about how you can apply that to your own life. I recommend starting with the command to 'obey your parents. Honor your father and mother.'"

He slammed Joe into an old wooden chair in the middle of the room. He opened a cabinet, pulled out a thick, white rope and slowly walked around him. "Did you know that the commandment, 'Obey your parents in the Lord,' is the first commandment with a promise?"

Frank stopped behind him, looped the rope around his chest and pulled him against the chair. He leaned into Joe's ear and whispered, "That you may live long on the earth."

As he spoke the words, he tied Joe's hands behind his back and tightened the rope, then he took a torn sheet, twisted it into a tight roll and wrapped it around Joe's mouth as a gag.

"The nice thing about using a large cotton rope and a torn sheet is, if you do it right, they don't leave any bruises."

Joe tightened every muscle and leaned back against the chair as Frank's silhouette loomed over him.

"I don't want to leave any bruises. I just want to teach you a lesson. You will learn respect if you want to live in this house."

The cold air and concrete walls felt like they were closing in as Frank tightened the gag. "I could've let you scream. There's no one around to hear except me, but I'm not going to listen to you scream like a girl."

Each step creaked as Frank climbed the stairs. He stopped at the top and said, "Goodnight, Joe." Then he slammed the door.

One solitary lightbulb was all that protected Joe from the utter darkness he already felt.

Chapter 40

Nathan and Donna

Nathan slept in his recliner with his oxygen tank beside him. He could barely walk, but in his dreams, he could fly. One night he was playing croquet and commanding the Starship Enterprise. Another, he was running across America with Forrest Gump and a herd of middle school cheerleaders. He'd eaten too many onions that night.

But in the morning, everything was the same. Always the same. His living room had turned into a hospital room. His walker beside him. Wheelchair by the door. Plastic urinal on the floor next to his chair.

Sweat beaded on his forehead as he tried to sit up. He strained and panted, but his strength failed, and he sagged into his recliner.

Tears flowed as he thought about how easily he'd been able to run around the furniture store just weeks before. Imprisoned in his home, he couldn't even get out of his chair by himself.

He wanted out. He wanted to go outside and breathe. He wanted to run, and if he couldn't run, he wanted Donna to push him in his wheelchair so he could pretend to run or even fly.

He missed the store. He missed the smell of the stains and solvents. They'd become like friends. He missed digging through other people's trash and uncovering discarded heirlooms. He missed bringing new life to old and weary furniture, but he missed something else even more, something he couldn't share with Donna.

Trembling and short of breath, he strained to reach his phone.

* * *

Donna rested her hands on the bathroom counter and hung her head over the sink. Her back ached and her eyes begged for more sleep. She scarcely recognized the woman in the mirror.

It had been a long night. Up and down as Nathan had coughed and sputtered through the night. Every cough, every pause between breaths, and every groan set her on pins and needles.

"Breathe, Donna," she told herself. She looked at those tired eyes in the mirror. "You can handle anyone for eight hours, but 24 hours a day, every miserable day?" She shook her head, took a deep breath, and splashed cold water in her face.

She missed the girl she used to know, the girl who hung the moon for the boy she used to know. Those days were never coming back, but she hoped the feelings somehow could.

She used to take the time to make herself beautiful. That girl in the mirror used to do the same. She studied those tired eyes. *I know you're in there somewhere.* "Girl, you've got to remember who you are and where you came from. You didn't get this far to sit down and give up."

She took a deep breath, pulled her make-up from the drawer, and forced a smile. She brushed life into her eyelashes and freshened her cheeks while she imagined Nathan sitting in that chair, barely breathing, never moving, occasionally calling for her, sometimes cursing or yelling, but all the while, sinking into the chair. It was his prison.

She feared death would be his only escape.

As she added the finishing touches to her makeup, the doorbell rang.

She shouted, "Nathan, I'm coming." She wrapped herself in her bathrobe, scampered down the hall, and started toward the door, but Nathan waved his hand to stop her.

"It's okay. I'm wearing my robe."

He scowled and shrugged her off with another wave. His gravelly voice said, "The door's unlocked. Pretty sure it's Uncle Charles."

The doorbell rang again, and Nathan strained a shout. "It's open."

Donna squeezed her robe a little tighter as she imagined Uncle Charles stepping through the door. Initially his smile and his kind eyes had been a comfort to her, but the flirtatious, old man had slowly become more of a dirty old man to her. His eyes no longer wondered but wandered. His voice no longer warmed her heart but warned her to keep an eye on him. She couldn't put her finger on it, but something felt wrong, and her gut begged her to stay until Uncle Charles was gone.

She ducked around the corner and back to the bathroom.

* * *

Nathan perked up as Uncle Charles twisted the knob and nudged the door open with his foot. "Hey, Nate. Sorry I took so long." He looked around. "Donna home?"

Nathan motioned for him to talk softly and nodded toward the bathroom.

"Oh. I won't stay long." He stepped back outside and waddled through the door dragging an old chair into the house.

"Where are you planning on putting that?"

Uncle Charles nodded toward the basement door.

Nathan shrugged and nodded his agreement.

Uncle Charles hefted the chair, half-carrying, half-dragging it. Nathan covered his face, thinking about the work piling up. Dragging that relic here meant Uncle Charles was running out of room at the store. Nathan shook his head. It was no use. The work would continue to pile up since Uncle Charles had neither the skills nor the gumption to do what only Nathan could do.

Nathan cringed at the clunks and bumps and scrapes as Uncle Charles dragged that old chair down the steps. One loud clunk and scrape of wood on concrete. Then footsteps clomped up the stairs.

Nathan said, "Not sure what creaked and cracked more,

the stairs or your knees."

Uncle Charles hobbled over to the sofa and sat next to Nathan's recliner. He glanced over his shoulder toward the hallway, then pulled a plastic bag out of his jacket and handed it to Nathan. "Sorry if it's not enough. It's best I could do."

Nathan looked disgusted but forced a half-smile as he examined the bag. Two pill bottles. He guessed about 150 hydrocodone. He lifted his eyes with some effort and leered at Uncle Charles. "It'll do for now." He thumbed through the pills, counting them again and glancing toward the closed bathroom door. He leaned toward Uncle Charles and whispered, "I'm going through these things like mad, and the doctor won't give me enough to do squat."

Uncle Charles patted his shoulder. "I'm glad I could help, Nathan. So, when's the doc say you'll be back to your old self and back to work?"

Back to work? Nathan sighed. "It ain't that easy. He hasn't given me much hope."

"You mean you could be stuck like this forever?"

"Until I die… Maybe."

Uncle Charles stuck his hands in his pockets and shook his head. "Sorry. Wish there was something I could do."

Nathan lowered his footrest, leaned forward and grabbed his glass of water from the side table. The bathroom door remained closed, but the faucet had stopped running. As he listened for the door, he quickly popped two hydrocodone and washed them down.

The bathroom door swung open, and Donna rounded the corner.

"Oh, hey, Donna," Uncle Charles drew his hand from his pocket and waved.

She waltzed into the kitchen all made up like she was going out. "Anything I can get you, Charles? Something to drink?"

"Nah. I'm good. Thanks." Uncle Charles leaned over and whispered to Nathan. "She doesn't know about the drugs?"

Nathan grabbed Uncle Charles's arm and snarled, "And she'd better never find out."

Uncle Charles frowned and jerked his arm free. "Sometimes, I don't know you, Nathan." He stood and ambled toward the door, flung it open and hollered, "Bye, Donna. You're still the prettiest thing ever. Don't let old grouchy pants tell you any different."

He closed the door, opened it again and hollered. "If he gives you too much grief and you decide to leave, you know where you can find me."

Donna waltzed out of the kitchen, followed Uncle Charles out the door and gave him a peck on the cheek before he walked to his car. He was an old softy with a big, warm heart, a heart that still worked—unlike Nathan's.

The house seemed so dark when she stepped inside and closed the door. She'd done her best to cover the menthol-sweat-and-urine smell that clung to everything, but it was still there.

She plodded back into the kitchen and stared at the clumpy oatmeal and egg whites with avocado slices. She poured two glasses of skim milk. No comparison to the sausage, biscuits and gravy, and scrambled eggs she used to make, but it was what the doctor ordered.

She loaded two plates, took a deep breath, and headed toward the living room and "old grouchy pants."

But he was smiling and sat up without a struggle. His hands were steady, resting on the armrests, and his forehead was dry.

"You look like you're feeling better."

"Seeing Uncle Charles always makes me feel better. I think today's going to be a good day." His half-smile had been replaced by a real one, for a change. He chuckled and said, "I guess I haven't had any good days lately."

Donna kissed his forehead as she balanced their breakfast.

He didn't grab her the way he used to. She missed the tussling between breakfast and the bedroom. Most of the time breakfast had won, but sometimes the biscuits and gravy had grown cold, and both of them had been late to work.

As she studied the warmth in his eyes, she hoped those days weren't gone forever. The flame was not dead, but she wondered how long the smoldering coals could survive.

She leaned across him and set his plate on the end table. Her chest in his face, she smiled as he sniffed her subtle perfume.

Maybe there was more life in his heart than she realized.

Chapter 41
Joe and Peggy

The solitary lightbulb dangled over young Joe's head. The glow became a blur as tears streamed. His throat ached from swallowing sobs. He didn't scream against the gag. He didn't fight the ropes. He surrendered to their grip.

Minutes turned to hours. Finally, he heard the rattle and felt the vibration of the garage door opening. He wanted to scream, but he heard a thump against the door, and his one lightbulb flicked on and off, Frank's signal to keep quiet.

Mom! The silent shout echoed in his head. *Why did you marry him? Why did you marry a monster?*

Faint footsteps came from the garage. They clomped through the kitchen, grew louder, then stopped outside the basement door.

Frank's voice sent fire through his veins. "Margie, I'm sorry. I don't know what I was thinking. I lost my temper. I've had so much going on with the business. I shouldn't have let the stress get to me, and I certainly shouldn't have let it pour out on you and Joe."

Joe wanted to scream, but he knew fighting with Frank was only going to make it worse for his mother and for him. He surrendered to the silence. *You win, Frank.*

"I will never raise a hand against you again. Please forgive me."

The soft thud and jingle were her purse and her keys hitting the floor. Joe was glad he couldn't see them making up.

Then his mother asked, "Where's Joe?"

He heard the swift thud of Frank's boot against the door.

"I was kind of hard on Joe. I realize that. We had a little talk to sort out our differences. I think he understands, and I expect us to get along much better from now on."

"Oh, Frank. I'm so glad. Joe!" She called.

"Shh. After we talked, I walked him to his room and put him to bed, but I left a nightlight on for him."

"Frank, I'm sorry. I was scared earlier, but I forgive you. Now let's forget about it and move on."

Her footsteps clicked over the hardwood then softened as they reached the carpet.

Joe's hope faded as the light flicked off, then back on. The knob on the basement door rattled. Frank's footsteps thudded overhead then stopped. The glow beneath the basement door vanished.

The house fell silent.

No one is coming.

Acid rose in his throat. He choked, sputtered, and swallowed. Joe had never felt more alone. He strained against the rope, but it was no use. He was strapped in tight. Only his tears could escape.

He imagined Frank dead, and his mind spun. As the lightbulb gently swayed, the basement seemed to move. The amber light cast shadows through the exposed studs like a harvest moon deep in the woods.

* * *

The quiet drew him into a dream. The basement disappeared, replaced by the forest.

He awakened to the soft crushing of leaves. Beyond the edge of his chair, a yearling doe slowly approached.

"Dad. Dad." He nudged his dozing father. No movement. Just slow, steady breathing.

The doe inched closer, nosing through the leaves, nibbling on acorns. His father snorted, and the doe paused.

She stood perfectly still, looking straight at the tree stand. Joe closed his eyes and gently elbowed his father, who opened his eyes without a sound, without any other movement.

The doe darted into the woods.

"It's okay, Joe. We can't shoot until 30 minutes before

sunrise." His father pointed at the horizon through the trees. "When that purple turns to pink or orange, it'll be time," and he folded his arms and went back to his nap.

As twilight hung on, Joe's mind continued to drift. The doe was not coming back, but he heard a snort. It was not his father. It was low-pitched, forceful, and it came from the woods.

The deep blue on the horizon had turned to a golden ribbon, and the purple above was being invaded with a growing wave of light blue. A ten-point buck strode out of the thicket and stood between two tall oaks. His antlers rubbed against a low hanging branch, and he pounded the ground with one hoof.

Joe's heart climbed into his throat and pounded furiously. *I should wake Dad, but if he snorts, that buck is gone.* He reached for the gun lying across his father's lap, but his reach stopped short because of his harness. He was fastened in snug.

He wrestled against the harness.

He scooched back in the seat, tried to raise up, and stretched as far as he could to grasp the gun. He bumped it, and it slid.

His father awakened and tightened his grip on the gun that wasn't there. The gun slipped from his knees and fell from the stand. His father lunged to grab it, not awake enough to remember he was not wearing the safety harness. As he gripped the barrel, his weight pulled him over the rail. The trigger caught a lower branch and unleashed a hot lead slug into Joe's right knee.

Joe screamed as he strained against the harness, watching his father plummet. He saw his body crumple against the cold, wet ground as pain ripped through his knee and vibrated through his body.

The warmth of blood poured over his legs, but it was not blood. This time it was his bladder surrendering to pain. As the wetness cooled against his skin, he awakened in the basement.

New tears somehow spilled from his tear-spent eyes.

It was my fault.

It was all my fault.

His mind had suppressed those fatal moments, but the ropes and the light awakened his pain, and his pain turned to seething hate. He no longer *imagined* Frank dead. He *wanted* him dead.

He imagined the chair as his tree stand, and Frank as his prey. He wished he had his father's 12-gauge. He would wait for Frank like he'd waited for that deer, but the ropes restrained his anger. The quiet and the dark protected him from himself and forced him to be patient.

He set his mind to a ruse of cooperation, feigned respect, and rebellion concealed in obedience until the time came.

"You are going to die, Frank," he whispered. "I promise. You will die."

* * *

The door swung open. Two feet clunked down the stairs as the door closed.

"Good morning, Joe. Did you sleep well?"

Burning eyes offered their surrender. Joe heaved a sigh as Frank removed the gag and tossed it into the trash, then untied and unwound the rope and stuffed it on a shelf.

Joe stayed in the chair as though still tied down.

"Now, that's a good boy. I think you may have learned your lesson."

Joe slowly nodded.

"It's too bad you couldn't wait to go to the bathroom. It looks like you've got laundry to do. You wouldn't want your mom to know her almost full-grown son is still wetting himself."

Frank knelt beside Joe, patted his dry leg, and whispered in his ear. "If you so much as drop a hint about any of this to your mother, you will think this was Disneyland." He patted Joe on the head and said, "I think you know what I mean."

Frank disappeared up the stairs.

Joe sat still until the house grew silent.

Chapter 42

Nathan and Donna

Nathan held the memory of Donna's kiss.

It was her first day back to work since his last hospitalization, his first day alone.

Her perfume lingered. He closed his eyes and imagined her still there. Whenever he thought of her, he remembered that young woman he'd met almost twenty years ago. He dreamed of that young beauty leaning over to kiss him. Her gentle hand stroking his cheek. Her fingers running through his hair. Her supple chest setting him on fire. Her lips consuming him.

He stayed in his dream until his pain dragged him back to reality. It shot through his knee as he straightened his leg. He grasped the armrests on his chair and tried to scoot forward and stand. His legs wobbled. His heart raced. And he broke into a sweat. His stomach lurched, and his throat burned. White spots flashed, yet the room suddenly looked dark. Breathing turned to panting and gasping, and he collapsed into his chair.

Tears washed over his face. He smacked the armrest. "There's nothing easy about this chair." The room seemed smaller and darker, the walls closing in as he sat alone. Home had become his new prison.

Nathan glanced at the clock. "Six hours until she gets home. What I used to accomplish in six hours. Now. Nothing. I sit here and breathe. Hope it gets better or hope I die. Don't much care either way. Just so stinking tired of this chair. Tired of waiting. Tired of hoping. Ready to be done."

He popped another hydrocodone and flipped on the TV. "Thank God for the remote."

Not two minutes into *The A-Team*, the phone rang.

He stared at it. The ringing taunted him. He knew it wasn't Donna. She would call, let it ring a few times, hang up, and call again. The phone kept ringing. He stared at it, not wanting to answer. But it could be someone calling to tell him Donna was hurt or ill. He grabbed the phone.

When he heard that same harassing voice, his face tensed. He said nothing and hung up.

Just in time to hear Mr. T say, “I pity the fool.”

Nathan imagined finagling some kind of explosive to blow up his stalker, but he wasn’t part of the A-Team, and he couldn’t do much from his chair.

Chapter 43

Joe and Peggy

Joe sat alone in the cold, musty basement. He'd tried to hold his urine until morning, but he'd soaked himself, and he sat there. Numb. Forgotten. And lost. His neck stiff and sore. Shoulders throbbing. Hands and feet swollen. Heart broken. Empty.

The solitary bulb slowly swayed like a pendulum keeping time—hypnotizing him. The house was still, so still he could hear his heartbeat. His pulse pounded like the slow, monotone tick tock of time counting every miserable second.

The doorbell rang and snapped him back to reality.

Peggy?

It had to be her.

Joe clambered out of the chair, stumbled, and fell on his face. His legs tingled with sleep. He brushed the dust off his knees and hands, and hobbled up the stairs as the bell continued to ring.

Pounding mixed with muted screams. "Joe, are you in there? Are you okay?"

He looked down and patted his jeans. *Almost dry.* He felt a sudden embarrassed warmth at the idea of Peggy seeing him this way—smelling him this way. But he had to see her. He needed to see her.

He rushed toward the door and opened it part-way, hiding his lower half behind the door.

"What are you doing here?"

Peggy pushed through the door. "Is that any way to welcome a guest?" She frowned and rubbed her belly. "I told the nurse I didn't feel well."

Joe wanted to hug her more than anything, but he could smell himself and didn't want it to be their last hug.

"Would you like a drink? There's milk or Coke in the

fridge."

She nodded. "Milk, please."

As he poured a tall glass, he asked, "Do you mind if I run upstairs for a minute?"

She gave him an awkward look and shrugged, then he darted up the stairs.

Joe was pretty sure he just set the world record for fastest shower. He threw on some clean clothes and hurried back down the stairs.

"Sorry, I didn't sleep well. I just needed to freshen up."

"You are a terrible liar, and since when have you worried about how you look?"

Heat filled Joe's cheeks. The light in his dark universe stood right in front of him, but he didn't know what to say or where to begin. He knew Frank would kill him if he breathed a word to anyone. He felt like his heart had been ripped out—like his mother had married Frankenstein and moved into his castle. Still, everything inside him wanted to tell Peggy. He wanted to share everything with her.

Peggy reached out and held his hand. Her warm and gentle touch brought life to his weary heart. "Is it Frank?"

Tears welled and trickled down his cheeks. "I wish Mom had never met him." *I wish Dad were still here.* His lips trembled, and the shaking spread even as Peggy pulled him close.

Her arms wrapped around him and held the weight of his world. He didn't want her to ever let go. Nothing was the way it had been. Frank's house would never be home. And Peggy was no longer next door.

He took a step back, slid his hands down her arms, and grasped her hands. She smiled and lifted his hands to her lips, kissed them and held them there. He looked into her eyes. Studied them. He could see that she loved him. He prayed she loved him as deeply as he loved her.

He wanted to talk. He wanted to tell her everything he was feeling, everything that had happened, his fears, his hopes.

But the lump in his throat made it impossible. Peggy closed the gap.

Her eyes said, *but I'm here now*, and she kissed him.

The world disappeared for five heavenly seconds, but Joe couldn't keep it away. His cold, angry world weighed on him, squeezing the life out of him. He felt cold and limp.

Peggy stepped back. "Joe? Are you okay?"

Her words seemed as distant as an echo. His cheeks felt clammy, and sweat ran down his face. His throat suddenly dry and his head spinning, he plodded toward the kitchen to get a drink.

He fought more tears as he leaned over the sink. Hands trembling, he reached for a glass but knocked it over. He felt Peggy's hand on his.

She grabbed the glass as it rolled across the countertop. The sink seemed to move as she turned on the faucet. Her face became blurry and shrouded in fog. Everything disappeared.

"Joe?"

Her voice seemed far away but grew louder and clearer as she called his name. His body shook as she jostled him. He coughed and sputtered, then spewed his emotions all over the floor and all over Peggy.

* * *

Peggy didn't push him away. She held him close. His head lay across her lap. She stroked his forehead and ran her fingers down his cheek. She would never let him go.

Even though he was no longer right outside her back door, he was the same Joe who'd always been there for her. She'd always be there for him.

Joe coughed and opened his eyes wide with a start.

Peggy lifted his head, and he turned to look at her. Fear turned to a frown when he looked at the mess he'd made of her sweater.

He said, “I’m sorry.”

“It’s just a sweater.”

Joe closed his lips tightly, strained to sit up, and grabbed his stomach.

Peggy leaned him against the cabinet, and rushed to the sink. She flipped on the faucet with one hand and opened the cabinet below with the other. As she soaked a washcloth in the sink, with her other hand, she plucked the trashcan from beneath the sink and shoved it in front of him in case he needed to throw up again.

He looked so pathetic sitting on the floor. She knelt beside him and washed his face with the damp washcloth.

He forced a smile and slowly stood. Peggy wrapped her arm around him and walked him to the sink so he could rinse his mouth. She grabbed a chair and eased him into it.

Peggy scrubbed the floor while Joe sat in silence. As she worked, she caught a glimpse of his weary face, etched and worn, emotionless. What had happened to the boy she knew, the boy she had grown to love?

Their eyes met, and they stared at each other as though they were worlds apart, unable to touch, unable to speak, afraid, and lonely.

Joe’s face tightened. His lips quivered, and he choked as he spit his words. “He’s a monster.”

Peggy squeezed beside him on the chair. Leaning her head on his shoulder, she reached for his hand and bumped the crook of his elbow.

He grimaced.

She pulled up his shirt sleeve, and her heart sank as she saw his bruises. Streaky bruises on his forearm and five bold fingertip bruises near his elbow. She gently wrapped her hand around his elbow. Her fingers weren’t quite long enough to touch each bruise with a firm grip, but she was sure Frank’s hand would fit perfectly. "Did he do this?"

He nodded, his face unchanged. She slid her hand to the irregular streaks on his forearm. She couldn't stop her tears. "Rope burns?" He nodded again, and he was crying too. Then he opened his hands, and she could see the scrapes and left-over grit from the basement floor.

Peggy stiffened and swallowed angry tears. "We need to call the police."

She stood, but he grabbed her arm. "It's no good." He shook his head, eyes pleading. "He's too smart, and he knows everyone. He'll just make up a story, and I'll look like the disturbed kid who can't get over his dad dying and his mom getting re-married."

Peggy let go and folded her arms. "So, what are you going to do?"

His unfazed eyes looked through her. "Nothing. Absolutely nothing." He half-smiled with a hope-you-understand look. "I'm going to be a good little boy and do everything Frank tells me." *For as long as I can stand it, then, when he least expects it, I'm going to kill him.*

She stood and put her hands on her hips and tilted her head. Her anger split between Frank and Joe. "You're going to do absolutely nothing?" Peggy closed her eyes and bit her lip as she turned around. "I can't let that happen." She tapped her foot. Her mind racing. She wanted to smack Joe, hug him, run away with him, steal him away and hide him in her family's guest room. She wanted to smack Frank, kill Frank, start all over. She wanted it all to go away, for the two of them to just be kids again. She wanted to run through the backyard, splash in the creek, and fall down laughing.

But there was no laughter at the sound of tires edging onto the driveway.

"Frank!" Joe jumped and shoved the chair back to the table. He glanced at the clock. "It's not even eleven yet. He should be at work." He snatched the soiled washcloth and towels and dashed to the laundry room. When we returned, he grabbed Peggy's shoulders and looked squarely in her eyes. "You need to go." Then he disappeared up the stairs.

Peggy stood, befuddled. She had never seen Joe snap to attention so quickly. She'd never seen such fear… in anyone's eyes. She heard water running upstairs as Frank killed his engine. She listened as his car door opened and his feet plopped onto the driveway. Footsteps outside and thumping upstairs.

Peggy dashed toward the stairs and saw Joe at the top of the stairs. His eyes widened. "What are you still doing here?"

Tight lipped, she glared at him. *I'm not going anywhere.*

"You don't understand." Joe lifted praying hands and begged her with his eyes, but Frank's keys rattled, the lock turned, and he glided through the doorway.

He glanced at Peggy. She felt exposed as a creepy smile matched his stare. Frank studied her with judgment as though she'd sneaked into the boy's locker room.

Joe cleared his throat and nodded toward the door. Peggy shook her head and mouthed the words, "Not leaving."

Frank's eyes narrowed. He turned towards Joe and stepped between him and Peggy. "I knew you had a rough night last night, so I thought I would stop by to check on you."

Frank walked toward the phone, eyebrows raised toward Peggy. "Shouldn't you be at school? I expect your parents are worried." He picked up the handset and punched the numbers, but Peggy noticed his left thumb resting on the cradle.

Coward. Peggy stepped beside Joe and rolled up his sleeve.

Frank stared at her and swallowed. As he lowered the phone, she held up Joe's bruised arm. "I wonder how you're going to explain Joe's arms to the sheriff."

Peggy smiled at the fear in his eyes.

Frank's blank stare disappeared with a raised eyebrow

and a smile. "My goodness, Joe! What stories have you put in this girl's mind?" His voice sounded like a preacher or a politician. He slowly closed the gap between them as he continued. "Let me see those marks."

He gently grasped Joe's arm. Melodramatic concern dripped from his face. "What did I tell you about that rope swing? Don't wrap your arms around the rope. If you slip, this is what happens."

Peggy backed towards the door as Frank continued his charade.

"I'm still unclear as to why you're not at school, and you, Peggy, why are you here? I'm picturing Joe showing off with the rope swing while the two of you are skipping school. Not exactly model students, but don't worry. I'm not as stern as Joe might think."

He winked at Joe and whispered in his ear.

Peggy felt a sickening chill as the color washed out of Joe's face and fresh tears appeared. She stopped with a thud as she backed into the front door.

Frank released Joe's arm then gripped Peggy's shoulder and opened the door. He looked at Joe as he said, "Be careful going home, Peggy. We wouldn't want anything to happen to you."

"It's too long a walk. We should take her home."

Frank squeezed her shoulder a little tighter and motioned her toward his car. Peggy had never felt more powerless. As much as she wanted to be home, she felt terrified as she imagined what might happen to Joe.

* * *

Joe stared at the floor mat during the ride home. He was glad Peggy was safe and away from Frank. He could still picture those spindly fingers squeezing her shoulder. He imagined clipping them off one at a time with pruning shears.

He jolted in his seat as the car pulled into their driveway

and Frank patted his knee. "Joe, you barely said a word. It's like you've been gagged or something. I should be taking you to school, but I understand why you might not be feeling so well."

His voice sounded so disgustingly normal, Joe wanted to throw up on Frank's hand. How could he do the awful things he'd done and pretend everything was normal. He wondered what other terrible things Frank had done.

As the car rolled to a stop on the spotless garage floor, Frank looked him in the eyes. "I think we understand each other. Don't we, Joe?"

Joe nodded.

"Don't we?"

Joe lifted his eyes and answered, "Yes, we have an understanding."

Frank raised his eyebrows.

"Yes, sir. We have an understanding."

Joe felt his stomach roll at Frank's satisfied grin.

Chapter 44
Nathan and Donna

Nathan stared at the wall in the cardiologist's office. Certificates and posters. A painting of a couple dancing in a downpour. No clock. "I know why they never have a clock on the wall. It's so you don't go mad waiting on the doctor."

Finally, the door opened. Dr. Jackson half-smiled and set his tablet on the counter. "Nathan, your echo has not improved. Your ejection fraction is about twenty percent."

Nothing like getting right to it. Nathan's already sluggish heart sank into his toes. He wished Donna had been with him to hear and help him understand. He couldn't understand the jargon, but the doctor's face told him it couldn't be good. "What does it mean?"

Another half-smile. "Your heart is pumping less than half as much as it should. That's why you can't walk from your bed to the bathroom without stopping to breathe."

"I needed"—Nathan coughed—"a fancy test to tell me that?"

The doctor looked him in the eye. "There's a strong possibility it'll get worse, especially if you continue smoking."

"Quit smoking?" *I've never heard that before.* "I know you're right, doc, but isn't there more we can do?"

"Mr. Fortune, I can't help you if you're not willing to do your part."

Nathan opened his mouth, but Dr. Jackson raised his hand to stop him. He turned his head slightly then continued. "We have to work together. I am not your enemy. I am not your friend. I am not your boss. I am your doctor. Think of me as an advisor. I can tell you what is wrong and what can be done about it, but *you* have to make the tough choices, and *you* are ultimately responsible for your health."

Nathan tightened his lips and stared.

The rest of the visit was a blur. All he heard was "Bad heart. Blah blah blah. Quit smoking." Oh, and "Here are some new pills."

"Do you understand our plan? Mr. Fortune?"

His words broke the stubborn trance, and Nathan raised his eyebrows.

"Mr. Fortune, I've written down the instructions and printed a current list of your medications. I think it would be best if your wife came with you to your appointments from now on."

Nathan half-scowled as he grabbed his walker and shuffled out the door.

* * *

The clock ticked slowly as Donna tried to distract herself. It was hard to care for her patients when the only patient on her mind was Nathan. She muddled through her day then rushed to get home before Nathan.

The house was empty and felt undone. Caring for him had meant not caring for much else. Dishes in the sink. Laundry sitting in the washer. Trash overflowing.

Nathan used to help her with the chores, but he was no longer able, and she was no longer motivated.

It was her first time alone in the house in a long time. She snatched up scattered newspapers and junk mail and tidied the living room.

Bubbles rose beneath the hot running water as she tackled the dirty dishes. She mused to herself as she washed the soup tureen they'd received as a wedding gift from a now-divorced couple.

She shoved the dish back into the suds and wondered if her own marriage could last. Her vibrant husband was withering, becoming an old man. She could handle the aging, the heart failure, but the growing doubts and bitterness made her own heart feel like it was failing.

The man she'd married was slowly dying inside and out.

His agitation, harsh tone, and coarse words felt completely alien. She couldn't remember a harsh word or angry look before his heart failed. This disease was not only killing him but slowly replacing him with a monster.

Who knew heart failure could make you heartless?

She stared through the ceiling, silently screaming at the heavens. *I want my Nathan back.*

Tears fell like raindrops in her dishwater.

Chapter 45

Joe and Peggy

Joe stood in front of Frank's house for the longest time. It was the house where hate was born, and the house where hate must die. He rued the day his mother met Frank, the day his life lost all meaning and all hope. Frank was the devil in the flesh.

And the devil had to be exorcised and eliminated.

Joe wished his dad's shotgun had hit a little higher. It would've been so much easier if his life had ended that day when his heart was destroyed. Instead, Joe felt like the walking dead. Heartless, with every emotion crushed or stolen, he felt no motivation to do anything except to kill Frank.

You stole my life, Frank. It only seems fitting I should steal yours.

Chapter 46
Joe and Peggy

As Joe stood in front of Danny's old house, he hoped it wasn't Danny's mother who'd opened the curtain. It had been so long, and he wasn't even sure the Misers still lived there, but he wouldn't dare wait to find out. His welcome had been buried long ago.

As he turned to head back toward his car, a siren yelped, and a police car headed toward him. He whispered to himself, "Don't run," and walked steadily toward his car.

The police car slowed and pulled up beside him.

"Joe, we got a complaint from one of the neighbors. You'll need to move your car." The officer sneered as he continued, "I can't tell you what to do, since you are a free man and all that, but, if I were you, I would move that car to another county. It's not going to get any easier around here, and I don't think it's ever going to feel like home again."

"Yes, sir," Joe nodded.

His stomach all in knots, he wanted to collapse as the siren and flashing lights brought back such painful memories.

* * *

As he stared at his car sitting in front of Peggy's house, he remembered the first time he saw her behind her new wheels. When she turned sixteen, her father bought her a Mustang convertible. Used, of course, but still a Mustang—cherry red with racing stripes.

He could still hear the purr of that engine. That sweet sound rounding the corner and heading down his driveway. Frank and the rest of the world disappeared whenever he heard that sound. His heart rumbled with the engine. Everything about that car screamed "Peggy." He would run to the front door and disappear into her car as quickly as possible.

More than once those familiar flashing lights had popped

up behind them. He'd teased her endlessly, imitating a police officer. "Young lady!" He'd scrunch his face, pucker his lips, and use his deepest voice. "You're driving too darn fast. This is a neighborhood. Were you aware you were speeding? May I see your license and registration? Are you old enough to drive?"

He'd go on and on until she'd smile and punch him.

That cherry-red Mustang became an escape for both of them. Guys made fun of him for riding in her car, but he couldn't care less. Peggy was his best friend, if not his only friend.

Summer nights in small town Indiana meant cruising the countryside with the top down. The hot, sticky air blew through their hair as they flew down the country roads.

Maple Grove Road was the best. When he could coax her into it, Peggy would punch the gas. If she could hit the top of the hill going eight-five, they'd get airborne for three full seconds and gently touch down on the other side. It was the perfect hill.

To make it "safer," Joe would convince her to flick off her headlights to see if there were any oncoming cars.

"Keep your hands on the wheel and keep it straight," he'd say as they left the earth for that brief moment. It was their Mustang rocket ship, and young love had them in orbit.

After cruising the back roads, they'd stop at Sweet Treats for homemade ice cream and a soda.

On Sunday nights, they'd count the minutes until church let out, then they'd hightail it to the drive-in for popcorn and a movie.

Joe didn't need anything more than to hold Peggy's hand. The movie never mattered. Just their two sweaty palms and pounding hearts.

* * *

Danny Miser always counted the minutes as well. He would wait until the other kids had left, then he'd hop in his car and follow them to the drive in. Watching. Loathing. Plotting.

Waiting.

He'd grown to resent Joe. They'd been friends, but Danny was always jealous of Peggy. He'd struggled to make friends and could never keep one for long. He'd always find something wrong with them, something he was better at, and if he couldn't find something, he would pout or call them names. Joe had been the only friend who would put up with him, and that was only because their moms were in a Bible study together.

When Danny started to take an interest in girls, none of them took an interest in him. None. But that didn't stop his interest or his jealously. He'd always had his eye on Peggy. He followed her every chance he could. And he'd made it a habit of following Peggy and Joe to the drive-in.

That Sunday, Sky-Line Cinema was playing a double feature. *The Love Bug* and *Herbie Rides Again.* He chuckled—sitting in a car watching a movie about a car. He imagined himself as Dean Jones but less awkward and better looking, and he pictured Peggy as Michele Lee but with blue eyes.

During a quiet scene, he could hear Peggy laughing. His cheeks felt hot. He tightened his fists and his jaw. There they sat. Joe and Peggy in her convertible. Top down under a cloudless, starry sky. He cringed as they snuggled—oblivious to the larger-than-life screen.

They didn't need to enjoy the movie. They were enjoying each other. And there he sat. Alone. Pathetic. Staring at his former friend and his neighbor. Hating them both.

Jealously turned into obsession. He imagined himself in that car. He and Joe making fun of the movie, or he and Peggy making their own fun. He let his mind run. She was no longer that bratty girl who stole his friend. She was a head-turner, and she had a super-hot car.

* * *

A hot-blooded young man can only take so much rejection. Danny's only friend had moved and no longer called or came over.

Joe only had time for Peggy.

Peggy never had time for Danny. Ever.

Danny decided to make his own time.

As the credits rolled, engines started and headlights flicked on all across the drive in. Lovers turned on the defrost or rolled down their windows.

Danny slunked in his seat, peered over the dashboard, and waited until Peggy started her car. His pulse quickened as Peggy and Joe joined the line of cars. He wanted to follow them in the worst way. He wanted to toss Joe out of that car and drive away with Peggy and never come back. But he was still Danny Miser—awkward and unsure.

The exhaust fumes and engine rumbles faded. The credits turned to previews. The previews turned to a dark screen. And he felt even more alone.

He finished his Coke and tossed the cup out the window. He may have been the last one to leave. He didn't care. Everyone had left him anyway.

* * *

"Peggy, I feel bad you always driving."

"It's not a big deal."

"Maybe not, but I feel like I should be taking you home instead of you taking me home." He couldn't shake free of a nagging worry about her driving home late at night by herself, but the nagging feeling didn't keep him from kissing her as long as he could.

* * *

There was no need to follow them. Danny knew where they were going. He knew exactly what they would be doing, and he knew exactly when Peggy would be leaving to head home. He had followed them enough to know all he needed to know.

The drive-in went dark in his rearview mirror as he

slowly pulled onto the road. Their kissing marathon would give him plenty of time to get things ready.

As he turned into his driveway, he checked his watch. Ten-fifteen. Peggy had to be home by eleven. He imagined her dad watching the clock and pacing.

Danny turned off his headlights and rolled into his driveway slowly—trying to make as little noise as he could. He killed the engine and snuck in through the garage. His parents were no doubt asleep, unfazed as usual at his comings and goings. He tip-toed into their bathroom. Opened the medicine cabinet, praying it wouldn't squeak.

Diazepam.

His mother's sleeping pills. He snatched four of them. Surely, she wouldn't notice. He shrugged and dropped the tablets into a sandwich bag. He crushed them, sealed the bag, and stuffed it in his pocket.

With each step toward his truck, his smile widened. He felt like a kid burying dog poop in Peggy's sandbox, but the stench from this plan would last much longer.

When Joe moved to the country, Danny thought the door would open for him to swoop in and steal Peggy. But without Joe around, Peggy never came around either. It felt like she had moved away too. He felt invisible, unwanted, and forgotten.

But he would never forget her and never let her go. He imagined her stealing away with Joe every time she hopped into her convertible and headed past his house without as much as a wave or a glance. His lust danced with its partner, resentment. What could have been love turned into hate. And he decided he was going to have Peggy even if she wouldn't have him.

He had waited for the right moment. Watching them smother each other at the drive-in for the umpteenth time was the final push he needed. He seethed as he imagined them inhaling each other in her sweet convertible. Those lips should be his.

He clenched his teeth as he slid into his car once more.

He drove down Sweetwater Pass toward Joe's house. Just off the road, a lonely stretch of gravel wound its way back into the woods toward the lake. It used to be a favorite spot for watching submarine races at night until Farmer Jenkins put an end to it with his camera and his Rottweiler, but Danny knew the old man was in Indy for the State Fair.

He stopped his car near the lane, not quite a mile from his home. He knew Peggy would be coming by soon. He turned on his caution lights, popped his hood, and waited. A couple of cars slowed as they passed. He ducked his head under the hood and waved them on, acting like he had everything under control.

When he heard the familiar purr of Peggy's Mustang, his pulse surged. As her headlights neared, he stepped toward the road to wave her down, but she accelerated and sped past, ignoring him once again. He seethed and glared at her rear bumper.

Then her brake lights flashed.

"Yes!" he almost shouted.

Her reverse lights kicked on, and her car backed up and parked.

Peggy left her car running and walked toward him, shielding her eyes with her hand. "Danny? Are you okay?"

He smiled at the darkness, knowing she couldn't see his smile or what was coming. "Yeah. Just broke down. Do you mind helping me push it off the road? Then, I could sure use a ride home."

"Let's do it."

They pushed his car off the road. As he turned off the hazard lights, he asked, "Do you mind if I drive your car?

Her voice quavered. "Yes."

Danny smiled at the hint of fear in her voice. Even before she answered, he had slid around her, hopped over the door and into the driver's seat.

"Brat." Peggy muttered as she climbed into the

passenger's seat.

Danny smirked, revved the engine, then shifted into gear. The controlled power of that beast felt good in his hands. He eased off the brake and tossed dust and gravel until the tires caught pavement and dug in.

The speedometer climbed as they flew down Sweetwater Pass.

The night air calmed Danny's nerves as it roared in his ears and blew through his hair. "I'm thirsty. Mind if we swing by Sweet Treats and get a Coke before we go home?"

"I have to be home by eleven."

He smiled and patted her thigh. "It'll be okay. If we're late, I'll tell your dad you stopped to help me."

* * *

Danny chose Sweet Treats because everyone would be there and would see him with Peggy. Sweet Treats was a 1950s-style drive-up restaurant with curb service. Danny parked beneath the neon sign and flashed the headlights.

"Two Cokes please. Make that two Cherry Cokes." Sweet Treats was famous for their flavored Cokes. They added their own syrup. But no amount of sweetness matched the feeling Danny had as he showed off his prizes in front of the summer Sunday night crowd.

Danny made googly eyes at the carhop wheeling toward him with two tall Cherry Cokes. He ignored her eye roll and snatched the drinks. He turned to hand Peggy hers, but she frowned, hopped out of the car and trotted toward the restroom.

As she walked away, Danny slipped the sandwich bag from his pocket. Looking around, he smiled and nodded as though he were everyone's friend, as though this were a perfectly normal event. He felt collectively ignored as everyone looked away—their eyes followed Peggy. A smug smile covered his face. He didn't need them any more than they needed him. He just wanted them to see Peggy with him instead of Joe. As everyone watched Peggy's walk, he lowered her drink into his lap and dumped in the powdered sleeping pills.

His heart leapt as the bathroom door swung open and she walked toward him. He watched her walk. Her stern eyes. Deliberate steps. Even when she looked disgusted, she was stunning.

When her gaze met his, she looked down and kept marching toward her car. It was obvious by the way she avoided the other kids' gazes and by her quick steps that she was mortified to be seen with him. His pulse raced. His face warmed. He squeezed the steering wheel with his left hand, imagining his hand around her throat.

Peggy slid into the passenger's seat. "You've got your drink. Let's get out of here."

He handed her the Cherry Coke. "Drink it while it's cold." He waited for her to take a few healthy sips, then he backed out of their spot and eased her Mustang around the building, waving at everyone—everyone who knew that Peggy was Joe's girl.

Peggy slid down in the seat and slurped that Cherry Coke. He felt his smile stretch a little more each time she sucked on that straw. He couldn't wait 'til she was passed out cold.

He drove as slowly as he could while she downed her entire soda.

Peggy made a sour face with the last few slurps. "They put a little too much syrup in mine. It had a bitter taste."

"Yeah, but it was still good. Wasn't it?"

She shrugged. "Where are you going? My house is that way."

"My mistake." He took the longest route possible back toward her house.

And timed it perfectly. By the time they turned down her street, she was out cold.

Danny giggled with excitement. He burned past the

house, knowing her father would hear the car and wonder why she wasn't pulling into the driveway. He could picture Peggy's father looking at their silhouettes through the window. He'd surely think it was Joe up to no good with his daughter.

Danny hammered the pedal, driving as fast as he could to get back to Jenkins's lane—the perfect set up—the place Joe would take Peggy if he were going to have his way with her. He pulled off the road and followed the winding lane toward the creek.

"Well, here we are sweetie. We don't have much time. Your daddy will be looking for us." Danny leaned toward Peggy. He chuckled at her limp face. "You're not nearly as pretty when you're passed out in the dark." He unbuttoned her blouse, slid his hand down her back, and unsnapped her bra. He held his breath as he pulled up her bra and stole a quick feel.

"No time for that," he said. "At least not on our first date."

She wore a simple decorative red scarf around her neck. He slipped it off and stuffed it inside her jeans. In the dark, he could barely see the hickey it had been covering. Danny pulled her into the driver's seat, then dashed back to the road and his car.

He hopped in and drove to Joe's house.

* * *

Danny took a deep breath as he squealed his tires and pulled into Joe's driveway. He panted and smacked his cheeks. He had to sell Frank on his story.

He ran to the door, rang the bell over and over and pounded the door until it opened.

"What are you doing here at this hour, Mr. Miser?" Frank rubbed his eyes and scratched his head.

"I'm really sorry, sir. I passed Peggy Landrum on my way home. She was having some car trouble down by Farmer Jenkins's lane. I know it's late, but I thought maybe Joe could come help me get her out of a tight spot, so she's not too late getting home."

Frank Mueller glanced at his wrist—no watch—not quite awake.

"I'm sorry, Mr. Mueller. It's almost midnight, she was supposed to be home by eleven."

Frank scowled. His usual look. Then he shouted, "Joe, get down here."

Joe was already halfway down the stairs. "Peggy's having car trouble? She just got that car."

"Yeah. Well, you can't trust a used car salesman," Frank said. "You boys get going and hurry back." He swatted Joe on the behind as they scurried out the door.

"Yes, sir," Joe said. "We'll be back in no time, sir."

Danny loved watching Joe cower like Frank's little, abject slave.

"Joe!" They turned around as Frank tossed Joe a flashlight.

Joe caught the light, then the two boys climbed into Danny's car and took off.

"Where's her car?" Joe asked as they approached the lane.

"She pulled off the road right here, but I don't see her car. I didn't want to leave her, but she said to come get you."

* * *

Joe shot out of the car and ran down the lane. His gaze followed the gravel until it disappeared around the bend. No sign of Peggy's car. His stomach knotted. Heart pounded. Head throbbed. He felt alone like a child in the dark.

A car door shut behind him. He spun around. Danny had barely stepped out the car. Why had he seemed so frantic at the house and almost complacent here—where he said he'd left her?

A chill swept over Joe. Something was terribly wrong. He could feel it. He balled his fists and sprinted toward Danny.

“Where is she?” Joe spit his words through gritted teeth and tried to not throw up. “You had better not be messing with me.”

Danny stepped back, bumping into his car. He shielded his face with his hands and started to cry. Joe cocked his fist—unfazed by the phony tears. “Start talking!”

Danny’s eyes widened. He was trembling, cowering. “I was afraid this might happen.”

“What might happen?”

“Well, she was out here alone with her top down—her convertible top down. I shouldn’t have left her alone.”

Joe turned his flashlight toward the lane. He caught the reflection of her taillights through the woods and ran toward her car. He heard the door shut behind him. The engine started and Danny sped away.

But Joe kept running. His heart pounded even faster when he saw the car. From a distance, it looked empty. He screamed her name and almost fell on his face as he tried running faster.

“Peggy!” He kept calling as he ran, but she didn’t answer. His mouth instantly dry, his heart pounding out of his chest, and his thighs burning, he feared the worst.

His light danced around the woods as he looked for any sign of her or anyone else. Finally, he reached her car.

Peggy.

His heart stopped. The woods fell silent. There she was—lying in the passenger seat, limp and exposed. He quickly pulled her shirt together and patted her cheek.

“Peggy, wake up. Wake up! Oh, God, please!”

Her cheek and her hand were damp and cold, but she was breathing, and her pulse felt strong. He shook her shoulders. “Peggy.”

She moaned and blinked.

“Wake up. What happened?”

Her hand dropped when he let it go. She moaned again as though trying to speak.

Fear turned to anger as he realized she'd been drugged. Her belt and jeans were still fastened, and her shoes were still on. It didn't look as though she'd been raped, but someone had certainly undressed her and fondled her.

Danny. "You tried to set me up, you little creep. Well, it's not going to work."

No time to waste. Joe opened her door, reached into her shirt, and pulled her bra back into place. He pulled her against his chest, slid his hands down her back and fiddled with her bra strap. As much as he'd wanted to, he'd never had his hands on it before. It took a minute to hook those little devils together. Not what he'd imagined for his first time inside her clothes.

He buttoned her shirt, then lifted her into the passenger's seat. When he got her settled, he slid into the driver's seat and started the car. He'd always wanted to drive her car but had felt strange asking. It felt much stranger than he'd expected.

Distant headlights flickered through the trees and moved on down the road. Joe waited until the taillights faded, then he turned on the lights and put the car in reverse.

He backed around and headed toward the road. Nothing. No cars. No noise. No Danny Miser. He turned left toward Peggy's house and prayed her dad wouldn't be home. Despite what Peggy might remember, despite what she might tell her dad, Joe knew it wouldn't look good. And he feared her dad wouldn't believe their story.

When he pulled up to the house, there were no cars in the driveway, but the lights were on. He parked the Mustang, hopped out, and went to retrieve their house key from under the rock. He chuckled at himself as he realized he was holding Peggy's keys. He unlocked the door then ran back to the car.

Peggy was out cold. He pulled her toward the open passenger door, lifted her onto his shoulder, kicked the door shut, and carried her into the house. No one was home.

"They must be out looking for you, kiddo." He swatted her on the behind, half-hoping she'd wake up, and half because he wanted to. He took a deep breath as he faced the stairs then carried her up to her room.

Her door was open. There was a note on her bed. "Peggy, if you get home before us, stay in your room until we get back. We are out looking for you. P.S. Your dad is not happy."

Ugh. I'm dead.

And so are you, Danny.

As softly as possible, he lay Peggy on her bed. He slipped off her shoes and left everything else alone. As much as he wanted to linger, he knew doing so would be suicide. He wanted to watch her sleep, to look at her peaceful face, to watch her chest rise and fall as she breathed. He wanted to remember their long passionate kiss before she'd said goodbye. He wanted to turn back the clock and let her parents take him home after the movie or walk home from her house. If only he hadn't left her alone.

As he watched her sleeping, he thought of sitting beside her and waiting for her parents, but the idea of getting caught in her room again sent a chill through him, and all he could think of was Mr. Landrum and his shotgun. As much as he'd like to tell him the truth, Joe wasn't convinced Mr. Landrum would be patient enough to listen. He imagined him pumping the shotgun and charging toward him. As he would point the finger at Danny, Mr. Landrum would point the shotgun at him.

He swallowed and took a deep breath. He had to get out of there, let Mr. Landrum cool down, let Peggy sleep it off—surely she would remember enough to pin the blame on Danny. He decided to wait until morning. Maybe after a good night's sleep, Mr. Landrum would be patient and understanding.

Joe gave Peggy one last look. Even passed out asleep,

she was beautiful to him. Nothing could taint that—not even Danny Miser. He imagined Danny stuffed into his pathetic orange plaid suit, laughing incessantly.

I'm not going to let you get away with this, Danny.

He closed her bedroom door behind him and hurried down the stairs to the kitchen. His first thought was to dash out the back door and head home through the woods, but he was afraid Frank might be waiting for him. As he reached for the door, he saw the phone on the wall. He'd seen Mrs. Landrum on that phone a million times.

He wanted to call Mom. But Frank might answer.

"Jane! I'll call Jane." She would be at her boyfriend's—anywhere but home with Frank. If he could only remember her boyfriend's name. Then he remembered it rhymed with jerk. *Kirk.* But what was his last name?

Kirk Williams, you idiot, he could hear Jane say.

Kirk Williams. He grabbed the phonebook from the cabinet where Mrs. Landrum always kept it. He flipped through the white pages. Williams. Williams. Williams. He had no idea what Kirk's dad's name was, but he knew they lived on Partridge Circle. "Got it."

He peeked out the window. No headlights.

He punched the numbers and waited. "Hello, Mrs. Williams, this is Joe Novak. No, everything's fine. I just need to talk to my sister, Jane if she's there."

His heart picked up a few extra beats as he waited in silence.

"Jane, I'm sorry. I really need your help. I need you to go home and talk to Mom."

Chapter 47
Nathan and Donna

Donna quietly opened the door. As she imagined, Nathan was asleep in his chair. The TV was on. Andy Griffith.

She knew it was late, but she couldn't pass up the overtime, and working felt like a vacation compared to caring for Nathan.

She tiptoed past him, avoiding the creaky spots in the floor. She paused on the unfamiliar bottle nestled between his thigh and the chair. It was a different label than their pharmacy.

Leaning for a closer look, she noticed the name had been blacked out. *Strange*. She gently wiggled the bottle free and held it up to the light coming from the kitchen.

"Hydrocodone." She covered her mouth, realizing she'd said it out loud. She tried to replace the bottle, but Nathan grabbed her wrist.

"What are you doing?"

"Your pills fell onto your lap. I was just going to put them back on the nightstand."

"Is that why you were holding them up to the light?"

Her heart sank at his words, and a cloud of fear and doubt engulfed her. His eager grip and sharp words told her he'd been using drugs and hiding them from her. For how long? And what other secrets did he have?

She jerked free from his grip and held the bottle in his face. "Where did you get these?"

"Dr. Wells." He sniffed, rubbed his nose and averted his eyes.

Donna twisted the bottle so he could see the black streak across the label. "Did Dr. Wells mark out your name?"

"You think because you're a nurse, you know everything?"

She swallowed the lump in her throat. "I'm not stupid.

It's hydrocodone, and it's not your prescription." She blinked to hide her tears. Her jaw tightened, trying to hide her anger and her hurt. She took a deep breath and blew it out slowly. "You couldn't get enough from Dr. Wells, so you're buying on the street."

"What do you know about my pain?" His voice cracked.

"I'm not going to talk to you when you're like this." Donna stormed into the kitchen.

"Like what?"

"You heard what I said. Good night." Donna stopped in the hallway, turned, and said, "I hope you don't need anything tonight, because you're on your own."

"I need an empty urinal, unless you want me to dump this one and start over."

Donna grabbed both of his urinals and went to their bathroom. Down the drain with one big flush. She felt like she was watching her life swirling into the sewer.

She walked into the front room with a urinal in each hand—something she had never imagined doing. He wasn't the man she'd married, wasn't the man she'd fallen in love with, and he was barely a man at all. He was disappearing into that chair. He may as well have been strapped to it. He looked as pathetic as she felt about their marriage and about herself.

He half-smiled and reached for her hand as she placed the empty urinals beside him.

"Nathan, I'm sorry." She didn't feel the least bit sorry for anything she'd done or felt, but she was sorry for the way things were shaping up. She hated heart failure and chronic pain and what they were doing to her husband. "I don't want things to be this way."

She sat on his armrest. "You're right. I don't understand your pain, but I'm going to try." She leaned and kissed his forehead. "But you have to understand there's a right way to treat your pain and a wrong way. Buying pills from a friend or anyone other than your pharmacist is not only wrong, it's dangerous."

Nathan curled his lip, showing his teeth as he squeezed the pill bottle.

"Don't scowl at me, Mr. Grouchy Pants. You are at my mercy." She looked at the urinals and looked at him as if to say, *you can't do anything without me.*

She leaned toward him, placed her hands on his hands, then stood toe-to-toe as he sat in his chair. He was powerless. He couldn't grab her, kick her, or lift his hand to throw anything. He could still spit, but she prayed he wouldn't dare.

"Mr. Fortune, you are one lucky man because I still love you. I don't love your pain, your misery, or your self-pity, but those things are not you. You are much bigger than your pain, and your heart is much bigger than the one inside your chest."

She looked into his eyes, making hers as wide as she could and smiling. "I know you're in there somewhere. I just have to believe that one day, you'll find your way back out here."

A tiny smiled worked its way into the corner of his mouth.

"Oh! There you are."

The smile stretched across his face. It felt good. She hadn't seen it in a long while.

She patted his thigh and tapped the pill bottle. "You know I think it's a mistake, but you should also know that I am going to let it go for now because I want you to know that I'm trying to understand your pain. You will have to confront your pain and"—she looked at the pills then at him—"and your addiction, eventually." A solitary tear dripped down his cheek as he stared at the bottle resting in his open hand.

He lifted it. "Take it."

"Are you sure?"

"You're right. The pills aren't controlling my pain.

They're controlling me, and I don't want to be Mr. Grouchy Pants anymore."

Donna tossed the bottle over her shoulder, leaned in, and kissed his cheek. "I knew you were still in there."

Chapter 48

Joe and Peggy

Peggy felt like she'd slept on a cloud. Her dreams jolted to a stop as she awakened to two silhouettes above her.

"Look who's finally waking up."

She rubbed her eyes as her mother touched her cheek. When she could see clearly, she felt the piercing gaze of her father and shrank at his clenched fists.

"Peggy, tell us what happened last night." His stern voice echoed in her foggy head.

"She's not quite awake yet. Give her some time."

"She hasn't got much time. I need to know which boy to kill before I kill both of them."

"You'll do no such thing." Her mother turned back to her. "Peggy, don't listen to him." She glanced at Dad. "Please, go in the other room and let me talk to her. Please."

His fists relaxed and he plodded into the hall, leaving the door cracked.

Her mother gently shut and locked it.

"What is Daddy talking about? What is he going to do?"

"Well, that may depend on what you tell us about last night. I see all your clothes are on. That's a good thing."

Peggy blushed, not with embarrassment but with hurt. "You don't trust me?" She couldn't look at her mother. "What do you think happened?"

"I honestly don't know. We were looking for you because it was well past eleven-thirty, and you were supposed to be home at eleven. We drove to Joe's house, but you weren't there. Joe's stepdad said he had sent him and Danny to go look for you back by Jenkins's place. We went, but no one was there. We came back home and found your car, and you were sound asleep in your bed. We tried to wake you, but it was like you'd been drugged. I pulled back the covers and saw you were fully dressed, so I guess I have no idea what happened. Do you?"

Her father's voice was muffled through the door, "We need to take her to see a doctor."

"Please don't stand there listening." Her mother shouted, then took a deep breath and tried to smile.

Peggy couldn't listen to them shouting at each other through the door. Her head spun as she tried to sit up. She heard them talk about Joe, Danny, Jenkins's place, but the last thing she remembered was drinking a Cherry Coke at Sweet Treats—with Danny. Why would she be with Danny Miser at her favorite hangout? And what made him think it was okay to drive her car?

What did he do? How did she end up at home in her own bed without remembering anything? She could only think of one reason Danny would have drugged her.

She cried into her hands. "I don't know what happened, Mom. I dropped Joe off at home, and on my way home I saw Danny standing beside his car, and I stopped to help him."

She scratched her head and nibbled her lip. Visions of friends laughing and waving. Cars. Short shorts and roller skates. "Sweet Treats! I took Danny to… No. Danny drove my car to Sweet Treats. That's the last thing I remember."

* * *

Joe sat at the island, head in his hands. Frank's footsteps paced behind him and around the island like an impatient prosecutor. Joe took slow deep breaths and waited for the footsteps to stop—hoping they would stop by the sink and not behind him.

He looked up at the sound of the faucet. Frank stopped at the sink, poured a glass of water, and took a swallow. His dagger eyes glared through Joe.

"You didn't touch her? You expect me to believe that."

Joe nodded. "I apologize, sir. I can only tell you what I know. You were here when Danny came looking for me. That should tell you that he was with her, and since she was passed out when I found her and remained passed out until her parents finally got her to wake up this morning, that should tell you Danny lied about Peggy sending him to get me."

Frank just shook his head.

"I think he drugged her," Joe said.

Frank clapped his hands once and laughed. "Danny Miser drugged your girlfriend?" His eyes narrowed. He pressed his hands against the island, clenched his teeth and leaned towards Joe. "Give me one good reason?"

Joe leaned back and winced, ready for a backhand across the face. Frank didn't blink but opened his eyes wider—waiting for an answer. Joe stammered. "I don't know. He hates both of us and would like nothing better than to come between us."

"I'm not convinced. For one thing, I know you're a lot smarter than him, and I'm not sure he's got what it takes to pull a stunt like that."

* * *

Joe sat beside his mother while Frank kept his vigil around the corner, his footsteps wearing a circle in the floor. Each step kept pace with the ticking of the clock. And each step sent a ripple of fear through Joe. He knew Frank would be listening to every word, and he could explode around that corner any second.

But Peggy was more important than Frank. And his love for her was greater than the worst of his fears. He looked into his mother's eyes. A mix of kindness, sadness, and fear stared back at him. Her hand trembled as she touched his. The woman who had loved his father had sold herself for fear of being alone and poor. She was a shell of the woman he'd known, but he could still see that loving soul in her eyes.

She smiled and tears filled her eyes. "Joe." She patted his hand. "What happened?"

He blinked through his own tears. His mind whirling through the last few hours and landing on the image of Peggy passed out in her car. His beautiful, best friend unaware and undone. That desperate image would stay with him forever. As much as he'd dreamed of seeing all of her secrets, he had wanted it to happen the right way—not like this—not at Danny's hands.

Mom squeezed his hand. "You can tell me."

Joe glanced toward the entryway and the kitchen. Frank's footsteps stopped. He pulled his mother close and whispered in her ear. "Danny drugged Peggy and took off some of her clothes."

His mother stared at the floor. Her lips quivered. Eyes tightened—unable to stop her tears. She wrapped her arms around him. Tears swelled, and their bodies shook.

Joe looked into her eyes. "He tried to make it look like I did it. Then he took me back there and left me, hoping Peggy's dad would find us and think I was..."

The words stuck in his throat. He shook his head, his eyes pleading with his mother to believe him. He mouthed the words, "I love her." Mom had to believe him, had to believe he'd never do anything to hurt Peggy.

"Joe, it's okay. Peggy's okay. She wasn't hurt. She doesn't remember, and she doesn't ever need to know what Danny did. You said Danny took off some of her clothes, but her mother said she was fully dressed when they found her in her bed. She did say she had a hickey on her neck." He caught a split-second smile when she said *hickey*.

Joe shook his head and smiled through his tears and sniffles. "That was me." He almost snorted as tears mixed with a momentary chuckle.

His mother squeezed him like she hadn't in years. It had been too long, and it felt good.

Frank stepped around the corner with his usual smug grin. "It was *you*. You even snort and chuckle as you say it."

"No! That's not what I meant. I…"

Frank talked over him. "Peggy's dad wasn't chuckling

when he took her to the doctor."

"The doctor?" Joe jumped out of his seat. "Why does she need to see the doctor? Is she hurt?"

"Did she get raped?" Frank narrowed his eyes and glared at Joe.

Joe's stomach rolled. His skin felt cold, and he broke into a sweat as he imagined Danny having his way with her.

Frank stepped toward him, raised his fists, and snarled. "You little…"

Joe's mother stepped between them. "Frank! That's enough. You need to mind your own business."

He pressed his chest into her face and looked past her at Joe. "What happens in my driveway *is* my business. And as long as *your* spoiled brat lives in my house, whatever he does is my business."

"Frank, please. He's *my* son."

Joe tugged her shoulder. "Did Danny rape her?" *I'll kill him.*

She turned, grabbed his shoulders tightly, then wrapped him in a hug. Joe closed his eyes, swallowed his tears, and held her close. He wanted that hug to last, but Frank dug his thumb and fingers into his shoulder and squeezed until Joe let go.

As Frank grabbed Mom's arm and swung her around, she said, "You think I married you because I needed a husband. I married you because I loved you and thought you were a good man, but I'm not sure I even know you. And you certainly don't know my son if you think he would hurt anyone, let alone Peggy."

Frank loosened his grip and looked at Joe. "I'm supposed to believe your little boy is a saint?"

Joe swallowed as Frank slipped around his mother and stepped toward him. Mom tried to step between them again. She rested her palm on Frank's chest. "The way Joe and Peggy get along, do you really think he would have to slip her some drugs?"

Frank slapped her face and shoved her to the floor. "How dare you, woman." As he stepped toward Joe, she scrambled toward him and grabbed his ankle. He gripped her wrist, jerked her hand free, then kicked her.

Joe charged at him and felt a sharp sting in his nose as Frank punched him and sent him stumbling. He collapsed, grabbed his nose and squeezed against the pain. But no amount of pain could keep him from protecting Mom. He leapt to his feet and lunged at Frank, his shoulder hammering Frank's side, driving him into the kitchen counter.

Mom lay on the floor near his feet. Out of the corner of his eye, he could see her holding her stomach and digging her heels to back away.

Joe clutched the counter and the sink and pressed all his weight into Frank, hoping he could hold him until Mom could slip away.

Frank laughed and just stood there. He grabbed a damp wash cloth from the sink and flung it at Mom. "You think your brat's little mess is funny."

Joe's head throbbed with every heartbeat as Frank laughed. When that washcloth struck Mom's face, Joe unleashed his frustrations through his fists. He shoved Frank and punched him in the gut. Warmth surged through his fist and arm and into his whole body. And it felt good.

He'd never wanted Frank in his life. Now he wanted him dead, and nothing would stop him. He swung and punched and flailed—unleashing all his hate.

Frank shoved him and sent him stumbling out of the kitchen. Joe crashed into the back of the sofa and fell to the floor. Frank sprinted toward Mom, stood over her, thrust his foot into her side and shouted. "I took a chance marrying you. You needed everything I had, but I didn't need you." He turned and scowled at Joe, gritted his teeth, and kicked her again. "And I certainly don't need your baggage."

Joe pushed away from the sofa and charged toward Frank again. But as he pounced, Frank spun around him. Joe felt two sturdy hands slam into his back. Frank grabbed his shirt, whirled him in a circle and hurled him toward the stairs and into the banister.

The room was suddenly dark and silent.

He opened his eyes to warm, damp carpet against his face. His head splitting. The room moving, spinning. He struggled to keep his eyes open. He lay still. Moaning and footsteps awakened his memory. His mother's moaning. Frank's footsteps. His heart raced, drumming its beat into his pounding head.

He lifted his head and touched his face. Warm blood oozed through his fingers and dripped on the carpet. He grabbed the neck of his T-shirt and squeezed his nose. As he turned his head, his eyes met Frank's, and he felt like he was staring at the devil. And the devil was going to kill him.

Mom looked at him and tried to move toward him, but Frank grabbed her wrist and squeezed until her hand was white. "You're hurting me."

Joe stared at her—wanting to help but not sure he could stand. Her eyes begged him to save her. He tried to stand, but his head spun, he collapsed to his knees, and vomited. He couldn't see, but he heard laughter far away. The laughter drew closer, then he heard his mother's voice like an echo or a distant scream. "Run, Joe. Run." Her voice grew louder. The smell of his own vomit whirled in his nostrils. His stomach rolled. His head swam. He felt the pain of Frank's hand gripping his neck, but he couldn't react.

Frank threw an arm around him and hauled him up the stairs.

Mom's voice cleared his head for a second as she shouted, "I'm calling the sheriff."

Frank shoved him onto the landing and stormed back down the stairs. Joe heard a loud slap and the clang of the phone crashing.

He wanted to run down the stairs and save her, but he wasn't sure he could stand. He pushed himself onto his hands and feet and crawled up the stairs. He heard a thump and a crash. The floor quaked. He cringed and pressed on, imagining his mother dragged from the kitchen and slammed into the bookshelf. Books and knickknacks falling to the floor. Her head bleeding.

He's going to kill her. He's going to kill us both.

He reached the top of the stairs—his heart pounding out of his chest, his head throbbing, sweat pouring, body shaking. He used all his strength to stand and lean against the wall. It shook behind him as he imagined Satan unleashing his fury beneath him.

His only thought was saving Mom. He hobbled into Mom's and Frank's bedroom. The phone sat beside the bed. He grabbed it, ready to call, but he heard a fast busy signal. Frank must have taken the phone off the hook. His heart sank and he flopped onto the bed.

Joe felt like he was in that tree stand again—just waking up. The shotgun was falling away—his dad tumbling after. *Not again.*

It can't happen again.

Joe ignored his pain—ignored his spinning head, his spinning world—ignored his grumbling stomach, and he dashed down the hall and into his bedroom. His mind set on one thing. The only way to save himself and his mother. Dad's shotgun.

He ducked into the closet, and pushed his clothes out of the way.

There it was. He grabbed the smooth wooden stock and backed out of the closet. His hands trembled as he held it.

His stomach knotted at the scent of gun powder and the

feel of the cold steel and wood. He gripped it tight as he heard his mother screaming. Her voice, the air around him, the room, everything was becoming clear.

He took a deep breath and hurried toward the stairs. *Four slugs.* He remembered. Only one had been fired. The other three should still be in the gun. He would wait to pump it. He didn't want Frank to hear it and use his mother as a shield.

With renewed strength and resolve, Joe flew down the stairs—pausing near the bottom to listen and catch his breath. He cringed as his mother screamed again, then he heard another loud smack, a crash and a thud.

His heart pounded out of his chest. His pulse whooshed in his ears. Face hot. Palms drenched. Throat dry. He wanted to rush in with the shotgun blasting, but he couldn't afford to make a mistake. He'd have to shoot him point-blank to avoid hitting Mom.

He peered around the corner. Mom was on the floor, backed against the wall, one arm stretched over her head. He caught site of her bloodied face, eyes swollen, nose bent, blood streaming.

Frank kneeled in front of her, clutched her throat, pulled her toward him, and stood with his right arm cocked and ready.

Joe pointed his gun at Frank. "Mom! Stay down."

She closed her eyes and fell limp.

Frank released his grip and wheeled around. His face was red, his chest heaving. Blood covered his face—Mom's blood.

Joe readied every muscle and shifted his gaze from Frank's dark eyes to his darkened heart. He pumped the 12-gauge as Frank lunged toward him. In that split second, he was at the firing range with Dad, and Frank was his target. His world stood still and silent until one ear-shattering blast exploded into Frank's chest.

Frank dropped to the floor.

Joe dropped the gun and ran to his mother. He cradled her head. She was limp and lifeless. He looked past the blood, bruises, broken skin, and swollen eyes and saw the pure and gentle face of his mother. The smiling face that had buttoned his top button before church when he was too little to do it himself. The eyes that had looked at him knowingly every time he'd talked about Peggy.

She'd spent her life on him and Jane, and she paid the ultimate price.

A cold wave rushed over him. He felt her slipping away. Her limp body careened as he shook her and screamed. He laid her on the floor and bent over her, praying to hear a breath.

Nothing.

He tried to feel her pulse—unsure if he was even doing it right. In desperation, he gave her two breaths and started chest compressions.

She gasped.

"Mom?" His pulse, already racing, flipped into overdrive, and he sprinted to the phone. Still off the hook, he depressed the receiver and released it. Fast busy signal. Frank must have taken the garage phone off the hook.

He glanced at Mom. She was barely breathing—but breathing. He scurried out to the garage to call for an ambulance.

Chapter 49
Nathan and Donna

It took everything she had to get out of bed. Donna had never been a twenty-four-hour-a-day nurse until Nathan got sick. Everyday had become a double shift and overnight on-call. When she wasn't at the hospital, she was tending to his every need.

The fiery passion in his eyes had reduced to smoldering coals, but Peggy knew even smoldering coals could erupt in flame if given enough fuel. She stared at his eyes and said, "We've got to get you fixed, old man. This girl ain't ready to be old yet." She straddled his dwindling thighs.

She knew he had no energy to react, but she hoped he still had the want-to. He smiled and puckered his lips.

She chuckled and kissed him.

"We'll get you back in the saddle someday, cowboy." She kissed him again and climbed off the chair.

Nathan smiled and reached into the seat beside him. His face strained as he pulled out his slender stash of cigarettes and handed them to Donna.

She saw *her* Nathan. The same eyes she'd fallen in love with years ago. The same smile. He handed her hope when he handed her his cigarettes. When she'd wondered if there was anything left between them, he'd shown her the only thing keeping them apart was stubbornness.

Donna didn't toss the cigarettes. She tucked them into her purse, and for the first time in a long time, they both said, "I love you."

All of a sudden dreading going to work had become dreading leaving him.

* * *

Donna felt a twinge of fear every time the phone rang at her nurse's station. It seemed strange that none of her patients seemed as sick as her husband.

Gallbladder surgery and hernia repairs seemed mundane. Compared to Nathan's failing heart, her patients' complaints felt like whining.

"This tape is too tight."

"Where's my shot?"

"I'm not sure I can make it to the bathroom."

She fought the urge to scream. Maintaining a smile, she forced herself to meet their every need.

The clock moved a little slower each day. Closer to the end of her shift, time seemed to stop.

Her patient sat comfortably in his bed. As he smiled, she hoped Nathan would be smiling again soon. This patient would be going home in the morning. Nathan, on the other hand, could be coming to the hospital at any moment.

She pictured him on a tightrope without a net and blindfolded. He was going to fall. It was not a matter of if but a matter of when.

"Donna? Hello."

She hadn't heard any footsteps and barely heard the other nurse's voice.

"There's a phone call for you."

* * *

"Donna, I'm sorry. It's Charles. You know I wouldn't call you at work unless…"

"Is Nathan okay?"

"He's… I think he will be. I called an ambulance. They're loading him on a cart to go to the hospital."

"What happened?"

"I came by to check on him, and he was almost blue. He was alive but cold, sweaty, and barely breathing."

Barely breathing. Those words stung and the tears flowed. Nathan's heart was the one that was failing, but she clutched her chest—not sure how much more her heart could take.

"Don't cry. He's breathing okay now. They cranked up his oxygen and gave him some kind of shot or something. They're taking him out to the ambulance. He's coming your way. I'll follow them and see you at the hospital. Gotta go."

Donna slumped into the nearest chair and covered her mouth. The noise of the hospital faded as she replayed Uncle Charles's words. *He was almost blue.*

The nurse beside her asked if she was okay.

Without looking, she answered, "I've got to clock out. It's Nathan." Her tears muffled her words.

* * *

Donna and Uncle Charles sat together, waiting.

Hours felt like days.

Finally, the nurse came out of the ICU. "Mrs. Fortune? You can see him now. He is stable, breathing on his own, but he is probably going to be with us for a few days."

A few days? That might be all he has.

Chapter 50

Joe and Peggy

Peggy and her mother huddled together on the edge of her bed. Her father paced outside her bedroom. She clutched her mother's hand and forced herself to breathe. She tightened her grip as he walked into the room.

Veins popped from his temples. His jaw clamped shut. He pounded his fist in his hand.

His eyes searched hers for answers—answers she struggled to remember. Her lips quivered as she and her father looked at each other. Her mother pulled her closer.

Her father drew a deep breath and stepped toward her.

Peggy couldn't speak, and didn't know what to say. She blinked through her tears and shook her head.

He spun, tore out of her room, and thundered down the stairs. Peggy sat paralyzed beside her mother. Her mother kissed her cheek and cradled her.

The house shook as the front door banged open and slammed shut. Her father's car started. The engine revved. Then wheels screamed out of the driveway and onto the street.

Peggy and her mother flinched as the car backfired.

Peggy's eyes widened. The sound reminded her of a shotgun, and she pictured her father standing between her and Joe, brandishing his 12 gauge—the 12 gauge he kept under his bed.

She pulled away from her mother and dashed toward her parents' bedroom.

Her mother shouted, "Don't worry. I hid the shotgun." Peggy stopped in the doorway, and her mother continued, "He didn't look for it, so I don't think he'll do anything too rash, but I would make myself scarce if I were Joe or Danny."

Her mother patted the empty spot on the bed beside her. Peggy sat, and they held each other in silence staring at the memories on Peggy's wall.

Half of the pictures captured Joe smiling—always. A picture of Peggy's grandmother in her favorite chair, holding them both and reading a picture book. *We were so cute.*

Her eyes stopped on the photo of her and Joe in the sandbox. "That must have been the last time I wore a dress except to church."

Her mother shook her head. "Those guilty smiles should have told me there'd be trouble someday." She kissed Peggy's forehead. "I don't ever remember having two boys fighting over me."

"Mom, you don't understand. Joe was trying to protect me."

* * *

Lights and sirens flew past Peggy's window.

"You said you hid the shotgun, right?"

Her mother ran from the room.

Peggy followed.

Her mother rolled back the covers on her bed, lifted the mattress, and sighed. "It's still there."

Peggy grabbed her hand. "Let's go. I want to see Joe. I have to know he's okay."

Chapter 51
Nathan and Donna

Nathan opened his eyes and stared at the clock. He felt those deceptive hands grip his throat. Each tick squeezed another moment. The clock's uncaring face taunted him like death waiting its turn. The hour hand barely moved. He would nod off, and when he would awaken, the hour hand had moved. But he hadn't.

Trapped in that hospital bed, he listened to the steady *beep beep beep* of his pulse mixing with the various alarms and sounds throughout the ICU.

"Good morning, Mr. Fortune."

His nurse was cute, but he couldn't smile or react. He was doing well to open his eyes, and he was glad he didn't have to have a tube down his throat. A catheter was bad enough, but at least that meant he didn't have to get up to use the bathroom. Lifting his eyelids took all his strength.

"You slept well, I see." She had to smile for both of them.

He raised one eyebrow to let her know he could hear.

"Oh. There you are. I knew you were in there."

The nurse had kind eyes and a soft voice. He felt safe with her at his bedside, and he drifted back to sleep.

* * *

Donna and Uncle Charles waited in the family consult room—the dreaded bad news room. Donna paced and Uncle Charles sat and stared out the window. She glanced at the unmoving clock as they waited for Dr. Jackson. As she walked by Uncle Charles, he reached for her hand. She stared at his hand. She wasn't too sure about him. He had to have been Nathan's source for drugs. But she could see the worry in his eyes. Regardless of what else he was, or what he might've done, he loved Nathan, and she needed a hand to hold onto.

She sat beside him and held his hand. They stared out the window together. Grandparents and parents smiling and laughing as they leave with a newborn. Families huddling together—crying together as leave their loved ones. Cars coming and going like the lives that came and went.

She let go of his hand and stood facing the window. Uncontrolled tears. “I don’t know how much more I can take. It’s killing me—just watching him die slowly.”

She felt Uncle Charles’s hand on her shoulder as he stood behind her. “Don’t talk like that, Donna. He’s going to be—”

“He’s going to be what? Okay?” She shook her head and resumed pacing. “He’s barely alive *now*. What do you think he’s going to be like in a few weeks, in a few days? He may not even last the night.”

She stopped cold as Uncle Charles gripped her arm.

“Maybe you don’t know him as well as you should, Donna. He’s been through worse—a lot worse than you’ll ever know. He’ll beat this. I know he will.”

Donna jerked free of his grasp, chilled by his words, wondering what they meant, and hoping he was right. “I know him well enough, and there’s no will left in his eyes—when he has the strength to open them.”

The door swung open, and Dr. Jackson came into the room. He set down a stack of papers and a pager and shook hands with each of them. “Please sit.”

Donna’s eyes trained on his lips, afraid of what they were going to say.

The doctor smiled and held out his hands, palms down. “Take a deep breath. He’s holding his own. We have him on all the right medicines and oxygen. Most importantly, he’s breathing without any machines, and his heart is in normal sinus rhythm.”

“But?” Donna said.

He nodded. “But, I don’t know how much more his heart can take. He’s been through all the tests. We’re just waiting and hoping for a donor heart.”

Donna’s stomach lurched, but she held herself together. “The idea that someone has to die so Nathan can live…” She looked Dr. Jackson in the eye. “How do you do this? Every day, how do balance life in your hands? I couldn’t do it.”

He looked at floor then looked at Donna. “It’s not easy. Someone always loses, but I’m thankful for the individuals and the families who care enough about others to become donors. Just because one life is lost doesn’t mean another isn’t worth saving. I had a patient last month who was one of nine people saved by the same donor. It’s a great way to make something beautiful out of a tragedy.”

Dr. Jackson grabbed the pager and handed it to Donna. “This is your lifeline. When this pager goes off, that means we have a heart, and you must call the number on the display immediately.”

Donna clutched the pager. “We will be packed and ready.” She kissed it and added. “I pray this baby goes off soon.”

“There’s one more thing, Donna.” He looked at Uncle Charles and continued, “Nathan got lucky this time. Charles found him before it was too late. He can’t be left alone, not anymore. How you do it is up to you. I can have a social worker come talk through the options. You can take a leave from work. You can hire a home health nurse or an adult sitter. Whatever works for you and Nathan, but he should never be left alone.”

Donna nodded. Closing her eyes to hide her tears, she’d never felt more alone.

Chapter 52
Nathan and Donna

Nathan sat alone in his chair. He could hear Donna shuffling in the other room. She hadn't said a word all morning. He figured she was mad about something.

He chuckled.

She can't be mad at me. No way to make her mad when you can't do anything.

"Why are you so quiet?" he shouted.

She slammed a kitchen drawer.

"I know you can hear me. I love you. Don't be mad." He smiled, almost laughing. "Don't be mad," he muttered to himself. *That always gets her.*

A car slowed, stopped on the curb. The engine silenced. A car door squeaked and shut with a thud. Nathan tensed, slid his hand between the cushion and the armrest and gently gripped his revolver. He couldn't hold his breath to listen, and he could barely hear anything else over the hiss of his oxygen.

He breathed a little easier when he saw a young woman step onto the porch. Light brown, smooth, wavy, shoulder-length hair. About five-and-a-half feet tall. Slender. She stopped at the door.

He didn't wait for her to knock but said, "Come on in."

The young woman awkwardly pushed open the door and stumbled into the house. Too many things in her arms, but her awkward beauty was not lost on Nathan.

Her smooth curls bounced on her shoulders. Her scrubs covered everything else, but her hands looked soft. She smiled as she bent to set her supplies on the floor.

He warmed at her gentle smile. She had no worry lines, and her face held no fear. He tried to push himself up in his chair as she bent forward.

She caught him staring at her chest, and he raised his

eyebrows and looked away, acting innocent.

Her blush made him feel alive.

"Are you my new nurse?" He tilted his head toward the kitchen and raised his voice. "I guess my old nurse has more important things to do."

Some dishes clunked in the sink.

"Oh!" The young nurse's eyes were wide. "I didn't realize I was replacing anyone. I thought…"

Donna walked through the living room. She avoided Nathan and shook hands with the nurse. "Thanks for coming. I'm Donna. You're not replacing anyone." She turned to Nathan, tears swelling in her eyes. "I'm sorry. I couldn't think how to tell you. Dr. Jackson said I can't leave you alone, so Uncle Charles is helping us hire a nurse." She closed her eyes for a moment and shook her head. "I can't afford to lose my job."

Nathan smiled at his new nurse, then focused again on Donna. "Everyone knows I need a nurse, and you need a break."

Donna left the room to finish getting ready.

He coughed and waved his nurse closer, feigning his need already.

She looked at him with soft sorrel eyes, so innocent. "Are you old enough to be a nurse?"

She blushed but stood her ground. One hand on her hip, the other pointing a finger at her new patient. "Don't think you can use that tired line on me, Mr. Fortune. I may look young, but I've been around the block a time or two." She bit her lip at her own words.

He smiled. Again.

"I know where your mind is going, and just stop. You know what I meant." She opened her oversized bag and pulled out her stethoscope and blood pressure cuff. "I'm not here for your entertainment. I'm here to make sure…"

"I don't die."

She frowned. "Not exactly. I'm here to make sure you

stay alive."

"To make sure I don't die. I get it."

She shook her head and wrapped the cuff around his arm. She carefully held her arms far enough from her chest so he couldn't steal a side rub. He wasn't the first old codger she'd seen.

Donna strolled back into the room, pecked Nathan on the forehead, and smiled at the lipstick smudge. "It looks like you're in good hands. I'll be back around three-thirty."

She whispered to the nurse. "Thanks and good luck." Then she slipped out the door.

After the door closed, Nathan said. "Well, now it's just the two of us. I guess we can stop pretending and reveal our true feelings for one another."

His nurse propped her hand on her hip again and shook her finger. "I thought they said you had heart failure, but I'd say yours is pumping pretty well right now. Maybe I don't need to be here."

He clutched his chest and waved his arm. "Oh no! It feels like the big one. Donna come back." He stretched out his hands and stared straight ahead. "I can't see. Donna is that you? Donna, I'm sorry." As his nurse stepped toward him, he let his head drop to one side and held his breath. He couldn't keep a straight face as she leaned over to check his pulse. He inhaled her subtle fragrance and smiled.

He opened one eye and caught both of hers staring him down with a knowing look.

He panted his words. "I hope you're that fast when it's real."

"Hmpf." She whirled around and waltzed into the kitchen. "I need a glass of water."

"Help yourself."

After she left the room, his thoughts slowed just enough to realize how fast he was breathing. That little bit of excitement, and he was exhausted. It didn't take long for him to fall asleep.

Chapter 53
Joe and Peggy

Tears dripped on his bloody hands as Joe held his mother in his arms.

"Mom, don't leave me," he cried. His eyes fogged over with tears. He could hardly breathe. The phone receiver buzzed on the floor next to him as the operator shouted to get his attention.

He picked up the phone. "I'm still here. Are they coming?"

He dropped the phone as his mother gasped and coughed.

"Mom!" He shouted and wrapped his arms around her. "Mom, it's Joe. You're safe." He lightly jostled her head. "Keep your eyes open. The ambulance is on its way."

He picked up the phone. "She's breathing. Please hurry."

His blood froze at the voice of Peggy's father behind him.

"What on earth?"

Joe whipped around, still holding his mother. Her blood clung to his hands, his clothes, and his cheek. The receiver lay still on the floor with the distant squawk of the operator.

When his eyes met Mr. Landrum's, the flood gates opened. Joe stuttered through his tears. "Frank almost killed her."

Mr. Landrum's face softened, and he rushed to Joe's side. "Is she breathing?"

She gasped and coughed.

"Barely."

Mr. Landrum snatched the phone and asked Joe, "Where's Frank?" Joe's eyes pointed him past the sofa to the blood-spattered mess and Frank's gray, empty face.

Mr. Landrum kept his eyes on Frank as he lifted the

phone to his ear. "You'd better send a sheriff along with the ambulance."

* * *

Peggy sprinted to her car and flung open the door. She had never seen her dad so angry. She imagined him cornering Joe. Frank would no doubt oblige and offer the back of his hand. She couldn't get there fast enough.

As she slid into the seat, her mother said, "You're not driving."

Peggy looked at her mom and turned the key. "Better hop in, Mom." As soon as Mom was settled, she popped it in reverse.

As they peeled out of the driveway, Peggy saw flashing lights coming up fast in her mirror. She swerved, almost hitting the Miser's mailbox as the sheriff whizzed past.

Peggy hammered the pedal, almost tailgating the sheriff. She shook her head, fighting tears, and rubbed her face as she imagined her father standing over Joe and punching his face. She bit her lip and punched the gas, edging closer to the sheriff. The speedometer climbed.

Her mother gripped the dashboard and door handle. "Peggy! That's close enough."

She caught the sheriff's eyes in his mirror and eased back on the accelerator.

The oaks lining the road blurred past.

Please be okay, Joe.

* * *

Joe rested his mother's head on his lap. He gently stroked her face and watched her breathe. His hopes rode on the rise and fall of her chest. His ears trained on the sound of her breathing.

He turned to the sound of Mr. Landrum's footsteps through the kitchen.

"They should be here any second." Mr. Landrum hung

up the phone and hurried to the front door.

Joe took a deep breath when he heard the sirens and sound of tires on the driveway.

Mr. Landrum hollered from the front door. "They're just sitting there."

"Why aren't they coming in?" Joe asked.

"Don't know. Let me check."

The siren stopped, and the door closed as Mr. Landrum stepped outside. Joe held his mother. "Don't leave me, Mom. Don't leave me." He turned his head toward the entryway. Nothing. A minute felt like an hour.

He heard the door swing open. Mr. Landrum swung around the corner out of breath. "They have to wait for the sheriff."

"What?" Joe felt his mother slipping away. Eyes closed. Barely breathing. "Oh, God!" *Please. No. I can't lose my mom too.* "Come on, Mom. Hang in there."

More squealing tires and sirens.

"I think they're here." Mr. Landrum dashed back to the door.

He backed away from the door with his hands up. "Don't shoot. It's all clear. Please send in the…"

Two deputies with guns drawn. "Step aside. We have to give the all clear before the paramedics can enter."

"She's dying." Joe shouted. "What are you waiting for?"

"Calm down, son. We heard there was a shooting. We have to make sure the scene is safe."

"Please." His eyes pleaded, but the deputy didn't budge. Joe pointed across the room.

Frank's body lay slumped against the hearth. His face sallow. Pale, dry lips. Sunken eyes.

The deputy gulped like he had never seen a dead body.

"He tried to kill her, so I shot him."

As the deputy stepped toward Frank, he stumbled over

the shotgun.

Joe shouted. "He's dead, but my mom is still alive. Will you *please* help her?"

"Send them in." The deputy spoke into his radio.

* * *

Peggy screeched to a stop just behind the sheriff's car. Her heart sank at the sight of the ambulance and paramedics scurrying into the house. She hopped out of the car, slammed the door, and sprinted toward the house.

The sheriff opened his door in front of her. As she dashed by, he grabbed her arm. She looked into his eyes. All business. No hint of a smile. His eyes looked past her, and she felt a familiar squeeze on her shoulder. As she turned to see her father coming out of the house, her eyes filled with tears.

He grabbed both of her shoulders and looked into her eyes. His face flushed, and his tears matched her. He bit his lip and shook his head. "You can't go in. And you don't want to go in."

The sheriff glanced at her and her dad, then he nodded at her dad and walked toward the house.

Peggy twisted, trying to free herself. Nothing mattered but seeing Joe and making sure he was okay. Her father gripped tighter. "The deputies are in there and…."

Peggy dipped and twisted out of his grasp. But as she darted toward the house, her dad caught her wrist and wheeled her around. She jerked, but his grip held fast. "Let go. I have to go in. I need to know Joe is okay."

Sweat beaded on his face. Eyes red and swollen. Jaw muscles quivering, her father gently gripped her other arm and looked her in the eyes. "Joe is not hurt, but he's not okay." She'd never seen her father so shaken. He could barely speak. Swallowing between words. "His mother is hurt badly. Frank tried to kill her, so Joe…" His eyes glossed with tears. His lips quivered. And his words stopped.

Peggy fell into his arms and buried her tears in his chest. He held her close while she stared at the open door.

A deputy stepped through the door. Over his shoulder, she could see Joe walking out with another deputy behind him. Her fears melted when she saw his face, but he wasn't looking up. He was staring at the pavement. He was that same perplexed little boy she remembered from his daddy's funeral.

Her father relaxed his grip, and she ran toward Joe. Her heart leapt into her throat when she realized he was in handcuffs.

"Joe," she whispered.

The deputy stepped between them and nudged Joe toward the cruiser.

* * *

Joe plodded slowly. Head down. Dried blood spattered and streaked across his face. Eyes swollen and exhausted. Every tear spent.

He stared at the ground, still seeing his mother's eyes and battered face. He was numb to the handcuffs, numb to the deputy's grip, and numb to anyone around him. He felt like he was passing from one world into the next as the deputy opened the cruiser's door. The bars between the front and back reminded him of a dog crate. He was the dog.

He felt the deputy's hand on his head and followed the nudge into the back seat. The door shut. He'd never felt so helpless. He closed his eyes and flopped onto his side. "Why couldn't it be me?"

He looked through the ceiling and beyond the clouds, straining to see the invisible face of God. "You know I'm talking to you. Why couldn't it have been me? Why her? Why Frank? Why did you let her marry him?"

Tears dripped onto the vinyl seat. He sniffed, frustrated he couldn't wipe his eyes or rub his nose. He let the tears fall.

He lurched at the loud thump on the window. "Peggy." He caught a glimpse of her tormented smile as she tried to reach out to him, but her father pulled her away.

Joe saw anger and compassion in his eyes, eyes that wanted to hug him and crush him at the same time. Eyes that softened as Peggy wrestled free to press her face against the window.

Both hands flat against the window, she looked into Joe's eyes, smiled, closed her eyes and kissed the glass. She bit her lip as she waved a gentle good-bye.

His eyes followed her until she was gone.

She came. Of course, she'd figured out it was Danny Miser who'd plotted the mess from the night before.

Danny. "If it hadn't been for him, none of this would have happened. Mom would be fine." *But Frank would still be alive.* He felt a hint of guilty joy knowing Frank would never torment him again. He'd never felt such a rush of warmth until he'd lifted that shotgun and leveled the barrel toward Frank's chest. His sweaty shaky hands had felt cool and calm as he'd held that gun. As he'd imagined the first time his dad took him shooting. It felt as though his father was there, holding the gun with him. *Food for the table and defense for the home,* he could hear his father say.

Over and over his mind replayed that split second: his eye trained on the sight, hands firm on the shaft and the grip, butt of the gun snug against his shoulder, jaw clenched, strong stance, deep breath, slow exhale, Frank's cold stare, and one gentle pluck of his finger.

It felt good.

No more Frank.

He regretted not killing him sooner. He'd wanted him dead so badly. Joe had hated that monster from the moment they met. He'd prayed his mom would never bring Frank home again, then he'd prayed she wouldn't marry him, then he'd prayed Frank would just leave him alone.

When Frank had started beating his mother, Joe had

become the answer to his own prayers, and his father's shotgun had become the transcendent tool to send Frank to meet his maker—and as far from Joe and his mother as possible.

Chapter 54
Joe and Peggy

"Can we go to the hospital?" Peggy asked as her father drove toward home.

His stern look was not the answer she wanted.

She turned on her daddy's-little-girl voice and said, "No one is going to be there for Joe's mom when she wakes up. Please? I want to make sure she's okay. Someone needs to be there."

"What about Joe's sister?"

"Jane probably doesn't even know anything's happened yet. When she finds out, she'll need someone there for her as well."

He continued driving in silence until they reached home.

She stared at the dashboard. Hands praying. Tears trickling.

Her father's hand rested on her shoulder. "Stay here. I'll get your mother."

* * *

Arbor County Hospital was only six miles from their home, but the drive felt like forever.

They parked in the emergency lot.

The normally quiet ER was buzzing. Gawkers and news crews vied for position.

"It looks like the circus has come to town," Mr. Landrum said.

Peggy scowled at the rubberneckers and reporters blocking her path. She squeezed through the wall of people, ignoring the looks and the cameras until a reporter grabbed her arm.

"Can you tell us anything about the murder?"

"Murder?" *It can't be true.* She knew the evil things Frank had done to Joe, but she couldn't believe he would kill his own wife. She imagined her tears and tortured expression all over the news, but she didn't care about anything but getting to Joe's mom.

She pulled free of the reporter's grasp and sprinted into the ER. "Where is she?" Peggy asked, but no one seemed to hear. Nurses scurrying, alarms beeping, then she spotted a brown-and-tan uniform guarding one of the rooms.

"You can't go in there," the deputy said with his hand raised. "The doctors are working, and she's not allowed any visitors until she's been questioned."

"She's still alive?" Peggy covered her mouth and sputtered. "They said she was murdered."

The deputy's expression remained firm as he shook his head. "She is still alive." He raised an eyebrow. "You her daughter?"

"No. Her daughter's name is Jane."

"Do you know how we can reach her?"

"She's probably with her boyfriend, but who knows where."

As the deputy turned to walk away, Peggy asked, "What about Joe?"

"Her son? He's been taken in for questioning."

"Questioning for what?"

"His stepfather was shot. I can't tell you anything else."

Her heart sank as she realized Joe must have killed his stepdad to protect his mother. *Joe, what did you do?*

* * *

Peggy rushed to her father when he entered the waiting room.

"Daddy, you've got to help Joe." She clutched his suit jacket and begged.

Her father looked away. "Do you *not* remember what he did to you last night? Don't you remember how we found you this morning?"

"Daddy, you haven't been listening." Her tears won as she continued. "Danny did it. He tried to set up Joe to make it look like he…" She shook her head. She couldn't bring herself to say the words. She wanted to run, run out the door, out of the hospital. Grab Joe out of jail and keep running.

Her father lifted her chin. She met his eyes, and his face softened. He hugged her, and said, "I'm sorry, Peggy. I thought the worst. And I should've listened to you." He nodded toward his wife and said, "Let's go get Joe."

Peggy tried to follow, but her father stopped her with his open hand. "You stay here. His mother will be happy to see you when she's awake, or when they let her have visitors." He pointed at one of the green vinyl chairs. "Stay right there until the nurse tells you it's okay to see her."

* * *

"Joe, why don't you tell us what happened?" the detective asked.

"I've already told you guys what happened." Joe was no expert in interrogation, but he'd seen enough movies to know they were going to ask him the same questions over and over just waiting and hoping he would make a mistake. He refused to look at the redundant detective. Instead, he spoke to the stark walls in the little cube of a room. He rested his elbows on his knees. The wooden grade-school-sized chair was not designed for hours of use.

"You haven't told *me*." The detective scooted his chair closer to Joe and forced a smile. "I know it gets tiresome, but we have different people ask the same questions to help us understand the truth."

Joe buried his face in his hands and shook his head. "I can't," he whispered.

"I'm sorry. You're going to have to speak up."

"I want to see my mom."

"You'll see your mom as soon as you tell us what *really*

happened."

Knock. Knock.

A deputy peered through the tiny window, then the door swung open.

Joe's eyes brightened. *Mrs. Landrum.*

Instant tears.

"Sorry." The deputy shrugged his shoulders. "I wasn't going to allow this lady and her husband to see the accused—the person of interest, but the Sheriff said to let them come in here."

Mrs. Landrum stepped between the detective and Joe. "He's not a whatever you said. He's a boy." She gave her best don't-mess-with-me look then pulled Joe from his chair and squeezed and smothered him with a hug. Joe didn't care that he could hardly breathe. Mrs. Landrum was his second Mom. He would hold that hug as long as she would allow. His chest heaved and his body shook as he sobbed against her chest.

"You've no right to question him. I'm taking him to see his mother." Her voice rumbled in his ear as she held him close.

Mr. Landrum spoke sternly—a voice Joe was all-too-familiar with. "I've spoken to my lawyer and the prosecutor. You don't have enough to arrest him, and you can't question him without parental permission. So, we are taking him to the hospital to see his mother."

Chapter 55

Joe and Peggy

Rain pelted the sidewalk and the street in front of the jail. Joe stood beside Mrs. Landrum under the awning as Mr. Landrum scurried through the Autumn rain toward their car. The rain seemed appropriate and certainly matched how Joe felt. Miserable. Gray skies, low-hanging clouds, and drizzle mixed with the occasional downpour.

Headlights flickered through the rain as Mr. Landrum pulled up beside them.

Despite the topsy-turvy, world-flipped-upside-down day, Joe had just enough normal in him to remember to open the car door for Mrs. Landrum.

They drove in silence until Joe said, "Thanks for bailing me out."

"No bail necessary. You weren't under arrest."

"Thanks for whatever you did." His voiced cracked. "I really need to see my mom right now."

Joe rested his head against the car window. Streaks of light whisked by as Mr. Landrum drove in silence toward the hospital. The windshield wipers thumped a slow steady beat. The wet pavement reflected headlights and taillights.

Joe's tears mirrored the drizzle on the glass. He wished he could turn back time and start over. His heart still ached from the loss of his father. He refused to imagine losing his mother. He looked at the silent silhouettes in the front seat, Peggy's parents. Her mom was his second mother—always looking after him, feeding him, keeping him out of trouble. Surely she knew how much he loved Peggy, knew he would never do anything to hurt her.

Here he was in her mother's car. She and Mr. Landrum had gotten him out of jail, and they were taking him to see his Mom. He felt their love. They didn't have to say anything.

He caught Mr. Landrum's eyes in the mirror. He wasn't smiling, but his eyes weren't angry either. Joe realized Mr. Landrum's unyielding approach was his way of protecting Peggy.

"Thank you," Joe said.

Peggy's mom answered, "No need to thank us, Joe. You're like part of our family."

He saw a hint of a smile with Mr. Landrum's raised eyebrow.

Joe felt a tiny smile, his first smile all day.

He took a deep breath and imagined Peggy standing next to Mom, holding her hand. He could hardly wait to see them. His heart warmed at the thought of Peggy being there for Mom and for him. He wanted to wrap his arms around her and hold her close, but he imagined tears streaming. He imagined her running her fingers across Mom's forehead, lifting hair from her eyes—hollowed and fixed.

The car bounced over a pothole, thumping his head against the glass. He rubbed away the pain, and his thoughts shifted from Mom to Frank. His lifeless body. His boots covered in blood. Streaks and spatter all over his pants and soaking through his shirt. He imagined Frank's rigid stare, but saw Danny's face. Danny's sneer. Danny's scowl. Danny belly laughing. Danny resting comfortably in his own bed with his mom and dad, both alive and healthy.

He imagined him lying in bed, arms folded behind his head, staring at the ceiling with a gloating smile. Danny had always been there like a tiny rock in his shoe. But that rock never went away. It became a splinter, a sprain, a punch in the gut, a black eye. Danny had become a threat to everything Joe loved.

His little prank almost cost him his relationship with Peggy, his mother's life, and his freedom. He imagined his fingers gripping Danny's throat, pressing and squeezing as hard as he could, choking the life out of him. *It's all his fault.*

"All who's fault?" asked Mr. Landrum.

Joe didn't realize he'd said it out loud. He caught Mr. Landrum's eyes again in the rearview mirror, but he shook his head and said nothing. He stared at the cold, wet street until they reached the hospital.

The rain slowed as they pulled up to the aging limestone structure. Joe slid out of the car—the hospital towering over him like a giant tombstone. Dark clouds hovered over it. And a misty haze hung around every light.

The imposing building brought back painful memories. He relived the pain of waking in that cold, sterile hospital room only to hear his father was dead.

Rain mixed with tears as his eyes searched the night sky.

He whispered into the darkness. "I don't know how much more I can take."

Silence.

The cold, gray clouds hung over him, unmoved by his words. Even the air was still.

He'd scarcely uttered a prayer since his father's burial, but he stared at the clouds, hoping God was somewhere listening. *Are you even there?*

A sigh and a headshake, then he lowered his gaze, paralyzed by fear until he felt Mrs. Landrum's hand on his shoulder.

She leaned into his ear. "Your mother's alive. Peggy is with her. It's going to be okay." She hugged him and gave him a gentle nudge.

His body trembled as she hugged him, then he grabbed her arm like a frightened child, held her hand, and they walked into the hospital.

* * *

Passing the nurse's station, he spotted the deputy who'd escorted him out of Frank's house.

The deputy raised an eyebrow. "Didn't expect to see you

here."

Joe wanted to slap the grin off the deputy's face and tell him where to go, but he buried his anger, held his tongue, and stepped past the deputy into the doorway of his mother's room.

Peggy rushed toward him and consumed him with a hug. Her body shook with sobs that matched his. As she held him, he looked over her shoulder and saw his mother lying in that hospital bed.

Joe had enough bad memories of the hospital already. He couldn't bear any more. He held Peggy tighter as he stared at his mother. He cringed at her marred and swollen face but felt some relief from the steady beep of her heart monitor. He loosened his grip on Peggy. She lifted her head and looked into his eyes. He tried to smile but tears prevailed. She slid her hand into his and led him toward his mother.

Joe inched closer in quiet disbelief. None of this should've happened. Life was supposed to be easy. He was still a kid. He wanted his mom and dad and the happy life he'd always imagined. But his dreams lay tangled in a web of tubing and electrodes—each breath and each heartbeat monitored.

He stepped closer, grabbed the bedrail and looked at his mother.

Eyes closed. Barely breathing. He watched her chest rise and fall, and he listened to the blip blip blip of her heartbeat as the monitor showed each pulse.

She gasped, and so did he. Her breathing paused. She opened her eyes, and he heard her raspy whisper.

"Joe."

Tears streamed. He breathed for what felt like the first time all day. He looked past the bruised cheeks and torn lip and saw her gentle eyes, the same eyes that had greeted him in the hospital that dreadful morning so many years before, the same eyes that had ached to see his father.

She lifted her hand. As he leaned closer, she gently

grasped it. “I’m sorry.”

He sniffed, and his lips trembled.

Her voice quavered and cracked. “I’m sorry I married Frank. It wasn’t fair to you or Jane. I—”

“It’s okay, Mom. You couldn’t know.” He choked on his words. *No one knew what a monster he was.*

Chapter 56
Brooke

Brooke opened her eyes to darkness. Her head spinning and pounding. Gut aching. Every nerve awake and screaming. She expected to find herself in the woods, but she felt cool, damp earth and hay beneath her. A chill ran through her. She choked on the smell of mold and hay, coughing as she strained to sit up. Her pulse quickened at the utter darkness around her.

She rolled onto her knees and tried to stand. Her hand slipped as she touched a damp wall. *Dirt.* She ran her hands up and down, beside her, and behind her. The dirt and darkness seemed to swallow her. She collapsed onto the floor and felt like she was in a freshly dug grave—her grave.

She heard a creaking sound like a wooden door, then a click. Tiny threads of light shone through slits above her.

Footsteps crunched over straw. *I'm in a barn.* She held her breath and prayed.

God, get me out of here...

...or let me die.

The footsteps drew near, then she heard tires on gravel, and the footsteps stopped.

In the spotty light, she saw fresh streaks of blood on her arms. She felt for new wounds, but there were none. Her legs wavered. Her head throbbed. And she wanted to go to sleep and never wake, but fear and the desire to live kept her fully awake.

As the sound of tires on gravel grew louder, the light switched off, and the barn door slammed shut.

Time to move.

Chapter 57
Nathan and Donna

Donna felt like a deflated balloon—exhausted at the end of her shift. She used to watch the clock, but going home no longer meant getting to rest and relax. Going home meant exhaustion and stress. She couldn't escape the image of Nathan in the hospital—clinging to life. His stagnant eyes had looked through her as all his energy had gone to breathing.
She saw those same eyes in her patients—clinging to life, hoping for another morning, longing for a return to normal—or even a new normal. Every failing heart. Every cough. Every wheeze. Everything she did and everyone she cared for reminded her of Nathan. And the clock reminded her that his clock was winding down.

At the same time, she couldn't stop thinking about the random family who would lose their son or daughter to a motorcycle accident or a drowning. And Nathan's life would depend on their loss.

* * *

Donna drove home as the sun sank behind the naked trees. Gray clouds pressed against the waning light.

Leaves blew across her windshield as she sat in the driveway staring at her house. She was late, but the nurse's car was still there. The house was dark except for the kitchen light, which meant Nathan was asleep. Donna stared at the house—not wanting to move. She wanted to savor every moment she had left with Nathan, but there was nothing left to savor. Every moment was a struggle, a painful reminder that he was dying. Her own heart felt like it was failing as she sat in the dark listening to her engine rumble.

She killed the engine, slid out of the car, and trudged toward the front door. She opened the door and stepped in quietly. There Nathan sat in his chair in the same T-shirt and sweatpants. Passed out. The steady rise and fall of his chest was the only sign of life.

Donna breathed a sigh of relief. He'd made it through one more day, and he was resting without coughing or laboring. She set down her things and softly kissed his forehead. Almost unconsciously, she touched his hand and his wrist.

His skin felt cold and dry, but there it was—a tiny thread of pulsating life.

She whispered, "I miss you, Nathan."

His nurse peeked around the corner.

Donna stared at him in yesterday's clothes, unshaven, crumbs on his shirt. And she clenched her teeth, tightened her fists, and tiptoed toward the nurse. "He hasn't moved, and he's wearing the clothes he slept in."

The nurse stepped back. Hands up. "I'm sorry. He seemed a little too eager for a bath. I called our nursing manager, and she told me to hold off on bathing and changing his clothes for now."

Donna unleashed her tears and looked at her ghost of a husband. He had little energy for her, barely a smile or a kind word, but he was more than willing to have a pretty young thing take off his clothes and give him a bath.

"I'm sorry, ma'am. I know he's no danger to me, but it's my first day here. I'll make sure he gets a bath and fresh clothes tomorrow."

Donna nodded. "It's okay." She covered her tears with a laugh. "At least he's showing some signs of life."

"You're not mad?"

"I'm glad you're here. I needed a break. He's not too much work, but seeing him like this all the time is taking its toll."

They shared a smile.

"I'll see you tomorrow then." The nurse opened the door and stepped into the night.

Chapter 58

Joe and Peggy

Joe sat at his mother's bedside with his head in his hands. His hope rested in the steady beeping of the heart monitor.

The door creaked, and soft footsteps perked his ears. Looking between his fingers, he spied Peggy's canvas tennis shoes. He felt her hands on his knees as she squatted in front of him. Her smile warmed his heart, but he closed his eyes and kept his face in his hands.

She sat beside him, and wrapped her arms around him. His floodgates opened. Tears and uncontrollable shaking. The pain of losing his father, the never-let-you-forget ache in his leg, and the threat of losing his mother erupted together in Peggy's arms.

She touched his hands. "Let me see your face."

He closed his eyes tight, squeezing out more tears, but Peggy softly pulled his hands away. "I'm sorry, Joe."

He blinked and stared at her supple hands. She lifted her hand to his chin, and he looked at her warm smile. Her smooth cheeks. She pushed a few stray strands of hair behind her ear, and he looked into her blue eyes, losing himself in those deep wells.

He couldn't think of an adequate measure for how much he loved her. He pulled her close and never wanted to let go.

"I'm sorry"—he sniffled—"about last night."

Peggy squeezed him tightly then planted a solid kiss. "It was Danny's fault."

She wiped his tears and straightened his hair. "It's going to be okay, and nothing and no one will ever come between us again."

Chapter 59

Joe and Peggy

Joe cradled his coffee and stared out the café window. Jane sat across from him, but he could barely look at her. A few days had passed, and Mom was slowly recovering. Jane had invited him to meet her for a cup of coffee and some catching up.

There were only a few local restaurants—all of them known for gossip and gawking, neither of which they wanted. But the Village Inn was the least crowded, and they served a decent cup of coffee. They chose the booth in the back corner.

"How long has it been?" Jane asked.

The three feet between them may as well have been a mile. Joe hadn't forgotten her words from when Dad died. The blame. The hurt. He'd wanted to forget, but it was constantly there, like the ache in his leg. He ground his teeth and tasted bitterness darker than his black coffee.

Neither said anything, but when he looked at her face, something inside him softened. He wasn't the only one hurt. His jaw relaxed when he saw her tears. Her eyes softened, and she smiled as they stared at each other.

Her hand reached for his. "Joe, how long has it been since it was just you and me, and we could just be normal?"

Normal. What did that even mean? He held her hands and looked out the window. The red and green traffic lights took his mind back to their last normal Christmas. His father reached under the tree and pulled out two boxes, one for each of them.

He remembered their half-smiles, half-frowns as he and Jane looked at each other. It was their Christmas Eve tradition.

His tongue stuck to the roof of his mouth as he tried to speak. He chuckled and almost cried. "Christmas Eve." He looked into her eyes and couldn't stop his tears.

Jane nodded. "Dad gave us our jammies."

"Every year the same thing. Pajamas," he said with the

same fake sound of surprise that they'd made every Christmas Eve.

"Had to look good for those Christmas morning pictures."

The table wobbled as Jane slid around it and sat beside him.

They buried each other in a hug.

Jane said, "Let's not let it happen again."

"What?"

"We can't let anything come between us. You're my brother. I need to be normal with you. And someday, we may only have each other."

"Don't say that."

"Joe." She lay her hand against his cheek and looked him in the eyes. "I'm sorry I wasn't there for you, but I will be from now on. I love you."

His smile was short-lived.

The bell clanged against the door as Danny Miser pushed it open and walked toward a lonely table. Danny had alienated every friend he'd ever had. It would be no surprise to see him having breakfast alone on a Saturday morning.

Joe hid behind his coffee, hoping Danny would just walk past, but his old friend stopped and rested a hand on his shoulder. He bristled at Danny's hand and shrugged it off. Joe stared at him with daggers.

"Hey. I was only going to say, I'm sorry about your mom."

When Danny touched him again, Joe stood, grabbed Danny's hand, twisted his arm behind his back and shoved him. "What about Peggy? Are you sorry about her too?"

The unfortunate loner smirked, and Joe lunged toward him, hurtling him into the next table. As Joe cocked his fist, Jane jumped between them, wrapped her arms around him, and pulled him toward the door.

Every muscle tensed as he watched Danny begging sympathy from everyone in the restaurant. He wanted Danny out of his life. He imagined a nice, soft spot of earth right next to Frank.

Jane grabbed his arm and shook him until he met her eyes. "I don't know what you're thinking, but let it go. Danny will be his own undoing. You just steer clear of him." She clutched his elbow and dragged him to his car.

* * *

Despite the years, Joe remained unable to let go.

He clutched the steering wheel as he sat in front of Peggy's house, reliving all the painful memories. The officer's words rang in his ears. *"I don't think it's ever going to feel like home again."*

The engine whined as he turned the key. The curtain moved again, and he saw the little girl in Peggy's house one last time. How he wished she was Peggy and he was that little boy again. The moments he'd missed and the moments he'd never have. How his heart ached.

Then he saw her. Peggy.

She stood beside her daughter. She'd pulled the curtain open. Their eyes locked. He wanted to freeze that moment, just seeing her face one more time.

He couldn't see her tears, but he saw her waving good-bye, and he knew there was no coming back.

As he shifted into gear and pressed the gas pedal, he pictured a smiling Danny Miser standing in the middle of the street. He ran him over in his mind, and he'd do it all over again and again—anything to get that sarcastic freckle-faced smile out of his head.

* * *

Danny waited until Jane had dragged her brother out of the restaurant. He watched them leave, then he hobbled toward the door, wincing with each step, smiling inside at the sympathy oozing from everyone in the restaurant.

When he stepped outside, he laughed out loud, pretending to cry for the sake of those inside who might still be watching. Joe was making it too easy. It was to the point, all Danny had to do to spark Joe's temper was to show up.

So, Danny decided to show up as often as he could find an excuse.

* * *

The following Tuesday, Danny and his family were part of the few who gathered to remember Frank Mueller. Mrs. Mueller, Joe's mom, was still in the hospital and couldn't come to the memorial service or the graveside. The drizzling rain was enough of an excuse for most anyone else to avoid paying their respects when they actually had none to pay.

Umbrellas bunched together around the casket.

No one spoke.

After the pastor prayed, one-by-one people left the graveside, but Danny lingered.

He didn't care for Frank any more than any of the others. He was there to see another grave—Joe's dad.

There it was. The nearby oak tree had grown quite a bit, making it harder to find by memory. He stood in front of the stone. It was nothing special and not extra wide—only enough room for one name. He guessed Joe's mom had expected she'd remarry and wind up buried next to another man.

Danny grinned as he read the gravestone. *Edward Novak. November 17. That's right. It was opening day. How could I forget?*

Opening day of firearms season for whitetail deer would be the perfect day to unleash havoc on Joe and what was left of his family.

Chapter 60

Joe and Peggy

It had been a little over a month since Joe's mother had come home from the hospital. Her lips no longer swollen, her face no longer bruised, she was starting to look like herself again.

But the house remained quiet. Neither Joe nor Mom talked much about anything, and neither of them had talked about that day. The wounds were too fresh and too deep.

They shared frequent hugs and tears, knowing looks, but few words. Joe watched the marks on her face slowly fade, but the pain in her eyes remained the same. He felt a twinge of guilt every time their eyes met, knowing she was seeing his father every time she looked at him.

Frank's house seemed colder and emptier than before. Joe and his mother had become untouchables. No one came to visit except Peggy and Mrs. Landrum. Even Jane had left to move in with Kirk.

Joe sat at the kitchen table sharing coffee with his mother.

No words. Just time together and coffee.

But that Sunday morning was different.

Joe watched his mother stare out the window. She looked past the trees with their leaves just starting to turn, past the winding creek, past the fields beyond, and past the distant clouds. It seemed she was looking into another time or another world.

"How are you feeling, Mom?"

She sipped her coffee and nodded to say she was fine.

Not even a word. Joe wondered if he would ever get his mother back again—if life could ever resemble some kind of normal. He looked past her blank stare and spoke to the woman he used to know. "You feel like going to church?"

Her eyes followed the steam rising from her cup. "Do I feel like it, or do I feel *up* to it?" Before he could say anything, she said, "Neither. I don't want to go. Have you seen any of *those people* here since…?" She couldn't say *since you shot Frank,* so she said, "since I came home?"

"No."

"Then let's just forget about it. I'm not ready to face them either."

"I remember you telling me more than once not to make decisions based on what somebody else does or doesn't do."

She frowned and drew a deep sigh, keeping her eyes locked on her coffee. She curled her fingers around the warm mug, lifted it, and looked at Joe as she sipped. No smile. No wink. But he saw a look in her eyes he'd not seen in a long time—that knowing, I-raised-you-right look.

He smiled at the tiny glimpse of the mom he thought he'd lost. She downed the rest of her coffee, set down her mug, and said, "Well, I guess we'd better get ready."

He smiled. "Peggy is coming to pick us up."

"Peggy? Here I thought it was Jesus who had you wanting to go to church."

* * *

Peggy's tires squealed onto their driveway.

Joe hopped up from the table and dashed out to meet her.

His heart melted as she twisted out of her car. He barely noticed her mother in the passenger's seat, smiling and waving. He waved, but his eyes were glued to Peggy. Her smooth, silky hair bounced as she walked toward him.

Her everyday look was enough for him, but her Sunday best was almost too much. Even a modest dress couldn't hide everything he imagined underneath.

And her eyes and her smile told him she knew exactly what he was thinking.

Hallelujah.

Peggy lifted her hand to his chin. She touched him softly, then closed his gaping mouth. They both chuckled.

Joe's cheeks felt instant warmth. "Mom's not too sure, but she's coming."

"It'll be good for her to get out." Peggy nibbled her lip and smiled. She gently tugged on her dress and did a little twist as though he wasn't already completely enthralled.

Joe reached for her hand and gently kissed it. "Thanks for coming." His eyes fixed on hers. Nothing else mattered when looked into her eyes. *I can't say it, Peggy, not yet, but you are my world, my whole world.*

She cocked her head to the side. "Are you okay?"

He squeezed her hand. "More than okay. You're here."

Peggy blushed and gave her mom a quick glance.

Joe smiled at Mrs. Landrum and dropped Peggy's hand. "We would be utterly alone if not for you and your mom. It's like the rest of the town forgot we existed."

Peggy lifted his chin and blew a subtle, Mom's-looking kiss. "Forget about this town. You and I know what happened. This town doesn't want to know or admit that one of their 'upstanding citizens' could've been such an evil man."

Joe looked down. His thoughts swirled. He couldn't forget Frank soon enough, but he could never forget this town. Every good memory he'd ever had involved this town. And leaving would mean leaving Peggy. *Never.* He'd rather die.

Peggy said, "I'm sorry, Joe. I know it's disrespectful to talk ill of the dead, but Frank was… He certainly didn't deserve the family your mom tried to give him."

"Peggy." He pressed her hand against his cheek and kissed it again. "It's okay. This town may never get over it, but we will. Frank tried to ruin our lives while he was alive. I'm sure not going to let him ruin us now."

She hugged him. He squeezed her tightly and never wanted to let go.

Chapter 61

Nathan and Donna

Once the nurse left the house, Donna took a deep breath and slumped onto the sofa, exhausted. Another long day. Another long night.

Nathan slept, but at any moment he could cough himself awake, or the pager could go off. His heart rhythm could trigger an alarm. The pulse oximeter might fall off and start beeping. It was always something—something besides sleep.

"I might just go to sleep right here." She kicked off her shoes and laid her head back. She closed her eyes and listened to Nathan's rhythmic breathing. His wheezing reminded her of an old-fashioned tea kettle that hadn't quite reached the boiling point.

How am I supposed to sleep with that? She leaned down and grabbed her shoes then watched him. His cold gray face almost lifeless. She hoped the young man she loved was still in there somewhere.

Then she remembered the bottle of pain pills. She'd tossed it over her shoulder. Scouring the dimly lit living room, she couldn't find it anywhere. Fear twisted her gut as she imagined him using every ounce of his strength to find that bottle himself.

She began to feel as though he'd already died. His chair had swallowed him, and this ghost of a man had taken his place.

As she walked toward the bathroom, she listened to his oxygen hiss. The mix of hissing and wheezing sounded like a snake of death coiling around him, squeezing the air from his lungs, squeezing the life from his body, and squeezing hope from her heart.

She looked into the bathroom mirror. Washed off her makeup and brushed her teeth.

As she stared at those worry lines in her reflection,

something inside her said *don't give up*. She stiffened at those words. They'd popped into her mind like a whisper echoing from miles away. She felt a chill over her skin and a warmth in her heart.

A big part of her wanted to give up. Go back home. Find a solid farm boy turned farmer. Adopt the kid she'd never had. Backpack Europe. Find a travel nursing job. Or just run as far away as she could.

But the bigger part of her could never give up. Nathan had been her world, but even as her world seemed to shrink and darken, it was still her world. And a thread of hope was still hope. And she would hang on to that thread until it snapped.

Donna chose to forget the way he'd shouted at her about not understanding his pain. He hadn't been able to raise himself to walk to the kitchen, but he'd raised his voice, and his face had reddened. Closing her eyes, she fought every ill thought, determined to remember him as he'd been and hope that someday he be that man again.

When she was finally ready to go to bed, she couldn't. She hated the empty feeling of that bed without him, and she felt guilty leaving him alone in the living room.

She grabbed her pillow, tiptoed back into the living room, and slept on the sofa.

* * *

Nathan awakened, expecting Donna to be in their bedroom, but there she lay, mouth open, sound asleep on the sofa. He watched her effortless breathing and felt jealous and helpless. He imagined wrapping his arms around her and carrying her to their bedroom. Even the thought felt exhausting.

His back ached from life in the chair, but when he reached for a hydrocodone, they were gone.

* * *

The next day started like so many others. Nathan woke in his chair—already exhausted. Donna fixed his breakfast, gave him his morning meds, and prepared for work.

Someone knocked on the door. She opened it for the nurse, blew Nathan a kiss, then left.

But it wasn't just another day. Nathan was sweating, shaking, and ready to kill for one of his pills.

When the door closed, Nathan glared at his nurse. "You think I'm an idiot?"

Her face flushed, and her eyes opened wide. "No."

He coughed and sputtered, his face red. "You think because I'm…" He panted between words. "Stuck in this chair that I can't look out for myself, that I can't tell what's going on."

She gulped, looked away, and opened her bag. "I don't know what you're talking about."

He pounded the armrest with his fist. "You know exactly what I'm talking about. Now hand them over." He held out his right hand and reached for the phone with his left.

She pulled his bottle of hydrocodone out of her bag. "I must have put this in here by mistake."

Nathan snatched the bottle from her hand, opened it, and popped a couple of pills.

Her eyes narrowed. Hand on her hip. "I didn't see that on your med list. I should call your doctor and make sure it's okay."

He stuck his hand between the seat cushion and the armrest and watched her eyes widen as he patted his revolver. "I've got six reasons why you'd better not."

She stumbled backwards, almost falling. "Mr. Fortune, maybe I'm not the nurse for you."

A smile stretched across his face. "You know you are." He lifted his hydrocodone bottle and gave it a little shake. "I'm sure we can work something out."

"Don't expect me to do anything illegal."

Nathan coughed between laughs.

Chapter 62
Brooke

When he heard the engine rumbling and the tires on gravel, he flipped out the lights and left Brooke in the barn. She wasn't going anywhere, but he didn't want any visitors either. He stood in the shadows and waited for the car to pass. He saw another set of headlights in the distance and decided to wait until there was no traffic at all.

After the first car had passed by, he jogged toward the house and slipped around to the back porch. His head throbbed. His heart raced faster than his mind, and he needed it to stop. He'd never imagined his past coming back to haunt him. He'd never imagined abducting anyone. And he couldn't imagine killing anyone—at least not without some help. He reached into his cooler, grabbed a beer, and sat on the porch swing.

He let out a deep breath and held the cold can against his head. He looked at the can. Cold sweat dripping down the side. He glanced at his eleven friends still in the cooler. *I'm gonna need all the help I can get, boys.*

He chugged the first can then tossed it onto the porch.

He opened another can and took a deep slurp. He turned sideways, leaned back, and lifted his feet onto the swing. Four beers. Five. The eighth beer was enough.

He stared at the barn knowing what he had to do, and he'd done everything he could to stifle his inhibition.

"You shouldn't have crossed me, Brooke. It's gonna cost you."

No mistakes this time.

"No mistakes." He slurred his words and his thoughts. But he shivered as he remembered the frightened little boy he had been, stiffening every muscle, bracing for those words and the blistering pain that followed them. *No mistakes.* His ears still rang from those words shouted into his young ears.

He set down his beer and remembered one of the many painful moments when the old man had slammed a beer down onto the table then flung it across the room. His eyes burned and his heart still felt the hurt from when the foam had run down his face.

He could still see the old man collapsed on the sofa, drowning the world.

Chapter 63
Brooke

Brooke set her mind on one thing: survival. Adrenaline suppressed all her pain and fear. She stood and felt the dirt walls on both sides. She took a deep breath, pressed one foot against each wall, and pushed herself up with all her strength. She reached for one of the slats overhead and pulled hard. Nothing.

She braced against the walls and tried pushing each slat. The first three were fixed, but the fourth gave. It was a door. It rose a little, stopping with a thud of wood against metal. *His car.* She inched up as high as she could and lifted the door with her head. It was tight, but she was determined to squeeze through the gap.

She could barely see in the dim light. Aged wooden walls and a smattering of scattered hay on the ground. Brooke held her breath and listened. Then she shimmied out of her pit and closed the door quietly. Her heart pounded with the fear that he might hear then burst into the barn.

Out of breath. Freezing. And feeling every little scrape, she lay under the car on the hay-covered floor until she caught her breath.

She slid out, clamored to her feet, and bumped into the wall behind her. She fell over an old, wooden chair into the barn wall. Her hands swept across the rough wall, feeling for a door. She found a hook-and-eye latch and tried to lift it, but the hook was tight. She jerked it loose, and it rattled against the opening door. She stepped outside, tripping over a shovel and into the darkness.

The air fell quiet as a passing car moved farther down the road. She caught a glimpse of taillights rounding the bend.

As she closed the door behind her, she felt a rain drop and leaned against the barn. She looked toward the stars too numb to pray—almost too stunned, too dehydrated to clearly think. Raindrops mixed with fine drizzle. She rubbed her arms and wished she had a jacket.

But she breathed a sigh realizing the rain tapping on the tin roof would cover any noise she would make.

Her heart jumped as she heard the barn door slide open, and the lights turn on. He'd have to pull the car outside before he could open the pit and check on her. The cool air and rain on her skin awakened her and helped her think. She decided to wait until he'd parked the car outside the barn and gone back inside. Then she would sneak around the barn, jump into the car and take off.

* * *

He thought he heard a crash, as if something had fallen over in the barn. He set down his cold little friend and staggered into the drizzle. Sliding the barn door open partway, he stepped inside and flicked on the lights. His old car stood guard over the root cellar, but something didn't feel right.

The back door was hanging straight, and the shovel wasn't where he'd left it. He blinked his eyes to focus and stretched out his arms for balance. Shaking his head only helped slightly as he shuffled his feet toward the back of the barn. The straw seemed more scattered, and he noticed some blood spatter.

Anger and fear were perfect stimulants to lift him from his haze. He looked over his shoulder and whirled around—not wanting to be surprised. No one was there. Not a sound. Not even breathing. As he stood silent, listening, the gentle tapping of rain turned to loud drumming. Even if there were something to hear, it would be impossible to hear it.

He scurried past his car toward the back of the barn—checking constantly to make sure no one was ready to pounce on him.

The shovel was still there but laying on the ground. He breathed a sigh, knowing at least he would not suffer death by shovel. The small wooden chair lay on its side. And the back door was shut but not latched. He shook his head, wondering if he could have forgotten to latch it.

He stuck his head out the door and looked toward the dense woods. It was too dark to see anything, but if she had somehow escaped, he doubted she'd get too far. The woods were a mess of briars, and she was dehydrated and barefooted.

He went to the car and grabbed his flashlight. Then he stuck his head out the back door squinting at the steady rain. He shone the light on the edge of the woods. The rain made it almost impossible to see anything.

He took a deep breath, gritted his teeth, and wished he'd killed her sooner. He stepped back inside and slammed the door. The old wood creaked. The hinges and hook rattled. And the door bounced open.

"It's no use, Brooke. You can't escape."

* * *

Her feet slipped from under her as she dashed around the side of the barn. The pain of the fall awakened her pain and fear. She had barely enough strength to stand, but she dug down and mustered every ounce of courage.

She peeked around the corner of the barn. His flashlight darted back and forth against the trees. She hoped he would step outside and head toward the woods. But he stood there—hiding from the rain—perhaps hiding from her. She was mad enough to kill him, though she wasn't sure she could bring herself to do it.

Even in the heavy rain, the old barn shook when the back door slammed and rattled. She knew what was coming next. He was going to check the pit to see if she was still there, which meant he would have to pull the car out of the barn. So, she slipped around the side of the barn, and waited for the right moment.

Her heart began racing as he slid the barn door open the rest of the way, started the car, and pulled it partway out outside. She could hear the rumble of the engine despite the pelting rain.

She glanced around the front of the barn. The car was sticking out about halfway, and he'd left the driver's door open—apparently not planning to take too long checking the pit.

Now or never. Those words had never felt so real or so final before. She took a deep breath and ran to the edge of the open door. She glanced inside—toward the back of the barn. She couldn't see him. He must have been opening the pit.

She slid around the front of the car, unable to duck beneath the headlights, and hoping he wouldn't notice the flicker of the lights. She climbed into the car and reached for the gearshift. She touched the brake, shifted into drive, then she crushed the gas pedal. The tires spun on the hay sending the car a little sideways as she sped out of the barn. As the car left the gravel and rambled onto the road, tears began to stream. Her heart pounded faster at the thought that she had escaped. *I thought I was gone. God, I thought it was over.*

The wipers beat back the rain as she wiped her tears to see. The road was lonely yet somehow familiar—even in the dark and in the heavy rain. Even as she drove, fear hung on. She imagined him breathing against her neck, watching her drive, waiting for her to find a gas station or another car—someone she could stop to ask for help—to borrow a phone and call 911.

Her stomach rolled. She tasted salt and bitterness, and tried to not throw up. She shook uncontrollably and tried to tell herself she was okay. She had gotten away, and he could no longer hurt her.

Fighting tears and fighting the rain, she had to pull over. She couldn't see, and whatever country road she was on had no white lines to show her the edge of the road. She was only a few miles away from him and did not want to stop, but she slowed the car to a stop and threw it in park. Sobbing, she planted her face in her hands. "I can't believe it." Laughter mixed with tears as she felt free even if it might be short-lived. She drew a deep breath and tried to gather herself. In the rearview mirror, she caught a glimpse of distant headlights. Her pulse quickened. She knew it couldn't be him. She had his car, but she couldn't escape the fear that it somehow was him. She wanted to hop out, wave them down, plead for help. But fear overcame hope and she put the car in gear in case it was him—in case the car slowed down and pulled off the road behind her.

But the car sped by—as fast as one could reasonably speed in a heavy rain. As the taillights fade, she pounded her fist against the steering wheel wishing she'd had the courage to wave them down. Then she saw headlights approaching in the distance.

This time, she had no doubt it couldn't be him. This car was coming from the wrong direction. She flung open the door, ignoring the rain, and stepped into the middle of the road to wave down the oncoming car.

As the car approached, the rain grew louder, and the engine died.

She climbed back into the car. It was still in park, headlights on, but the ignition was empty.

The keys were gone.

She startled at the sound of jangling keys next to her ear. He leaned over the seat holding the keys. His warm breath sent a chill down her neck. "Did you think I would let you get away?"

He climbed out of the back seat and stepped into the downpour, laughing at the rain. He opened the door and shoved Brooke across the seat. "Stay down, or this night's gonna get even longer for you."

The oncoming car slowed as it got closer, but he smiled and waved, then waved them on, and down the road they went.

He slid into the driver's seat and started the car. "Where do you want to go?" He laughed. "Back to the barn?"

"Just kill me now, please."

"You know that's the problem with youth today. You've got so much to live for, but you just can't see it. Don't worry.

You’ll die when it’s time.”

Chapter 64

Joe and Peggy

It was an ordinary October Sunday. Church bells rang. Crisp morning air whirred about those gathering to worship. Joe's mother held his hand and squeezed firmly as they walked toward the church's front step. He could feel her angst in her shaky grip and uncertain footsteps. But no amount of nerves could keep him from noticing Peggy's honeysuckle perfume as she and her mother followed close behind.

The couple assigned to greet stood at the door with their pasted smiles, shaking hands. One of them reached for Joe's hand. "Good morning. It's good to see you." The man nodded at Joe and his mom.

Joe shook the man's wet-noodle hand and glared at him, wilting that sickening smile. *You're not fooling me. Where were you?* He dropped the man's hand and looked into the sanctuary as he stepped into the tiny foyer. *Where were any of you?*

He cringed as that same sappy voice greeted Peggy and her mom. "Peggy, Mrs. Landrum, it's good to see you too. Thanks for letting us borrow your husband this morning."

The four of them climbed the stairs and went inside.

The church felt cold, but no one was wearing a coat. It felt empty, but almost every seat was full.

Mrs. Landrum walked toward their usual pew near the front, but Joe's mother stopped at the back row. Her head down, she stared at the distressed wood floor.

Joe squeezed her hand. "Mom, it's okay. It's going to be okay."

Her eyes told Joe it was never going to be okay. He felt the pain. Her eyes had watched his father die, and he felt as though she were looking right through him. He felt invisible, as if she were looking at his father, wishing he would come back.

Chatter bounced about the tiny church as the bells

stopped ringing. The sudden silence cued the organist to begin the prelude.

His mother let go of his hand, plodded into the back row and sat. She folded her hands and stared at the floor. Joe heard the familiar footsteps of Mrs. Landrum clomping back towards them. Her face tight, fighting tears for his mother—her friend.

Joe stepped out of the pew and let her slide in beside Mom. Peggy followed.

"Blessed Assurance" groaned from the aging organ. Heels clunked and shoes squeaked as the people made their way to their seats.

As all eyes turned toward the front of the sanctuary, Joe felt a familiar sting in the back of his head followed by a familiar laugh. *Danny Miser.* A quick flick of the finger was one of Danny's favorite annoyances. Joe's pulse soared. His face flushed, and his fists tensed. The momentary pain only added to his growing mountain of hatred for Danny—a mountain that was ready to erupt.

Joe stood and whirled around—fist loaded and ready, but Peggy grabbed his arm and dug in with her nails. Joe glared at Danny, took a deep breath, sat, folded his hands in his lap, and held his tongue.

But his eyes followed Danny all the way to his seat.

* * *

After the final amen and the closing chorus, Joe walked his mother out to the car. She was pale and trembling.

Mr. Landrum came alongside and helped Joe practically carry her to the car. They eased her into the backseat. She wore no expression, stared at nothing, said nothing.

Joe stood holding the door and hoping his mom would give him something—a smile, tears, anything. "Mom?" Joe said it loud enough to startle her, but she barely moved. Her eyes widened for a second—then nothing.

Mr. Landrum stepped close and squeezed Joe's shoulder.

"You okay?"

Joe nodded. "Yeah, but I'm worried about Mom."

Mr. Landrum gave another squeeze and waited until Joe looked him in the eyes. "Joe, I'm sorry I didn't have more faith in you. Peggy told me you tried to help her. She told me it was Danny's fault." He lay both hands on Joe's shoulders and said, "I still don't know exactly what happened that night, but I'm trusting Peggy, and until I know otherwise, I will assume she is telling me the truth."

Joe held his gaze and said, "Mr. Landrum, I don't want anything to ever happen to Peggy. I would never do anything to hurt her." He looked past Mr. Landrum and saw Danny Miser trying to steal Peggy's attention. "And I won't let anyone else do anything to hurt her either."

He slipped away from Mr. Landrum and started to run towards Danny, but Mr. Landrum grabbed his arm. "Son, you need to leave Danny Miser to me."

* * *

Peggy had watched her father grip Joe's arm. She'd edged back toward the wall as her father led Joe outside. Her eyes followed them to the door, but she'd stood paralyzed—afraid her father hadn't believed her—that he'd thought she was simply protecting Joe.

She'd cringed as her daddy's hand clutched her world in his fist and dragged him out of the church. Joe had glanced over his shoulder. His eyes a mix of sadness, love, and fear. Her heart ached as she'd felt him slipping away. Panic seized her. Trembling. Sweating. Panting. She'd stared at the church doors. People leaving. Everyone leaving. She imagined the doors closing and feared she might never see Joe again.

Her pulse out-of-control, she'd darted toward the door, but a hand grabbed her wrist and jolted her to a stop.

"Peggy." Danny's shrill, whiney voice shot through her. She'd sooner stomp on his face than look at him after what he'd done. She jerked to free herself, but he squeezed tighter.

"I'm sorry about the other night."

His words shot a chill through her. She caught the wary glances of other churchgoers filing out of the tiny sanctuary and forced a smile. Then she turned toward Danny. Finger in his face. "Don't even pretend, you son of a—"

"I'm sure Joe didn't mean to go that far."

The church fell silent. She felt every eye on her and imagined every cutting word in every thought and whisper. But she ignored the stares and whispers and focused her fury on Danny.

She grabbed the wrist that held hers, dug in with her nails, and yanked free, raising her hand like a catapult ready to be cut loose.

His cheesy smile and raised eyebrows dropped, and his freckled face paled.

Peggy smacked him hard enough to silence the rumors. Anyone who hadn't yet noticed the two of them couldn't help but notice now. The smack rang like a stack of hymnals striking the hardwood floor.

His cheeks flushed, and he lunged at her, grabbing her throat.

Mrs. Landrum dashed toward them shouting. "Get your hands off my daughter."

Danny let go immediately and feigned his best guiltless smile. "I'm sorry, Mrs. Landrum. I just wanted to apologize to Peggy for the other night."

Mrs. Landrum glared and motioned for him to leave. After he walked out the front doors, Peggy collapsed into her arms, soaking her blouse with tears.

Chapter 65
Brooke

Brooke opened her eyes to darkness once more. The sting of duct tape pulled her lips and her cheeks. A zip-tie once again bound her hands behind her, and duct tape bound her legs.

The cold, damp ground chilled her skin. Her throat ached as she swallowed her tears. Her only comfort was the darkness and silence telling her he wasn't there. She lay perfectly still. Holding her breath, she wondered if she would be better off dead. She felt swallowed by the cold, unfazed earth. She imagined the dirt walls closing around her, burying her. She pictured her mother standing on the earth above her, crying.

She closed her eyes and wished for that tunnel of light, a heavenly choir, a welcome-home hallelujah moment, but there she lay against the damp earth, choking on the smell and taste of mold and dirt.

Jesus, help me.

How long had it been since she'd heard a sound? Sure, an owl's hoot, an occasional distant bark, but nothing from him. No doors. No footsteps. Not even a car driving down the road.

If he's not here, I still have a chance.

She tried to twist her wrists, and they moved. She curled into a ball and tried to pull her bound wrists under her bottom and over her legs, but it was no use.

She wiggled her wrists but could not break the zip-tie. The dirt walls felt like they were closing in on her as she collapsed on her bound hands.

God, I'm still here. Where are you?

Chapter 66

Joe and Peggy

Peggy finally got some rest. Nothing is quite as cozy as a warm bed on a late Autumn morning. Leaves covered the fading grass. Darkness held its grip a little longer each night.

As morning dawned, Peggy lay fast asleep. It was the kind of morning she would've loved to sleep in, snuggle her age-old Teddy bear and read a book. But she awakened to the rumble of her father's car and her mother's clomping footsteps. She glanced at her clock. *Seven-thirty on a Saturday*? *Why can't they ever sleep in?*

Her mother tapped on her door and stuck her head in. "Peggy, I'm going to breakfast with my Bible study. I'll see you this afternoon. Your father had to run to the office."

And you had to wake me up.

Her head flopped against the pillow. Grabbing the covers, she rolled onto her side, closed her eyes, and prayed sleep would find her once more.

Her mother shouted good-bye as she left the house.

Peggy smiled at the silence. *They're gone. I can go back to my dream.* She'd been dreaming of riding horses with Joe. She chuckled thinking it must have been her mother's clomping that stirred the dream.

It didn't take long to return to her dream. She rode a pure white mare. Joe rode a solid black stallion. All at once, his horse began to limp, and Joe climbed down. Checking his hoof, he found a rock wedged under the horseshoe. He used a stick to pry it loose.

As he was tending his horse, Peggy's mare whinnied and raised on its hind legs. She patted the mare's neck to calm her, but there was no consoling her. The mare sidestepped and jumped as though she had seen a snake.

Peggy managed to turn her around. Her pulse pounding.

Sweat pouring. She looked around for Joe, but he was nowhere in sight. Her spine tingled and every hair bristled at the sight of Danny Miser slowly plodding toward her on the black stallion.

She dug her heels into her mare, but the horse couldn't budge. The mare's legs were galloping, but she wasn't going anywhere. Meanwhile, the stallion grew closer. The air grew strangely thick, and she felt like she was choking.

Peggy startled awake. Danny Miser stood over her with his hand pressed firmly against her mouth and a knife dancing in front of her eyes. His hand, his pressing weight, and his sharp blade suppressed her scream.

"Good morning, Peggy. I came to finish what we started the other night."

* * *

Joe had his own dream. He was a little boy, and he felt the gentle touch of his father's hand and heard him whisper, "It's time to get up." A cold sweat and nausea washed over him. He'd had the same nightmare many times, and each time, the terror felt fresh and real.

In his nightmare, his father would lead him by the hand into the woods. As they would walk, his father's hand would grow colder and weaker with each step into the silent, deep, dark forest. His father would stumble again and again until they'd finally reach the tree stand.

This time, the dream was no different. Darkness turned to a shadowy blue, then twilight. A crisp Autumn wind rustled the falling leaves, and frost clung to the ladder.

Joe grasped the rung as he did every time in his nightmare, but he refused to climb. He gripped the ladder with both hands.

"You have to climb, Joe." His father's voice sounded hollow and far away.

I can't. I won't.

His hands began to tremble. He was hanging on for dear

life. Looking down, he realized he was at the top of the stand, and on the ground lay his father's cold, stiff body.

Joe awakened in the same cold sweat. Heart pounding. Head throbbing. Mouth dry. Panting. But this morning was different. The nightmare hurt more than usual because it was the start of deer season, and a gunshot had awakened him—a *real* gunshot.

Opening day. No one had to remind him. It was a day he could never forget. Another anniversary. Another year, another opening day without his dad.

How he wished he could have that day back.

Sadness and guilt ran together with the thought of his mother someday living alone. She had lost two husbands, both dead because of him.

He sat on his bed, drenched with sweat. He took a deep breath, stood, and walked to his mother's bedroom. She slept so peacefully, her chest slowly rising and falling. She was alone, but at least she would forever be without that monster.

He warmed at the idea of Frank out of their lives forever, but he stared at the empty spot beside her and wished his father was there.

Opening day. He couldn't get the thought out of his mind. Many of his friends from school and their dads were already out in the woods. Even inside his house he could hear the scattered gunshots, constant reminders of that horrid day.

The phone rang.

He snatched it quickly, hoping his mother would not awaken.

"Morning, Joe."

Danny!

"Just wanted to wish you the best of luck."

"You know I don't hunt."

"Oh. I forgot. Sorry." He laughed as he hung up the phone.

Joe imagined his hands around Danny's throat, squeezing that putrid smile from his face.

His mother rubbed her eyes and sat up. "Joe, who was on the phone?"

"No one important."

* * *

Peggy choked on her tears as Danny pressed his hand harder against her mouth. Lying on top of her, he set down the knife and pulled a small roll of duct tape from his pocket. He tore off a pre-cut strip, smiled, raised his eyebrows, and stretched the tape across her lips.

Grabbing the knife with his right hand, he said, "Don't even think about touching that tape." He smiled as her eyes screamed with fear. "I can see it in your eyes. You know right where this is going."

As she shook her head and moaned against the tape, he climbed off and flung her to the floor. "Hands behind your back." He almost shouted, startling himself. He needed to quiet down. He didn't want to alert any neighbors.

He straddled her and sat on her legs as he held her wrists together tightly and wrapped them several times with the duct tape. His pulsed raged as he felt her warm body shaking beneath him.

Her wrists firmly bound behind her back, he hoisted her back onto her bed.

"It's pretty convenient that you're already dressed for bed." His knees pressed into her legs, and she wrestled pointlessly at the sounds of his belt unbuckling and his jeans unzipping. He grabbed her waist and her pajama pants. As he pulled them down, he said, "I know why you're crying. I didn't want our first time to be like this either."

* * *

The phone rang again.

Danny, I'm going to kill you. Joe answered the phone.

Stone cold silence. "Danny, this isn't funny. You know what day it is, and you're being an…"

"Joe." Her voice broke. Her attempt at words cracked into sobs, and the phone fell silent.

"Peggy?" He paused and listened. But all he heard were sobs. His heart pounded and his stomach rolled. She tried to speak but only blubbered. Then she drew a deep breath—a slow, stuttering deep breath.

He gulped. "It's okay. I'm here." His thoughts ran wild as he anticipated what she was going to say. Ten seconds felt like an hour.

Then she took another deep breath and blurted it out. "Danny raped me."

Joe couldn't breathe. He couldn't think. His mind jumped back into the tree stand. His thoughts gripped the shotgun. He imagined his knuckles turning white against cold steel.

In his daydream, Dad wasn't there, and he wasn't hunting deer. He was hunting Danny.

"Joe? Are you still there?"

He snapped back to reality and whispered, "Still here." His mind let go of the shotgun. He pictured it falling from his grip—like the rest of his world. Nothing was right. Everything had fallen apart, and Peggy had become his world. Now, his whole world had been violated. *Today of all days.* Danny had chosen that day to hurt them both.

"I'm sorry, Peggy. Are you okay?" He couldn't catch his reckless words. "I know you're not okay, but I mean are you hurt, are you bleeding? Um..." He stammered. "I don't know what to say."

"Joe. I'm scared. I don't know what to do. Can you come over."

"Shouldn't you go to the hospital?"

"You're the only one who knows. I'd like to keep it that

way." Her voice dissolved into tears.

"I'll come right now. I won't tell anyone." *And I'll make sure Danny never tells anyone.*

"Joe?"

"Yes."

"Do you still love me?"

They'd never spoken the words. They'd never had to. They just knew. Their whole lives growing up together, almost inseparable, each there for the other in their darkest moments and on their best days, side-by-side and hand-in-hand. Today would be no different.

"I will always love you. No one can change that. Not Danny. Not anyone." He spilled his tears and sputtered his words. "I. Love. You. I'm coming over right now."

* * *

Peggy opened the door. Joe had braced himself for scrapes, bruises, and torn clothes, but she looked like herself with her messy black shag and scant makeup. Tight jeans. Soft-collared shirt. And sandals. But her eyes and her smile melted into tears and quivering lips, and she fell into Joe's arms.

Neither of them said a word.

Joe held her tight as he kicked the door closed behind him. Her tears soaked his neck and shoulder. He let her cry as long as she needed. When her sobbing and trembling faded, he lifted his arms to her shoulders and looked into her eyes. "You are still you. Danny can't change that. No one can change that."

Joe touched her face and tried to wipe her tears with his thumb, but he stopped and leaned back. "There's something sticky on your cheek." His eyes widened. *Duct tape.* He couldn't say it. As angry as he was, he had to be calm and unfazed for Peggy.

Joe licked his thumb and rubbed her cheek.

Peggy giggled. "You're such a redneck."

"I got it off, didn't I? Were you chewing gum in your

sleep?"

She stretched out her arms, turned over her wrists, and whispered. "Duct tape."

Joe lifted her hands and shuddered at her raw, tender skin. The duct tape had peeled off a few layers. "You're not going to tell your mom and dad?"

She covered her mouth and shook her head. Eyes closed. Tears streaming. "I can't." She opened her eyes and looked at Joe.

Her tears and the utter sadness in her eyes broke his heart and ignited his anger. "Afraid of what your dad might think?"

She nodded. Her lips quivered—unable to speak.

He held her hands. "How are you going to hide this from your mom and dad?"

She pulled her arms away. "Long sleeves."

Joe nodded.

Peggy kissed his forehead. "Thanks for coming, Joe. Thanks for…" Her eyes studied his bewildered face. Love, frustration, anger, and hope all at the same time. "Thanks for everything. You should go before my dad gets home. Remember. Nothing happened, and no one needs to know."

He nodded. *No one will ever know.*

Chapter 67
Joe and Peggy

"Mom?" Joe stepped inside. The house was quiet. Her car was gone, but she'd left a note.

"Joe, sorry to leave you alone today. I know it's a hard day for both of us, but I figured you were with Peggy, and her mother invited me to lunch. She's so thoughtful. We may run to the store after, but I should be home by six."

The long November shadows would not give him any extra daylight. He glanced at his watch. One-fifteen. That would give him about four hours.

Joe dashed up the stairs and dug through his closet. He pulled out the box of his father's things, some of Joe's most treasured possessions: his dad's old wrist watch, a few pens, his belt. Nothing special, but they were reminders of the man he loved and missed more than anything.

The small box within the box jumped out at him. *Remington.* He took four slugs from the box and tucked them in his pocket. If his mother had known he had more ammunition, she'd surely have taken it years ago. Good thing she didn't know.

When the sheriff's office had returned Dad's shotgun, she'd asked them to keep the slugs. She thought they were all gone.

After grabbing his backpack, he rushed to his mother's bedroom to find the shotgun.

Guilt could not keep him from digging through her closet, under her bed, in the attic, and finally behind the tiny door in the wall where she kept a card table and a broom.

Reaching through the tiny door, he slid his hand up the wall. The gun rested upright atop a brace in the wall. He couldn't imagine how his mother had thought to hide it there, but he'd checked there because he knew it was something his father would've done.

She had done her best to hide the awful memory, but she couldn't sell it or give it away, because it was Dad's, one of the last things he'd held. It was a part of him, and she would never let go.

The cool metal and smooth wood felt good in his hands. Love and hate swirled in his head. He hated the gun for what it did to his leg and to his father, but he loved it for the freedom it gave him. The freedom and the power.

Gripping the gun, he felt a warm surge, and he pictured Frank's fixed stare as he lay stiff in his own blood. He shook off the thought and pulled the four slugs out of his pocket. His pulse accelerated as he shoved the first slug into the shotgun. With each one, he pictured Danny with the same fixed stare—color draining from his face. Mouth gaping—lips darkening, stiffening, waiting for the mortician to close them forever. No more annoying smiles. No more sarcastic quips. Arms flopped at his sides—splotchy pale with livid streaks. No more finger flicks on the back of the head. Never another finger on Peggy.

He shoved the last slug into the gun and slung it over his shoulder. Then he ran to the garage, grabbed a tarp, a roll of duct tape, and some rope and stuffed them into his backpack. He threw on his father's hunting jacket and orange hat, and stared at Frank's truck.

No, you can't borrow my truck. Those words no longer stung. He marched to the cabinet where Frank had stashed the keys, opened it and plucked the keys from their hook. *One more good reason you're dead, Frank.* He slammed the cabinet shut—hoping everything inside fell out of place. He clutched the keys. "It's my truck now."

He stowed his gear on the seat, hopped in, and drove toward Danny's house. Parking alongside the road was nothing unusual on opening day of firearms season. He stopped between Jenkins's place and his old neighborhood about a half mile from the Miser's house.

He hopped out of the truck and trekked into the woods. He didn't see another person, but he counted at least a dozen shotgun blasts. Boom. A single blast. *Someone must have gotten one.*

Three shots in a row. He chuckled. *They missed.*

He tightened his jaw and pictured Danny's snarky smile. *I won't miss.*

Following the creek, he knew he was getting closer. He and Peggy had played in that creek so many times. He'd never forget it.

* * *

No one was foolish enough to hike through the woods without wearing hunter orange on opening day or any time during firearms season. As much as he wanted to take off his bright orange hat, Joe knew the best way to avoid suspicion was to stick out like any other hunter.

Hidden in the woods behind Danny's house, Joe slid the tarp out of his backpack. He laid some sticks on it, folded the tarp around the sticks, and wrapped the tarp in his rope. He pumped the shotgun and fired a shot into the ground.

He has to hear that one. He imagined Danny, the ever-inquisitive brat, running to the window because that gunshot was so close.

Joe grabbed the rope and slowly dragged the bundle toward Danny's house. He stopped every few feet, acting as though he were hauling a huge buck through the woods.

He smiled at the creak of Danny's back door, an old familiar warning to make himself scarce, but today, it was a most welcome sound. Danny thundered across his backyard into the woods.

Joe left his bundle and walked a few steps toward Danny, trying to avoid eye contact—pretending he hadn't noticed him.

Danny charged into the woods panting and wiping sweat from his forehead. He slowed to a walk as he drew closer and strained to see what Joe had been dragging through the woods. Joe stepped between Danny and the tarp-wrapped bundle. "Pretty stupid to be out in the woods without wearing hunter's orange. Might get yourself shot."

Danny smirked. "Didn't expect to see you hunting again—ever." He stepped closer and leaned around Joe to see the tarp. "Did you get one?"

Joe squeezed his gun and stared at Danny. No racing pulse. No queasy stomach. Only cold determination. "Wasn't going to hunt Danny, but you talked me into it."

"Me?" Danny laughed.

"After you called this morning, I got to thinking my dad would want me to use this shotgun today." He looked into Danny's soul, smiling at the eyes that would soon be dried and hollow. "You want to give me a hand?"

"Too heavy for you?"

As Danny took one step past him, Joe buried the butt of his gun into Danny's skull with all of his strength. Danny wilted onto the ground. He would never touch Peggy or anyone else ever again, and Joe would never have to see that snarky smile for the rest of his life.

Joe peered through the trees. The brush and the lengthening shadows were such good friends. They kept him well-hidden, but he didn't see any movement behind the houses anyway.

He grabbed Danny's wrist and dragged him toward his tarp. He untied the tarp and dumped out the sticks.

Rolling Danny onto his back, Joe stared at his face. He was out cold—barely breathing. He smacked his cheek for good measure and to see if he would respond. Nothing.

No time to waste. He rolled Danny's limp body into the tarp. In case he woke up, Joe bound his hands and feet with duct tape and taped his mouth. One eye tried to open as Joe stretched the tape across Danny's lips. Anger swelled at the thought of him still breathing, at the thought of what he'd done to Peggy, at the thought of what he'd done to both of them his entire miserable life.

He wouldn't need the shotgun after all. He unloaded the roll of duct tape with all of his anger. He covered Danny's eyes and his nose. He wrapped the duct tape around Danny's head and neck until the roll was empty. He looked like a redneck mummy.

Joe laughed and cried at the same time. Part of him died as he watched Danny's life fade away. Part of him felt more alive than ever. Free of Frank. And now free of Danny Miser.

He wrapped Danny's body in the tarp as quickly as he could. He threw a bundle of sticks into the tarp as well to give it more bulk in case anyone spotted him. It had to look like he was dragging a deer and not a human.

* * *

Joe took a deep breath. He was well away from the nearest house. Another fifty yards and he'd see his truck. He stopped to catch his breath. Exhausted and drenched with sweat, he leaned against a tree to rest and gather his thoughts.

He grabbed the rope and dragged the body until he was almost close enough to see his truck. He could see the occasional passing car, but the gunshots had stopped. The sun was down, and the light was fading. His eyes had adjusted. He could still see well enough to make out his truck, but his stomach leapt into his chest as he saw a white pickup with flashing lights behind his truck. He dropped the rope.

He waited a few minutes to see if the truck would leave, then it hit him. With the sun down, there was less than thirty minutes left of legal hunting time. The conservation officer would not be going anywhere. He was waiting to catch a poacher, listening for a gunshot at night.

Joe left Danny's body and slowly walked toward his

truck. A fanning flashlight stopped on his face, but he kept walking, trying to put as much distance between himself and Danny as possible.

"Any luck?" the officer shouted.

"No, sir. Struck out."

"Did you see any?"

"Saw one but didn't have a clear shot."

As Joe neared his truck, the officer said, "For not getting a deer, you worked up a pretty good sweat."

Joe leaned the shotgun against his truck and bent over with his hands on his knees. "Yeah. I forgot my flashlight and thought I might lose my way if it got too dark, so I ran until I could see my truck." He smiled. "Plus I didn't want a conservation officer to think I was hunting after dark."

The officer nodded. "Fair enough. Glad you made it back. Better luck tomorrow."

"Thanks."

As the officer walked away, Joe collapsed against his truck. His heart pounding, sweat dripping, he choked on the sour, salty taste in his mouth, holding it in until the officer's truck disappeared around the bend.

Unable to contain his tears, Joe collapsed on the ground and sobbed. *That was close. Too close.* His chest heaved as his breath ran away with his pulse. He rubbed his eyes. His tears shrouded the fading horizon.

Danny! Dead and still causing trouble.

He jumped to his feet, opened the door of his pickup, and shoved the shotgun across the seat. As he stared at the shadowed woods, he wished this day had never happened. He wished it'd go away forever. Opening day was supposed to be a day of excitement and anticipation. A day surrounded by planning and reward. But for him, it opened a gaping wound that would never heal, a wound that just kept getting bigger.

He wanted to escape with Peggy and never look back,

but the sun was down, and darkness was falling. He buried his thoughts and sprinted through the woods to where he'd left Danny. He hoisted his body onto his shoulder and carried it towards his truck.

Headlights flickered through the trees. He dropped the body and pretended to drag a deer. The car barely slowed as it passed his truck.

His furious pulse showed no signs of slowing. His head pounded with every heartbeat, and his tongue stuck to his dry mouth. The truck seemed miles away, but he finally reached it as the last hint of daylight disappeared beyond the horizon.

The woods were still and dark. No gunshots. No song birds. No moon. A subtle wind caressed the trees. Clouds hid the stars.

In complete darkness, Joe lifted Danny's body into the truck. The steel bed shook with a clunky thud.

He wasted no time climbing into the cab to take off, but when he reached into his pocket, his keys were gone. He slammed the steering wheel in frustration, flipped on the light and looked everywhere. No keys.

Panic turned to sheer terror. He couldn't tell if the world was black because of night or because he was passing out.

"I'll never find those keys in the dark."

He climbed into the back of the truck, untied his bundled friend, unrolled the tarp, and pushed the lifeless body to one side. Tucking one edge of the tarp between the body and the truck, Joe stretched the tarp across the bed and lay his backpack on top.

It was still obvious that something was under the tarp, but hopefully no one would see it or think to ask.

"I got a small doe. Not worth seeing. That's what I'll say."

How could he expect to find his keys in the dark?

He knelt on the ground beside the truck and felt around. Opening the door to get a little light, he studied the spot where he collapsed. "Maybe they felt out of my pocket."

Joe jumped out of his skin as headlights pulled up right behind his truck.

"Joe, is that you?"

He wiped sweat and tears from his face as he squinted and walked toward the headlights.

"Mr. Landrum?" His silhouette was unmistakable.

"Are you broke down?"

"No. I lost my keys?"

Mr. Landrum laughed. "How'd you get this far from your house and then lose them?" He looked at Joe's orange hat and hunting jacket. "I didn't realize you were a hunter."

"Haven't hunted since Dad died, but I thought it was time to give it a try. Thought it might help me remember him."

"Your dad loved to hunt. I know he really looked forward to the day you could—"

"I couldn't do it."

He paused, and the two of them stood in awkward silence until Mr. Landrum said. "Couldn't—?"

"I couldn't shoot him." Joe pictured Danny as he spoke of the buck he never saw. "It was a ten-pointer. There he stood. He didn't even know I was there. I wanted to shoot, but I couldn't bring myself to do it. The gun was loaded and ready, but I let him go. He saw me. He looked right at me." *He smiled, then I smashed his skull with the butt of my gun.* "And he was gone. Just like that."

"Sounds pretty intense." Mr. Landrum stepped closer and said, "Let's find those keys."

It was hard to tell if the headlights helped much. They weren't really pointed at the ground, and they were almost blinding. They scoured the ground with no luck, until Mr. Landrum said, "Let me run home and grab a flashlight. I'll be right back."

"No, really, it's okay. I'll look a little longer. If I don't find them, I'll walk home and get a light myself. You don't need to stay out here."

"Nonsense. I know you would do it for one of us. You would certainly do anything for Peggy, I'm sure." As he patted Joe on the shoulder, they both heard a tiny clink.

Joe reached up to the breast pocket and remembered following his father's advice to stow his keys in a more secure pocket when hunting. His racing heart slowed for that brief moment, and he actually chuckled.

"Are you kidding me?"

He sniffed and wiped his tears, laughing as he said, "Dad always put his keys in this pocket when he went hunting. I guess I did too and just forgot."

"Oh, well. I'm just glad you're safe and you found your keys. Now go on home."

Oncoming headlights slowed, then stopped, followed by flashing lights.

The conservation officer.

"Everything okay? I thought you'd be home by now."

Mr. Landrum stood next to Joe, patted his shoulder. "Everything's fine. He just misplaced his keys."

Joe walked around the front of the truck, hoping to get in and drive away, but the officer whipped out his flashlight and pointed the beam at Joe's face.

"You look absolutely exhausted for a young man who didn't even get a deer. What time did you get out of bed?"

"Been up since three AM, sir. Like I said, I ran to get back to my truck before dark."

"Yes. You did," said the officer as he turned the light toward the truck. "Shotgun on the seat. Not the best way to stow your firearm. Hopefully, you have a better plan than that for your drive home." As he lifted the flashlight, he caught a glimpse of blue in the truck bed. He shined the light on the bed.

"I don't remember seeing this tarp in the back of your

truck when I stopped earlier."

"No, sir. It was wadded up in my back pack. It seemed a little damp, and I wanted to air it out."

"Good enough. Mind if I look at your license."

Joe pulled out his billfold and handed him his driver's license. He squinted at the flashlight in his face.

"Your hunting license." The officer leaned closer.

Joe couldn't hold it in any longer. "I'm sorry." His words sputtered through tears, and his body shook. He felt a wave of darkness and knew he would pass out, but Mr. Landrum's hand squeezed his shoulder and pulled him from the edge.

"Officer. I'm sorry to interrupt, but what Joe can't tell you is this is the first time he has tried to go hunting since his father died in a hunting accident."

Joe felt unexpected kindness in Mr. Landrum's voice. Half of his heart melted as he spoke. The other half kept racing—hoping neither the officer or Mr. Landrum would want to see what was wrapped in the tarp.

Mr. Landrum stepped between Joe and the officer. "He's really not himself today. Can you understand?"

The officer lowered his flashlight. "I'm sorry you've had a rough day, young man. If you go out tomorrow, make sure you have your license on your person, and…" He chuckled. "Don't lose your keys." Handing him his driver's license, he said, "Now get out of here."

Mr. Landrum wrapped his arm around Joe and pulled him close.

Joe buried his face in Mr. Landrum's chest. His tears soaked his coat. He held on until the sobs turned to sniffles and the shaking stopped.

"Joe, I know your dad would be proud. I never thought you would hunt again, but you've proved me wrong. Now go home and get some rest."

"Thanks, Mr. Landrum." Joe tightened his lips and tried to smile.

Mr. Landrum nodded and turned toward his car.

Joe climbed into his truck and watched Mr. Landrum drive away. As the car shrank in his rearview mirror, warmth crawled up his spine. He felt no pain, no remorse. The all-over warmth erased his fear, and a smile stretched across his face.

He tilted the mirror to look at the crumpled blue tarp. He would never have to endure Danny Miser's ridiculous smile again.

Chapter 68

Nathan and Donna

The phone rang again.

Nathan glanced at the caller ID. “Nope.”

“Don’t you ever answer the phone?” his nurse asked.

“Wrong number. They call all the time.”

“Hmm.” She shrugged and brought him his pills and a glass of water.

“I’m not sure why Donna thinks I need you.”

“I’m not sure either, except that she must want you around for some reason. I’m here in case you pass out or have a heart attack, so someone can call 911.”

“You’re a real joy. Glad you’re here.” Nathan glared at her, pulled his hydrocodone bottle out of the seat, and popped two more.

“You take way too many of those pills.”

“You need to mind your own business.”

“Excuse me? Your health *is* my business.”

“Is that what you were thinking when you stole my pills? You were thinking about my health.”

She looked away.

As Nathan tried to stand, his face warmed, and he felt his eyes bulging. He groaned until he’d made it. Wobbly as he was, he stood on his own and scowled at his young nurse. He lifted his shaky hand, gritted his teeth, pointed at her, then pointed at the door.

His breathing accelerated as he leaned against his walker, trying not to faint.

She moved toward the door, grabbed the handle, opened it, and stretched one leg across the threshold. With one hand on the door she turned and glared at him. “You feel like such a man, now don’t you?” She scowled. “Don’t need a nurse? Ha. You can barely even stand.” She smiled, stepped back inside and shut the door.

Startled, he collapsed back into his chair.

She stepped toward him, stiffened, and pointed her finger. “Don’t you worry, Nathan, I would never leave you. And I don’t bow to empty threats.”

As he tried to stand again, she snatched his pills, opened the door, and tossed them into the yard. “I told you I wasn’t stealing your pills, I was just looking out for your health, and that’s what I’m going to do whether you like it or not.”

He fell back into his recliner and coughed. “I’m going find a new nurse.”

“You’re going to find yourself without a nurse, period, if you don’t straighten up.”

She stormed out the door.

He raised his eyebrows thinking maybe she was leaving after all, but a moment later, she was back inside with his bottle of pills.

She toyed with the bottle as though teasing a puppy with a ball. “I know how bad you want these. And I know I could get in trouble for not throwing them out and for not turning you in.”

She walked around his chair dangling the pill bottle. “Because I can tell you have legitimate pain, and because—believe it or not—I like being your nurse, I’ll give them to you—but only when you need them. One peep. One complaint to your wife or my boss, and these are going in the toilet, and I will let your doctor know I quit because you’re taking narcotics from who-knows-where.”

She smiled and tapped his nose.

He stared out the window. As much as he hated her, he liked her. Witty. Smart. Full of spunk. But she had him under her thumb, and he knew it.

* * *

The next morning, Donna woke to find Nathan asleep in his chair as usual. He’d barely spoken to her the night before.

When she looked at him, she saw herself withering away with him—in that chair. He was her heart, the love she thought she would never find, love now faded and dying.

That wiry dreamy-eyed boy was nowhere to be found. Heart failure had stolen him, sucked the life out of him, and buried him in that recliner.

Tears clouded her vision as she watched his chest strain for every breath. Oxygen hissed like a snake coiled around him.

A twinge of guilt followed her to the bathroom. How could she go to work and leave him alone? Did it make sense to hire a nurse to care for him when she was a nurse herself?

She ignored her own tears as she stood in front of the mirror.

At the sound of tires on her driveway, she buried her guilt, finished her hair and the tiny bit of makeup she wore for work, and started toward the door.

As the nurse opened the door, Donna whispered, "It was a rough night." Her voice broke. "I'm not sure he's going to make it much longer… without a transplant."

The nurse gave her a gentle hug. "I'm so sorry, Donna. We'll keep praying. Maybe today will be the day."

Donna smiled and left for the hospital.

* * *

Nathan opened his eyes in time to see Donna sliding out the door. He feigned sleeping and listened.

She closed the door quietly. He smiled inside, knowing his nurse thought he was still asleep. Her footsteps tip-toed into the kitchen. The coffee pot clacked against the coffee maker followed by the sound of a cup filling.

Then the phone rang once, and she grabbed it.

She whispered, "Hello. May I ask who's calling? I'm sorry? Who were you calling? No." She turned and caught Nathan's icy stare. Her face paled, and she shook her head. "There's no one here by that name. Yes, I'm sure."

Nathan cleared his throat and snarled, “Hang. Up.”

Eyes wide and color draining from her face, she stood silently holding the receiver to her ear.

Nathan strained to stand. Anger warmed his face. His breath and his heart sputtered. He ignored his failures. His shaking hands gripped his walker, and he started to move toward her.

The nurse stepped backward and quickly said, “No one here by that name.”

As she hung up, Nathan shouted “Don’t. Ever. Answer that phone!”

“You were asleep, and I didn’t want the phone to wake you.”

“I’m awake.” He slumped back into his chair, panting and holding his chest.

“Are you okay?”

He glared at her. Stomach whirling. Cold sweat. Chest heaving and aching.

Chapter 69

Joe and Peggy

Mrs. Landrum hung up the phone and stood in silence.

"Mom, is something wrong?"

"Have you seen Danny recently?"

Peggy looked out the window. "No. Is he in some kind of trouble?"

"I'm not sure. His mother seemed upset. His car is at their house, but he's nowhere to be found. I thought maybe you'd seen him."

"I do my best to stay away from him. I wouldn't be disappointed if I never saw him again."

"Peggy! He's missing." Mrs. Landrum grabbed her keys, slung her purse over her arm, and headed toward the door. "Well, I'm going to visit Mrs. Miser to see if there's anything I can do to help."

* * *

Peggy picked up the phone. Her stomach leapt into her throat as she punched the numbers, and she felt like the phone was going to ring forever—until he finally answered.

"Joe?"

Peggy trembled at the silence. She imagined Joe standing over Danny's cold body with blood spattered on his shirt and dripping from his hands. "Joe! What did you do?"

"What did I do? I think it's what Danny did."

"Danny's missing." She closed her eyes and bit her upper lip, but she couldn't bury the horrifying image. "What did you do?"

"Don't worry, Peggy. He's gone."

"Gone! Gone where? Did you kill him?"

"I saw him leave his house and take off into the woods."

Tears streamed as she imagined Danny running away. "What if he comes back?"

"He's a coward. He'll never come back."

Chapter 70
Joe and Peggy

Seven years had seemed like forever. Prison had burned the memories into Joe's mind. He glanced back at Peggy's house one last time before he climbed into his car and started his last drive out of town. The curtain quivered. He smiled at the thought of the little girl sneaking one last look. He imagined a young Peggy waiting for him to come over and play.

Those days were gone, long gone, and never coming back.

He started the car, drew a deep breath, and headed toward Frank's house.

Emptiness grew as he drove further away from Peggy and every wondrous memory he'd shared with her. She was his life. Without her, his life was over.

Along the way, he stopped at Jenkins's Place. It looked so different. Most of the trees had been cleared, replaced with asphalt. And Wal-Mart stood right in the middle—right where all the kids used hang out.

He slid out of his car and imagined walking through the woods toward the creek. He imagined standing over a small white cross in the woods instead of a huge store. As he stared at the parking lot entrance, the police cruiser pulled up beside him and flashed his lights.

The officer stuck his head out the window. "I thought you were leaving town—for good."

"Just thought I'd get a Coke."

The officer leaned back against his car. "Kind of ironic, ain't it? Coming to the very spot where we found Danny Miser."

Joe looked him and faked a smile, trying not to glare, figuring the officer was a few years younger than him and must've recognized him. "I served my time."

"You did. Tell you what, Joe. Let me buy you that Coke

and I'll give you a police escort out of town."

Joe half-smiled. "All right, but I want to stop by Frank's one last time before I go."

"You got it."

* * *

As they walked back to their cars, Joe felt the same panic that had shot through him when he'd heard Wal-Mart was considering Jenkins's place.

As soon as he'd heard the news, he'd driven there, but he'd been too late. Surveyors had already walked the property and staked it. It had been less than a year since Danny had gone missing. His body would be right under the front entrance. Joe had tried coming by at night, but crews had already been working around the clock to stay on schedule.

There'd been nothing he could do but wait and hope, hope they wouldn't find the body and hope they couldn't link the murder to him.

Hope had fizzled when he'd heard that fateful ring of the doorbell and that deep no-nonsense voice.

"Joe Novak?"

"Yes."

"You need to come with us."

* * *

Joe sat alone in an eight-by-eight room with white walls, a small table in the corner, and three chairs. After almost an hour, a detective entered and sat beside him.

"When was the last time you saw Danny Miser?"

Joe had practiced the interrogation a hundred different ways, knowing it was inevitable, but he still felt completely unprepared.

"Danny? Has he come home?"

The officer sneered. "That's a nice try, Joe, but I think you already know the answer."

"What do you mean?" He was more ready than he'd

thought as the tears began to flow. "Tell me he's okay."

"When exactly did you last see him before he went missing?"

His eyes darted about as though he was trying to remember. "A few days before, I suppose. I don't remember exactly. Why is that important?"

The officer grimaced and leaned forward. "Daniel Miser is dead."

Joe gasped, choking back tears. "Oh, my God! No! He can't be dead." He cried into his hands, almost believing his own grief.

"I'm afraid so."

Joe stifled his tears as he lifted his head. "Why are you telling me this?"

The officer smiled. "Gotta hand it to you, kid. You are either really sincere or a really good actor." He leaned back and folded his hands behind his head. "I think you're acting, and I think you know exactly why you're here."

Joe chewed his lip and sniffed. Tears dribbling down his cheek, he stuttered. "Y-you think I killed my friend." He covered his mouth. His eyes widened. "You think I killed him." He shook his head. "I've seen enough death in my life. I don't need to see any more. Why would I kill him?"

"Funny you should ask." The officer pulled out a folded sheet of note paper. "The medical examiner found this in Danny's shoe."

Joe felt the color drain from his face. Danny had pranked him one last time from the grave. If only he could kill him again.

The officer unfolded the note. "Kind of amazing what a kid will hide in his shoe when he's afraid for his life. Let me read it… well, part of it anyway. *If you found this note, I'm dead and Joe Novak did it because…*" The detective set the note on the table, face down. "See what I mean. That's kind of amazing. He was alive when he wrote it, but he somehow thought you were going to kill him. Why do you suppose he thought that?"

A deputy's face popped into the window, and the door opened. "I need you for a second."

The detective sighed, folded the note, and smiled as he left the room.

The bright room seemed dark, and the walls felt like they were closing in on him. His breathing quickened. He closed his eyes, hoping to escape, but he felt like he was back in Frank's basement, tied to that chair.

* * *

Joe jumped at the sound of the door opening, but it wasn't a door. It was the thunk of a Coke falling out the pop machine. He was standing in front of Wal-Mart. The officer snatched the can and popped it open. "Here's one last Coke on me."

Joe nodded. "Thanks."

The officer shrugged his shoulder and motioned him towards the car. "Always liked your mom's old car." Joe stopped and bent down with his hands on his knees. Unable to stop his tears. "Sorry, Joe. Didn't mean to stir things up. I mean you have to look for the positives. Life never really turns out the way you plan. Everyone in this town expected you and Peggy to be together forever. Until Miser did what he did."

The walk toward his car felt like the long, slow walk to prison. Joe was supposed to be free, but he certainly didn't feel it, and the officer couldn't seem to shut up. "Nobody questioned why you killed him. I'll bet you 'bout died when you found out Peggy was pregnant with his kid."

Joe couldn't handle it anymore. He lowered his head, tossed the Coke in the nearest trash can, and did a fast walk the rest of the way to his car.

He hopped in and slammed the door shut.

He'd wanted to take responsibility for Peggy and her baby, but he couldn't imagine Peggy marrying a murderer, and he couldn't imagine raising Danny Miser's child. That baby should have brought life and hope, but Peggy's pregnancy and his murder conviction were more than enough to dissolve the un-dissolvable.

He could still hear Mr. Landrum's crushing words after everything was out in the open. *I don't want to ever see you around my daughter again*. Those words stung like it was yesterday—as they stung each and every day.

He might as well have still been wearing an orange jumpsuit and shackles. He wasn't free. His mother was dead. He wished he was dead. Life without Peggy was his new prison.

* * *

It had been seven long years since he'd seen Frank's house. It was his now, but he could never live there. It had never felt like home, and it never would.

He felt a strange comfort knowing the officer was following him. Frank was long dead and could no longer hurt him, but, as Joe passed Frank's old house, those old fears were still terribly alive.

As Joe slowed his car, he noticed the white picket fence was spattered with dust, not pristine as Frank would have liked. He smiled at the hint of green clinging to the white shutters. Haze covered the windows. They probably hadn't been cleaned since the last time Frank had made Joe do it years ago.

Joe stared at the front door for the longest time. Every scream, every slap, every shove, every harsh word, every look, and everything Frank stole from him was trapped behind that door.

The only thing he wanted from that house was his father's shotgun, but he was a convicted felon, and the police officer was right behind him. The gun would have to stay locked inside the house.

His pulse raced as he remembered his father kept his handgun locked in the glovebox. He doubted his mother even knew, so it was probably still there. With the police officer in tow, he couldn't check to make sure.

With one last glance at the house, he realized he only had one way out, one shot to escape his painful past and his fears forever. His way out was locked in that glovebox.

* * *

It was mid-afternoon when Joe pulled away from Frank's house. He felt nothing, empty. His whole life faded to black in his rearview mirror.

The police officer flashed his lights as he slowed and made a U-turn after they were well beyond the town limits.

When the cruiser was out of sight, Joe stopped the car and folded his arms across the steering wheel. After a few slow, deep breaths and wishing he hadn't tossed that Coke, he unlocked the glovebox and dug through the registration and driver's manual until he found his father's .357 magnum. No messing around, that gun could drop a man with one shot.

He held it on his lap admiring the smooth stainless steel. The gun felt solid and sturdy. He pressed the cylinder release and flicked his wrist. Six rounds, loaded and ready.

He would only need one.

Closing the cylinder, he rubbed the gun to remove smudges and residual oil just as his father would have done. As he leaned to open the glovebox, he heard the high-pitched chatter of a bald eagle.

He rolled down the windows, and more sounds filtered into his mind. Crows mobbing the eagle. He stuck his head out the window and looked toward the sounds in the treetops. The crows showed no fear as they swarmed and bombed the larger bird.

When one of the crows landed on the eagle's nest, the female eagle's head popped up.

All at once, the male eagle swept over the nest, poked a single talon in and out of the crow's head, and kept flying. The dead crow crashed to the ground, and the other crows scattered.

"You can only take so much." Joe closed the glovebox and put the car in gear.

Chapter 71

Nathan and Donna

As Donna stepped onto the porch, the nurse burst through the door and brushed past her without even a glance.

She watched the young woman jog to her car, throw it into gear, and peel away.

Then Donna stepped inside. "What was that all about?"

Nathan shrugged one shoulder and closed his eyes. Donna wasn't disappointed at the lack of conversation. She felt completely spent. Patients calling her name all day. Alarms beeping. Hour glasses spinning or freezing on every computer.

She dropped her purse and jacket and collapsed on the sofa.

Nathan coughed and opened one eye. He muttered, "Long day?"

Before she could answer, he was asleep. His eyes and mouth partially opened, barely breathing, panting. Beads of sweat clung to his pasty gray skin.

She felt a chill, not as if she were cold, but as if Death were walking by, waiting for Nathan's turn. She scooted next to Nathan's chair and laid her hand on his. Ice cold. Her heart jumped as she grabbed his wrist to check his pulse.

His eyes opened, and he gasped at the sudden movement and the squeeze of her warm hands on his arm.

Donna counted each beat. Fifty-six beats per minute. How much longer could this go on?

The end table and everything on it shook and rattled as his pager bounced with vibration and blared its alarm. Donna's heart leaped out of her chest and Nathan's eyes opened wide.

"It's time."

Chapter 72

Nathan and Donna

Nathan lay on his back, gown around his waist, wires across his chest. There was nothing stale about the hospital air. He felt like a newborn breathing for the first time. The air felt cool in his lungs, yet he felt warmer and more alive than he had in ages. Life was starting all over.

He watched his heart rhythm on the monitor. Smooth and steady. He drew another deep breath with no effort, simply because he wanted to. The deep breath felt fresh and reminded him of early Spring air when the snow is melting.

A twinge of pain pinched his chest, but he didn't care. It was a small price for feeling alive again.

His heartrate picked up when a smiling twenty-something nurse tip-toed into the room.

"If my heart stops, it's your fault."

She feigned a smile and motioned for him to whisper as she pointed to Donna, asleep in the cramped vinyl chair beside him.

He tried to say something, but the nurse shoved a thermometer into his mouth. "Your heart's not stopping today. Dr. Murphy will be in shortly."

* * *

Nathan sat on the side of his bed—ready to leave the hospital whenever they would let him—ready to take on the world. He smiled at his nurse as she checked his vital signs.

As she felt his pulse, a hand reached around the curtain and thrust it open, waking Donna and startling the nurse. Dr. Murphy slid around the curtain, smiling ear-to-ear. Nathan was not only his patient but one of his many proud achievements.

"You made it."

Nathan smiled, and Donna cried.

"Your heart was much worse than we realized. Your

ejection fraction was fifteen percent. Your pump was broken, and you had a large collection of blood and fluid around your heart."

Nathan squeezed Donna's hand as they listened.

"When I cut through your breast bone, blood started spurting. Spurting doesn't even cover it. It shot out of your chest, even splattering on the lights and the ceiling." Dr. Murphy took a deep breath. "I thought that was it. I thought you were done, but once the sack emptied, I was able to contain the bleeding and proceed with the transplant. It took a little longer than expected, and it was a little scarier, but you made it."

"You make it sound like I dodged a bullet."

"More like you dodged a train. You were done without this new heart." The surgeon patted his leg. "You'll be up and out of here in just a few days." He looked at Donna with a grin. "Part of me feels like I should apologize. I think you're going to have your hands full with this one. He's a fifty-year-old man with a twenty-one-year-old heart."

Chapter 73
Nathan and Donna

Three weeks later Nathan awakened in the middle of the night drenched in sweat and shaking uncontrollably. He rolled onto his side, reached under the bed for his shoe, and pulled out his pill bottle.

Only two pills left.

He popped one and saved the other. *One last pill.* He stared at the lonely pill wondering where all the others had gone. His surgeon had cut him off. "You shouldn't need much pain medication after *my* surgery," he'd said.

He'd have to have more, for the pain, of course. He sat on the edge of the bed. Donna slept soundly beside him. She looked so peaceful. He felt happy and jealous as he watched her breathing.

Sliding quietly off the bed, he stowed the bottle in his shoe then snuck into the living room. He leaned over his chair and shoved his hand between the cushion and the arm rest, hoping he'd misplaced his other pills. No luck. It was going to be a long day, and he wouldn't be able to do anything about it until Donna left for work.

He scrambled some eggs, sliced an avocado, and brewed a pot of coffee. Breakfast would provide a distraction, and coffee would provide an explanation for his sweating. He always sweated if he drank too much coffee.

Donna smiled as she waltzed into the kitchen. "You still make this girl feel special." She kissed his cheek. For a second, Nathan didn't think about his pills. Her kiss still owned him, and her finger tickling its way down his neck didn't hurt either.

When she sipped the last of her coffee, she gave him another peck on the cheek and bounced out the door. His smile followed her to the car. But when she was gone, so was his smile.

He began his search.

Nothing. The pills were gone. He hated to admit it, but deep down he knew he'd eaten them, popping one at every ache, every pain, every whim, every I-just-want-to-feel-normal moment.

As the day wore on, worry turned to panic. Shaky hands. Nausea. Sweat. Irritability. Panic turned to paranoia. What if Donna had found out about his problem? What if his home nurse had snuck back into the house and stolen his pills? She'd been gone for a week, but he clenched his teeth and imagined her waving them in his face then tossing them outside as she'd done before.

He didn't want to believe he'd taken all those pills.

He called Uncle Charles. No answer. He didn't trust voicemail, although he couldn't imagine anyone else listening to Uncle Charles's voicemails. He'd wait and call again later. He checked the clock—only twelve-forty. Donna wouldn't be home until three-thirty. He decided to save his last pill until about three o'clock to minimize his symptoms when Donna came home.

Finally. Three o'clock. He took the pill, opened the fridge, and pulled out a package of ground beef. "It's going to be spaghetti tonight, Donna."

As he set the table, the door opened, and he stuck his head out to see Donna stepping through the door. No bounce in her step. Eyes glazed and mouth opened, but her exhaustion turned into an instant smile as garlic and basil wafted from the kitchen. "Mmmm. That smells good."

Nathan met her just inside the door with a no-hands hug. "Sorry." He held up his hands, which were covered with bread crumbs and garlic butter.

Donna smiled and hugged him anyway. She cradled his face in her hands and kissed his garlic-buttered lips. "Thank you." She looked him in the eyes. "It's been a long day. I had no idea what I would've fixed for dinner."

They watched an episode of *Monk* after supper. Donna fell asleep on the sofa. Nathan wanted to scoop her up and carry her to bed, but she was over his weight restriction for another three weeks. He sat beside her and watched her sleep. She was so *out*, he could have put her in different positions, taken pictures, and posted them on social media. But he just watched her sleep. Mouth open. Slight drool. Hair a mess from a day's worth of patients. None of it mattered. She was the woman he loved, and everything about her was beautiful.

He woke her with a gentle kiss and helped her to the bedroom.

She fell asleep as soon as her head hit the pillow.

Nathan tip-toed back to the kitchen. As he cleaned up from supper, he felt the crash coming. Too much effort—too soon after his surgery, but no more pain pills. He lay beside his snoring beauty, but he was wide awake.

Wide awake and out of pain pills. He felt the cold sweat first, then nausea, then the shakes and irritability. Without any more pills, whisky would have to do.

He grabbed the bottle from the pantry then opened a cabinet to find his whisky glass. Tucked in the corner behind some tumblers, he found a bottle of pills. *Xanax*? He read the name *Donna Fortune* and cursed under his breath. *She acts like everything's perfect, but she's been hiding these from me.*

He curled the bottle of Xanax in his fingers wondering how she'd so easily deceived him. But as he studied the bottle, he realized he had the perfect cocktail.

He popped two pills and downed a healthy dose of whisky. He planned to climb into bed beside Donna, but she was sprawled across the middle of the bed, and he didn't want to wake her. Quietly, he strode to his all-too-familiar chair, sat, closed his eyes, and tried not to think. The sweats and shaking gradually eased, and he fell asleep.

* * *

At five-thirty, Donna startled at the alarm. She silenced it, hoping Nathan would stay asleep, but he wasn't there. His side of the bed was cold.

The house was still dark, so she imagined he was asleep in his chair.

She felt a strange comfort in the darkness, knowing she was alone and free to do as she pleased while he slept. Each day he was getting better, stronger, more mobile and active. But something was missing.

She appreciated his hard work, his thoughtfulness, making meals she hadn't expected, touching her gently and often, and the unmistakable love in his eyes. But she also felt like a prisoner, alone and afraid she might wake the beast within. He'd tried so hard to hide his drug habit from her, but she was a nurse, and she saw right through the façade. She'd decided to overlook everything and love him—even when he seemed unlovable.

Donna tiptoed into the bathroom, gently closed the door, and turned on the light. She drew a deep breath as she looked in the mirror. Then she readied herself as quietly as possible.

Finally, she smoothed her eyeshadow and applied her lipstick. She was more than ready to go back to work.

As she sneaked through the living room, Nathan breathed quietly in his chair, sound asleep. Peaceful. Almost smiling.

She paused and watched his chest slowly rise and fall. It was good to see him sleeping and breathing without effort, without worry. No more pager. No more fear that the next breath might be his last breath, but she worried about the man he'd become—one day he's vibrant, fixing dinner, cleaning the house, but the next he might be irritable and sloth. She didn't know which man she should expect, so she tried to leave for work without waking him.

As she unbolted the door, Nathan gasped. She whirled

around, her heart thumping.

He coughed, opened his eyes, and blinked.

"Are you okay?"

He frowned and spoke gruffly. "I thought you were going to work."

So much for not waking the beast. She flung open the door. "I'm going to miss you too, Nathan." Her heart ached. She wanted to kiss him good-bye. She wanted him to hop out of his chair, wrap her in his arms, study her eyes and her lips, plant a deep, passionate kiss, and beg her to skip work like he used to. But he sat there with no excuses. Breathing like a twenty-one-year old. But he folded his arms, closed his eyes, and pretended to sleep. Not so much as an "I love you" or even turning his head to offer a good-bye kiss.

She slammed the door behind her.

* * *

As Donna turned onto the street, she noticed a black sedan in her rearview mirror. She didn't think much of it until she was about two blocks from home, and the sedan pulled away from the curb. She gradually sped up. The car matched her speed.

Rounding the corner, she lost sight of the it. As she started to take a deep breath, blinking headlights danced in her mirror, and she noticed blue and red lights flashing through the car's grill.

Her stomach knotted as she bumped the curb and her car stopped. With trembling hands, she grabbed her license and registration, lowered her window, then planted her hands on the steering wheel.

Her heart thumped with each approaching footstep. She jumped when the officer spoke.

"Mrs. Fortune?"

How did he know her name? Her mind raced. "Yes?"

"I'm special agent Austin Turnbill from the DEA"—he

flashed his credentials—"Your husband is"—the agent looked at his smartphone and said—"Nathanial J. Fortune?"

"Yes." A salty brash climbed up her throat, and her mouth was suddenly dry.

"How well do you know your husband, ma'am?"

A cold sweat rushed over her. Her left arm and her jaw tingled. Her chest ached, and a sense of doom filled her like ice water. "I'm sorry. I don't feel…" But the world darkened, and she couldn't finish the sentence.

* * *

Donna opened her eyes. She felt weak—her heartbeat erratic and much faster than she'd ever felt. Her chest ached. Sweat soaked through her scrubs.

Her eyes widened and she jumped in her seat as she realized the agent had opened her door, unfastened her seatbelt, and was leaning over her.

When she locked eyes with him, he said, "You passed out."

She tried to move, but the agent insisted, "You need to sit and try to stay calm. I really caught you off-guard." He smiled, and she noticed beads of sweat on his forehead. She wasn't the only one caught off guard.

Donna forced a smile. She rubbed her face, shook her head, then took a sip of yesterday's water bottle. The cool water seemed to slow her heart a little. "You were saying something about my husband."

"It's okay, ma'am. We can save it for another time. You're not feeling well."

"No. I'm fine. I need to know."

As the agent spoke, his face and his words became a blur. Donna could hear his voice far away asking if she was all right, then her world went dark.

Chapter 74

Nathan and Donna

Nathan took a deep breath. How good it felt. No effort. No pain.

He walked to the kitchen, opened the fridge. *No beer.* He laughed. It had been so long since he'd had a beer, so long since he'd stood in front of the fridge.

No shaking. No dizziness. No shortness of breath. He grabbed the jug of milk.

His eyes clouded with tears as he stared at it. Something as normal as milk. But it had seemed like forever since he'd poured a glass of milk, since he'd felt the cold jug or the cold air from the fridge.

He lifted the glass and guzzled. Cold and refreshing, it felt like life pouring through him, like life starting anew. He wanted his old life back and his miserable life over and forgotten. He closed the fridge and looked at his old chair, his prison, a part of his life he needed to bury.

Nathan slammed the glass on the table and ran to the living room. He grabbed the chair with both hands and dragged it towards the basement. He shoved it through the door and watched it bounce down the stairs, nicking and scratching the wall as it tumbled.

His cell phone rang as he flipped on the basement light and ambled down the stairs. He ignored the phone as he watched the chair slide to a stop.

He kicked it, scooting it to the center of the room. Fire rushed through his new heart as he punched his fist through the back of the chair, tearing the worn, stained fabric. He grabbed the tear and ripped it.

He stripped the chair down to its bare frame and imagined it raging in flames and crumbling to ashes. When he'd torn away the last strip of fabric, he bent down and rested his hands on his knees. He smiled as sweat dripped on the floor, sweat he'd earned from hard work, not from trying to breathe. Tears streamed as he stared at the old chair and saw his old self.

But he saw something more—something even better than he'd imagined when he first saw the chair. Something new that no one else could see. He saw what that chair would become.

Restored.

He licked his finger and tapped the dangling bulb—just for fun—to watch it sway. His work was done for the moment.

As he climbed the stairs, his phone rang again. He glanced at the unfamiliar number and let it go to voicemail. Before he could check the message, he heard the doorbell and stuffed the phone in his pocket.

Nathan peeked through the window. His nurse stood on the porch, nervously tapping her foot and nibbling her lip. He hadn't seen her in weeks. She drew a deep breath and tucked her hair behind her ear. He smiled and opened the door. "How's my favorite nurse?"

She blushed and diverted her eyes.

Something didn't seem right, but he couldn't put his finger on it. "What are you doing here?"

She still didn't look at him but fidgeted with her purse. When he caught her eyes, it was obvious she'd been crying and was trying to hide it.

He stretched out a welcoming hand. "Come on in."

As she stepped inside, her eyes fixed on the worn carpet where his chair had been. "I thought I might have forgotten my sweater."

"Your sweater?" He faked a frown. "I thought you came back because you missed me."

Her puffy red eyes and trembling lips seemed like too much for a lost sweater. And something about her silent stare felt strangely familiar—and disheartening.

She opened her mouth as if to speak, but nothing came out. Her hands over her face, she shook her head, sniffed, half-cried, half-smiled, and finally said, "I need some answers."

His blood froze. He remembered how she'd reacted to his hydrocodone. The confused way she'd looked after she'd answered the phone and he'd scolded her. The way she threatened to expose his habit to his doctor—to Donna.

He scowled and stepped toward her. "What kind of answers?"

Her eyes widened, and she opened her mouth, but he leaned near her face and looked straight into her eyes. His face flushed, and he gnashed his teeth. "I'm not sure you really want to ask the questions."

Tears streamed as she shook her head and covered her mouth. Nathan's phone rang, and she stumbled backward and dropped her purse. The snap popped open when it hit the floor.

He motioned her toward the sofa as he bent down to pick up her purse. He grabbed his phone with his other hand and answered without checking the number. "Hello." While he spoke, his eyes focused on her spilled purse. She slid from the sofa and knelt to pick up her purse. As she quickly grabbed it some old newspaper clippings fell at Nathan's feet.

"Mr. Fortune?" a man said.

"Yes. Who is this?"

"Special Agent Turnbill. Your wife has…" The words blended together and made no sense.

Nathan focused on the newspaper clippings at his feet. He snatched them before his nurse could stop him, and he flipped through them—staring at images of himself in disbelief—wondering why his nurse was prying into his past. As he glanced back and forth between her and the headlines, he heard the agent say "You need to come to the hospital…"

He stared at his nurse—both of them trembling as he spoke a distracted, "Thank you" and hung up.

His nurse squirmed as he lay the loose pages on the sofa beside her and kept his eyes on her. She said, “Who was that?”

He shook his head as though trying to wake up. His mind raced through everything before him—DEA agent calls about his wife—nurse shows up with incriminating stories of his buried past. He imagined an investigation unfolding and exploding—ruining any chance of restoring his life.

Anger surged through his brand-new heart. But anger would have to wait. He needed to get to the hospital. In the meantime, he had to quash whatever dirt his nurse was trying to dig up and pour all over him. He’d buried that old life. No one was going to dig it up and use it to bury him.

He faked a smile and quickly conjured a way to deal with his nosey nurse. “It was a customer. I’ve started working on reupholstering again.” He stepped back onto the empty spot he’d called home for too long. He stood, stretched out his arms, and took a deep breath. “It’s good to feel free. I couldn’t look at that old chair anymore.” He glanced at her purse. “I can’t look at that old life anymore.”

He swallowed as fear rose in her eyes. Everything he’d buried stared him in the face, but he was new man with a new lease on life, a twenty-one-year-old heart in his otherwise middle-aged body. His past could no longer hurt him. He would never allow it.

He stretched a wide smile, spun, and walked to the basement door. “Would you like to see what I’m doing with my old chair?” Opening the door, he flipped on the light. He paused like a maître d’ waiting on his guest. His eyes did not let go of her until she moved. He led her down the steps to his workshop.

* * *

She felt a strange chill as she looked at the naked chair, stripped to its frame. Alone in the middle of the sterile room, beneath a solitary bulb.

Nathan smiled and stretched out his arm as though he

were showing off a trophy. “This chair was my prison. No more. I’m going to make it look more like a throne.”

He slid behind her, gently but forcibly nudging her. “Why don’t you have a seat?”

Chapter 75

Nathan and Donna

Back on the main floor, Nathan locked the basement door, walked straight to the sofa, picked up the purse, and pulled out the loose newspaper clippings. His pulse raced as he studied the aging photo. His hair stood on his neck as he remembered the young man leaving that courthouse. The orange jumpsuit. The handcuffs. He shuddered. His throat ached, and sweat beaded on his forehead.

He glanced at his watch, grabbed the nurse's keys and her purse, and stepped to the basement door to listen.

Silence.

He walked through the kitchen into the garage. His spotless '67 Ford Fairlane sat untouched. He opened the glovebox and lifted his revolver just enough to remove his gloves.

The smooth black leather felt good on his hands and would leave no fingerprints.

He checked his shoes. It wouldn't be too hard to explain fibers from his house, since she'd been there every day for months, but he brushed his shoes clean anyway.

He climbed into her Prius—her little blueberry as she'd called it. Gripping the steering wheel, he took a deep breath and let it out slowly.

He looked up and down the street. Everything was so quiet; he could hear his pulse. His hands trembled. He gripped the steering wheel harder.

As he slid the key into the ignition, sweat dripped from his face. His stomach lurched, and his tongue stuck to the roof of his mouth.

"You can do this," he whispered as he turned the key. The soft rumble of the engine drowned the beat of his heart. He drew another deep breath and eased out of the driveway.

It was his first time to drive with his new heart. He'd hoped for a Sunday drive through the country with Donna, but that hope had died.

You need to come to the hospital. Those words played over-and-over, strangling his mind. Once he was out of the neighborhood, he hammered the pedal. As he tested the limits of that little Prius, he pictured his smug little nurse digging up dirt to bury him and wondered why she would do such a thing. His pulse accelerated with the car. It felt so good to have a rigorous heart, but Donna was testing his heart as he wondered what was wrong and why he needed to come to the hospital.

He distracted his fear with anger towards his nurse. He imagined grabbing her and throwing her down the stairs, smashing her into the chair. He could feel his hands around her throat as he squeezed the steering wheel—his thumbs pressing until her purple face foamed and gasped.

Squealing tires and a blaring horn snapped him back to reality. He slammed the brakes and stopped as a red car blurred past. *Thank God for a new heart. Pretty sure the old one couldn't take that.*

He loosened his death grip on the steering wheel and stepped on the gas.

* * *

As he neared the hospital, he turned onto a side street and drove past the home health agency. He parked her car on the street about half a block from the hospital.

No surveillance cameras.

No people.

He left her purse in the seat, minus all of the incriminating documents. He lowered the windows slightly and left the doors unlocked and her keys in the ignition.

Nathan climbed out of the car and took once last glance. No one in sight. He closed the door gently, leaving it slightly ajar.

Chapter 76
Nathan and Donna

"I'm here to see Donna Fortune."

"One moment, sir." The receptionist tried to hide her frown as she looked at the computer and picked up the phone. "Mr. Fortune is here."

A nurse forced a smile and led him down the hall. But they walked past all patient rooms and stopped at the consultation room—*the consultation room*—the soul-sucking void where they leave you until a random doctor enters to drop a devastating truth bomb on your heart. His heart raced and his stomach leapt. He could already hear the news.

The nurse ushered him into the quiet, empty room. A person wearing blue scrubs and a white coat walked in behind her. Nathan couldn't look up. He dropped his face into his hands. The tears started before the doctor uttered a word. The only words that mattered were the ones he'd never wanted to hear.

The doctor said, "She didn't make it."

Everything else was a haze, and nothing else mattered.

* * *

As he stood over her unscathed body, he felt his pulse thumping, climbing his neck, and pounding through his ears.

"Nurse."

No response.

"Nurse!" he shouted.

Every eye in the ER turned, and the nurse rushed to his side.

Nathan shook his head. "They said she had a heart attack while she was driving." The nurse stumbled backwards, grabbing the bedrail as Nathan spit his words. He continued as the wide-eyed nurse nodded. "Where are the bumps and bruises? Cars don't automatically stop when someone has a heart attack." The nurse opened her mouth to speak, but Nathan kept going.

"Someone needs to tell me what happened."

Black leather shoes slapped the tile floor as a plain-clothes officer stepped between Nathan and the nurse and flashed his credentials.

"Mr. Fortune, I'm Special Agent Turnbill, the one who called about your wife."

Nathan stared at Donna—his world—unravelling. They were about to rebuild their life together. He was ready to toss the drugs for good, ready to hold her in his arms, ready to pick up where they'd left off. Six months earlier, his heart wouldn't have been able to handle the news. He would have immediately shared a grave beside her, but his new, youthful heart would last longer than he would. His new heart was strong enough to hold on even though he felt like letting go—giving up.

Heartache turned to hate as he gripped the rails and rocked back and forth against her bed—knuckles turning white—anger turning red hot.

His world wouldn't stop this time. He glared at the agent. "What happened?"

"Mr. Fortune, I know you're upset."

"Upset?"

"Please calm down. Please."

Nathan bit his lip and swallowed his tears. He sniffed and sputtered as he clung to the bedrail. "But she's my wife. She's dead, and no one can explain why it doesn't make sense."

He stared at the agent, a hefty, taller man stuffed inside a second-rate suit. But behind the suit, his deep-set eyes seemed kind and understanding.

Nathan drew a deep breath and softened his tone. "Please—tell me what happened."

"I stopped her to ask some questions. After I introduced myself, she passed out. I opened her door and gently shook her. She woke up briefly, then she collapsed. She had no pulse, so I called for paramedics and began CPR. I'm sorry."

"You're sorry. Everyone's sorry." Nathan looked at Donna. He wanted to rip his new heart out of his chest and give it to her. *You deserve it more than I do.*

"Mr. Fortune, I'm truly sorry. I'm going to leave you alone with your wife. I can ask my questions later."

"No." His raised hand, signaling the officer to wait. "What do you need to know?"

"Are you sure?"

Nathan scowled.

"We received an anonymous tip that Charles Fortune was using his store to sell drugs and launder money. What can you tell me to support or deny these allegations?"

The answers didn't matter. Nathan was certain the anonymous tip had come from his nurse.

"When I was in pain, Uncle Charles gave me some pain pills, but I can't believe he was selling drugs or laundering money."

"You didn't think it was strange that you were selling a few chairs a week and an occasional bed, yet Charles Fortune always had his bills paid on time and always drove a nice car."

Nathan stared at Donna as the agent spoke. His voice seemed distant, hollow, unimportant. Nathan blamed himself. He blamed Uncle Charles. But most of all, he focused his blame on the young woman strapped to the broken-down chair in his basement.

He could slap all the answers out of her. Why was she meddling? What was she trying to prove? Was she working with the DEA? It didn't matter. None of her answers or excuses would matter. Donna was dead, and soon she would be too. *I need to get home and finish my work on that chair.*

Nathan rattled his head back to the moment and looked at the agent. "You're right. Maybe now isn't the best time to ask your questions."

Agent Turnbill nodded. "Good enough. I'll give you a

few days. Just don't go anywhere."

* * *

Nathan's nurse would keep a little longer. His world had stopped at Donna's bedside. He wanted to lie down beside her. He wanted everything else to stop. He wanted to lie there stiff and cold. He wanted the world to go away once and for all.

He didn't see the pallid face with livid streaks. He saw the girl he'd met in Farmer's Park, her smile that danced around him and went right through him. But she was gone, and he felt more alone than ever.

He wished he had that revolver from the glovebox, but he heard a whisper. *Don't do it. No one else needs to die. Not you. Not your nurse. No one.* He felt that voice more than he heard it—like the eyes of a ghost staring the words into his soul—like the whisper of a young girl searching for answers yet hiding.

He closed the curtain, lowered the bedrail, and inched Donna's body toward the other side. Looking to make sure no one could see, he climbed onto the gurney and lay beside her.

* * *

Nathan squinted as the nurse pulled back the curtain. He rubbed his shoulders, wiggled his cold toes, and blinked as light followed the nurse into the room.

"Mr. Fortune." Her soft, dark eyes met his. "I'm so sorry for your loss." She stood beside him and placed her hand on his. "It's obvious you loved her very much."

"Still do," he muttered through tears. "I can't believe this happened."

"No, sir. It's never easy." As Nathan grabbed the rail and started to sit up, she said, "You don't have to get up yet."

"I can't stay here forever." As he sat up, the nurse lowered the bedrail and he turned to sit on the side of the bed, he looked over his shoulder. Donna was no longer there, just an empty, lifeless shell. All the warmth of life had retreated. Her soft, rosy cheeks were stiff, mottled gray. Her sweet perfume had faded.

He looked at the nurse who was fighting tears herself. He shook his head. "She's gone. It's time for me to go too."

As he stood and started to leave, the nurse said, "Someone called for you."

"For me?"

"When your wife arrived, I checked her phone. She had you listed 'in case of emergency,' but when I called no one answered, so I called the alternate number."

"Uncle Charles?"

"A woman answered. I told her I was calling because of an emergency, but she said she didn't know anyone named Donna Fortune. I thought I'd called a wrong number, but she asked me to read the number back to her, and it was the same number your wife had entered."

"Why are you telling me this?"

"She asked to speak to you."

"And?"

"You weren't here yet. I told her I couldn't release any information, but she insisted on leaving her phone number."

Nathan stared at the phone number. *Area code 812.* He crumpled the note but stuffed it in his pocket.

* * *

The sterile lights reflected off the floor as he plodded down the hall. He cursed his pulse with every step. His new heart, already broken, grew colder as his thoughts moved from Donna to his nurse.

Despite the usual alarms, patients calling, and chatting visitors, the hallway felt empty and silent. Nathan was still walking, but he wasn't moving. Time had stopped. The world had stopped. Ended.

His musing stopped at the sound of a familiar voice—*Jane*. "Why didn't you call?"

Tears streamed as he turned and saw her. For the first time in years. Her brown eyes, long brown hair, and even her awkward half-smile softened his pain. "I couldn't call you. I was dead."

Her eyes clouded with tears. "*I* wasn't dead, but I thought *you* were."

He looked away. "That was the idea."

Closing his eyes, he swallowed fresh tears and sniffed. He winced as he took a step toward the window, wishing it would open, wishing he could fall and disappear. He thunked his head against the glass and stared at the sea of blacktop.

Her hand gently squeezed his shoulder, and her breath warmed his neck. "Please come back."

His shoulders quivered and his chest heaved. Tears flooded, uncontrolled.

She hugged him tightly as they crumpled to the floor together. Their tears mixed as she pressed her cheek against his.

"I'm sorry," he whispered. He lifted his chin and looked deep into her eyes. "I want to come home, but I'm not sure I can, and I'd have to tie up some loose ends first."

Wiping away his tears, sniffing, and almost finding a smile, he stood and helped her stand. "Can you give me a ride to my house? I took a cab, so I could drive Donna's car home, but the police have it impounded."

"Impounded?"

"You don't want to know."

Chapter 77
Nathan and Donna

Jane drove in silence as the sun sank close to the horizon in her mirror. So much she wanted to say but knew he wouldn't want to hear. At least, not yet. So, she drove, thinking of how much she'd missed, how much he'd missed. Her throat ached from swallowing tears.

He pointed toward a mailbox and motioned her to turn. "So this is where you've been hiding all these years."

The car rolled to a stop. She popped it into park and stared at the quaint little house—enough daylight left to see light green siding and white trim, the cozy porch swing, and fake shutters. She took a deep breath and turned toward him. He was miles away yet right beside her. His vacant eyes peered through the house to who knew where. His lips moved, but nothing came out.

They sat in silence, staring at the house. Finally, she asked, "Why did you leave without saying good-bye?"

His eyes popped wide open like someone startled from sleep. He grimaced and the tears ran.

Her stomach reeled at his instant pain. He looked as though she'd plunged a blade into his gut and twisted it.

"Nothing turns out the way you planned," he said. "Nothing."

Without another word, he opened the door and climbed out of the car. She followed him into the house. Light green walls. A few pictures. No kids. No grandkids. Old photos of him and his wife. Not one recent photograph.

"Want something to drink?" he asked.

"Sure." She continued to look around the room. Behind the sofa, she saw an image of him and Donna in front of Fortune Furniture. An older man stood beside them leaning against the door. She stepped back and turned toward the kitchen. She was poised to shout, but here he came with two glasses of milk and a bag of chips. *Weird combination.* As he handed her a glass, she pointed at the photograph. “Is that Uncle Charles?”

Nathan sat on the sofa, nodded and motioned for her to sit beside him. “I’m glad you came, but I’ve got no place for you to stay”—she stared at him in disbelief—“The guest room’s a mess, and I can’t expect you to sleep on the sofa.”

“I’m not asking to move in. I just got here, and I barely sat down. I’d like to at least spend a little time with you.”

“Me too, but now’s not a good time. My wife just died, and I’ve already got enough to think about without digging up my ghosts.”

She slammed her glass on the end table ignoring the milk running down her hand and all over the edge of the table. “I’ve never understood you! Haven’t seen you since you blasted out of town after Mom’s funeral. Everyone, including Peggy, thought you were dead. Your hospital calls to tell me my sister-in-law, whom I’ve never met is dead, and you ask me to leave before my butt even sinks into the sofa.” Nathan looked down—eyes filling with more tears. “And I’m not a ghost, but I feel like I’m staring at one.”

She watched him sulk—hands folded—staring at the floor. Not one word from his mouth. She stood and grabbed her purse, but as she started towards the door, he gently gripped her arm and looked into her eyes.

“Jane. I’m sorry. For everything.”

She dropped her purse, collapsed beside him, and wrapped her arms around him. “You should be.” Her tears dripped onto his neck as she leaned back and looked into his eyes. “I had nothing when you left. Nothing.” She looked right through him. “Nothing. And no one.”

He rested his hands on her shoulders. “You can stay. You can sleep in my room. I’ll sleep out here.”

She nodded. *I can’t lose you again, Joe.*

He grabbed her hands, pulled them to his chest and kissed them. She smiled and almost giggled inside. He hadn't done that since he was a little boy and they pretended to be prince and princess. She couldn't imagine he would even remember those days. He would've been four or five years old—still young enough to play with a princess.

He popped her fairytale bubble when he said, "I want you to stay, but I've got some things I have to get done before Donna's funeral."

She gave him a questioning look, and he answered, "Just some work stuff."

"It can't wait?"

"I need to finish one thing, then we can talk."

Jane munched her chips and shrugged.

As he walked toward the basement door, he said, "Don't come down here. There's some fumes and dust and not the best ventilation, and I've only got one mask."

She shrugged again and thought it strange that he closed the door behind him before turning on the light. Then she heard a click. *He locked the door?*

Clunk clunk clunk. She listened until his footsteps faded. Shaking her head, she sipped what was left of her milk. It was already getting warm.

She went to the kitchen to grab a towel for her mess and to see if he had anything besides chips.

The refrigerator looked like a health food store. "Donna's been watching out for you," she muttered. She grabbed a package of blueberries and opened the freezer to find some low carb ice cream.

"Mrs. Johnson's Organic. Sounds—healthy." She pulled the yellow vinyl-covered chair from the 50s-era yellow table and sat by the window with her berries and ice cream.

Occasional headlights broke the darkness. *Nice, quiet street. I bet nothing ever happens here.* "Looks like you found a simple life," she whispered.

Her mind wandered through the empty years of living without him. The pain she felt wondering if he'd died, if he'd run away, if he'd killed himself. She'd tried to imagine him happy. Wife and kids and a great job. Nice house in a cozy suburb, but her heart always knew better. She knew that whatever he was doing, wherever he was, his hopes and dreams had died, and any life he'd had was playing pretend.

On one hand, she was relieved to find he'd started a new life. On the other hand, she wanted to shove him down the stairs or barricade the door and leave him locked in that basement.

"No!" she shouted, startling herself and covering her mouth. "Not locked in the basement. Never." She downed the rest of the milk, wishing it were something stronger that would dull her pain and quiet her thoughts.

The last blueberry rolled in a puddle of cream. She finished it off and said, "Mrs. Johnson's Organic, not bad." She smiled and took a deep breath, wondering how long he was going to piddle around in the basement.

Her phone chimed. She frowned as she read Joe's message. "Need cold beer. Left two blocks. Right. Two lights. On left. Pay you back."

She shook her head. *Some things never change.* Her fingers tapped a few choice words that she deleted before sending *Get it yourself.* She stared at her phone. *He's had my number for all of two hours, and he's already asking me to get beer.* Then she wondered how Donna had gotten her number. She didn't get it from Joe. Jane didn't even have a cellphone the last time she saw Joe. *Wow. It's been so long.*

She figured Donna must have dug into her husband's past and uncovered his secrets. Why else would she have her number? And why else would she have it as an alternate emergency number.

With nothing else to do, she decided to go buy his beer.

She slung her purse over her arm, grabbed her keys, and headed toward the door, but she paused at the sound of footsteps coming up the stairs.

The basement door rattled as he unlocked and opened it.

With one hand on her hip and the other on the door, she asked, “What have you been doing down there?”

“Working on that old chair.”

He flipped off the stairwell light and shut the door.

“What old chair?”

He shrugged and pointed at the four impressions in the carpet. “The one I called home for six months before my heart transplant.”

Her jaw dropped. “Heart transplant? What the—?”

He raised his hand. “Don’t ask me to explain. It would take more time than we’ve got.”

“Time is all any of us has, Joe. And you’re right it’s running out. Clock’s ticking. And I can see you don’t want to waste any of your precious time on your sister. You don’t want me here, so there’s no point in me staying. You obviously have my number—though I have no idea where Donna got it—so you can call me when you decide to come back to life.”

Jane paused, watching his eyes, hoping for a spark of life, some recognition, anything. Nothing. She was right after all. Her brother had died years ago, and she was staring at a corpse. It was way past time to stop looking for him.

“Good-bye, Joe.”

She slammed the door behind her.

* * *

When the door slammed, a picture of him and Donna bounced off the wall. Glass splintered as the frame broke.

He stared at the door, wanting her to come back and wanting her to go away. Her engine started, revved, and she peeled out onto the street. He kept staring until the sound of her car had faded.

His eyes turned to the shattered glass on the floor. His life in pieces.

He plopped onto the sofa and rubbed his face. "No one has called me Joe since…"

His mind raced through every horrid memory he'd tried to bury. His father's death. His pain—the daily reminder of the gunshot to his leg. His stepfather's cruelty. His mother beaten so badly.

Joe pounded his fists against his head, but his thoughts wouldn't stop. *Call me when you decide to come back to life.* "She's right. I'm dead. My life didn't just end. It ended a long time ago. I was fine pretending with Donna. Donna was a good woman, a good wife, and…" Tears took over. "I thought she'd saved me, what was left of me."

He turned and shouted at the basement door. "Until *you* ruined everything."

Heat rushed through his face, his arms, his whole body. He wanted to run down those stairs and choke the life out of her, but he forced himself to breathe—not sure if he wanted answers or just wanted her dead. *Deep breath. Hold. Blow it out as slowly as possible.*

He held out his hands. No tremor, but everything inside him was shaking. As much as he wanted to choke the life out of her, his nurse would have to wait. He couldn't be sure Jane wasn't coming back.

As though everything were normal, he got ready for bed. Pajamas. Meds. He brushed his teeth.

As he headed toward his bedroom, headlights panned across the living room windows, and a car rolled into his driveway.

Jane.

Despite everything, she came back, and he rushed to meet her, opening the door as she hopped up the steps carrying a twelve-pack of ice cold beer.

“I couldn’t leave,” she said.

He stepped out onto the porch, closed the door behind him, and motioned her toward the porch swing. His internal earthquake settled as she ripped open the box and pulled out two beers.

They both smiled. He couldn’t remember the last time they’d both smiled.

They sat on the porch swing for most of the night until the beer was gone and neither of them could keep their eyes open for a full sentence.

“Let’s get some sleep.” Joe laughed, stumbling and pointing, as Jane sat completely passed out with her mouth hanging open. He jostled her shoulder and helped her up, half-supporting, half-dragging her, and laughing all the way into the house and into his guest room.

His laugh was more of a squeal as he shoved everything off the bed and flopped her onto it. He lifted her legs to join the rest of her on the mattress and took off her shoes.

Her empty shoe struck him as hilarious. The tragic loss, the girl in the basement, the beer—they were all messing with his sanity. “You need a bath,” he said to the shoe.

* * *

The morning sun burst through his window. His head splitting, he squinted, laid his hand over his eyes, and hoped the sun would go away.

He swung his legs off the bed and sat up slowly. When he turned to see if Donna was still asleep, the space beside him was empty, and that emptiness surged through him like a dark pulse chilling his soul. He cursed his new heart as he stared at her empty pillow. Anger roared like a fire, consuming and controlling him. His gut wrenched. Every muscle tightened.

He clenched his teeth and his fists, fighting against the uncontrolled shaking. Soaked in sweat and panting, the room spun. He closed his eyes, but his whirling world wouldn’t go away. The emptiness wouldn't go away.

He thought about Donna's stash of Xanax. He thought about his father's .357. He hadn't been able to do it before, and there'd be no Donna to rescue him this time. He opened his eyes, but the room was gone. He was staring into the void, his mind set on ending everything.

The clunk of the icemaker startled him, and the room reappeared. His favorite picture of him and Donna stared him in the face. Her eyes said *not here, not in my house.* He swallowed and looked away as though she'd really said it, as though she were staring into his soul.

He glanced at the picture one more time. "Why did you have to die?" *I just came back to life, and now you're gone.* He pictured Donna driving to work as usual. Not a care in the world until a siren and flashing lights in the mirror stopped her cold. His mind raced through every possible scenario. He blamed himself for taking drugs from Uncle Charles. He knew she'd known. And he knew it bothered her. She didn't like what the drugs were doing to him—to his attitude. He felt like hydrocodone had destroyed them both.

But what had prompted the investigation? Who'd tipped off the DEA? What was Uncle Charles doing and how did he get caught? Joe wanted to grab those pills and heave them into the.... He stopped mid-thought and closed his eyes. The only thing he could see was his nurse curtly smiling. *She did it. She tipped them off.* Her nosiness and deceit had stolen the only love he had left. He felt no reason to live and every reason to crush her sickening smile and cast her into the emptiness he felt.

Drenched in icy sweat, he stood and set his mind toward the basement. But he froze at the sound of footsteps and a woman's voice.

"How did my shoe get in the bathtub?"

Jane! His head pounded as she laughed. He stumbled into the bathroom. "You can't stay."

Jane whirled around and pointed her shoe at his face. “I haven’t seen you in years. Your wife, whom I never met, just died. I finally found you, and all you can say is ‘you can’t stay.’ Really!”

“Jane, I’m sorry. Now is not a good time.”

“It’s never a good time when someone close to you drops out of your life. I understand. We’ve both been there before. I want to be there for you now.”

“It’s not a good time.”

“Will there *ever* be a good time?” She stomped on his foot and shoved him against the door frame.

He smiled at the pain, remembering how many times they’d fought as kids. She didn’t smile but shoved him again, grabbed her things and darted out the door, slamming it behind her.

Engine started. Tires squealed.

He breathed a long sigh and walked to the basement door. As much as he would have liked to reconnect with his sister, he had a greater desire to avoid prison and couldn’t risk her finding out about his nurse.

Chapter 78

Joe clutched the empty glass and beer bottle in one hand as he closed the basement door. He walked to the kitchen and tossed the bottle into the trash. He set down the glass, lifted the trash bag and knotted it tightly. How many months had gone by that he'd helplessly watched Donna take out the trash and do every chore while he'd sat in his chair?

He dumped the trash in the bin and wheeled it to the street then casually walked back to the garage. With each step, he thought through his plan. He'd make no mistakes this time.

His nurse was going off-duty for good, and no one would ever find her.

He closed the garage door and pulled the blind on the side door. He grabbed the leftover carpet they'd used for the living room, unrolled it, and laid it over the trunk of his Fairlane. He cut a section about the right size. He flipped the carpet upside down, mashed it into the trunk, and traced the contours with a Sharpie. He clicked open his utility knife and followed the line with his blade. He flipped the carpet and gently tucked it into the trunk. Perfect fit. He closed the knife, grabbed a brand-new tarp, opened it and spread it over the carpet.

He dashed into house, and down the stairs. He hefted his cooler full of snacks and beer and clomped up the stairs and into the garage. He stashed the cooler in the passenger's seat, took a deep breath and smiled.

After shutting the trunk, he gently patted his car. "A quiet ride in the country is just what the doctor ordered."

Chapter 79

Joe ignored his phone. His mind was in a different place, a much darker place.

He sat in the quiet country house—Frank's house—untouched for years. Jane had wanted nothing to do with anything of Frank's, including the house, and neither did he. They'd sold most of the land to the county. Farmer's Park. At least one good thing had come out of the mess of their lives, but the house and the barn had never sold.

The stain of Frank's death left a myriad of stories. Some said the house was cursed. Others said it was haunted. Others said you could still smell death in the air.

To Joe, the house was hell on earth. The place where his life had ended and where it would end again.

Everything had been going just fine. Past behind him. Donna was the woman—the wife—who'd saved him. Life was good. Even through heart failure, Donna stood by him, nursed him, loved him. Then Brooke came into his life—that meddlesome nurse who had stir things up. The DEA investigation. Donna's heart attack.

He blamed it all on Brooke.

But as he pictured Brooke alone beneath the barn, he saw himself—a terrified child, alone in the dark, on damp earth. His mother had grown wise to Frank's abuse. She'd seen the chair and the ropes. The basement was spooky enough without being bound and left alone for hours.

He remembered overhearing his mother yelling at Frank. *It's got to stop.* He remembered his fear for her as she raised her voice, but Frank had been devious and clever. He'd agreed to stop and had indeed stopped tying him to the chair and leaving him in the basement.

But it hadn't ended there. Joe still felt the sting of Frank's words—*I have a new punishment for you, Joe.* Frank had called it the pit. He'd told Joe's mother he was digging it to make it easier to change his oil. He'd slide a ladder into the hole for when he needed to use it, and when it wasn't in use, he had a door he could close and latch, so no one would fall in.

Joe spent many nights locked in there. "Oh, he's gone to a friend's house to spend the night," Frank would say. "He said he cleared it with you."

Joe had always suspected his mother knew better, but she was just as afraid of Frank as he was, if not more so.

His stomach roiled as he realized he'd become the monster he'd hated. Never would he have imagined doing the same cruel thing to anyone as Frank had done to him. "Not a chance," he would have said.

But there he was, sitting in Frank's dust-covered chair, staring at the barn, knowing another human being was suffering the same horror he'd suffered. The damp darkness, the smell of mold and dirt, the tight walls and utter loneliness still clung to him. There was no escape from the pit. Frank had forever removed the ladder and buried his heart.

Even a new heart couldn't raise him from that pit.

Chapter 80

Brooke

Brooke sat on the cold earth, arms wrapped around her knees, trying to stay warm. Trying to understand why. She'd been shocked when she discovered those newspaper clippings and old photos. She hadn't been able to imagine Nathan as a murderer, and she'd wondered how a convicted murderer had been eligible for a heart transplant. She still couldn't understand what it had to do with her, and why Nathan wanted to kill her.

She held her breath when she heard footsteps outside the barn followed by a latch opening. Tiny streams of light shone through the slats above her as the barn door opened. Footsteps crossed the dirt floor, shuffling through the loose straw. His shadow stopped over her. She smelled his beer and felt his eyes peering through the slats.

He said nothing.

His breathing was terrifying and hypnotic. She was a tiny rabbit caught in the thicket, and he was the wolf panting, waiting, his eyes fixed on her.

He took a deep breath and leaned down to unlock the latch.

This is it.

Unlike the frightened rabbit, she didn't quiver. Her eyes didn't widen but remained fixed on her killer, only blinking to shield them from falling dust. She couldn't understand it, but she felt a strange sense of resolve, almost peace.

Finality felt less painful than she'd expected, almost like a relief, knowing her suffering was about to end.

As he unlocked the latch, his phone rang with "Sweet Child of Mine." He dropped his beer and plucked his phone from his pocket.

Her pulse raced as he sat directly above her. She held her breath, straining to listen, but everything was silent, even the birds.

Hints of light and dust came through the slats above her as he stood once again. She took a deep breath, expecting the door to fling open and praying he would make it quick, but he walked away.

Listening intently, she could hear him muttering, almost whimpering. A car door opened. Shuffling noises. The door closed. Footsteps grew louder, and his shadow stood above her once more.

He flipped open the door, and she caught a glimpse of his face. He was still mostly silhouetted, but his cheeks were not taut. His brow was not wrinkled. What she could see of his eyes seemed strangely alive, but they weren't looking at her.

He slid down into her grave and stood beside her. Breathing. Staring at the exposed earth. No eye contact. No words. It was as though he couldn't look at her or felt guilty looking at her.

As he closed his eyes and leaned into her, she recoiled. He grasped her waist and hoisted her from her grave.

She sat on the edge. Her legs dangling over the pit and her body trembling as he pulled out a knife. She imagined the stinging warmth of the cold blade on her neck. Every muscle tightened as the blade came closer.

He grabbed her leg and with one swift movement, he thrust the blade upward, cutting the zip-tie that bound her feet. He set the knife beside her and placed his right hand on her thigh. She felt his weight as he pressed down and climbed out of the pit. He sat next to her, leaning against her right shoulder, catching his breath.

Brooke studied his face. Still no eye contact. He just stared at the pit.

Her fear shifted to stilted compassion. She somehow felt sorry for the monster who had strapped her to a chair and locked her in his basement. She stared at his hollow eyes wondering how he could be the same man she'd cared for, the same man she'd been curious enough about to call her grandfather. How could this man who sat beside her—seeming to be lost and distant—how could he have shoved her in a trunk, chased her through the trees, and dumped her in this pit.

She'd imagined firing a slug through his chest and a hundred other ways to kill him, but her anger faded as he sat beside her in silence.

He was in another world. His eyes were hollow. He cleared his throat and opened his mouth but didn't speak. Coughing and trying to swallow, his eyes swelled with tears, and he reached behind his back and pulled out a revolver.

She gasped behind the duct tape and trembled as he rubbed the revolver in his hands.

She couldn't breathe. Everything inside her screamed as he reached for her with his left hand, holding the revolver in his right.

She closed her eyes as he grabbed the back of her neck and squeezed. Then he peeled the duct tape from her mouth. She opened her eyes. The gun lay in his lap—his hands resting at his sides. The knife lay between them under his left hand. She stared at the gun. It was right there—if only her hands were free, she'd grab it and run.

Her heart—already racing—broke into a full sprint. Mouth dry. Her bound hands dripping with sweat. She glanced at his face and caught his eyes. She couldn't help but glance at the gun, then he grabbed it and set it on his right.

He looked at her. His eyes seemed hollow and distant. No fire. No life.

Her lips throbbed and burned but felt numb at the same time. She captured a glimpse of her own blood on the loose duct tape as he grabbed it, wadded it and tossed it into the pit. Then he folded his hands in his lap.

The knife lay between them. Maybe he'd forget about it.

Maybe she could turn, grab the knife, and free herself. She bumped his shoulder as she tried to turn her back to the knife—reaching for it with her fingers but coming up empty. She turned and looked at him.

But he didn't move. He didn't look away. He simply stared into the pit like a ghost dreading the grave.

Without turning his head, he said, "I'm sorry."

Her heart thumped, and she blinked through fresh tears. *I'm sorry, I'm about to plunge this knife into your chest? I'm sorry I did this, you can go?* "What do you mean?"

He turned to face her, his eyes watery, pleading, but she couldn't trust that look, and she couldn't run either.

She trembled as he grabbed the knife once more. But he leaned behind her and cut the zip-tie holding her wrists together. Then he flung the knife into the pit without a word.

There she sat unbound. His silence told her it was over. She was free to go.

But she couldn't leave. She had to know. "Why?"

No response. It was like talking to a ghost.

He turned his head and looked at the old chair near the back door, the one she'd stumbled over when she'd tried to run. Her fear slowly melted as the man she'd nursed to health seemed to slowly die before her eyes. He was still there. Still breathing. His new heart was still pumping, but the man she'd known was gone. She was staring at an empty shell.

His shoulders quivered, and his hands trembled. A sniffle muted his tears. He stared at the chair as he slid his hand behind his back and laid his phone between them.

She stared at the phone. Was this a test or an invitation to call for help? The screen was lit with a text. Timidly, she picked up the phone and read, *My daughter is missing.*

The screen cracked when she dropped it. Her trembling hands covered her blistered mouth. Too dry to speak. No tears left to cry, she shook uncontrollably.

Her hand tight across her mouth, she held her emotions like a lid on a steaming pot. She grabbed his half-spilled beer bottle, wiped it off and took a sip. The alcohol burned her lips, but it felt good going down. She tipped the bottle and downed the rest, tossing the bottle into the pit.

* * *

He heard the bottle thud against the cold earth, but nothing else. No footsteps. No screaming.

He turned around slowly. Staring through a veil of tears, he looked into her eyes and shook his head. His sweaty palms gripped the revolver and flipped open the cylinder. *Six rounds*. He flipped it closed and gave it a spin.

Her eyes widened with fear and doubt. Keeping his eyes fix on hers, he cocked the gun then un-cocked it.

Slowly, he turned back toward the old chair and stared at the reminder of suffering and shame. For the first time, he stared at the chair without feeling fear or intimidation. The wear from ropes and residue from duct tape were obvious, but none of it mattered any more.

Listening, he expected to hear a mad dash toward the door, but he heard nothing.

For two minutes, he heard nothing.

Without turning around, he said, "Why are you still here?"

Timid footsteps crept toward him. A trembling hand rested on his shoulder. Standing beside him, she leaned forward, placed her other hand on the revolver and gently pressed downward.

The gun fell from his hands.

She grabbed the old chair, sat down and faced him.

"The text was from my mom, wasn't it?"

He nodded. More tears than ever. He couldn't look at her. "I didn't know."

"You didn't know what?"

He buried his face in his hands. Silent tears shook his entire body. He moved his lips without a sound.

"You didn't know what?"

Shaking his head, he said, "Please go." He closed his eyes and pointed to the door. "Please."

He listened as Brooke slid from the chair—her fingers rustling over the ground to pick up the gun. He imagined her aiming at him as she spoke. "You wanted to kill me and had several opportunities. I think you owe me a reason."

His ears perked at the sound of the cylinder revolving. Two little clicks meant she had cocked the gun. His eyes remained closed and he nodded. "Please." *Please shoot me. End it.* Sweat clouded his vision as he blinked. He wiped his face with his sleeve, caught a glimpse of her holding the gun, then closed his eyes again.

The gunshot jolted him. His ears rang, and he collapsed, but he felt nothing, no pain, no warmth, nothing. Opening his eyes and patting himself, he couldn't see any blood and couldn't feel any wounds.

Looking up, he noticed a gaping hole in the chair. Splinters dotted the ground and the wall.

"Stop looking at the damn chair," she said, her hands trembling, tears pouring as she pointed the gun at his nose. "You didn't know what?"

He studied her eyes, her bloodshot, hazel eyes.

His mind drifted as he mumbled, "I didn't know."

"Didn't know what?" Her scream mixed with tears. Her lips and the gun shook together.

He opened his mouth but couldn't speak. He felt as empty as the day he'd stood on Peggy's porch knocking and waiting, ringing the doorbell, and waiting, never seeing anyone but the young girl who peeked around the curtain. "I…"

Her face fell. "You're him."

She dropped the gun. "You're the man I saw that day

from the window. Mom wouldn't let you in. You're him. I knew I'd seen those eyes."

Tears streamed down his face, but he didn't bother to wipe them away. What would be the point?

She picked up the gun again and motioned for him to sit on the ground. As he sank to the ground, she slowly sat down on the chair. "Start talking. Who are you, why were you at our house, and what is it you didn't know?"

"Brooke, I'm sorry."

"Talk!" she said through gritted teeth.

"When I saw the newspaper clippings, I thought you'd betrayed me. You'd dug up my past, and I was afraid you'd tell Donna everything. When I talked to the police, I thought you'd turned in Uncle Charles, and I blamed you for Donna's death."

Her mouth fell open. She smacked her lips, swallowed, and shook the gun. "Go on."

He looked down and shook his head. "I've ruined every good thing I ever had." *Including you.*

He looked her straight in the eye, stepped toward her, and gently grabbed the gun. As her grip loosened, he squeezed his hands over hers, pressing them against the gun and pressing the gun against his chest.

"You have every right to kill me."

She pulled the gun away from him and tossed it into the hay. "Your name isn't Nathan. It's Joe, isn't it? Joe Novak. My mother never talked about you until that day you came to our house. I pestered her for days until she finally opened up."

"She said you used to be neighbors and best friends, but something happened. Something terrible, but she would never say what it was. Then one day, when she was out with grandma, I snuck into her room.

"I'd seen her put away the same book several times when I'd come into her room. I went straight to that book. When I opened it, newspaper clippings fell out. Every article was about—you. Boy Shot in Hunting Accident. Father Falls to His Death. Every article.

Then I found it. Body Found: Novak Arrested.

I should have put it together, but heart failure had stolen some years from you, and I didn't recognize you. I thought you turned on me because of those drugs, but it was those clippings. You thought I'd figured it all out. You thought I knew your sordid past and knew a murderer would never have been accepted into the transplant program."

He stood dumbfounded, locked onto her hazel eyes.

A whirlwind of memories spun. All those times playing with Peggy, chasing Peggy, looking into her eyes, her deep blue eyes. Every annoying thought of Danny Miser, his red hair and freckles, his irritating laugh, and his blue eyes.

He imagined those eyes, dark and lifeless, sunken into a cold, sallow body, bloated with thin, cracked skin from weeks under water. He'd buried that fateful day deep in the recesses of his mind, but the day he'd hoped to forget, now haunted him through Brooke's hazel eyes.

* * *

The phone had rung early that morning so many years ago. He'd answered.

Peggy's voice had been so warm and enticing. "Thank God it's you. Come over now."

It had seemed like a normal Saturday morning with the usual guilt that followed him everywhere since he'd murdered Danny, but that Saturday had been different. It had felt like a dream, a dream the rest of his life had buried. He'd driven the pickup to Peggy's house, parked on the street, and run inside.

She'd locked him in an unrelenting embrace. "Mom and Dad are gone." He'd never seen her smile quite like that. Her face warm, eyes glowing, and her tongue tickling her teeth. She'd tugged his shirt and pulled him toward the stairs. "Come with me."

He'd followed like a bottle-fed lamb. Nothing and no one could've cured his worries like Peggy. His eyes had followed her bouncing black hair and the twist of her hips up each step. His mind had locked onto her subtle yet disarming perfume and the warmth of her hand.

She'd backed him into her bedroom, closed the door, and wrapped her lips around his. Every thought had melted into one emotion.

No one else in the world mattered. No one else existed.

He and Peggy had become one.

It wasn't how he'd planned it, though he'd imagined it over and over, and it was every bit of what he'd imagined and more. Every inch of his skin had pulsed for her. He felt warmth all over like never before. His lips felt swollen and numb. He floated above the bed, above the house, somewhere in the clouds.

She'd kissed him again, her body sliding on his as they'd both dripped with sweat.

That moment could've lasted forever, he could've held it, cherished it, relived it over and over, but the startling ring of the doorbell had buried that bit of heaven until now.

* * *

That bit of heaven stared him in the eyes.

The trance briefly ended as he and Brooke turned toward his phone, chiming, vibrating and bouncing near the pit.

He leaned down, grabbed it and read, "Joe. Please." Pressing the home button to silence the phone, he stared at the message, but the sound continued in his mind.

* * *

He remembered Peggy's arms around him even as the doorbell had kept ringing. She'd handed him his clothes.

"You'd better hurry."

"It's your dad?"

Peggy had frowned. "Daddy wouldn't ring the doorbell."

A loud voice barked up the stairs. "Anybody home?"

She'd covered his mouth and hollered. "I'll be right down." She'd tucked in her shirt and glanced in the mirror to jostle her hair, then she'd turned and faced him.

He'd stood dumbfounded, a bottle-fed lamb with mouth and eyes wide.

As footsteps had clomped up the stairs, she'd squeezed his face and planted one last firm kiss. Then she'd looked him in the eyes and said, "No matter what happens, I will *always* love you." She'd kissed him again as the door swung open.

"Miss Landrum, step away," the officer had said as he nudged her away with one hand and reached for Joe with the other. "Joe Novak! Hands behind your back. You're under arrest for the murder of Daniel Miser."

He remembered the sting of the cold steel cuffs like it was yesterday. Even more, he remembered the instant tears in Peggy's eyes, the way her hair had swayed, as though in slow-motion. The room had gone dark. The memory buried. The officer's voice sounded like a distant fog horn. All he could see were Peggy's blue eyes. All he could hear was her tender voice breaking through her tears. "I love you."

* * *

The day he'd never wanted to forget had become the day he'd buried forever, until he saw the truth in Brooke's eyes.

Glancing at his phone, he entered a message then tapped the screen to send it.

"Was it her again?" Brooke asked.

He couldn't look at her. He only nodded. "You should go. Your mom will be here soon with the police."

As she walked past, he lifted his head, and she gave him a bewildered look. "If she's coming, do you mind if I borrow your phone to call her?"

He closed his messages, tapped the phone icon and typed in the number without thinking.

As he handed her the phone, she said, "You still remember the number after all these years. I can see you were best friends." She stepped outside as the phone started to ring.

As soon as the ringing stopped, she said, "Mom!" but her grandpa's voice interrupted.

"You've reached the Landrum residence, please leave a…"

She lowered the phone as the sirens grew closer. Red and blue flashing lights flickered through the trees and slowed at the end of the driveway.

A strange sense of calm came over her, and she lifted the phone, touched Messages and read, "Our daughter is safe at Frank's barn. Please forgive me."

Our daughter. The words burned into her soul. Every empty memory, every time she'd wondered who her father was, why he'd left, did he love her, did he love her mother, was he dead? Every single thought she'd ever conjured of him raced through her mind and crashed into the monster who had tortured her and brought her to this pit to die.

Rage, confusion, and utter sorrow whirled within. She wanted to run into his arms. She wanted to find the revolver and kill him.

The flashing lights and sirens drew closer, and the cars stopped in front of her. For the first time in days, she knew she was going to live. Shaking uncontrollably, she dropped the phone.

The police officers held their guns at the ready and aimed their flashlights at her. She stood perfectly still with her hands shielding her from their lights and pointed them towards the barn.

They spread out and slowly moved that direction. Their flashlights lit up the side of the barn and the open door. One of the officers motioned for her to get behind them.

As she followed the officers, the blast of a revolver

startled her. The officers stood still. None of them had fired a shot.

She screamed, "No!" turned and ran into the barn. The officers followed, their flashlights bouncing on the uneven ground.

She cringed and jumped as he fired four more shots. Leaning through the doorway, she expected to find him lying in a mix of straw and blood, but there he stood. The gun smoking. A spray of splinters and gaping holes riddled the old chair.

Her heart sank as he turned his gun on himself, pressed it against his temple, and turned to face his audience.

* * *

Joe had bound every painful moment of his life to that worn and abused chair. His young heart had been broken too soon. The first shot was for his father. *You died way too soon, Dad.*

The next was for his mother. *Frank stole you from me, then prison took me away from you, and I wasn't even there to say good-bye.*

The next shot was for Danny Miser. *I would have killed you twice if I could.*

He paused to think about Donna. She'd had such a beautiful smile. She'd loved him deeply and was an amazing lover, but Peggy was the love who would never die, the love stayed with him yet left him feeling alone. He felt his heart failing all over again as he wondered why he'd never thought the girl in the window could be his daughter, and why Peggy had never told him.

"I wasn't there," he'd muttered as he'd fired his fourth shot into the chair for Peggy.

He'd paused and let the shot ring. Taking a deep breath, he'd cocked the gun one last time to make the last shot count. He'd gritted his teeth and strained to steady his shaking hands. "This one's for you, Frank."

There are not enough awful ways to die to satisfy what he'd wished he could have done to Frank. If he could spend his eternity killing him, it wouldn't be too long. The memories of his step-monster still haunted him daily.

Every twinge in his wrist reminded him of the ropes, cable ties, and duct tape. Every shadow, every dark corner, every night reminded him of the stale darkness in Frank's basement and in the pit. Every stitch in every chair and every cushion was his attempt to cover Frank's memory and conquer that miserable chair.

Boom! The seat split and the fractured chair collapsed.

Five rounds gone. One left.

As footsteps thundered into the barn behind him, he cocked the gun, lifted it to his head, and turned around slowly. One hand in the air, the other holding the gun against his head. He looked at Brooke through his tears. She was the embodiment of the life and love that he'd missed.

Her eyes told the story. She couldn't be Danny's as he'd thought. Danny and Peggy both had blue eyes. Their daughter would have blue eyes as well. He looked at Brooke's hazel eyes, the same eyes that had watched him through that window so many years before.

The ache in his heart was too much as he stared at the daughter he'd never known. *My daughter. The nurse who cared for me when I didn't care for myself. The woman I blamed for Donna's death. My innocent child whom I almost killed.*

All his pain melted into one final lump of molded lead in one powder-packed cartridge. One last breath. One last look at the daughter he would've loved. He cocked the gun and said, "Brooke, I'm sorry. I loved your mother. I would've loved you too, but I didn't know."

He closed his eyes and tightened his grip on the revolver.

* * *

Brooke eased toward him, waving off the police officers. "Joe, don't. Please don't. It's no good."

She winced as he pulled the trigger.

Click.

She ran to him, smiling. There were no bullets left. She'd fired the first round into the chair.

Brooke wrapped her arms around him as he dropped the gun and collapsed into her. Fear and anger melted as the monster died in her arms. She felt as though all the pain and evil pent up inside him had exploded with that miserable chair.

As they sunk to the ground together, she gently squeezed his face with both hands, tilting his head and shaking him until he opened his eyes. "Look at me."

He blinked, closing his eyes and straining against her grip, trying to turn his head.

But she squeezed harder. "Look. At. Me."

They locked eyes. Father and daughter for the first time. The pain and the questions didn't matter anymore. She looked at him with all the love her mother had borne into her. She finally understood the quiet moments when her mother would sneak away by herself and cry. She understood the book with the clippings. She even felt like she understood the silence.

"My mother always talked about you. When you left, part of her died, and now I realize why she sometimes struggled to look at me, and why it felt like she was sometimes looking through me to some far-off place, some far away memory. She saw you. She was looking at you in my eyes."

Brooke continued to speak to him as the police quietly surrounded her. She paused at the hand on her shoulder.

"Ma'am. We have to do our job."

"Just one more thing, officer." She held out her raised hand. "One more thing."

She stood and lifted Joe by his hand, walked him to the chair. Grabbing his hand, she placed it on the chair. They gripped it together. Lifting it, she nudged him toward the pit.

He smiled as she looked into his eyes, then they tossed the chair into the pit. What was left of his pain crumbled against cold earth.

The grave that he'd meant for her is where they buried his pain together.

Chapter 81
Six months later
Edinburgh Correctional Facility

"Novak," the guard shouted, then tossed him a package.

Joe smiled as he read the return label. *Brooke.*

He tore open the package and discovered an envelope and a book.

A note fell out of the book.

Joe, I stole this book from Mom's room. She doesn't write much anymore, and this book is full anyway. It's all about you.

I think she wrote every memory of everything the two you ever did together. Don't worry. I made a copy for myself, but I thought you deserved the original, since it's all about you.

When she ran out of memories, she started writing her dreams. She wrote about the three of us. We lived in a mansion on a hill overlooking a valley of wildflowers. I know you'll have plenty of time to read it.

I truly wish I had known you after reading her words.

He smiled at the smudged letters from tear stains. He had forgotten what is was like to feel loved.

Joe opened the envelope. It contained a photograph and a letter.

Dear Joe, Mom said you would like this picture. She's reading a book to my son and the little girl from two houses down. She said you would recognize the book and get a chuckle. Alexander and the Terrible, Horrible, No Good, Very Bad Day.

Joe smiled and chuckled.

You may not recognize the chair. It was my great-grandmother's, the one you and Mom used to sit in when she would read to you, the one you collected from her garbage. Uncle Charles helped me find it. He worked diligently to repair and reupholster it. He said he couldn't do as good a job as you would have done, but I think it looks perfect.

Uncle Charles said you were going to sell it for $3500, but he wouldn't take a dime. He said it was my chair to begin with and let me have it for free.

It's ready for you when you get out.

Sorrow and joy drizzled down his cheeks as he put himself in that picture. The family he'd always wanted. The woman he'd always loved.

As he studied the photo, his heart melted at the pictures within the picture. On the wall behind the chair, he saw a portrait of his mother and father together. *Their wedding picture.* Next to it hung the picture of him and Donna in front of Fortune Furniture. Beside that one, he saw himself.

He flipped the letter to read the second page.

I hope you like the portraits on the wall. It was my idea. Mom seemed to like it. I told her, since you are my father, you are part of this family.

As you read Mom's book, you'll realize she never married. I'm her only child. Everyone assumed I was the product of rape, that Danny Miser was my father. No one bothered to look me in the eye or get to know me. That's why I always studied. I wanted to succeed and get away from my lonely past.

As soon as I graduated from nursing school, I left and never looked back. Sure, I missed my mom and grandpa. I would see them now and then, holidays and such, but I lived with great grandmother.

She used to say, "Maybe someday, you'll meet a fine boy like that little neighbor who used to play with your mother. He was a sweet boy." If only she'd known. Ha.

Great grandmother didn't have to know anything else about you, Joe. She knew your heart, and I do too.

I hope that when you are finally released from your prison, we can be the family mother dreamed of.

The End

ABOUT THE AUTHOR

John Matthew Walker writes
to inspire hope amid despair, to reveal light in the deepest darkness, and to prompt compassion in a world filled with contempt
and disregard.

Follow the author at johnmattewwalker.com

More Books by John Matthew Walker

Moonlight Awakens: a sex-trafficking story

At only seventeen, Emma is used, abused, and discarded. She runs a thousand miles away from shame and judgment and falls into the arms of a stranger. One careless mistake, and she plummets into the hellish world of sex-trafficking. Her pimp takes everything from her, starting with her name. Deep in that darkness, Emma must find herself and find a way out. Her story is a tantalizing suspense that awakens hope.

Fire in the Moonlight: a story of persecution

Sometimes faith calls us to walk on water. Sometimes, to walk through fire. Andrea Widener drifts to sleep while studying. A vivid dream takes her to India, a burning church, and a whisper through the flames. She awakens, unable to escape the feeling that the church and the voice were real. *Fire in the Moonlight* is a story of reckless compassion. Follow Andrea as she abandons her own dreams to follow the unrelenting dream that whispers her name.

Tiny Blush of Sunlight: a slave story

Nkembe is a young slave in South Carolina's lowcountry in the 1830s. After witnessing a murder, he runs for his life. Hounds chase him through the woods and into the marsh. Trapped between a bitter past and a desperate future, his only hope is to find a place to hide and someone who can help him escape the reach of his master.

Made in the USA
Las Vegas, NV
09 February 2023